MW00611274

The
UNFORTUNATE LIFE
of
GENEVIEVE RYDER

The
UNFORTUNATE LIFE
of
GENEVIEVE RYDER

A Novel

SAMMY BEUKER

credo
house publishers

The Unfortunate Life of Genevieve Ryder
Copyright © 2023 by Samantha Beuker
All rights reserved.

Published in the United States of America by Credo House Publishers,
a division of Credo Communications LLC, Grand Rapids, Michigan
credohousepublishers.com

ISBN: 978-1-62586-247-1

Cover and interior design by Frank Gutbrod
Editing by Elizabeth Banks

Printed in the United States of America
First edition

For Eric,
Who has always believed in this story
And has always believed in me.

Part
ONE

One

November 1946
Medford, Wisconsin

The way her mother saw it, Genevieve Ryder at twenty-two had lost her chance at a respectable marriage, which was the only thing that mattered. However, Gen had different ideas. Bobby McFadden, the last eligible bachelor left in her small Wisconsin town, was going to be her fiancé, tonight.

Staring out of the living room window, Gen saw the dairy cow barn and the kitchen garden and the piles of hay in the field. This wasn't a life for her, outside of town, wearing homespun skirts and hay in her hair. She was meant to be an in-town wife, with stylish clothes and adoring children. Even now, as she closed her eyes, she could picture her wedding day, her neat little house full of handy appliances, the life she would build.

The banging of kitchen cupboards and the screech of her mother's voice from the kitchen crashed into Gen's thoughts. "Genevieve, come set the table for dinner."

"I'll be there in just one minute." A gurgle made her hand fall to her stomach. It hadn't lost that hollow, metallic feeling for a few weeks. Uncomfortable as it was, this was her plan to get Bobby to marry her.

Antoinette stamped her foot on the floor and said, "Now, Genevieve!"

When she walked into the kitchen, all the dishes for dinner were stacked on the sideboard. Antoinette stood with arms crossed, glaring at her oldest daughter. "I'm waiting for you to do what's expected. Your time for daydreaming is over." Her eyes flitted to Gen's waist. "I thought I raised you to know better."

Her dream ripped from her, Gen fought back tears which threatened so often these days. Her mother's condemnation was not subtle. As Gen carried the pile into the dining room, her younger sister, Marie, laid a gentle hand on her arm. "Are you okay?" Gen grimaced, shook her head and set the family dinner table for four.

She examined her work. The table was simply set with white plates and plain silverware. The linen napkins were well used, but clean and pressed. She adjusted the vase of black-eyed Susans to make it look fuller. "Table's set," she said as she walked back in the kitchen. Marie was buttering the mashed potatoes. Antoinette bustled around the kitchen, loading food onto serving platters. Her white apron was stained, a dirty kitchen towel and her cherished rosary beads tucked in the side. Wrinkles etched her Mother's mouth and forehead. Genevieve couldn't help but think she looked like the simple farmer's wife she was and that Gen never wanted to be.

Antoinette frowned and took the plate of roast into the dining room. Gen watched as her mother's severe bun disappeared through the swing door separating the two rooms.

"Genevieve, get in here," Antoinette called from the dining room. Gen felt lead settle in the bottom of her stomach. Being used to criticism didn't mean she was immune to it. No one could measure up to her mother's exacting standards. Except Marie, the golden child.

Gen and Marie exchanged knowing glances. "You probably left a crumb on the carpet." They shared a bitter laugh, united only as sisters are in the face of unearned criticism.

Gen grabbed the pitcher of milk from the counter to take with her and pictured Bobby's smiling face looking at her across the altar. As she turned to push the swing door open, Gen caught her foot on the floor and stumbled into the dining room. Milk sloshed onto the floor.

"Clumsy girl." With arms crossed, Antoinette waited next to the table, an angry scowl carved into her face. Jabbing her hand toward the place settings, "How many times do I have to tell you? The napkin goes under the fork on the left side of the plate and the knife edge is always turned in."

"I'm sorry, Mother. I'll fix it." No matter how hard she tried Gen was never as precise as her mother demanded. She couldn't wait to get married so she could be her own woman.

"I'll do it. I should have just done it in the first place. Tonight it has to be perfect. Nothing out of place. We'll all be ruined if the McFadden's don't accept you."

Gen reached toward the table to adjust a glass, but Antoinette slapped it away. "But they're not even coming for dinner. Why does this matter anyway?" Just then, the back door slammed shut. Relief flooded through her. Dad was home.

But tonight, he didn't bring his usual cheer. A biting November wind swept in behind him, chilling the kitchen. The dark, gray clouds filled the space with a gloom that threatened to consume Gen. Len's shoulders were hunched more than usual and his face had aged ten years in the days since Gen had risen from her sickbed and tiptoed down the stairs.

Her parents' reactions were seared into her brain. No matter how hard she tried, she couldn't unsee her father's disappointment or her mother's condemnation. Gen knew, somehow, she'd proven to her that she was every bit of the disappointment her mother believed her to be.

But she had a plan worked out in her head. After confronting Bobby at his job a few days ago, his parents called, inviting themselves over for coffee after dinner. Tonight, she knew, Bobby was coming to propose. They were going to get married, raise this baby together, as they should, as man and wife.

The doorbell rang as the grandfather clock in the hallway struck 7:00. The house was warm and welcoming for a dark November night. Len answered the door. When he opened the door, Bill and Caroline McFadden stood in the doorway, sandwiching Bobby. "Welcome. Glad you came over tonight, Bill," and nodding at his wife, "Good evening, Caroline. Please come in." A taut smile covered Caroline's face. "Evening, Bobby. Nice to see you here again," he said to the young man.

"Good to see you too, Len," Bill said. "Although, I must admit, I wish we were meeting under different circumstances."

Bobby stood silent behind his parents, looking like a whipped puppy. Gen's heart ached with compassion, wanting to sweep him up in her arms. His parents must be pretty upset. Maybe the Hudson's hadn't taken the breaking off of the engagement well. Gen shrugged her shoulders knowing that should be expected, at the least.

Len led the trio into the living room where Bill and Caroline sat on the couch. Again, they kept Bobby between their shoulders. Gen sat in Len's rocking chair across the room. She kept her eyes down in a flirtatious way, trying to appear innocent and loving. Bobby's eyes were downcast.

Marie scurried about serving coffee and cake, her movement the only one in a room full of statues. With stiff back, Caroline perched on the edge of the couch, holding her cup of coffee. Steam rose from the cup, tracing a path in the air. The cup itself never moved. Antoinette had parked herself in her rocking chair, arms locked across her chest.

Len and Bill made casual conversation about cows and the state of dairy farming, about business at the clinic. A "heh-hmm" from Antoinette and a stern look from Caroline focused their attention to the business at hand.

Rubbing his hand behind his neck, Bill said, "So, it seems that our kids have found themselves in a bit of trouble."

Len nodded and said, "Yes, they have."

Silence reigned in the room. Only the crackle of the fire in the fireplace broke the quiet. Gen lifted her eyes to see Bobby sitting with hunched shoulder. Not quite what she expected of her suitor at this moment.

Antoinette started to tap her feet, both in anger and nerves. "Can we just get on already?" Looking straight at Bobby, she said, "What do you have to say for yourself, young man? Are you going to accept responsibility for my daughter and your baby?"

Bobby's face turned crimson and his eyes grew wide. Stammering, "Mrs. Ryder, I'm sorry for what happened, but . . ."

Reaching over, Caroline laid her hand on Bobby's knee. "Not another word, Bobby." Caroline said. "You kids already made a mess of things. It's up to the adults to fix them now." Bobby sunk further into the pillows on the couch.

Antoinette pushed her feet on the ground and crossed her arms. "No, I want to hear what the boy has to say for himself," she said.

"He will do no such thing. I will not let him open himself to your vicious tongue, Antoinette. He's already suffered enough."

"Suffered, because he laid with my daughter? I don't think that's suffering. It's my daughter who's bearing the consequences for his actions." Antoinette's voice was rising, gaining momentum.

Len laid his arm on Antoinette and said, "Nettie, this is not the time or place for such words." Antoinette diminished under the scolding, but her rage simmered underneath a thin exterior. She pursed her lips and bore her eyes into Caroline who did not back down under the stare.

Len asked, "So what do you suggest we do about our situation?"

Bill looked at his wife, the two exchanging words with their eyes. Caroline said, "Well, I've made some calls and I found a home for unwed mothers in Eau Claire."

Gen leaped out of her chair, "A home for unwed mothers! In Eau Claire!" Eyes racing from face to face, "I'm not going anywhere!"

Len walked toward his daughter, "Gennie, please, let's listen to what they have to say."

Gen's eyes darted between Bobby and her parents. Her breathing grew ragged and rasping. Her hands seemed locked together, but also desperate to reach out to Bobby and grab on to him. "Bobby, aren't we going to get married?" she asked. "Aren't you here to propose to me?"

Bobby looked at her, his eyes full of sorrow. "Gen, I'm sorry," he said. "But, I'm still going to marry Susie."

At those words, panic fully engulfed Gen. Her heart hammered, ugly tears threatened the edge of her eyes. She threw herself at Bobby's feet. "No, that can't be true. That's not how it's supposed to work. You're supposed . . ."

Bobby shifted in his spot, pulling his feet away from Gen. The four parents sat unmoving. Marie, watching from the kitchen, came and pulled her sister off Bobby's feet. She guided Gen back to her chair and knelt on the floor next to her. A comforting arm hung on Gen's shoulder as she sobbed into her hands.

Wiping tears from his eyes, Len cleared his throat and said, "Go on, then, tell us about this place."

Caroline stared at Gen, unblinking. The sound of Gen's sobs filled the room. She shook her head and then continued, "There's a home for unwed mothers in Eau Claire called Bethany House. It's a good place, or so I've heard from," she hesitated, looking at her husband, "from others who have visited this home."

Antoinette leaned forward. "What do you know about this place?"

"It's a clean, safe place for young women who find themselves in this situation. Girls live there for one year. During the time they live at the home, they learn skills and are counseled about what to do with their babies."

"A year!" Len said. "That's a bit long, most pregnancies don't last that long, do they?"

Rolling her eyes, Antoinette patronized her husband, "No dear, only nine long months. And she's already a few months along." Turning to Caroline, she asked, "Why so long?"

Caroline cleared her throat by taking a sip of coffee. "The director says a full year will reform a girl from her waywardness."

Len looked between Gen and her mother and frowned, "A program like that must be expensive. I'm not sure we can afford something like this."

For the first time that night, Bill smiled. He reached into his coat pocket and said, "Not to worry, Len." He pulled out a white envelope and handed it to Len. "I spoke with the director of the home, Mr. Ronald, this morning. He assured me that, while there aren't any openings right now, there'll be a spot available right after Christmas." Placing the envelope in Len's hands, he said, "I'm sure you will find more than enough money to cover all of Gen's expenses."

Len opened the envelope and counted $200. Antoinette leaned over his shoulder and nodded her head.

"Well," Len looked at Antoinette as he considered the offer.

After a glance at his own wife, Bill added, "By accepting this offer you are freeing my son of any responsibility in this matter."

Genevieve hiccuped from her chair. "Bobby, this is your baby, it's our baby." Her voice was thick with her crying. Looking at him, she saw small tears in the corners of his eyes.

Bobby raised his hands, "Viv, what else you want me to do?" Regret filled his voice.

"I want you to marry me." Her desperation made her grow bold, even in this room with all the parents around, he had to know her heart.

"Gen, I can't do that. Susie knows and still wants to marry me. There's nothing I can do."

"At least, don't let them send me away. Please, let me stay here."

Raking both hands through his hair, he blew out a frustrated breath. Looking at her, he said, "Viv, you can't stay here. What will people say?"

"Who cares what people say?"

Caroline set down her coffee cup in a clatter. She stared at Gen and said, "I do. I care very much, young lady. And if you had any sense about you, you will accept our offer and get this baby into a good home. You can't raise a baby. How could a girl like you raise a baby?"

Antoinette jumped to her feet, "What do you mean, 'a girl like you'? What are you saying about my daughter?"

Caroline leaped to her feet in response, "Only what everyone has always said about her. That she's no good, she's just like her mother. It was only a matter of time before this happened. I'm just sorry Bobby got involved."

Antoinette put her hands on her hips, her nose flaring with each breath. "Are you calling her a hussy? Why if your son hadn't—"

Both husbands jumped up in front of their wives. Len stood in front of Antoinette, blocking her line of sight, and said. "Calm down, 'Nettie." Bill did the same, grasping Caroline's hands in his. "Caroline, you need to be quiet. You're not making this any easier."

Caroline said, "But, Bill, you know it's true. Now Bobby's involved. What will he do?"

"Mother," Bobby said. "I managed to make it through the war. I'll make it through this too. I'll be okay."

Genevieve sat in her chair, a whimper escaped from her lips. This cannot be happening. This is all wrong.

Picking up his hat from the arm of the couch, Bill said, "I think it's time for us to go. Len, let me know what you decide."

Looking the other man in the eye, Len said, "You'll hear from me in a day or so." Len shook Bill's extended hand, completing the business proposal.

Bill guided his wife toward the front door, her jaw set. "Goodbye, Antoinette," she said. "Thanks for your . . . hospitality."

Last to rise was Bobby. Looking at Gen, he walked toward her chair. Kneeling down in front of her, he grabbed her hand. "Viv, I'm so sorry. I never meant for this to happen."

He released her hand, turned his back, and walked out the door.

Gen remained in her chair and wept.

Two

en didn't know what to do. She prided herself on being a woman who knew her own mind and did what she set out to do. But she wasn't going to be allowed to make up her own mind on this.

Len and Antoinette reached their decision the morning after the meeting with the McFaddens. Gen seethed with anger, a restless energy pulsed through her exhausted, pregnant body. She didn't want to go anywhere, especially not to some boarding house two hours away from home.

The turmoil she felt was mirrored throughout the entire Ryder household. Traditionally, Thanksgiving was a jubilant time for the family, full of food and friendship. The house would be crowded with neighbors and distant family members making merry.

But not this year. Since the Ryders entrusted no one with the news of their daughter's condition, no extra faces would surround the Thanksgiving table. Indeed, Antoinette was convinced there was only one thing for which to give thanks.

"Thank goodness the McFaddens gave us that money so you can go away for a while." Antoinette ironed the napkins for their dinner with vigor, chatting with Gen as she worked.

"Mother, would you please stop!" Gen said. She was tired of her mother's continued harping. She was powerless to fight the plans her parents had made, but she didn't need her mother continuing to sing the praises of the people paying to send her away.

Setting down the hot iron to look at her daughter, Antoinette said, "We should be thankful for their help."

Gen ran her finger down a finished napkin's crease, refusing to make eye contact. "They could have helped by convincing Bobby to marry me."

"Genevieve Antoinette, you must be mad! It's clear Caroline doesn't like you. Why would she convince Bobby to marry someone like you? You didn't leave him anything to discover once you got married."

Gen gaped open-mouthed at her mother. Coming in from the barn, Len brushed fresh snow off his head. Looking between the two, he said, "Enough. Nothing left to say." He squeezed his wife's hand and kissed his daughter's forehead.

Every day was like that. Antoinette making comments about how horrible Gen was, Len putting down his foot that no more comments should be made. The house simmered with barely contained anger and hurt.

As the holiday season grew nearer, so also her leaving, panic rose up in Gen. She couldn't sit still. Her parents had forced her to quit her job shortly after her announcement so she had little work of meaning to do. Gen knew her mother would love her to spend her time scrubbing the bathroom or ironing some napkins, but she just wouldn't. There wasn't joy in the task for her.

Often, she found herself bundled up against the cold walking out. She had so little left, what was the cold to her. As she walked, she thought. Every thought circled back to Bobby and that he was the one who could fix all this. This was all his fault and he needed to answer for himself. Not hide behind the shield of his parents. A man who returned home from the war was a man unto himself and didn't need his mommy and daddy to protect him.

The more she walked, the more her anger grew until it was a blind rage which led her into Medford to the McFadden Veterinary Clinic. Without an ounce of hesitation, Gen pushed open the door. She couldn't even hear the bells hanging on the door tinkle, so thick was her rage. Walking up to the desk, she asked. "Is Bobby here this morning? I need to talk to him."

Nancy, the receptionist, narrowed her eyes at Gen. A shadow darkened Nancy's features. "Let me see if he's available." Drawing out her actions, she leaned over the intercom microphone. Without taking her eyes off Gen, she poked the button on the system. "Bobby, please come to the front desk. You have . . . a visitor."

She lifted her finger off the intercom button with a loud click. She turned to Gen and said, "I called for him." She snapped her mouth shut and stared. Her eyes issued challenge while she tapped her pencil on the countertop.

Gen didn't care about Nancy's obvious contempt. Always a busybody, she put her nose into other's business, then told anyone willing to listen. In their town, Nancy was popular only for the information she supplied, but no one ever wanted to be on her gossip list.

A few minutes later, Bobby appeared at the receptionist desk. Leaning toward Bobby, Nancy whispered loudly enough for Gen to hear, "Genevieve Ryder is here to see you. Should I send her away?"

Bobby glanced up and saw Gen waiting. Inside, her heart was racing. Her entire body stiffened, frozen in place. She was sure he could hear her heart pounding through her chest.

"Hey Viv. It's been a while." His manner was easy but he didn't reach out to touch her like he had before. He was so calm, Gen wanted to rip his head off.

"It has, Bobby." Her hands gripped her purse.

Gen looked around the waiting room. Except for the four metal chairs, the room was empty. The white tile floor and bare walls echoed the click of the clock on the wall. She tapped her foot in nervousness, the sound reverberating through the room. Bobby ran his hand through his hair. He looked down at his hands, pulling at the cuffs of his sleeves underneath his gray suit coat. The silver button cuff link was dirty and he spent uncomfortable minutes polishing it.

Gen broke the silence. "Do you have a few minutes? I need to talk to you."

Bobby hesitated. He glanced over to the receptionist's desk, Nancy flipped her head around to a book laying behind her. He looked up at the clock and sighed. "Sure, I have a few minutes. Do you want to talk out here or somewhere else?"

"Somewhere private."

Bobby fingered the scar on his face, a flush growing. "Well, Gen" he said loud enough for Nancy to overhear. "I'm not sure it's a good idea to go anywhere private. I'm engaged now, I don't want Susie to get suspicious."

Gen's blood began to boil. She fought to stay in control of her voice and emotions, but her anger prevailed. "Suspicious? Have you done nothing worthy of suspicion or have your actions always been aboveboard? I wonder how much Susie knows . . ." She let the threat hang.

Looking toward the desk, he said, "Not here, Gen." Bobby grabbed Gen by the arm, pulling her into one of the small animal examining rooms.

As she walked into the room, the smell of disinfectant overwhelmed her senses. She slammed her hands on the metal examining table, steadying herself.

"Viv, are you okay?"

Regaining control, Gen straightened herself. "No, Bobby, I'm not okay."

"Is there anything I can do to help? Would you like a glass of water or something?"

Gen's bitter laugh filled the small room. "Is there anything that you can do to help? You've done enough."

"What? What did I do?" His voice rose, but his hand stayed on the doorknob.

Gen's voice was tight with fury, weeks of anger, months of frustration pouring out. "Are you kidding? You never broke up with me. One fight, we don't talk for weeks. Then, I get the flu and when I get out of bed, I learn from my dad you are engaged to Susie Hudson."

"Come now, Viv."

"And now, I'm being sent away for a year. This is your fault."

"Viv, I'm—"

"Who the hell are you kidding? When did you court Susie? While you were dating me?"

Bobby swallowed hard. "Of course she knew we'd dated, but I told her that it'd ended."

"You selfish, self-centered bastard. Do you care about anyone other than you? What about me?"

Bobby lifted his head, "I know this is awful for you. I'm sorry. My parents got this idea in their head and well, I couldn't stop them."

Taking a deep breath and steadying herself against the wall, she said, "I had an idea." She paused to take another breath. "Bobby, we could still get married. We could say Susie was a mistake and that we really love each other." In desperation, she continued, "We could get married next month and then the baby would have both a mom and a dad. A real family. What do you say?"

Bobby's mouth dropped open. "Are you crazy, Viv? We can't get married. I'm engaged." His head sunk back into his hands. Again, silence filled the room.

Gen stood against the wall with her arms crossed. Her nostrils flared in anger. She stared at Bobby, sitting hunched in the chair. She sneered at him with his face in his hands, unable to be the man she needed. "You're weak," she snarled at him. "I'm sorry I ever met you." He raised his head to respond and she turned her back, opened and then slammed the door behind her.

Gen didn't need a man like that anyway. If she was going to be in this situation and Bobby wasn't going to be by her side, then she was going to do it her way, no matter the cost.

Three

Two days after Christmas, her heart heavy, Gen settled into the back seat of her parents' car and resigned herself to that which she couldn't believe: she was leaving home for an entire year, no one truly loved her, they were happy to be rid of her. The two-hour drive was dark, lonely, and quiet. Len and Antoinette sat in the front seat, silent as statues.

On the drive to Bethany House the roads were empty and the winter sky was dark. Gen noticed nothing, immersed only in her misery. By the time the three had reached Gen's new home, the sun had risen, but the skies were still overcast and gray.

Grim and foreboding, the long drive leading up to the House's main entrance were lined with dirty snow. Bethany House, a large three-story red brick building, rose up in the middle of a barren, snow covered lawn. Evergreen bushes were snowy mounds sprinkled with dirt.

In the past weeks, Gen had learned arguing was pointless. No one cared for her arguments about coming home immediately after the baby was born. No one listened to her desire to stay home and hide at their house. Instead, she was supposed to be grateful she could convalesce here, grateful to Bobby's parents who provided so generously.

Despite all his words to the contrary, Gen didn't think her father did anything to fix the situation. Despite her pleading, nothing changed. She couldn't believe he was so weak-spined.

He could put a stop to this, she knew it. As much as he assured her otherwise, Gen knew he was ashamed.

"We're here," Len announced as he parked the car in front of the large oak front doors. A tight smile played across his face. Turning to Antoinette, he said, "Let's get Gen settled." Locked in an upright and rigid position, she turned her head to meet Len's eyes. A simple nod commanded him to proceed.

"Don't you want to say anything to her before she goes?" Len asked his wife.

"No, I've said all I have to say. She knows how I feel. I wish her well." She turned her head to look forward again. Picking up her rosary beads, she closed her eyes and silently mouthed a prayer.

Hanging his head, Len sighed again. Turning to his daughter, he said, "All right, Gennie, they're expecting us. Let's go." He opened the door for Gen, reaching for her hand as he would an elegant lady. Accepting his help, Gen gave him a grateful smile.

As Gen shut the door behind her, her mother's unforgiving posture gave rise to her anguish. "Mother" she yelled through the door. "Mother, why aren't you coming?"

Antoinette looked straight at her oldest daughter. She set her face with displeasure. With a single shake of her head, she answered.

Placing her hand flat on the window Gen said, "I guess this is goodbye." Her shoulders slumped in recognition of another rejection. Turning away, she followed her father up the walk to the front of Bethany House.

The bell gonged and the heavy door creaked open. A middle-aged man wearing thin wire-framed glasses greeted them. "Come in, come in. We've been expecting you."

As Genevieve walked through the front door, she realized Bethany House was unlike any place she'd ever been. A tall, wooden greeting desk stood off to the right. Behind it was a set of French doors opening to a room dominated by a decorated Christmas tree. A fire crackled. The foyer smelled of lemon, pine, and smoke. To the left was a set of closed French doors. Ahead, a grand staircase rose to the second level of the house. Gen could hear the murmur of voices throughout the house.

The lobby was empty except for the man who welcomed them and a tall, spindly woman who stood behind the man with her arms crossed in front of her chest. "Welcome to Bethany House," his voice echoed throughout the foyer. "I'm Mr. Ronald, Patrick Ronald," he said, holding out his hand to Len.

"Nice to meet you. I'm Leonard Ryder, but my friends call me Len." As he shook the administrator's hand, he looked around. "Nice place you got here."

Mr. Ronald smiled and answered, "Thank you, we do our best, trying to make it like home for the girls." Turning to Gen, he said, "You must be Genevieve?"

She nodded, "Yes, but people call me Gen."

A firm voice interrupted and asked, "Excuse me, Mr. Ronald?"

"Oh dear me. I'm so sorry." Motioning to the woman on his left, he said, "This is Mrs. Beverly Skloot, our headmistress."

The woman stepped forward. A beige cardigan was draped over her thin shoulders. She extended her had. "Pleasure to meet you both." After greeting them, she said, "I'll excuse myself now. Ms. Ryder, I'll show you to your room once you're done meeting with Mr. Ronald." With that, she turned to leave, picking up a clipboard from the desk and heading through the doors on the left. A peek through them showed Gen the kitchen. The smell told her they were preparing lunch.

Mr. Ronald was silent for a moment before he continued, "Miss Ryder, you do need to make one decision before you can settle in here. Oftentimes, girls take false names for the duration of their stay. All the staff would use that name to address you."

She drew back in surprise. Gen hadn't expected this. No one said anything about taking a different name. She wasn't interested in hiding who she was. Gen lowered her head to look at her hands, her lip caught between her teeth. After a moment of indecision, she looked at her father, "Dad," she asked, her voice a whisper, "what do you think I should do?" Gen couldn't believe her own weakness. Since when did she need others' approval of her choices. If she had an ounce of real courage, she would have known without asking.

Len looked at her, his face soft with tears welling up in his eyes. "Oh, honey," he said just as softly, "you don't need my permission to make your choices. What do you want?"

Unbidden, Gen's eyes filled with tears. She looked away and wiped her eyes. Relief flooded through her, knowing she wouldn't have to hide. Looking back to her father, she nodded. Keeping her eyes locked on his, she said, "If it's all the same to you, Mr. Ronald, I'll use my own name."

Mr. Ronald coughed and pulled his glasses from his face. After blowing them with hot breath and wiping them with his coat sleeve, he said, "Miss Ryder, this is an unusual choice, nonetheless, we will see it done." He turned and led the two to his office.

Once they were settled, Mr. Ronald behind his heavy wooden desk and Gen and Len seated in leather armchairs, they talked about life at Bethany House, the details of which Gen knew nothing. She listened intently as Mr. Ronald described the business of housing young, unwed mothers. She'd be part of a small group of girls living in community with one another. She'd be required to do chores as assigned and expected to be an encouraging member of the community. He rattled through the business so quickly that Gen lost focus. Until he said, "Well, I think that covers everything. I'll give you some privacy to say your goodbyes before we settle you in."

After Mr. Ronald closed the office door behind him, father and daughter sat in their chairs. Neither made a move toward the other.

"So, this is really happening?" Gen said to no one in particular.

The two of them sat in silence again, neither wanting to say goodbye. "I guess you should go. No good leaving Mother alone in that cold car for too long."

He laughed and squeezed her hand. "I'll miss you. I love you, Gennie."

He stood and opened his arms to his daughter. Gen welcomed being enveloped in his strength and love. She held on as tightly as she could, burying herself in the familiar scent of his coat. The smells of a thousand mornings milking cows and tossing hay filled her mind. They stood silent for a few moments, only the sound of the cracking fire popping behind them. When she lifted her head, his jacket was spotted with her tears. She wiped her eyes with her sleeve coat. Len allowed a single tear to trace a track down his leathered face.

Picking up her bag with all the resolve she could muster, she marched toward the closed office door. "No better time than right now, wouldn't you say, Dad?" She swung the door open. The room, which had earlier been empty was full of girls in various stages of pregnancy. The office door swung shut behind them and the girls crowding the living room fell into silence.

Len followed Mr. Ronald, who had been waiting in the living room, to the front door. Gen stood in front of a rose chintz covered couch, both hands clutching her suitcase. She searched the room for a friendly face, but saw only curious stares. Turning, she found every eye zeroed in on her. She squirmed, readjusting her coat and shifting her feet. She'd never been good at making new friends. An entire room of girls to meet was overwhelming to her.

The room was quiet when the front door clicked shut. Although the sound was small, it reverberated through Gen's whole body. That click signaled the end of everything Gen had hoped for. The closing door shut Bobby out of her life permanently.

When Mr. Ronald reentered the living room, he addressed the group, "Girls, meet our new boarder, Genevieve Ryder. She'll be living here for the next year."

Murmurs of hello swept the room. Gen lifted her eyes as she heard the chorus of voices. From behind the Christmas tree, Mrs. Skloot appeared. "All right, Genevieve, let's get you up to your room," she said as she led the way out of the living room.

Gen carried her borrowed brown suitcase. In a flash, the sting of her humiliation renewed itself. She remembered Mr. McFadden standing in the doorway holding a beaten and battered hard suitcase. "We just got a new one, so we don't need this one right now." Mrs. McFadden sat in the car, her smug smile slapped Gen. They were so happy to help. And to rid Bobby's life of Gen forever.

Mrs. Skloot led Gen through the home toward her room on the third floor. Generally, she oriented Gen to the building, with the kitchen and laundry on the first floor, her office, classrooms, and the nursery on the second floor, and the clusters of suites on the third floor.

After 20 minutes of walking she opened the door to the third floor of Bethany House.

Gen looked down a long hallway. The wood floors were scuffed yet scrubbed clean. No light from the outside shone in, making the walls feel close and uncomfortable.

"This top floor is separated into four distinct areas we call pods. In each pod are rooms for eight to twelve girls, a common living area, a shared bathroom, and a kitchenette." As they walked through the pods, Mrs. Skloot named them: Peace, Friendship, Charity, and Unity. "You are the last boarder joining the Unity suite. All of you girls are expecting babies in May and June of this upcoming year." Finally, Mrs. Skloot motioned to a door about one-third of the way down the hall on the left. Knocking on the door, a quiet, "come in," sounded from within. Mrs. Skloot pushed it open and allowed Gen to enter her new room.

Gen walked in and first saw the furniture: two single beds, two desks with hard-backed chairs, two dressers and a large brown braided rug in the center of the room. Sitting on the edge of one of the twin beds was a slender, well-manicured and pregnant black woman.

Gesturing to the girl on the bed, Mrs. Skloot said, "Genevieve, this is your roommate, Jane Brown. Jane, meet Genevieve Ryder."

Gen set her suitcase down and extended her hand. "Nice to meet you," she said.

The girl gave Gen a limp handshake. "You too," she said without meeting Gen's eyes. Her eyes skittered across Gen's face to her suitcase and rested on her belly.

Mrs. Skloot said, "Genevieve, I'll let you get settled. Lunch is in about an hour. We can finish going over things after." She pulled the door shut behind her, but could be heard walking down the hallway. The noise of her footsteps swallowed up the silence in the room.

Gen tried to hide her surprise at this new development. She had never considered that there would be a black girl at Bethany House, and her roommate, no less. Gen had never had a real conversation with a Negro before. She had seen them around town, but they always lived in a different neighborhood. There'd been no reason to intermix.

However, if they were going to be roommates for an entire year, it didn't matter what color skin she had. So Gen swallowed her shock and asked, "How long have you been here?"

Jane looked down at her slightly protruding stomach. "Just a month. I got here just before Thanksgiving. My baby is due in mid-May."

"You've sure made this place feel like home." Jane's purple quilt lay across her bed and the lamp on her desk shone on the picture of a handsome black man.

Jane stared at the picture for a moment, "Nothing will make this place like home." She sighed and looked over at some stationery on her desk. It was half full of neat cursive.

As Gen took off her bulky winter coat and placed it on the empty bed, she turned her back so she could calm her thumping heart. Speaking to the wall, she said, "Boy, I sure am nervous to meet you."

Jane laughed lightly. "That's okay. I was nervous when I first came here too. Truth be told, I'm a bit nervous now."

Gen sighed in relief. "I can't tell you how relieved I am to hear you say that. I'm just not so good at meeting new people. First impressions are not my specialty." After sitting down on the edge of the bed and setting her head against the pillow, she began to relax. Closing her eyes, she blew out a deep breath and pulled her feet onto the bed. As she did so, the tension from the beginning of the day slipped away, replaced by a deep weariness. Within minutes, she curled up on the bare bed and fell asleep.

Four

From the peacefulness of sleep, Gen felt someone pulling on her shoulder. She opened her eyes to see the dark skin and doe-like brown eyes of her roommate bending down. "Genevieve, it's time for lunch."

As Gen rubbed sleep from her eyes, Jane checked her hair in the square mirror that hung on the wall next to the door. She raised her hand and smoothed the black hair back into place. Gen noticed a thin band with a small diamond on the fourth finger of her left hand.

"Just so you know," Jane said as she preened in the mirror, "my name isn't Jane Brown, I choose that name to protect the father of my baby. My real name is Carol Hammond." She turned to look straight at Gen, challenging her.

Gen sat up, surprised again. A flush crossed her neck. She'd assumed that Jane Brown was a real name. She had no right to protest someone else's assumed identity. "So what would you like me to call you?"

"If you could call me Jane around the other girls, I'd appreciate it. But when it's just the two of us, you can call me Carol, if you'd like."

Gen nodded, wondering what other surprises the day held. "You can call me Gen. It's what everyone calls me."

Gen adjusted her red sweater, pulling it down low to her waist. Despite being pregnant and away from interested eyes, she wasn't going to be sloppy in her dress. Looking in the mirror, she finger-combed her hair and reset the red headband she'd made to match this sweater. She'd always loved the way the color red made her look.

"Okay, I'm ready." Gen followed her roommate out the door and down the stairs. Walking down the stairs, Gen held the handrail and took small, careful steps. These steps were steeper and narrower than the ones at home. It felt like she was going to slip and fall down the whole set. Carol, on the other hand, kept her grip light and steps delicate, floating down the stairs.

Gen watched her roommate bounce down the stairs, aware of her own awkward movements. "These steps are steep. I'll bet lots of people slip on them."

"I guess girls have slipped," Carol said, "but no one should ever fall down these stairs unless they wanted to."

"Why would someone want to fall down the stairs? Wouldn't they get hurt?"

"Maybe, but not badly." Carol's voice trailed off.

"What aren't you saying?" Gen's eyes widened with alarm. "You mean, girls fall on purpose?"

Without turning back, Carol said, "That's what I've heard, but nothing like that has happened since I've been here." They turned down into the last flight of stairs. "If something does happen, you'll know. News travels fast around here."

Walking into the dining room the first thing Gen noticed was how many girls there were. She hadn't been in a crowd of girls like this since high school. Gen had never seen so many pregnant women in one place. And all of them in various stages of pregnancy. A few looked ready to burst, while others hardly looked pregnant at all. But they're all so young, Gen thought as she looked around the room. Why, some of these girls couldn't be halfway through high school yet. She didn't belong here with these kids, she wasn't even that kind of girl. Her fingers twitched at her sides as her eyes darted around the room.

It didn't take two seconds to locate Carol at a table on the other side of the room. Her brown skin stood out in the sea of whiteness. But she was chatting with another girl at her table. Gen saw one empty chair next to her and walked straight toward it. She sank into the chair when she reached the table.

Lunch was a whirlwind of soup, fresh bread, and new faces. Carol was patient in the introductions of every girl clamoring to meet Gen. But Gen couldn't keep all the names and faces straight. After meeting three different Bettys, one blonde, one with curly, dark hair, and another who looked barely old enough to be here without a chaperone, Gen realized that every other girl had taken a false name for her time at Bethany House. She wondered if anyone had ever used their real name.

Eventually, Gen was allowed to focus on her vegetable barley soup and crusty bread. A sudden wave of sadness crashed over her as she recalled her mother's anger-baking and the house smelling like a bakery. She would miss waking up to that smell.

She had hardly finished the last crust of bread when Mrs. Skloot stepped to the front of the room and cleared her throat. "Ladies." She waited until everyone had set down their spoons and the room was silent. "Good afternoon. A few announcements for today." Gen listened raptly. From the way she spoke, Gen knew Mrs. Skloot was the person in charge of Bethany House, and under her watchful eye, things happened as they were supposed to.

Her thoughts were broken when she heard, ". . . and please extend a warm welcome to our newest boarder, Genevieve Ryder. She will be staying in Unity suite for the next year. I'm sure that you will all make her feel welcome."

The room filled with polite clapping as Gen looked around the room and waved hello. "Now, lunch is over. You are dismissed." The room filled with the sound of chairs scraping over wooden floors and the pleasant jabbering of girls off to an afternoon of nothing.

Mrs. Skloot was at Gen's side guiding her out the door and up to her office on the second floor. Gen settled on a small love seat while Mrs. Skloot poured two cups of tea, handed one to Gen, and sat down, ready for a conversation.

Gen sipped the tea and waited for Mrs. Skloot to tell her why she was here.

Mrs. Skloot sipped her tea and regarded Gen.

"First," she began, "welcome to Bethany House. I hope that your time here, while not the same as being at home, is pleasant."

"Thank you." Gen took another sip of her tea. Mrs. Skloot kept her eyes locked on Gen.

Setting her teacup into her lap, Mrs. Skloot said, "Genevieve, you are the first young lady to ever come here and not take a pseudonym for her time here."

Gen steeled herself for criticism, holding onto her cup with both hands. Her eyes were laser focused down to the floor, studying the pattern of the carpet.

"Would you care to explain yourself?"

Gen stuttered, "Well, I guess, I just never thought about having a different name. So when the time came, it felt most natural to just be me."

"But aren't you worried about people finding out about you being here, pregnant?"

"I don't have many friends and I trust my family to keep this secret. They were none too happy about it in the first place." She took a sip. "Besides, a false name really isn't going to make a difference for when I take my baby home with me."

Mrs. Skloot nearly dropped her teacup. "Excuse me?" Her voice tremor a little. "Do I hear you saying that you are not going to be giving this baby up for adoption?"

Gen drew in a deep breath. "No, Ma'am. I'm not. I'm going to keep this baby."

It was Mrs. Skloot's turn to be silent.

Now that she was speaking, Gen rushed to get all the words out. "There's no reason I shouldn't keep this baby. I can raise a baby. Who says I can't?" Her voice grew higher in pitch, with every word she spoke.

Mrs. Skloot took a deep breath. "Genevieve, there's no need to get excited. I'm not going to take your baby away from you."

Chest heaving with deep breaths, Gen worked to calm herself. Every time she tried to talk about it, she knew she was being judged. "Well, why shouldn't I keep this baby?"

"For one, you are not married. And raising a child is best done when there is a mother and a father. Second, you do not have any of the necessary things to care for a child."

"Oh yes I—"

"Oh?" Mrs. Skloot raised an eyebrow. "Where would you live? What work will you do to earn a living? Who will keep the baby while you are working? These are serious questions that you need to consider."

"So you don't think I can do it, do you? You're just like my mother, who thinks I'm not good enough at anything or for anyone."

Mrs. Skloot recoiled as if slapped. She closed her eyes and took a deep breath. "I never said or thought anything of the sort." She glanced toward some framed photos on her desk across the room. "However, I do know a thing or two about raising children. I know that it is hard work that will be made much harder if you have to do all of it on your own."

Gen looked at the framed photos too. One photo was the framed head shot of a soldier. The other was of three teenagers, arm-in-arm, against the side of a car. "Is that your family?"

Mrs. Skloot smiled a weary smile. "Yes, my husband, Milton, was killed in the war. My three kids, well, they're older than that photo now, but are off making a life for themselves now." Her voice was soft and kind. "Yes, I know a thing or two about both those things."

"I'm sorry."

She was silent for a moment, then said, "We'll sort everything out in due time. However, for today's meeting, I have a few things to go over with you."

Gen rolled her eyes. She was tired of going over "things." Mr. Ronald had already made the rules and ways of life clear. Carol had filled her in on other things. She was a smart girl, she could figure everything else out.

"I would like to hear how you ended up in this situation."

Five

As she returned to the third floor, Gen was drained. Her eyes puffy and red, her splotchy cheeks streaked with tear tracks. She was looking forward to the quiet of her room, the relaxed unpacking of her suitcase, of making her tiny room home. She longed for quiet, but craved companionship.

Coming up the stairs, she could hear laughter. She paused, exhausted. Seeing no other way to her room, Gen continued up the stairs. At the top, before turning the corner, she steeled herself, knowing she didn't want to talk to anyone just then. She blew out an exasperated sigh and smoothed her hair, knowing the best she could do was to put on a brave smile.

Turning the corner, she saw six girls sitting around the room. One sat in a large, overstuffed chair in the corner with an open book on her lap. Two sat on a love seat, each with a basket of yarn at their feet and knitting needles in their hands. Two were seated at a small table with a chess board while another girl stood near them. Gen tiptoed, hoping to avoid their attention, but when she entered the room all eyes turned toward her.

Gen froze. Looking around the room, she recognized some of the faces from lunch, but couldn't remember any of the matching names.

A ponytailed girl sat at the chessboard. "Gen, I'm Emma Larson." Emma sat straight and tall in her chair. "Welcome to Unity." Her slanted eyes shone as she looked around the room introducing the others. The girl across the table from her was Sarah Smith whose wild ginger hair shot out in all directions. Sitting in the chair with a book, Marva Maple kept her head bent down, not even lifting her eyes. A mumbled "Hi" was all Gen heard from the girl. The two girls on the couch were Betty Jones and Shirley Temple. A loud snicker went up from Shirley as Emma spoke her name. "Sorry," she snorted and covered her freckled nose. "I laugh whenever I hear someone say my name." Her blonde curls bounced.

Laughter ringed the room. "Yeah," Betty said. "I'm never quite sure when someone's talking to me."

Emma finished by introducing Sally Smith, standing next to her table. Gen recoiled at the look of Sally. With a flat nose, flatter hair and a wide, broad shape, she was a girl who wasn't any cuter when pregnant.

Gen nodded to each girl, "It's nice to meet you all." Standing by the doorway, she rubbed her eyes, trying to make her escape to the privacy of her room. "I've just had a long meeting with Mrs. Skloot and—"

"I remember that talk," young Shirley Temple said. "I was so scared to talk to her, I hardly said a word. Especially when she asked me how I ended up in this situation, I just couldn't talk about that." She feigned a smile as her skin turned bright red.

A chorus of voices echoed her sentiment.

From out of their shared room came Carol. "Oh there you are, Gen. I was wondering what was taking you so long. Looking around the room, Carol lingered on Gen's face. "Why don't you come on in and unpack. You've had a long day. It'd be a good idea to rest before dinner and house meeting tonight."

Gen nodded, thankful for her new roommate's timing, and closed the door behind her when she walked into their room.

In the calm, quiet of their room, Gen took a deep breath and brushed stray hairs off her face. She studied her roommate who stared out the window. Carol's black shoulder length hair had texture. Her skin color wasn't pure brown, but variations from medium to dark. Carol turned back to see her roommate's eyes locked on her.

Embarrassment flooded over Gen, she hadn't meant to stare. "Carol, well, I um . . ." Her voice trailed off, she averted her eyes, finding a small knothole in the floorboards to study. She'd never met a black person before.

"Listen, Gen," Carol turned to face her, her eyes shining with strength. "I've been thinking. Being a roommate is new for me, probably like it is for you. And there's a lot we don't know about each other." Carol paused.

Gen searched for a correct response, but wasn't sure what to say. Even opening her mouth would reveal her naïveté. So she remained silent. She glanced at Carol and saw dignity in her roommate. Whatever she needed to say didn't make her look uncomfortable at all.

"I've never been in a situation like this before. Usually, I avoid white folk and keep to my own people. I don't know much about living with one." Carol started to chew at her nail. Maybe she was nervous after all. A rattle and hiss sounded from the wall underneath the window. The white metal radiator coil clattered to life.

"Neither do I. But it looks like that's what we're doing for the next year."

"Well, aren't we just two sad, pregnant women livin' far from home?"

Having nothing to offer, Gen was quiet. When Carol turned back to the window, Gen started unpacking her things. Her one borrowed suitcase held a nightgown, a few skirts and dresses, shoes, stockings and a few toiletries. Her skirts wouldn't fit her much longer, the waists were already getting a bit tight. If only she had access to a sewing machine, with a bit of fabric and time, Gen could whip a new wardrobe for her changing body. Good clothes mattered to Gen.

As she put her things away, she asked Carol, "You see that poster in the living room? The one with all the advice on how to dress when pregnant?" Gen pictured the poster, full of tips on how to dress to conceal a pregnant belly. She giggled as she recalled the fashion advice, as if wearing a sweater set would hide anything.

Carol's bubbly laugh filled the room. She said, "Yeah, as if clothes could fool people about us bein' pregnant." She snorted through her nose, covering her face. "Let me tell you, no one in this town is fooled when a bunch of pregnant girls come walking down the street, even if they are wearing wedding rings."

Gen smiled at the image of a gaggle of bundled pregnant girls waddling down the sidewalk. "Where do we get rings from?"

"Mrs. Skloot hands them out whenever we leave. They're kept in a basket at the front desk. When we return, it's put back in the basket."

"What about you?" Gen asked. "You're still wearing a ring. Didn't Mrs. Skloot make you turn it in after the last time you went out?"

Carol looked down at her hand. The thin gold band glinted against her chocolate skin. Pulling it off her finger, she caught it by the small diamond and spun it in circles. "This is mine. Jimmy gave it to me." She twirled it in silence.

"Jimmy?" Gen watched her roommate stare at her diamond.

Taking a deep breath, Carol said, "Jimmy and I are gettin' married. We've always known that, we talk about it all the time. The night Jimmy asked me to marry him, well . . ." Carol lowered her face. Although Gen couldn't see it, she knew her roommate was embarrassed.

"Why are you here, if you're getting married? " Gen asked.

"Jimmy loves me and we're still going to get married. The thing is, he's about to graduate from seminary and he'd be kicked out if they knew. And if we rushed a wedding, well, people can count backward." Carol stopped twirling her ring and straightened it on her hand. She studied the light reflected through the diamond's facets. "He's the first Negro to graduate from his school. He's worked so hard and nothing's goin' to get in the way. He's going to be a fabulous preacher someday."

"He's still going to marry you?" Gen asked.

"Yes, but I need to give the baby up for adoption first. Then after I'm home and he's graduated, we'll get married all proper with our friends and family." Carol's voice rose with hope and promise.

Gen shook her head in disbelief. She could hardly believe what she was hearing. How could a place like this really be part of someone's happily ever after?

Carol saw Gen's reaction and her body stiffened. "No one believes us, but you'll see. Even my mama doesn't think it'll happen." She stood and moved to the windowsill and said, her voice firm, "We will, we love each other."

"You don't have to convince me. I'm still working out if there's any way to get Bobby back."

"Back?"

"Yes, back. That's the way it's supposed to be. Bobby and I are going to get married and live in a cute little house and have a family together. It just has to happen." Even as she said it, Gen felt embarrassed. It sounded like such a childish dream.

Carol snorted. "Why would you want him back? You're here after all. There was plenty of time for him to do the right thing.

You don't believe my plan, but you think waltzing back into town after a year is gonna make Bobby want you?"

Now Gen's face flushed red hot. "Don't laugh." She turned her back so Carol couldn't see the tears rise. "You'll see, Bobby will see his baby and . . ." Her tears choked the end of the sentence.

Carol said, "Oh Gen, I'm sorry. I didn't mean to make you cry."

Gen turned away from Carol's concern and plopped herself down on a chair. Tears welled in her eyes and she sunk her face into her hands. She wanted to run and hide from everyone, seal herself up in darkness. This would have been different if it wasn't for Susie Hudson, if Bobby had proposed to Gen instead.

The radiator knocked again, interrupting the silence. Gen sniffed. "Is that always that loud?" she asked.

"Yeah, but like other things, you just get used to it." Turning to look at Gen, Carol asked, "So, what do you think about our suite-mates?"

Gen was glad for a chance to change the subject and searched for words, "They are . . . interesting?"

"It's amazing what you can learn when you just listen, but mostly I think they're just scared little girls. You're what? 20? 21?"

"I'm 22."

Carol said, "I'm 21 myself, but Shirley Temple is only fourteen and Marva turned sixteen last week. Sally and Emma are both 19, although Emma has a birthday soon. I'm not actually sure how old Betty is, but I would guess she's seventeen. Sarah, she's 16, but she doesn't give a hoot what anyone thinks about her. I've never met anyone so full of spunk in my entire life."

"They're so young. 14? 16? They're just kids."

"Yeah, kids having babies."

"Shirley ain't allowed to show her face at home until after the baby's born. It's her stepfather's and he threatened to tell the whole town she's a whore."

Gen raised her eyebrows as shock passed through her. She'd never heard of such a horrible thing.

Carol kept talking. "Marva just wants to go home. She doesn't care one bit about that baby."

"Does anyone want to keep their baby after it's born?"

Carol turned and looked straight at Gen. "Now why would anyone want to do that?"

A blush creeped up Gen's face. She hadn't been prepared for an answer like that. She stuttered, "Well, um, I just wondered, that's all."

Carol cocked her head to regard her more closely. The faint ring of a bell sounded from somewhere outside the room. She looked up at the clock on the wall. "Oh goodness," she said, "It's 5:30, time to get to dinner and meetin'."

Gen breathed a sigh of relief. She didn't have to explain herself again. After storing her empty suitcase under her bed, she said, "Okay, let's go." Carol led the way and Gen closed the door as they went down to dinner.

Six

After a weekend of getting acclimated to her new home, Gen couldn't wait for the new week to begin. On her way to breakfast on Monday morning, Mrs. Skloot handed her a single piece of paper. As she absent-mindedly spooned oatmeal into her mouth, she pored over the list in Mrs. Skloot's tidy cursive, wondering what it meant.

8:00 M–F: Chores
Monday, 9:00–11:30 Kitchen—Ms. Mavis
Tuesday, 9:00–11:30 Laundry—Mrs. Plumb
Wednesday, 9:00–11:30—Mrs. Skloot
Thursday, 10:00–12:30 Kitchen—Ms. Mavis
Friday, 9:00–11:30 Laundry—Mrs. Plumb

Gen deflated. Kitchen? Laundry? She already knew how to scrub pots and hang laundry. Years in her mother's home trained those skills into her fiber. Her mother's sole intent was to prepare her to be a wife. Gen was skilled in housework, even if she didn't care to be very good at it. She tried to remain open to new ideas, but already she was dreading these hours of work.

When the bell rang for chores, Gen focused on completing each one thoroughly, putting off the unpleasant hours ahead of her. However, sweeping the stairs just didn't take a long time. Despite her best effort not to, she arrived at the swinging kitchen door just as the grandfather clock in the foyer rang nine.

Standing in the doorway, Gen gaped open-mouthed at the sight before her. With a kerchief wrapped around her head and a white apron wrapped around her whole body, Ms. Mavis was directing a group of women cleaning the kitchen after breakfast.

Despite the chilly winter morning, the kitchen was hot and steamy. Ms. Mavis wore a light sheen of sweat across her brow. Using her sleeve to wipe her forehead, she looked up. "Well, don't just stand there, Miss Gen, come in. Welcome to my kitchen."

Gen was swept up under the hand of the small black woman. At first she winced to hear Ms. Mavis call out instructions to her staff, her voice loud and clear. "Nellie, yeast proofing yet? Holly, you started choppin' onions for the soup?" Ms. Mavis's voice thundered through the room.

Never before had Gen seen a room like this kitchen. Her mother would have been beside herself with envy. Long counters made of steel were covered with food in various stages of preparation. A freezer and refrigerator hugged an entire wall. A partially opened door led to a well-stocked pantry full of preserved food. Against the back wall was the largest stove and oven Gen had ever seen. Sixteen burners on the stove. Mother could bake cakes for an army in that oven!

Ms. Mavis's voice broke into Gen's amazement, "Come now, child, stop gapin' and get over here." Mavis led Gen to a corner acting as an office, with a desk covered in papers and a coat rack full of aprons. Pulling up a chair, she motioned for Gen to have a seat.

"Alrighty then, let's get to business. Beverly thought you could use some time here in my kitchen. So tell me, what do you know 'bout cookin'?"

Gen shrugged her shoulders. Using cautious words, she said, "Well, my mother doesn't seem to think I know anything about cooking."

"I didn't ask what your mama thought, I asked what you thought."

Gen reached up and grabbed a piece of hair resting on her shoulder. After fiddling for a moment, she said, "Well, I know how to boil water for tea and coffee. And I'm pretty good at mashed potatoes."

Mavis waited.

"I can make applesauce and a ham steak." She looked at Mavis, waiting for her nod of approval.

She didn't even blink. "Anything else?" Mavis asked.

"No, ma'am, not that I can recall right now," Gen answered. She kept her eyes lowered and fidgeted her hands. She wanted to sink into the floor.

Mavis burst out laughing. "Oh Lord, child, no wonder Beverly sent you here. You think you're gonna take your baby home and feed her only applesauce and mashed potatoes? It's not gonna take a week for her to throw 'em back in your face." She opened a drawer on her desk and pulled out three worn notebooks wrapped shut with twine. "These are my notebooks. They hold all my recipes and the recipes my Momma taught me. Now I'm gonna use 'em to teach you to cook. That's why you're here. Every Monday and Thursday, 'cept when you have your baby, you're gonna be here in this kitchen learning to cook."

Gen broke out into a wide smile. "That sounds lovely, Ms. Mavis."

"Lovely? I ain't so sure 'bout that, but it'll be fun. Don't misunderstand, though, I'm fixin' to make you capable in the kitchen, so you can feed that baby of yours and hopefully, someday, a man too. It's gonna be work, make no mistake."

Gen nodded, properly chastised.

"Here's your first assignment: take my notebooks and make a list of the recipes you want to learn."

"Yes ma'am," Gen said. And as she held out her hand to receive the books, Ms. Mavis pulled out a clean notebook. "What's this?" she asked.

"Why it's your own notebook. No use teachin' you the recipes if you ain't got a way to remember 'em."

Gen smiled, "Of course not, Ms. Mavis. Thank you." She stood to walk toward the door when she felt a hand on her arm.

"Now where do you think you're goin'?"

"Upstairs, to do my work."

Ms. Mavis shook her head. "Uh-un, darlin' we're just beginnin' to work 'round here. Now you set those books down, grab an apron and let me show you 'round my kitchen."

Gen obeyed and spent the next hour learning the intricacies of Ms. Mavis's kitchen. She whirled around the room so fast and spoke with such authority that after ten minutes, Gen's head was spinning. Even with the education her mother had attempted, nothing compared to this speedy tutorial. In the second hour, Mavis rattled off twenty meal combinations, named all the items for a well-stocked pantry, and gave tips for dealing with the continued rationing of sugar.

"Now, I hear the sugar ration is 'bout to end. Lord have mercy, the cakes and sweets I am goin' to bake for you girls, those babies will be jumpin' from all the sugar in you!" Her rich laughter surrounded Gen. Although she wasn't sure what Mavis was talking about, the laughter felt wholesome.

When she left the kitchen, Gen was exhausted but exhilarated. Her arms carried four notebooks, her head whirled with tidbits of kitchen wisdom. She spent the entire afternoon pouring over the tattered notebooks and making notes in hers. Exploring the kitchen under Mavis's guidance gave her a sense of freedom her mother never offered. Her head swam with the possibilities awaiting her. For the first time, hope flickered, maybe things would turn out okay after all.

The next morning dawned bitter cold. As Gen walked to the laundry, the second hub of Bethany House, she rubbed her hands together. After the energetic hours in the kitchen yesterday, Gen feared that the monotony of the laundry would be crushing. How could hours of sorting, scrubbing, hanging, and ironing ever compare to the wild exhilaration of Ms. Mavis's kitchen? She set her face for hours of mind-numbing work. When she pushed open the door to the laundry, a wave of warm, sticky air engulfed her. Gen wrinkled her nose at the acidic scent of bleach blanketing the room. Large industrial washing machines stood sentry along the side wall. Long lines laden with diapers, maternity clothes, and linens traced the room. In the back of the room was a closed door to a tiny office. Once standing in front of the door, Gen hesitated.

After taking a deep breath, she rapped her knuckles on the door.

"Come in," a soft voice called.

Gen pushed the door open to a crowded space. Piles of half-finished projects filled shelves that scaled the wall. Between the two sewing machines on one table was a jumbled pile of pattern papers. The other table was stacked high with a circus of fabrics and cut pattern pieces. Loose threads littered the floor. Baskets of pastel yarn were squirreled away under chairs.

As she walked between the tables, Gen tried not to bump any of the piles. But as she turned to shut the door, her swinging arm knocked a pile of pinned items to the floor. "Oh no" she cried. When bending down to pick up what she dropped, she knocked another pile over with her back.

The soft voice said, "Oh, don't worry about that. I'll get it. Come, sit down." As Gen sat in the only open spot in the room, a tall-backed wooden chair with arms, Mrs. Henrietta Plumb glanced up and said, "Welcome to my shop, Miss Ryder."

"Thank you, Mrs. Plumb. I'm glad to be here."

Silence descended upon the room. Mrs. Plumb sat still in her chair except for her hands holding flying knitting needles. A pair of glasses attached to a gold chain rested low upon her nose. Her blonde-gray hair was pulled into a bun at the top of her neck, loose pieces tucked behind her ears. She sat with ankles crossed. Her blue sweater was fastened with only one button at the top.

"Mrs. Skloot believes you may have some skills with fabric, is that true?"

"Yes ma'am," Since Mrs. Plumb didn't ask another question, Gen said, "My mother taught me some basics and I made clothes for our family throughout the war. I'm pretty good at making new clothes but not so good at straight hems." The words tumbled out and hung in the air. As the silence enveloped her words, Gen started pulling at her sweater. Soon, the faint tick of the second hand of the wall clock filled the entire room with an uncomfortable noise.

"Can you knit?" Mrs. Plumb asked. She counted off her row of pink yarn before she looked up at Gen, sitting in the chair next to her.

Gen answered. "It's not my favorite thing to do but—"

"In my shop, idle hands are not allowed. If you are ever not working on a project, you will have a set of needles in your hand and a basket of yarn at your feet." Her voice was quiet, but commanding.

Gen gulped. Obviously, Mrs. Plumb thought knitting was quite important. "Yes Ma'am," she said. Within seconds, a pair of knitting needles were placed into her hands.

"Every child leaving Bethany House goes with a handmade blanket. I believe a ball of yarn is in the basket under your chair."

Under her chair was a pastel green wicker basket with some rose decals on the lid. Pulling it out, Gen found it fit perfectly on her lap. Opening the lid, she found one ball of pink yarn and a set of knitting needles. There was room for much more in the basket: patterns, fabric, a small shelf for spools of thread or sewing scissors. It was easy to imagine it full of projects and designs for projects.

Gen retrieved the ball of yarn. She tied the yarn on and attempted a decent row of knots, but she kept having to start over. A low growl grew in her throat when she dropped her stitch for the fifth time. Plopping her knitting needles onto her lap, Gen huffed and said, "I'm sorry Mrs. Plumb, but I can't make a blanket for you. I keep dropping stitches."

Mrs. Plumb stared at Gen for a moment. Her eyes were wide and unblinking, like an owl's. She set down her knitting needles and sighed. "We'll just have to start at the beginning then, won't we?"

Over the next hour, Mrs. Plumb guided Gen's hands through casting on and counting stitches, how to purl and knit, how to add and decrease stitches. Not once did Mrs. Plumb raise her voice in frustration, nor did she roll her eyes at Gen's inability. She was perfectly patient the entire time.

At the end of their time together, she spoke in her quiet voice, "Why don't you take this basket with you until we meet again later this week."

"Yes, Mrs. Plumb, I'll do that," Gen said, rolling her eyes. A few days of frustrated practice was not how Gen wanted to spend her free time, but she gathered her supplies into the basket to take with her anyway.

"When we meet again, we will review what you know about sewing garments. Please be sure to bring the basket with you to all our classes, it's going to be the place where you store all your pieces while they are in progress."

Gen nodded. "Yes, Mrs. Plumb."

"You were an excellent student today, Miss Ryder. I look forward to our time together."

Gen left the room carrying the sewing basket and blooming with peace. She hadn't done anything well, but Mrs. Plumb's calm demeanor was soothing. In the few minutes left before lunch, she wanted to sit in the living room and practice what she'd learned. The calm spirit of Mrs. Plumb had infiltrated Gen's soul. Gen hummed as she walked, enjoying the peace she felt.

Seven

The chairs scraped across the cold, clean tile floor. A small child wrapped in a blanket whimpered. Loud, staccato coughs sounded through the frigid silence of the doctor's waiting room. With a straight back, Gen sat on a chair with her coat buttoned up tight and hands folded in her lap. Next to her, Mrs. Skloot sat with her ankles crossed, reading the latest issue of Time magazine.

Through Mrs. Skloot's connections, Gen had her first doctor's appointment two days after New Year's, 1947. The waiting room was crowded with young children and new mothers. Gen noted their superior airs, one that said they deserved to be sitting in this doctor's office waiting to be seen.

She rubbed her naked hands together. Mrs. Skloot had forgotten to give Gen a wedding band before leaving Bethany House. On the drive over Gen realized the mistake and mentioned it.

Mrs. Skloot was dismissive in her answer. "Don't worry about it, Genevieve. Keep your coat buttoned up tight and no one will suspect why we're there. For all anyone cares, we're a mother and daughter there for a 'personal matter.'" Gen protested, but Mrs. Skloot hushed her.

Gen had no idea what to expect at this doctor's appointment. She didn't know pregnant women went to the doctor before the baby was born.

Sitting in the waiting room, Gen steeled herself for condemning stares. The young mother whose baby was whimpering was so busy trying to calm her fussy child that she wasn't even aware Gen was in the room. The other pregnant women were focused on their magazines and swollen bellies.

As Gen sat waiting, nurses called names from the doorway. The waiting room emptied, only to fill up again. She took surreptitious glances around the room. The waiting room was continually occupied by harried mothers or pregnant women. Everywhere she looked she saw pregnancy and babies.

Finally, an older nurse in a crisp, white uniform called from the doorway, "Genevieve Ryder." Although she had been waiting to hear her name called, Gen jumped in her seat. "That's me," she said, rising to follow the nurse. When Mrs. Skloot settled further into her chair, she asked, "Aren't you coming with me?" Gen didn't want to do this by herself.

"No I'm not," she said. "I'll be waiting right here when you're done."

Gen swallowed hard, straightened her coat, and followed the nurse.

"So, Genevieve, you're a new patient of Dr. Rasmussen? What are we seeing you for today?"

"I'm pregnant," Gen said.

"How wonderful," said the older woman. She looked back at Gen over her shoulder. "New babies are so delightful. Is this your first child?"

"Yes, it is."

"The father, he must be very excited," she said as she led Gen back through a labyrinth of hallways.

Gen hesitated. "No, he's not very excited. He's engaged to someone else."

The nurse's face tightened. Looking down at the file in her hand, she said, "I see." She turned her back to Gen and quickened her pace.

"Stop here. I need to check your weight and height and blood pressure." She motioned to a scale set off into a small alcove. Gen stepped onto the scale.

The nurse rolled her eyes and let out a huffy breath. "Take off your jacket and shoes, and put your purse down." Her voice had lost its sound of humor.

Feeling reprimanded, Gen did as she was told. She watched as the nurse recorded her height and weight, shaking her head at the number on the scale. The nurse used quick movements to take her blood pressure. When they were finished, Gen slipped her shoes back on and followed the nurse to an examination room.

Closing the door behind her, the nurse directed Gen to sit on the edge of the examination table. When Gen was seated, the nurse battered her with a series of questions about her health.

"Where are you from? Date of birth? Have you ever been in the hospital before? Have you received any vaccines? When do you think your baby is due?" The nurse paused long enough to record her answers.

Gen answered each question, careful not to add personal details the nurse did not want to hear. When the nurse finished her questioning, she instructed Gen, "Put on this gown and wait on the examination table, the doctor will be in to see you in a few minutes."

Gen took the washed gray gown from the nurse's hand. "Can I wear anything under it?" she asked. She had no idea what to expect.

"No, you mayn't," the nurse answered. "But you should be just fine with that." She left, leaving Gen alone in the cold, sterile room. Gen removed her shoes and stockings and folded them into a pile on the chair in the corner. Putting on the gown, she made sure the opening was in the back. After making her belongings neat, she sat up on the examination table. The cold of the metal table sent a shock through her entire body. Repositioning herself, she tried to find a comfortable way to sit on the table.

It had been years since Gen had been in a doctor's office, but this one was similar to what she remembered from her childhood. A skeleton hung in the corner. A large, framed diploma hung above the head of the examination table. Attached to the end of the exam table were two long legs with straps on the end.

A light rap on the door filled the room with sudden sound. "Come in," Gen said, hugging herself.

Entering the room was a tall, handsome man with dark hair and a white medical coat. He greeted Gen, "Good morning, I'm Dr. Rassmussen."

"Hello," Gen said, averting her gaze from the doctor's eyes.

"You're Genevieve Ryder?" he asked, studying her medical chart.

"Yes."

"I see here you are pregnant with your first baby." Still looking at the medical chart.

"Yes."

"Do you know how far along you are?"

"My mother and I think I am due in mid-June."

"Oh," he said, glancing up from the chart. "Is your mother a mid-wife?"

"No," Gen answered.

"Well, we can't just take your mother's word for it, now can we? Let's do a proper examination." He commanded Gen to lie back on the exam table. As he started her exam, he looked down. "Your gown is on backward, it should open in the front," he said.

Gen's face blushed hot red. She stammered an apology, but Dr. Rasmussen brushed it off. "Next time," he said, "put the gown on correctly."

He pulled a sheet out of the cupboard and allowed Gen to cover her lap while he observed her stomach. Pressing down on different areas, he asked more questions. "Have you felt the baby move? How are you eating? Have you had any spotting or cramps?"

Eventually, he asked Gen to place her legs in the leather straps at the end of the table. She filled with shame at what followed. No words of comfort from the doctor, just silence as he completed his examination. Once he was finished, she put her legs down, squeezing them together to protect against more intrusions.

Clearing his throat, he said, "You are pregnant. I'd say by the size of your womb that you are approximately four to five months along, making your mother's estimate quite possible. I believe the baby is due sometime in late May or early June."

Gen smiled weakly at him, nodding as he spoke.

"Now, Miss Ryder, listen to me carefully. I'm a doctor who's studied all kinds of things, including complicated things like what happens during pregnancy, things you've never even thought about."

Gen nodded.

"I'll be giving you medical advice throughout this pregnancy. You need to pay close attention or you could put your baby in harm's way."

"Yes, sir," Gen said. "What do I need to do?"

"Are you and the father of this baby still together?"

"No sir, he lives in a different town."

"Good, because you're not to engage in any sexual activity during your pregnancy." Without pausing for a breath, he continued, "What are your plans for after the baby is born? Is it going to be adopted by a loving couple? To give this baby the life it deserves?" His gaze was intense.

Gen knew what he wanted to hear. She swallowed, nervous to speak honestly. However, she couldn't keep her choice a secret, despite what others would think. "Actually no, I'm going to keep the baby."

"Excuse me?" Dr. Rasmussen asked. "I believe you misspoke. Did you say you intend to keep this baby?" The sound of disapproval was distinct in his voice.

"Yes, sir," she said, lowering her head.

He cleared his throat and closed the medical file. "I believe we are done here. I need to speak with your mother."

"Sir, I am living at Bethany House. My parents are in Madison, but you may talk with Mrs. Skloot if you'd like."

"I most certainly will." He stood. "You need to see me once a month until we get closer to the baby's due date." Then he left the room, slamming the door behind him.

Gen began redressing. Her hands shook as she put on her skirt and stockings, blouse and shoes. She was buttoning her coat when there was a gentle knock on the door.

Mrs. Skloot spoke through the door, "Genevieve, are you dressed yet?"

"Yes, Mrs. Skloot. I'll be out in a minute."

"May I come in?"

Before she had a chance to answer, Mrs. Skloot walked in.

She said, "Dr. Rasmussen isn't pleased with your choice to keep the baby."

Gen was silent, but nodded.

"Does that make you want to change your mind, Genevieve?"

"No. Why would that make me change my mind? I don't care what he thinks, I'm keeping this baby."

"I was just checking. Let's get you back. I'm sure it's been a difficult morning."

Gen followed Mrs. Skloot out of the office maze and back to the car. On the way back to Bethany House, she stared out the car window as silent tears of humiliation traced paths down her cheeks.

Eight

After the trauma of her doctor's appointment, Gen was looking forward to a weekend of relaxation. She flopped onto her bed, thankful for some time alone.

No sooner had she closed her eyes to rest than Carol danced into the room, happiness emanating from every pore. In her hands, she clutched a letter. "He's coming this weekend!"

Gen sat straight up, startled from her rest and her exhaustion forgotten. "What? Who's coming this weekend? What's happening?"

"Jimmy!" Carol squealed. "He's coming for Open House on Sunday."

"For what?"

"Didn't Mrs. Skloot explain that on Sundays, Bethany House is open for family to visit us and for couples to visit the nursery?"

Gen tried to recall that part of their conversation. "No, I don't remember anything about that, I must have missed it."

Carol started to fan herself with the letter. "It's only the best day of the week." Gen burst into laughter as she watched her serious roommate dissolve into a sentimental, mushy girl, staring out the window, humming, and playing with her ring. "And Jimmy, he's coming to take me to Sunday dinner."

On Sunday, Carol spent the morning preening in front of the tiny mirror on the wall. Between long gazes, Carol kept glancing out the window, waiting. When she spotted Jimmy coming up the walk, she checked her face, smoothed her hair one last time, and bolted out the door.

Gen followed behind, curious to meet Jimmy. "Hey, wait up," Gen called as she ran through the living room. Carol was halfway down the stairs before Gen caught up. "Not so fast. I want to meet this man of yours."

"Of course, Gen. I'd love for you to meet Jimmy. I'm sure he'd like to meet you as well." As they walked down the stairs, Carol regaled Gen with more stories of Jimmy's many strengths. When they arrived in the foyer, Gen caught her breath. Standing at the front desk in a neat gray suit with his winter overcoat draped over his arm, Jimmy Wattson smiled at the sight of Carol.

"Now there's a sight for sore eyes," the deep baritone of his voice rang through the foyer as she ran into his arms. She disappeared against his chest.

Gen couldn't believe what she saw. A man who loved his woman and stood by her in times of trial. Jealousy shot through her. Although she kept a bright smile pasted on her face, Gen's heart threatened to burst with sadness. It just wasn't fair.

The sharp voice of Mrs. Skloot called out from the living room. "Ms. Brown. That's quite enough."

Carol pulled away from Jimmy, her eyes locked on his. "Sorry, Mrs. Skloot."

The prim voice said, "I know you are happy to see Mr. Wattson, but decorum must be practiced."

Jimmy stepped away from Carol and bowed his head to the older woman, "I'm sorry Ma'am. It won't happen again."

"I'm sure it won't, Mr. Wattson." As she turned back to the living room, Gen saw the hint of a smile cross Mrs. Skloot's face. When she looked back at Carol and Jimmy, their arms were linked around each other's waists, looking straight at her.

"This is my new roommate, Genevieve Ryder," Carol said.

"It's a pleasure to meet you, Miss Ryder." Jimmy said as he stuck out his hand.

Gen nodded as she shook his hand. His hand was large and his grip was strong. She laughed. "The pleasure's mine. I've been waiting to meet you." Their bright smiles lit the room. "But please, call me Gen. It's what everyone calls me."

Arching an eyebrow, Jimmy exchanged glances with Carol who said, "No, it's okay, it's her real name."

"Well, then, I'm more than pleased to meet my girl's new roommate." He grabbed Carol's hand and pulled her toward the door. "But now, if you don't mind, we're expected for Sunday dinner."

"Don't worry, Mrs. Skloot, I'll be back by curfew," Carol sang as they walked away.

Gen watched as they talked all the way to his parked car, where he opened the door for Carol. Joy radiated. Gen stood in the window until the car's exhaust disappeared into the cold January afternoon. Gen sighed as she turned away and trudged to the living room, her heart overwhelmed by her own sorry situation.

Gen stayed there for the entire afternoon, as others received their visitors. The excitement and nervousness cycling through the room was contagious. Gen wondered if her family even knew about Open House days. She watched as fathers stood uncomfortably against a wall while mothers made awkward conversation. Sometimes a sister or aunt would visit and the two would gab for a long time. Gen pictured her mother coming to this place and knew it would never happen. A comfortable afternoon with Marie would be lovely though.

Every girl sitting in front of the warm fire tried to share in the joy of the girls who had a visitor. They completed their rows of knitting in sad silence with eyes lowered and tears wiped from the corners of eyes.

Gen sat with the others who had no visitors. To distract herself from the sadness, she flipped through old magazines she found under the coffee table. Worn copies of *Look*, *Ladies' Home Journal*, and *Women's Home Companion* helped pass the time, but offered no respite from her feelings. Filled with articles on how to make marriage work and how to be more beautiful, Gen felt it was all just a rotten waste of time. Pregnant and single in a world that wouldn't accept that, she'd failed at the basic core tenant of being a woman: to have a husband, a home, and a family that she could care for.

However, the ads for clothes piqued her interest. Even though she couldn't wear any of the styles, she imagined what it would be like to create her own clothes for a magazine ad. Gen lost herself in her mind's eye imagining her clothes in the ads of a magazine. The palette of colors and variety of fabrics danced across her imagination. Slowly, single threads of an idea started to weave itself in her mind.

Flanked by Shirley on one side and Marva on the other, they all sat wordless throughout the afternoon. Each time another girl returned, their spirits deflated a bit more. By the time the dinner bell rang, two withdrawn creatures sat next to Gen. Refusing dinner, they plodded to their rooms and went to bed.

As the faint light of the day disappeared, the empty sound of the living room was a sad contrast to the joyous noise of returning girls echoing through the house. The heavy front door would open and close with a heartbreaking thud. Happy footsteps would skip up the stairs to share stories with friends.

Sitting at a half-full dinner hall, Gen wondered if every Sunday was like this: a painful reminder of the life that had rejected them. The bologna sandwich and wilted cabbage salad on her plate seemed appropriate. She pushed it around, pretending to eat. Despite her hunger, she had no appetite. Heaving her shoulders, she pushed her plate away and left the dining room. Her steps dragging, she made slow passage up to the third floor where her own roommate was waiting to regale her with tales of her own glorious day.

Six weeks of Open House Sundays had passed. Gen missed her family. She, along with a few others, had never had a visitor. Jimmy had whisked Carol away two more times. Gen spent those afternoons alone in her room, trying not to allow jealousy to devour her. That stack of magazines, full of pictures and stories of ideal lives kept her and her imagination company.

Otherwise, things at Bethany House were fine. Her room was comfortable. Carol was becoming a wonderful friend. Gen was learning a lot under the guidance of the staff.

But she missed the smell of the wood fire that warmed the living room and the squeak of the rocking chairs in the evening at home. She missed long talks with Marie, draped across her bed. She missed the smile her dad reserved just for her. She even missed the sound of her mother clomping around the kitchen.

Mrs. Skloot offered to let her use the phone in her office to call home, if she'd like. But Gen couldn't bring herself to do it. She was afraid that the sound of her family's voices would hurt more than they'd help.

Valentine's Day was just like any other for Gen and the girls at Bethany. But the bouquet of red rose buds in a vase on her roommate's desk made it impossible to ignore.

The morning had been spent with Mrs. Plumb, which usually quieted her spirit, but today there was no peace. In the afternoon, she sat in her room, fighting with blue yarn and a delicate diamond baby blanket pattern. After discovering a few extra holes that shouldn't have been there, she threw her needles onto her desk and dropped her head into her arms. Eventually Gen opened the sewing basket and rummaged through the growing collection. Her hand poked around pieces of scratch paper with sketches of dresses for a pregnant body, the crinkly pieces of pattern pinned to black rayon, and little bits of this and that. Nothing she touched gave her any inspiration.

While examining her most recent sketch, for a maternity dress wondering if there was any way to make it look less frumpy, there was a knock at the door. After a moment, Mrs. Skloot walked in, holding a package wrapped in brown paper. "A deliveryman dropped this off for you a few minutes ago."

Gen opened her arms to receive it. Turning the package over in her hands, she smiled. Mail from home! She ripped open the brown paper, letting pieces fall to the floor. The scent of gardenias rose through the air. Opening the box, flannel fabric pushed out first. Under that she found a bar of soap wrapped in white paper and a small silver hand mirror.

She picked up the soap and inhaled the familiar scent of gardenias. The only extravagance her mother allowed was a single bar of gardenia soap kept in the bathroom. A small note on the soap read: "This soap was hand milled in France and is quite expensive. Don't waste it.—Mother."

Gen laughed. Her mother didn't change, even when they were apart.

She pulled the flannel nightgown up to her face and rubbed the soft fabric against her cheek. Without looking for a tag, she knew this was from Marie. Her sister had a weakness for new pajamas. The white cotton had thin blue stripes and yellow rosebuds, a scoop neck and short sleeves. Holding it up against her, she could see there was plenty of room for her growing belly. Tied around one of the buttons with a blue grosgrain ribbon was a small white card written in Marie's hurried scrawl. "Gen, I hope you love it. I saw it and thought of you. I miss you. Marie."

Tears sprung to Gen's eyes. The ache in her heart grew as she pictured her sister making a special trip in the February weather to purchase it for her. She smiled through her tears and sat with the nightgown in her lap.

Looking down to study the gown again, she caught the glint of a silver hand mirror, petals growing up the handle and along the rim of the mirror. On the back of the mirror two roses were stamped, one in bloom, one still in bud. Turning it over, the mirror face was shiny and bright, a small envelope taped to it. Inside, an ivory card was full of Gen's father's chicken scratch.

Gennie,

I hope you are well.

We received an invitation for the McFadden/Hudson wedding, but declined. The wedding takes place on Valentine's Day.

The house isn't the same without you. Mother doesn't seem happy without you here. I know I'm not. I'm hoping to come visit for an Open House soon.

I love you,

Dad

Gen couldn't hold back any longer. Slumping over, she held the mirror tightly in her hands as she cried. Tears streamed down her face.

So it happened, Bobby really married Susie. Gen's hope to get him back was gone. Valentine's Day now tasted more bitter.

The baby started to kick. The little one had been more active lately, kicking, punching, and moving, as if it was announcing its presence. Gen's hand dropped to feel the jab of tiny feet push against its confinement. The sureness of the baby's presence in her pain brought a weak smile to her face.

Looking down at her growing belly, covered with gifts from her family, she said, "Don't worry little one, we don't need Bobby. You and me, we'll be okay. Look who loves us." And she spent the rest of the afternoon talking to the baby in her belly about their family.

Nine

To cover her homesickness, Gen threw herself into her weekly lessons. The trio of women acting as mentors each added something different to Gen's life.

Wednesday mornings with Mrs. Skloot were her anchor. Sipping tea and chatting, Gen was free to ask any question without fear of judgment.

Her weekly visits to Mrs. Plumb's sewing room were the cornerstone to who she was becoming. With joy, she worked to design new clothes for the girls to wear during their pregnancies. The work of creating was quiet, only the humming of sewing machines could be heard. Gen and Mrs. Plumb spoke in subdued tones.

Gen felt peace infiltrating her soul. When Mrs. Plumb asked if she could tutor some of the other girls in their sewing skills, Gen filled her afternoons teaching in the same patient, calm manner that had been used on her.

In complete contrast was Gen's time in the kitchen with Ms. Mavis. It was loud and fast-paced. After a few months of Mondays, Ms. Mavis taught Gen how to make loaves of bread, fried chicken, and sponge cake, and how to serve a proper afternoon tea. Gen filled her notebook with recipes and tips. Every page of the notebook reflected the love Mavis poured into creating food.

However, the pace of the kitchen work took its toll on Gen's body. By the end of each night, her ankles were swollen and her back ached from standing all morning. Even the baby protested the effort the work required, kicking and punching throughout her morning lessons.

Mrs. Skloot and Mavis had a special job in mind for her time in the kitchen on Thursdays when Gen's work time coincided with lunch service. The two women expected that Gen would help prepare and serve lunch every Thursday while all the younger girls were in their academic classes. Gen loved being able to participate in a useful way in the house.

When she rolled the cart out of the kitchen into the dining room on Thursdays, she stood straighter, knowing she had a hand in preparing the food. While today's menu sounded simple, Gen worked hard making the rolls and chopping the vegetables for the soup. Under the ever-watchful eye and interfering hand of her mother, she'd never made a full meal for others before.

As Gen rolled the cart to the first table she looked them in the eye and greeted them. "Hi girls, soups on!" She placed a basket full of hot rolls and a tureen of spring vegetable soup on the table. The looks on their faces were a mixture of awe, confusion, and respect.

"Gee, thanks Gen."

"Did you help make this yourself, Gen?"

She nodded and said, "Yes, I did and thanks. I hope you enjoy it."

Moving from table to table, Gen received the respect of all the girls and she reveled in it.

Springtime struggled to appear. One day the March air smelled of wet dirt and warm sunshine. The next, dark clouds blanketed the sky and rain fell in sheets. As the crocuses and daffodils pushed out of the black dirt, the girls of Bethany House blossomed into their pregnancies. The girls of Unity neared the final trimester of their pregnancies. As the babies grew, so did the list of complaints from the girls of Unity suite.

Sitting in the living room after dinner, Gen rubbed her swollen ankles. "These days with Ms. Mavis are killing my feet."

"Sitting in classes all day makes my back ache," said Shirley Temple. She placed a pillow behind the small of her back as she read her science assignment.

Sarah twisted a piece of red hair around her fingers. "Oh my goodness, I don't know what you girls are talking about. I feel great!" She stood to do a couple jumping jacks, a goofy smile plastered on her face.

"Knock that off, Sarah." Gen threw a crocheted pillow at Sarah's head. "You're just trying to make us jealous."

"Yep," Sarah said. Two jumping jacks later she collapsed on the couch, panting, her cheeks red from the effort. Throwing her hand up to her forehead, she said, "Phew, that's enough exercise for one day!" The girls burst into laughter.

But the mood wasn't always so sunny. On the spring days the rain fell like a thick curtain, the girls' mood darkened like the sky.

At a house meeting on one of those dreary evenings, Mr. Ronald announced that Marva had taken a fall down the stairs. Concerned murmurs circled the room. "She's been taken to St. Mary's for observation. Not to worry, we expect her back in a few days."

Gen closed her eyes and sighed. She'd watched the poor girl shrivel up inside herself, locked away in her room. Marva pushed off all offers to go out, to play games, to make up stories, or to sit together. She just wanted to be alone. And now she had fallen. Gen shook her head. Life had not been kind to Marva Maple.

Two days after Mr. Ronald's announcement, Mrs. Skloot pulled Gen aside after breakfast. "Genevieve," she said, "I'm packing up Marva's things this morning. I'd like you to help me."

Gen was shocked, unspoken questions written across her face.

"There will be time for questions later. I'll meet you in Marva's room in thirty minutes." Mrs. Skloot's sharp voice was quieter than normal. She turned on her heel and walked away. Dumbfounded, Gen watched Mrs. Skloot guide Shirley out of the dining room and up the stairs.

After finishing her chores, Gen found Mrs. Skloot and Shirley together in the girls' shared room. Shirley was crying, tears streaming down her cheeks. Her eyes were red and swollen.

Gen stood in the doorway, hesitant to enter. Mrs. Skloot leaned over and spoke into the girl's ear. She looked up and pointed out Marva's bed, desk and dresser. A single picture stood on the desk.

Mrs. Skloot laid a gentle hand on Shirley's shoulder. Her voice soft, she said, "Why don't you collect yourself for a few minutes, then take some time to freshen up. When you feel better, head to class." Shirley nodded. Gen moved aside to let the girl bolt from the room.

Mrs. Skloot waved Gen into the room. "Let's get to work," Mrs. Skloot said. After retrieving the suitcase and laying it open on the bed, she opened the top drawer to find a jumble of shirts, sweaters, and stockings. Gen watched the headmistress fold and pack each item jammed into the overcrowded drawers. Gen turned toward Marva's desk. The desk was cleared on top. But when she opened the top drawer, paper and pens and half-written letters exploded out. Papers seemed to be falling everywhere. She bent over to catch them, but her growing belly was in the way. Looking up, Mrs. Skloot said, "Let me get those for you."

"Thanks, Mrs. Skloot. But I can get it, just give me a moment . . ." Her voice trailed off. Standing back up with a fistful of papers, Gen turned to her mentor and said, "Why am I here? You don't need my help to pack a suitcase."

Turning toward the girl, Mrs. Skloot said, "I wanted to talk with you, and I thought we could do it while cleaning out Marva's things."

Gen looked down at the pile of papers she was attempting to corral. "Where is Marva?" she asked. "Why isn't she coming back? All she ever talked about was how badly she wanted to go home."

"I believe the correct word for her feelings about Bethany House is 'hated,' Genevieve." Gen flinched at the harshness of the word. Mrs. Skloot held her eyes. "I think you need to hear the truth about Marva."

"The truth?" Gen covered her open mouth with her hand as realization passed through her. "Her fall wasn't an accident, was it?"

Mrs. Skloot shook her head, but didn't remove her eyes from Gen's. "The truth is that sometimes a desperate girl will throw herself down the stairs."

Gen's eyes widened. An 'oh' formed on her lips, but no sound came out.

"Marva will be fine." Mrs. Skloot took a breath and said, "But her baby died, a beautiful, perfectly formed baby girl."

The room started to spin. Gen couldn't believe it. The baby was dead. Marva had done it on purpose. Her questions tumbled into each other. "Didn't she understand that the baby would be adopted to a family? Why wasn't that enough? This doesn't make sense."

Gen felt Mrs. Skloot's strong hands press down on her shoulders, lowering her to sit on the edge of the bed. Mrs. Skloot could make sense of this madness. She looked up at the headmistress, sitting on the edge of the other bed, so close their knees knocked. With hands clasped in her lap, she sat with furrowed brow and shiny eyes.

"Genevieve, oftentimes, in life, things don't make sense. Bad things happened to good people. Good people make bad choices. Sickness, unplanned pregnancy, heartache, and grief. All a part of life. If we rely only on what we can make sense of, we'll spend our lives lost and lonely."

Gen squirmed in her seat. These words made her uncomfortable, although she didn't know why. Her eyes darted around the room, looking for something to latch on to.

Without wiping the tears from her eyes, Mrs. Skloot leaned forward and put her hand on Gen's knee. Gen's eyes returned to the older lady's.

"Marva's not coming back, is she?"

Shaking her head, Mrs. Skloot said, "I called her parents. They're so distraught they took her home, against Doctor's orders, I might add."

"Will she be okay?"

"Her body will heal, but her heart will bear a scar. Losing a baby, whether by accident or choice, changes a woman forever. The same for those who have their children adopted."

New questions filled Gen's head, "Why are you telling me?"

"Your decision will mark you too, just in a different way. You can either try to do everything by yourself, or you can lean on the family around you."

In that moment, Gen was jealous of Marva. She got to go home.

Gen stood to resume boxing up the contents of Marva's desk, when Mrs. Skloot stopped her. "I'll finish up, I'm sure you have a lot to think about. Why don't you go rest for a while?"

Gen released the paper she'd been clutching. "Yes, Mrs. Skloot." She felt a bit off-center and could use a rest. Before walking out the door, she studied the family picture on Marva's desk. Just a smiling couple and three girls in front of a house. "I wonder what kind of family Marva had that she so desperately wanted to get back." A sigh full of longing escaped her lips. "Must be a good one."

Mrs. Skloot sighed. "More than that, it's a great one."

Gen left Mrs. Skloot to the sad work of cleaning up the rest of Marva's belongings.

The conversation with Mrs. Skloot left Gen unsettled. Beyond Marva's fate, Gen couldn't decipher the rest of the conversation. Did Mrs. Skloot tell her to convince her not to keep this baby? They'd had too many talks about the possibilities for that to be true. She lowered her hand to her bulging belly, feeling the sharp kicks beneath it. The way she'd talked, Gen wondered if she was also trying to tell her something about Carol who was having her child adopted. It all felt so conflicting. There were consequences for each decision and none of them seemed particularly kind.

Gen spent the next weeks moping around the house. Despite a growing hunger, food didn't interest her. She spent time in the living room talking with the girls, but she just wanted to be alone. She needed time and quiet to calm the storm Marva's loss had raised in her.

The next Open House Sunday, she sat in the parlor with the other neglected girls when Mrs. Skloot walked in, a wide smile plastered across her face. "Genevieve," she said above the noise of conversation, "you have a visitor."

Cheers erupted across the room. Gen's heart leaped in her chest. There hadn't been any letters or calls. Mrs. Skloot's voice interrupted her thoughts. "Don't just sit there. He's waiting."

At these words, Gen ran from the room to find her dad chatting with Mr. Ronald. "Daddy!" Her voice filled the foyer. She ran into his arms and hugged him tight. Burrowing her head into his jacket, she breathed in his familiar scent of fire and farm. Everything would be okay now, her dad was here.

When she pulled away, he took a step back. "My goodness, Gennie, look how you've grown. You're practically glowing."

Gen blushed and said, "Thanks, Dad. What are you doing here?"

"I'm here to see my girl, thought it was time for a visit." He smiled and looked past Gen's shoulder. Gen turned her head to see Mrs. Skloot standing at the Welcome Desk with shining eyes.

"Thank you," she whispered to the matron.

Mrs. Skloot nodded.

"So," Len said, calling the attention back, "why don't you show me around?"

"My pleasure," Gen said, as she slipped her arm into her dad's. For the next hour, Gen and Len walked the grounds of Bethany House. They followed the gravel footpath that circled the property. Their conversation wove a meandered path across life at home and at Bethany House. Their pace was unhurried, the sun high in the afternoon sky.

Len sat down on a bench in the middle of a green lawn, patting the seat next to him. Gen plopped down beside him. After all the catching up and family gossip, Gen needed to talk seriously with her father.

After a settling breath, her words tumbled out. "Will my life be horrible because I'm keeping this baby? Am I trying to fix things and making more trouble instead?"

After a deep sigh, Len took his daughter's hand between his own. "Oh Gennie, I don't know the right way to answer. Would it be easier to have this baby adopted? Probably, but then I think you would always wonder. Will your life be harder because of it? Yes, without a doubt. Parenting is hard work."

Gen leaned her head onto his shoulder. "How am I going to do this?"

"I don't know. But your mother and I, we'll be there to help you."

Gen popped her head up to gape at her dad, one eyebrow cocked. "Really, Mother, too? She'll help?"

Len chuckled and said, "Well, if nothing else, you and the baby will be well fed." He wrapped his arm around his daughter for a side hug. Turning his wrist, he caught sight of his watch and gasped. "But if I don't get you back for dinner, you won't be well fed." He stood and offered his hand. Gen laughed.

"Oh Dad, I love you."

"I love you too, Gennie."

Ten

The calendar pushed into May. The growing bellies of the girls in Unity suite proclaimed the nearness of birthing. While fear filled every heart, only Gen also carried fear mixed with anticipation.

As the others readied themselves to hand over their babies to new parents, Gen could no longer pretend she wasn't excited to meet the little person who kicked her all night long. She was ready to become a mommy. When she sat in a chair, her hand rested atop her growing belly. A smile lit her face as she tried to guess which bulging bump was what part of the baby. Her time with Mrs. Plumb had been spent sewing clothes, knitting blankets, and cutting diapers in anticipation for her little one's arrival.

While Gen acknowledged her life was changing even though her baby was not yet born, her roommate refused to acknowledge how her unborn baby had changed her too. She'd seen Carol cradle her belly, singing soothing songs.

"I don't understand, Carol. You and Jimmy love each other. Why can't you keep this baby? You'll be a wonderful mother."

Carol threw her hands into the air. "Why do you keep bringing this up? It's a done deal. I don't argue with you 'bout your choice, why do you continue to harp on mine?"

"'Cause it's wrong, that's why." Gen was tired of her roommate's denial.

"It don't matter what you think. I've made my decision. You don't have to like it."

The air between them was heavy and conversation sparse.

Carol's baby wasn't expected until the middle of May, but on the morning of May 2, as she stood in the bathroom brushing her teeth, water splashed onto the tile floor.

She called out into the living room, "Gen, Shirley? Anyone out there?"

Sitting on the loveseat, Gen was rereading the first chapter of *Baby and Child Care* during the quiet morning lull. Looking toward the bathroom, she answered, "I am."

"Could you come here, please?" she asked, a tremor sounding in her voice.

Gen heard the sound and asked, "Are you okay?"

"Could you get Mrs. Skloot? I think it might be time." Gen followed Carol's gaze down to the puddle around Carol's feet.

She gasped and said, "I'll be right back." Waddling out of the bathroom and down to the lobby, she found Mrs. Skloot chatting with the girl who tended the reception desk.

"Mrs. Skloot," Gen leaned against the desk to catch her breath. "Mrs. Skloot, come quick."

"Genevieve? Are you okay?"

"Yes, I'm fine, but Carol, I mean, Jane, it's her waters . . ."

"Say no more. I'm on my way." Turning to the girl at the desk, she said, "Get Donnie to bring the car around. I'm heading to the hospital with Miss Brown. Quickly now." She clapped two times, sending the girl on her way. Mrs. Skloot ran to Carol, Gen trailing behind.

By the time Gen arrived at Unity suite, Mrs. Skloot had helped Carol clean up and prepare for a trip to the hospital. Mrs. Skloot packed a few things into a small overnight bag. Carol gave Gen a nervous hug. As they disappeared down the stairs, Gen wondered when she would see her roommate again.

Five days later, Carol came back. Gen didn't see her return, but her bag appeared next to her bed. For the next few days, Gen only saw Carol when she slept, particularly during odd times of the afternoon. One morning as Carol tied a kerchief around her head, Gen caught her on the arm and asked, "Where are you going?

"To be with Charlie, in the nursery," she said, pushing a few stray hairs under the kerchief.

Gen felt stupid, of course that's where she'd be. Why hadn't she thought of it before? "May I come with you?"

"Of course," she answered in a soft voice.

Gen followed Carol down one level to the second floor. Although she knew where the nursery was, she'd never been in there. The nursery wasn't a place the girls went. The room held evidence of what they were going to lose. Under the cloying scent of baby powder lay the knowledge of coming grief. It was a private and personal space. With her head held high, Carol led the way into the nursery and walked straight to the third crib on the right. She picked up a small bundle wrapped in a blue blanket. "Good morning, little one. You hungry?"

Carol settled into a rocking chair and nursed the tiny bundle, her eyes never leaving his face. Her soft coos filled the room as she brought him to her shoulder to burp. He raised tiny arms with clenched fists, his legs curled up into his chest. After he burped, Carol asked, "Would you like to hold him?"

Gen looked at all the baby cribs, her heart racing. She didn't belong here yet. This wasn't her place. "I don't know if I can."

A gentle smile crossed Carol's face. "You're going to have one of your own soon enough. Doesn't hurt to practice. It's like"—she paused, searching for the right word—"I've always known I was supposed to be a momma." She looked down at the bundle in her arms.

Gen shrugged, but held out her arms to accept the babe. "As long as you don't think I'll hurt him."

Carol laughed, her voice floating through the air like a gentle breeze. "Don't worry, you won't hurt him." As Gen lowered her girth into a neighboring rocking chair, Carol handed her the baby, saying, "Gen, I'd like you to meet my son, Charles James Brown."

She looked down at the little boy to find his eyes open and searching. "Oh hello!" Gen said. With a reddish face and head covered with bits of dark curly hair, he was beautiful. Looking up at her roommate whose face radiated joy, she said, "Oh Carol. He's darling."

She nodded. "I know. Jimmy and I made a beautiful boy."

"Has Jimmy met him?"

Carol looked away before she spoke. "No, I called him from the hospital, but he refused to come," she said, her voice trembling.

Gen looked up, shock plastered on her face. "He's not going to be adopted, is he? Look at him, how can you give him away?"

"Oh Gen, I don't want to let him go, but I don't have any choice." Carol's eyes returned to her boy as tears traced down her face. "I just can't."

An incredulous anger filled Gen. Carol now had this perfect little boy, a symbol of his parents' love, and she would still give him away. Her voice shaking, Gen said, "You don't have to, really you don't." She pulled the little bundle closer to her chest, tightening her hold on him. "Start your family with this beautiful baby."

"I can't. It would ruin everything. Jimmy's ministry, our future." The sound of her voice was desperately sad.

"Carol, listen to me. Whoever they are, they're wrong. No ministry is worth sacrificing your son."

Tears streamed down Carol's face as she said, "I'm giving him a chance at life, full and free. I love him enough to know this is best for him." Gen heard finality in her words, and didn't pursue it any further. But her anger raged inside. No one should wrench a baby from the hands of a loving and capable mother.

In her heart, Gen knew Carol would tread this path to its brokenhearted conclusion. She handed the precious bundle back to his mother's arms.

Carol's next words were so quiet, Gen almost missed them. In a voice hardly louder than a whisper, Carol asked, "I wonder if anyone will adopt a Negro baby boy?" Her eyes were locked on newborn, wide-eyed brown ones.

"Why wouldn't anyone want to adopt him?"

"Come on, Gen. How many black couples you seen come through those doors? I'll count 'em for you. None. So I have to pray a nice white couple will adopt this baby, not to be their servant or their slave, but to be their son."

"I'm sure someone"—Gen's voice faltered—"I mean, someone must want to . . ." Words fell dead on her lips. Her roommate didn't deserve false platitudes. "Carol, I'm so sorry. I would take him home for you, if I could." She looked down at her own belly which was being punched and kicked by the tiny baby inside.

In the background Gen heard the bell for breakfast. "You coming to breakfast?" she asked her roommate.

"No, I'll get somethin' later. Ms. Mavis'll make sure I can eat when I'm ready. You go on." Carol turned back to Charlie, rocking him with a quiet lullaby. Gen tiptoed out of the nursery.

The next day was Open House Sunday. Only one couple, tall and lanky, came. She looked mousy and sad, he was gangly and unsure of himself. The gray in her hair bespoke years of monthly cycles and sadness.

Although it was sparkling clean, the nursery smelled of spit and poop and powder. The just-washed windows brightened the nursery with sunshine and hope. Some babies slept in their cribs, a few older babies sat on a play-mat surrounded by fabric balls and stuffed animals. One baby was being rocked by a nurse near the open window.

The couple walked from crib to crib, weak smiles on their faces. They waved their arms at the babies that cooed at them. Kneeling down, the woman shook a ball in front of a girl who squealed to have a playmate. The wife turned back to her husband looking for a response. He stood apart, arms crossed, face set.

The little girl turned away. The couple drifted over to the nurse holding a bundle near the window. They looked down to see a small reddish-brown face enveloped in a blue blanket.

"He's only a few weeks old," the nurse said. "A happy baby. Would you like to hold him?"

"Oh no, I, we couldn't," the wife demurred.

"May I, please?" the husband said. The wife turned to him, a kernel of hope in her eyes. The nurse placed the bundle into his arms, an awkward giant. But as he settled in, he watched the baby boy open and close his dark eyes, thick lashes sweeping up and down. The little lips pursed into a perfectly surprised "oh." The big, silent man with a broken heart fell in love with a little boy not of his seed.

Watching her husband, she knew right away. A son. They were bringing home a son.

He handed the baby back to the nurse. He met his wife's eyes and nodded. She blinked quickly to keep her eyes from filling with tears. Taking his hand, they left the nursery to see about bringing that baby boy home.

Gen watched as Carol worked to say goodbye. The tears falling freely onto the letter she hoped would help him understand someday. Gen heard the body-racking grief of a mother who would never watch her boy learn to walk or call her Momma. If any doubt remained about whether Gen should keep her child, it was erased by Carol's pain. Gen would do anything to keep her baby by her side. No one would take her child from her. Ever.

Eleven

B y the middle of June, only Gen was left waiting to have her baby. Her weekly doctor's appointments had revealed no progress at all. She felt as big as a milk truck. She hadn't been able to bend over and touch her toes in weeks, but she knew her ankles were the size of oranges. As far as she knew, this baby was stuck and was never coming out.

Gen was jealous to watch the girls' figures returning to their prepregnant shapes. Although they complained their bodies had changed, she didn't care. Her face was bloated, her feet swollen, and her belly threw her off balance. She was still pregnant and uncomfortable.

And then there was her back. Throughout her entire pregnancy, it ached, especially after her mornings in Ms. Mavis's kitchen. But since she'd gotten up that June morning, a new dull pain throbbed in her lower back. The smell of breakfast made her nauseous. After pushing away her plate of scrambled eggs and toast, she excused herself. She started pacing the lobby and parlor. The pain in her back was becoming too much to bear, even walking no longer eased her pain. Her breaths grew shallower and more frequent.

She blocked out the concerned voices around her, but the more she stood and walked, the stronger the pressure she felt. "I think I have to go to the bathroom."

"What did you say, Gen?"

She focused her eyes to find Carol standing next to her, holding her elbow.

"I have to go to the bathroom." She whispered into her ear. A look of concern crossed Carol's face. Placing both of Gen's hands on the reception desk, she said, "Stay here."

Gen grimaced as new pain pulsed through her back. "Don't worry, I'm not going anywhere," Carol ran up the grand staircase. When she returned with Mrs. Skloot, the headmistress looked Gen over. Gen's face and hair were slick with perspiration, the veins in her neck bulged from clenching in pain. Mrs. Skloot asked, "Genevieve, how do you feel?"

Gen took panting breaths, "It hurts." More panting breaths, "I feel like I have to go to the bathroom." Alarm crossed the woman's face.

Mrs. Skloot lifted Gen's face to look her in the eyes and said, "Don't. Genevieve, do not push." Looking at Carol, she said, "Don't let her push, keep her breaths shallow and quick." She ran away.

"How am I supposed to do that?" Carol called out after her. Looking back, she said, "Gen, stay with me. Can you hear me?" Using a handkerchief, she wiped the sweat from Gen's brow.

Gen answered with a deep, guttural groan.

After a few unbearably long minutes, Mrs. Skloot arrived with the car. She and Carol guided Gen into the back, telling her not to panic. Mrs. Skloot drove as fast as she dared to St. Mary's Hospital. Before she could even say goodbye, Gen was laid on a bed, wheeled into a room, and left alone. Mrs. Skloot and Carol were ushered away.

Told by the nurse to stay on the bed, Gen writhed in cycles of increasing pain while lying flat on her back. A nurse came in and asked her to keep the noise down, she was beginning to scare the other patients. Gen wasn't aware she'd been screaming. She only knew unrelenting waves of pain.

Finally a doctor came in and put her legs in stirrups. Noting the progress of her labor, he nodded to his assistant who handed him a syringe full of clear liquid.

"Don't worry, this will all be over soon." He stabbed the needle into Gen's arm and pushed in the plunger. Gen was unconscious within moments.

Whether it was minutes or hours later when she woke in a hospital bed, Gen hadn't a clue. She was groggy and sore. Looking down, her belly was smaller than before. Her back and legs ached. Her breasts felt heavy. After a few moments in the dark room she realized what she had missed.

"Where's my baby?" She searched the room but didn't see a bassinet anywhere. She wore a hospital gown and was covered by a thin blanket. The lights were out and the curtains drawn. The room looked dark as night. The partially opened door allowed a dim light. The clock on the wall pointed at 2:25, but Gen couldn't be sure if it was day or night.

"Where's my baby?" she said again. Panic set in. *They've taken my baby away. They decided I wasn't a fit mother after all.* Her panic gave way to hysteria. She tried to sit up and swing herself out of bed, but excruciating pain ripped through her abdomen. So she laid back down.

Looking around, she grabbed a red call button and started pushing, her desperation growing. After minutes that felt like hours, a nurse entered.

"Calm down, calm down," she said as she entered. "You've had quite the day, young lady."

"Where's my baby?" Gen screamed at the nurse.

Not wavering from her calm demeanor, the nurse said, "She's in the nursery. She's beautiful, came out squalling with a shock of dark hair." She laid her hand on Gen's arm, her touch soothing.

"A girl? I had a baby girl?"

"Yes, you did. And she's beautiful, just like her mama."

"Her mama?"

"Yes, you. That knockout drug really did a wonder on you."

Gen put her hand to her forehead. "I don't remember having a baby, I remember lots of back pain. And being left in here alone."

"Yes, when you were admitted, your labor was quite advanced. The doctor administered a drug to pacify you. She was born right around five o'clock last night, if I recall correctly." She looked at the medical chart hanging on the foot of the bed and said, "Yes, 5:06 p.m., to be exact."

"Oh, 5:06" Gen said, as if repetition would make it more real. Looking up at the nurse, she asked, "When can I see her?" She moved to push the blanket off her lap and put her feet onto the floor.

The nurse used a firm hand on Gen's shoulder to lay her back onto the bed. "Not now. Your body has been through quite the ordeal. You don't have the strength to visit the nursery right now." As she readjusted her covers, she said, "Go back to sleep now, your little girl will be brought to you in the morning. Get some rest, you're going to need your strength. New mamas always do."

Nodding at the nurse's wise and gentle words, Gen lay back down. Even though she wasn't awake to experience it, birth demanded every extra ounce of her bodily strength and she was tired. The nurse closed the door as she left and darkness lulled Gen into a deep, healing sleep.

Peeks of light snuck between the fabric curtains awaking Gen just past six thirty. Gen was eager to see her baby. As she waited for a nurse to bring her, she surveyed the room. After cataloging the contents of the room in the daylight, she glanced at the clock again. It read 6:32 a.m. This was going to take forever.

She was so deep in her thoughts that she jumped when there was a light knock on the door. "Yoohoo," called a voice from the hallway. "It's time to be awake."

Gen sat up. She smoothed her hair and rubbed away the mascara from under her eyes for the little girl she was about to meet.

"Good morning," said the chirpy nursery nurse. "I have a little girl who'd love to meet her momma. She's been an absolute peach in the nursery, but it's time for her to eat."

Gen's hands were greedy to touch her daughter. The nurse used gentle hands to pick up a tiny, pink bundle and placed it into Gen's outstretched arms. She pulled the bundle into herself.

"Hello, little one. It's nice to finally meet you."

Tears filled her eyes and a strange emotion overwhelmed Gen. She had never known such an immediate love, desire, and possession. She brushed her thumb across her little round cheek, down her sweet nose, across her puckered lips. She'd always thought her child would have smooth porcelain skin. Right now, she looked like a squashed tomato. "She's so red and wrinkly."

The nurse laughed. "Over the next couple days her skin will lighten and unwrinkle. Soon, she'll be the beautiful baby you already know she is." The nurse made a few notations in Gen's chart, then asked, "Is the proud daddy coming by today after work to hold his new little one?"

Gen couldn't look away from the blue eyes peering up at her. "No, it's just me and this little one, the two of us together."

The nurse's voice grew sharp. "I see." She made another notation, her pen scratching across the chart.

The baby squirmed in Gen's arms. Alarmed, she looked at the nurse and asked, "What's wrong? What did I do?"

The nurse laughed again, but this time her laugh carried a note of condemnation. "You need to feed her. She's hungry."

Gen looked around the room. Momentary panic filled her voice as she said, "What does she need to eat? Do you have a bottle for her?"

"She needs to nurse. Don't you know anything about how to care for this baby?" The nurse rolled her eyes. "I'll call the floor nurse, she'll help you." She turned on her heels to leave. Under her breath, but loud enough to be heard, she said, "Who does that girl think she is? She can't raise a child on her own." She slammed the door, leaving Gen alone with her hungry baby.

The slam of the door startled the baby who started wailing in Gen's arms. She tried to soothe her with bounces and calming noises, but nothing helped. The squalls grew louder and more insistent.

She didn't know what to do. The pats and bounces weren't working. Just then, she felt a leaking from her chest. Of course, breastfeeding was part of what she and Mrs. Skloot had discussed. As Gen opened her gown, the baby reached for the milk. Gen winced at the new sensation. No one told her that it hurt to feed a child. The baby sucked with loud smacking noises. "Shhh, little one," she said, embarrassed by the earthy noises.

As the baby settled in, Gen stared at the new child in her arms. Her thoughts drifted. What happened during her delivery? How many people had stared at her? How was she going to get a job and provide for this little one?

Her thoughts were interrupted by a steady stream of people. First, the floor nurse came to check on her. Next, an orderly arrived with a hot meal. The smell of bacon, eggs, toast, oatmeal, fruit, and coffee aroused her forgotten sense of hunger. Her stomach growled. Since it had been twenty-four hours since she'd last eaten, she was impatient for the baby to finish.

Another nurse came in to ensure she was nursing well. When the baby finished eating, Gen sighed with relief, she could finally eat. However, the nurse informed her that the baby was only half-finished, she needed to eat from the other side, especially if Gen wanted to remain evenly balanced.

The nurse was followed by the floor secretary. "Congratulations on the birth of your baby girl. I need to start some paperwork and her birth certificate. Do you have a few minutes to answer a few questions?"

"Okay," Gen said, pulling the blanket to cover her exposed torso with her child attached.

She waved a dismissive hand toward Gen. "Don't worry about that. I've seen it all." Gen relaxed a little, but not much. With that, she pulled out a sheath of papers attached to a clipboard.

Looking down, she asked, "Your full name is?"

"Genevieve Antoinette Ryder."

She followed with questions about her birthplace and her current address.

"Now the father. What's his name?"

Gen cleared her throat, afraid to tell the truth. "He isn't married to me."

The secretary didn't even flinch. She just said, "Even so, he still needs to be listed on the baby's birth certificate. You do know who the father is, don't you?" She tapped her pencil against the desk while waiting for Gen to answer.

"His name is Bobby McFadden. Capital F."

"Is Bobby his given name or a nickname?"

"A nickname, his given name is Robert."

She continued on with details about Bobby, where he lived and was born.

"Now dear, the best part. What's her name?"

"Her name?" she said. "I don't know, what is her name?"

The nurse smiled. "No, Miss Ryder, this little girl is yours to name. I won't know her name until you tell me."

Gen blushed. Looking at the little girl in her arms, she asked, "What is your name?" She sat silent for a few minutes, running through names in her head. The secretary waited, looking up at the clock on the wall, back to her paperwork, to the list of other patients she needed to visit, back to the clock on the wall. "If you need a bit of time to think about this, I can come back. I have other rooms to visit."

"No, that won't be necessary. Her name is Katherine. With a K. And her middle name is Antoinette, after me and my mother." She laughed out loud. "Katherine Antoinette Ryder." Did she really just give her daughter her mother's name? Gen broke into a fit of hysterical giggles over what she had just done. What would her mother say?

"As you say." The secretary completed her written paperwork. "If you need to change anything, you have a couple hours to let me know."

"I understand, but there won't be any changes." After the secretary left the room, Gen looked down into her wide-open blue eyes. "Hello there, Katherine Antoinette. I'm your mommy. It's very nice to meet you."

Twelve

en spent her days in the hospital eating and sleeping as much as she could. After five nights at St. Mary's she'd have to return to Bethany House. Katherine was brought to her at regular intervals throughout the day for feeding and kept in the nursery at night.

In the sweet moments when Katherine slept across her chest, Gen's thoughts turned to Bobby. This little girl would have captured his heart. Because she couldn't talk to him, she scratched out her thoughts to him on hospital stationery, describing the softness of her skin, the perfection of her face, the song in her voice. Katherine stirred in her arms. She reread the words on the page, flinching at their syrupy sweetness. Filled with embarrassment, she stuffed the letter into her overnight bag.

No one called on Gen, except Mrs. Skloot who visited every afternoon. While Mrs. Skloot cradled Katherine in her arms, the two women discussed what life at Bethany House would now be like for her. Gen's chores and suite responsibilities would remain, but she'd have freedom to spend time with Kat, getting to know her rhythms.

"She will have a crib in the nursery, but of course, she may accompany you whenever you would like, even around the house."

"How would I do that? I can't take a pram up and down all those stairs."

Mrs. Skloot looked up, a serious look on her face and said, "For centuries, women have kept their children near them wearing slings. If you want to keep little Katherine with you, you'll do that as well."

Gen did not like the idea. "No promises, Mrs. Skloot, but I'll think about it." She knew her mother would never approve. Only women who live with Natives would bind their babies. Not someone like her.

Mrs. Skloot held Katherine close and studied her face. She stroked the baby's cheek with her long finger. "Genevieve, this time will go so fast. When you look back you'll wonder what happened to the sweet babe in your arms."

Gen nodded in appreciation, but dismissed the words. The woman had grown nostalgic in her old age.

After placing the baby back in her bassinet, Mrs. Skloot picked up her purse to leave. "By the way, I called your parents. They said they'd come to visit this afternoon. I don't want them to catch you by surprise."

Gen was shocked. "Mother is coming here to see me?"

"I think it's more correct to say she's coming to meet her granddaughter. Babies have the incredible ability to usher in healing and forgiveness." Mrs. Skloot made sure she closed the door when she left.

The late afternoon quiet was interrupted by a knock on the door. Gen sat up and pressed her hair down with her hand. "Come in," she said. When the door pushed open, Len, Marie, and Antoinette piled into the room. Joy expanded through Gen.

"Hello, Gennie," Len said, looking around the room. "I hear I'm a grandpa!"

Her smile turned to soft laughter. "Hello to you too, Dad. It's good to see you."

Len grinned, "Nice to see you too." He looked around again. "So where is she? I don't see a bassinet."

She covered her nightgown with her housecoat, tying it tight around her waist. Past his eager face, Gen saw her mother standing off to the side, looking uneasy. "Hello, Mother," she said. Old angst rumbled inside her. It was only a matter of minutes before Antoinette would disapprove of Gen's parenting.

"Hello, Genevieve," her mother said. Her voice was as stiff as the stance she took in the corner of the room.

Marie jumped forward with a wrapped gift in her hands. Dropping it onto Gen's bed, she said, "This is for you. Where is she?"

At this, Gen laughed out loud, "You didn't come all this way just to see me?"

Len and Marie shared a mischievous look, but Antoinette locked her fists onto her hips. "Of course we didn't come all this way to see you." Her look was full of disapproval. Gen sighed. Nothing had changed. "If we wanted to see you, we would have visited you at that home."

Gen stiffened and said, "No, Mother, of course not. Why would you waste your precious time on me?" The birth of her own daughter mad Gen wonder about her own mother's attitude toward her. Her feelings toward Kat were possessive and protective. When did her mother loose those feelings for her?

"Now, now," said Len, placing his hand on Antoinette's back. "This is not the time to dredge up old grudges, it's a time for celebration. I have a granddaughter and I want to meet her."

Gen led her family to the nursery ward on the other side of the maternity floor. From behind glass windows, Gen pointed out the second crib back on the right. "That's your granddaughter, my little girl. She's beautiful and perfect," she said with pride. "Let me see if someone will bring her out."

The head nurse, the one who snubbed her the day after Katherine was born, answered the nursery door. During their conversation, Gen motioned to her family gathered at the window. Marie waved and Len blew kisses at the glass. Antoinette stood, eyes locked, on the bassinet. The nurse brought the bassinet to the door of the nursery with strict instructions to bring the baby back as soon as they were done.

As Gen pulled the bassinet, her dad ran over. Grabbing it gently and pushing it back toward the room, he said, "Let me, you've been through enough this past week." She wanted to protest, but the attention felt good. It'd been a long time since her family admired her effort.

Her hand rested on the edge of the bassinet as they walked. As soon as the door closed behind them, Len picked up the baby. She woke from sleep, stretching her arms and yawning. "Well, hello, little Katherine." His eyes sparkled as he cuddled the baby into his arm like a football.

Gen sighed. Her heart overflowed with love for both her daughter and her dad. She had no idea their interaction would be such a treasure.

"Let me in, my turn. I'm an auntie now," Marie said as she pushed forward. After scooping the baby out of Len's arms, Marie used her fingers to trace the line of the baby, from her dark curls to her teeny toes. She sighed. Her voice strained, she said, "Gen, she's perfect. I can't believe she's yours."

Turning to Kat, snuggled in her arms, Marie said, "Hello, little one. I'm your Auntie Marie. I'll tell you everything you need to know about life."

Gen groaned with a smile on her face. She reached her arms up to take her daughter back from her teasing sister, but Marie swung the baby away from Gen's greedy grasp. "Don't listen to her, Kitty Kat, I taught her everything she needed to know." Playful laughter filled her voice.

Marie pulled the baby up close to her face, "Between me and your momma, she's pretty, but I'm prettier. If you ever get in trouble, you come straight to me and I'll fix it for you. You can count on me, Katherine." She kissed the tip of her nose. Katherine let out a little squeal and hint of a smile. Bringing the baby close to her chest, Marie squealed in reply.

Antoinette cleared her throat. "Excuse me. I'd like to hold her now. You've had quite long enough." Marie looked at her sister. Gen shrugged. She was her grandmother, she had some rights to the child. "Go ahead," she said to Marie.

Perched in a chair in the corner of the room, Antoinette waited with outstretched arms. With practiced hand, she held the baby at arm's length, untying her sleeping gown and examining every part of her body.

Gen watched, curious to understand what her mother was doing. As her mother's fingers ran up and down Kat's belly, she knew her mother was falling in love.

Her child cared for, Gen looked at the wrapped box her family had brought with them. It had been expertly wrapped with a large pink ribbon. Under layers of white tissue paper she uncovered a white smocked dress. Tucked underneath was a hand-stitched bonnet. "Thank you, Mother. They're beautiful."

From her spot in the corner where she sat with a naked baby, Antoinette said, "I thought your child would need a dress for church."

Gen gulped. She understood what wasn't said. "Would you want us to attend at our parish?" Her voiced tightened a notch. "I would have to come back with Kat and present her publicly. Everyone would know."

Len said, "It doesn't matter, Gen, really it doesn't."

Antoinette snapped and said, "Don't worry, everyone already knows, After you left, word spread like wildfire."

"But no one knows that I'm going to raise her without a husband."

Antoinette looked down at the baby in her arms. Bringing her close, she whispered into her ear. "Don't worry little one, I won't let Genevieve have her way. I'll protect you." She was loud enough that everyone in the room heard her words.

"Mother!" Gen leaped from her bed. Her voice lost its laughter. "You have no right to speak like that. Give her back, now."

"What? I said I would look out for her, not let her make the same mistakes you did."

"You think she's a mistake?"

"She's not the mistake. Your actions were." Antoinette's voice regained its sharp edge. Gen wanted to plug her ears at the sound of it.

Len raised his hands between the women. "Stop. If you can't say something kind to each other, don't speak." His voice was forceful.

Antoinette gave the baby a kiss on the forehead, wrapped her back up and deposited her onto Gen's arms. "She's lovely," were the last words she said as she walked out the door.

Len's shoulders fell, "I'm sorry, Gennie. I didn't want this to happen."

"It's okay, Daddy. It's not your fault." Looking from her Dad to her sister, she was grateful they'd come at all. "Thank you both for coming. For meeting Katherine."

Len kissed his daughter on the forehead. "I love you, Gennie, and so does your mom. Sometimes it's hard to be a mother. Try to remember that. "

Before she left, Marie held her sister's hand. "She's beautiful, Gen. You should be so proud. I am." She looked into her sister's eyes and again at Kat.

In the silence that followed after Marie closed the door, Gen held her daughter close. Her joy at being a mother had been tempered by her mother's ever-present judgment. How could she ever raise a daughter when she had no idea how a mother loved? When the tears started, she let them spill until she fell asleep, a content baby sleeping next to her.

Thirteen

elief flooded Gen when she returned to Bethany House the next day. Walking through the giant oak doors, Gen breathed in the familiar scents of cleaned wood and simmering soup. She climbed the stairs holding her tiny pink bundle, she watched the activity in her suite swirl until Sarah walked by.

"Gen's back." In a voice loud enough to beckon the girls from their rooms. Eager fingers reached out, feeling the edge of the blanket wrapping baby Katherine. Gen felt like a Hollywood star. She stared into the open eyes of her daughter and relished the admiration. At the beginning of their life together, they were noticed for their worth.

She shared Kat with the girls, passing her around. Silence reigned as each girl greeted the child. On their faces, Gen could see so many things: joy, sadness, grief, greed.

Carol watched the party from the doorframe of the living room. Arms crossed in front of her chest, her face set in a frown. Even the sound of Kat's gentle coos didn't bring a smile. When Shirley offered Carol a chance to hold her, she stiffened in the doorway.

"Come on, just hold her, she's so sweet." Shirley said as she pushed the baby toward her.

Carol couldn't speak, she just shook her head, her jaw clenched.

The baby squirmed in Shirley's arms. They both looked down and saw Kat's head thrashing from side to side. "Gen, I think she's hungry." As Shirley placed the baby back in Gen's arms, Carol turned into their room and closed the door. The baby startled and started to cry.

Pain stabbed Gen's heart when the door slammed shut. Her roommate was hurting. She wanted to talk to her, but she couldn't right now, Kat needed to eat. She would catch her later, after Kat was sleeping.

But the days and nights flew by in a blur of feeding and sleeping. To help Gen care for her girl, the nursery staff set up a cot near a bassinette in a private corner of the nursery. When Kat was eight weeks old, Mrs. Skloot asked Gen to get back into the routine of life at Bethany House, reinstating her chores. The first weeks, Gen worked shortened hours, but Mrs. Skloot wanted to prepare her to be a mother on her own. She gradually increased her requirements to match what she'd be expected to do as a single mother. Gen was overwhelmed by everything she needed to accomplish in a day. Not only did she have to do her chores and work, but she also bore the responsibility of caring for Katherine.

As the summer months faded into fall, Gen learned the rhythms of her daughter's needs and how to fulfill them. Under the gentle tutelage of the nursery staff and Mrs. Skloot, she learned how to give baths, feed, put down to sleep, and care for her child. Splashing warm water over her daughter's porcelain skin, Gen watched Katherine's gummy smile light up her face. After Gen dried and powdered her bum, she blew raspberries into her belly. Her laughter rang through the nursery and echoed down to the foyer, bringing smiles to all who heard.

In the late nights, when the nursery was quiet after the hustle of the day, Gen would rock Kat to sleep after her midnight feeding. In these moments as she gazed at the round cheek resting against her, Gen's thoughts turned to Bobby. She knew, for all his failings, he would have loved their little girl. She wondered if he was happy with the choice he made. She knew, for all the work of it, she was.

Now that Katherine had arrived and Gen had settled into the routines of being a mom, she'd started welcoming Marie on Open House Sundays. She'd missed her sister so much that now she visited once a month. Gen and Marie spent lazy Sunday afternoons traipsing around Bethany House grounds.

On a blue-sky October Sunday afternoon, Marie and Gen took a long walk along the back side of Bethany's property. The path wound through a grove of oak and maple trees. The leaves had shed their drab green and were dressed in brilliant reds, oranges, and yellows. Gen pushed a pram with a sleeping baby along the gravel path.

Suddenly, in the middle of a wide-open space, Marie stopped walking.

Gen walked a few more steps before she realized. Turning to her sister, she saw that Marie had paled. "Marie, are you okay?"

Marie just looked away.

"What is it? Tell me."

Marie wouldn't meet Gen's eyes, but kept her gaze locked on a row of holly bushes. After a quick glance back, she cleared her throat. "Listen, Gen. I have something I want to say, but don't answer until I'm done, okay?"

Gen nodded.

Marie took a deep breath, "I'm sorry."

"What?" Gen looked over at her sister, trying to decide why she would apologize.

"I'm sorry," Marie said again. She kept her eyes down as she spoke. "I'm sorry Mother always picked on you. I'm sorry she favored me and made your life so hard. And I'm sorry Bobby didn't marry you and you were sent away. It was so unfair. I'm just so sorry." She took another deep breath.

Gen turned and said, "Marie, you have nothing to be sorry for. You didn't do anything wrong. You said it yourself, it was Mother." Marie fidgeted her hands in front of her.

"But I didn't stop it and I could have if I'd tried." Her voice sounded so anguished. Gen'd never seen her sister like this before. Laying a hand on her sister's arm, she said, "Marie, there's nothing you could've done."

"Wait, I'm not done." A blush crept over Marie's face. "There's something else. I've met someone and he wants to marry me. And we're so happy, it's just that . . ."

Gen was silent as the range of emotions whirled through her head. Anger. Happiness. Jealousy. Surprise. Sadness. "Marie, I don't know what to say." She paused. "Do Mother and Dad know yet?"

"That Cliff wants to marry me? Not yet, he's going to talk to Dad soon."

"Will Mother think he's a suitable match?" The words were delivered with a hint of venom.

Marie winced. "Yes, he's spent time at the house. She's given her blessing, as much as she ever will." Her voice turned crisp and said, "Well, he isn't who I would choose, but he'll do." An involuntary giggle escaped Gen. Marie did a fair impression of their mother.

Marie spoke again, "Gen, one more thing."

Gen stared, overwhelmed at the thought that there could be more.

"Cliff and I want to marry just after the New Year. I want you and Kat there to see me get married. We're choosing the date because I want you to stand next to me as my maid of honor."

Gen's mouth dropped open. She stood dumbfounded for just a moment. "Yiiiii," a high-pitched scream filled the air. Gen jumped and clapped her hands. "Oh Marie, of course! I would love to! Whatever you want or need. Just let me know." She threw her arms around her sister, embracing and dancing around in circles at the same time.

Marie laughed as she pushed her sister away. "Calm down, Gen, he hasn't even asked Dad yet."

Pulling her in for a tighter hug, Gen whispered into her ear, "May you find all the happiness that has eluded me." With a final squeeze and girlish squeal, the two girls continued their walk in the woods, their conversation full of the promise of an upcoming wedding.

As the leaves fell off the trees and the cool winter wind began to blow, Gen recognized that her time at Bethany House neared its end. Just as Gen was the last one to join the Unity House, she would also be the last to leave. But before it would be her turn to leave, she had to say goodbye to her roommate.

Carol had kept her distance in the months since Katherine was born. She always found a way to disappear whenever the baby was in the room. If they were in the living room, Carol excused herself to her bedroom. If Gen and Kat were together in their bedroom, she needed to study in the library.

On one hand, Gen understood how Katherine was a visible reminder of all that had been taken from Carol, that every cry was one she would never answer, that every laugh was gone forever. But Gen wanted her friend to share in her joy. The gap between them grew as their experiences tore them apart.

The afternoons were darkening early as winter neared. On a cold November morning, Gen excused herself from Ms. Mavis's kitchen to look after Kat for a few hours.

She hummed as she carried her daughter, now almost five months old, up to her room. "No one should be upstairs this time of day, we'll have the place to ourselves, little one," Gen said to the baby in her arms. Kat cooed in reply.

Swinging open the door to her room, Gen stopped when she saw Carol packing her suitcase. "Oh hey," she said. "What are you doing?"

"Packing, Jimmy's comin' to get me this afternoon."

Surprise flooded Gen. "I didn't know you were leaving today. You should have told me."

Carol stood and stared at her. Her eyes darted to the baby and back to Gen. "Why you think that? I don't owe you anything."

"But you're my friend. I would have regretted not having a chance to say goodbye."

Bitterness leaked into Carol's words. "You? Have regrets? I doubt that."

Gen stood dumbfounded. They'd hardly exchanged any words in the past few months. "What did you say?"

"You're so clueless sometimes. In the end it all works out for you, doesn't it Gen? Well, here's a clue. It doesn't work out for everyone."

Gen jumped back at Carol's anger. The baby startled and started to fuss. Gen gave her an absent-minded pat on the back.

"Carol, I meant . . ."

Carol put her hand on the back of the chair and took a steadying breath. "I know what you meant, but it's just that it hurts to see you lovin' that baby girl. I wanted to keep Charlie so bad, my guts ache. Every night I sleep alone in this room missing part of me. You'll never know that emptiness, because you kept her." Her anger had cooled and now tears carved a path down her face.

Gen never told Carol about the bitter tears she swallowed when she and Jimmy were together. All she ever wanted was for Bobby to love her. "You'll get married in a few months and live happily ever after. You'll have other babies, beautiful boys and girls."

Carol's tears had turned to sobs. Kat's cries rivaled.

Gen wanted to clear the air, to have it all said. She was acting like keeping Katherine made it all better. "But I sleep alone too. I see his smile in the shine of her eyes. It's you who has it all." She bounced to calm her crying daughter. "At the end of the day, all I have is her." Her words sounded so flimsy against her roommate's sorrow.

Carol sat down on her unmade bed, shoulders shaking with grief. She wiped her face, looked up, and said, "But Gen, that's all I've ever wanted, to be a momma. And now he's gone." A fresh round of wailing overtook her. In between sobs, she said, "When I go home, no one's gonna cry for me or Charlie. Not even Jimmy. No one wants to share my shame."

Carol's grief was too much for Gen to watch. Tears spilled down her cheeks too. Gen laid Kat in the middle of her bed and sat next to Carol on the other. She wrapped her arm around her shoulder and pulled her in close. Carol turned and wept on her shoulder.

Minutes passed as Carol emptied herself of months of grief and longing. Gen fell headlong into her friend's grief. If only she'd paid attention, she chided herself for not seeing the fullness of Carol's pain.

As Carols' tears lessened, Kat's fussiness lessened as well.

The room was quiet for a few minutes before Carol said, "Gen, I'm sorry." Her voice was raspy and quiet. "I shouldn't be so angry at you. You did what you felt was right, so did I."

Carol wiped her face again and stood to look in the small mirror. "Ugh, my face gets so splotchy when I cry," she said, patting her cheeks.

Gen laughed out loud. "I'm sure Jimmy thinks you're all the more beautiful because of it." She watched her roommate move about the room, packing her last few things. A pang pierced her heart. She didn't want Carol to go. They'd never see each other again.

"Carol, I'm gonna miss you." She turned to focus on the baby who was playing with her feet. Gen's voice faltered. "Can I . . . will we . . . Is there any way I can talk to you again?"

Carol's face softened at Gen's hesitant words. "Oh Gen, how we gonna do that? Outside of here, our people don't mix."

Gen felt desperation growing up in her. From their months of living together, Carol was the closest friend she had. She wasn't ready to let go of that. "But I can't forget our friendship because of what other people think. Why can't we?"

Carol turned to face her roommate, a half-smile on her lips. "Even my momma won't think this is a good idea. Nothin' good ever came from fraternizin' with white folk."

She raised her eyebrows and waited.

Carol bent over her desk and scribbled on a pad of paper. Ripping the paper and handing it to Gen, she said, "Here, call me if you need me someday. I'm not makin' any promises."

Hope rose up in Gen as she took the paper in her hand. Her heart was swamped with affection for Carol. "Thank you." Even Katherine squealed to say thanks.

Carol bent over Katherine and tickled her toes. A giggle rang around the room. She leaned into the baby's face and kissed her on the forehead. More giggles. "Gen, she is a delightful child." She paused, then asked, "May I pick her up?"

Gen nodded, a grin plastered to her face. "Yes, of course, please do." She sat down and watched the two of them. She'd been waiting for this!

Carol hugged Katherine tight in her arms and started to sway. Her hips moved to the smooth rhythm of a lullaby. Carol lifted the baby up to her face and looked her straight in the eyes. Holding one hand behind her head and the other at her feet, she said, "Katherine Antoinette, May the Lord bless thee and keep thee. The Lord make his face to shine upon thee and be gracious to thee. The Lord lift his countenance upon thee and give thee peace. Amen." Finishing with a soft kiss on the forehead, she handed the child back to her mother.

Gen couldn't move, stunned by the beauty of the moment. Although she wasn't quite sure what had happened, it was a holy moment.

Carol moved in silence, packing up the last of her belongings, a small sway in her step. "Well, I guess that's it," she said as she locked her case. Before she gathered her hat and coat, she pulled Gen into her arms, giving her a tight squeeze. Whispering into her ear, Carol said, "I'll miss you Gen Ryder. May the Lord be good to you."

Without thinking of her words, Gen said, "You as well, Carol. You deserve it." Their embrace lasted until the child squished in between them squirmed.

Carol laughed. "Now that's a send-off. A crabby baby on my last moment here at Bethany House." With that, she picked up her coat, hat, and suitcase. After a final look around the room, she walked out the door and never looked back.

Fourteen

Her time at Bethany House was almost over. In just a few weeks Gen would be free to go, her terms of confinement complete. Although her mother insisted she move home, Gen was fighting to keep that from happening. She was a grown woman who was perfectly capable of tending to all their needs. Her time at Bethany House taught her everything she needed to know. Mrs. Skloot had many friends and had found a seamstress near Bethany House willing to take Gen on as an apprentice, offering room and board to her and Kat in exchange for work. Mrs. Skloot arranged an interview between Gen and Lucy Young on the first day of December.

The day outside was windblown and snowy, making the fireplace in Mr. Ronald's office a comfortable meeting place. Pacing in front of the roaring fire, Gen rehearsed her speech. "I'm a very hard worker. I have some skills as a seamstress, as you can see by these samples. Katherine's a well-behaved baby girl. You'll hardly know she's there."

She stared out the window, mesmerized by the whirling snow. Her stomach twisted like the snow blowing in the wind. She tried to control her hands, but they fidgeted, patting her hair, rubbing her ear, smoothing her skirt. A sound outside the closed door made her jump. Whipping her head around, she saw the doorknob start to turn.

She quickly perched on the chair furthest from the door.

Mrs. Skloot ushered in Mrs. Lucy Young. Gen pasted a bright smile on her face.

Gen rose to shake her hand and said, "It's nice to meet you, Mrs. Young." Lucy's handshake was firm enough, but quick.

After brushing flakes of snow off the shoulders of her coat and removing her hat, Lucy settled in a chair next to Gen. Despite thickly caked makeup, dark bags shadowed her eyes. Gray hairs near her temple peppered her brown hair with light.

Mrs. Skloot took a few minutes to introduce them to each other. As the headmistress talked, Gen continued fidgeting, running her hands over the bundle of clothes she'd brought to display her talent.

Mrs. Skloot said, "Genevieve has a strong recommendation from our seamstress, Mrs. Janice Plumb. You may speak with her if you wish."

Lucy blew out a sigh. "If I must." But she turned her attention to Gen and asked, "Don't you just have some work I can look at?" Her eyes dropped to the pile on Gen's lap.

Although they had been neatly folded, Gen's nervous fingering of the items ruffled their appearance, making them look more like a wrinkled bundle of laundry. A hushed gasp escaped her lips. "Oh no," she said, keeping her voice quiet. Letting out a frustrated breath, she tried to smooth out a blue-smocked play dress across her lap.

"Don't worry about that," Mrs. Young's voice was sharper than Gen was used to. "It doesn't have to be perfectly neat for me to tell how well you sew." Holding out a dry hand with ragged cuticles, she said, "Hand those over here. Let me see them."

Mrs. Young turned the garments inside and out, tugged on seams, and checked the placement of the lace. The fire crackled in the long moments Gen waited, fingers still fidgeting. Looking up at Gen, she said, "You do very good work."

"Thank you," Gen said, her breath barely above a whisper. Her nerves had stolen her voice.

Mrs. Young laid the items in her lap. "Yes, you'll do very well." Her voice had a stony edge, although her face remained neutral. "I'd like to have you join me as an apprentice."

Gen's mouth dropped open. Her hand flew to her chest as she gasped. "Really?"

Mrs. Skloot and Mrs. Young shared a look and broke into soft laughter. Mrs. Skloot laid her hand on Gen's knee. "I told you that your work would speak for itself. You had nothing to worry about, Genevieve."

Gen blushed.

"Our tailoring business is run on the first floor of a three-story building on the corner of Lake and Acorn here in Eau Claire. My family and I live in the top two levels. There is a room set aside for you."

Gen didn't hear any mention of her daughter. Mrs. Skloot should have told her. She couldn't take this job, as wonderful as it was, if Kat couldn't come with her. So Gen said, "Mrs. Young, this sounds wonderful, but I have a young daughter, Katherine."

"Beverly told me about your situation and we'd be glad to have you both come live with us."

Gen breathed a sigh of relief.

Mrs. Young kept talking. "Before you move in, you need to know about our family. We have eight children. Our oldest two are out of the house—Peter is in college after his tour in Europe and Abigail is in college in Madison. But that leaves six kids still in the house. Our house is orderly chaos. Do you think you can live in such a situation?"

Gen laughed. "After living with eight pregnant women for a year, I'm pretty sure your house will be no problem, Mrs. Young."

Mrs. Young picked up her purse and started to dig through it. Without looking up, she said, "Please, call me Lucy. We're going to be living and working together, we might as well be friends."

"Okay, Lucy," Gen said, trying it out. Although it felt awkward, she did like being an equal and not a child.

Lucy looked up from her purse. "Drat, I can't find it. I wrote down all the details for this arrangement. Herman insisted I do that, he knew I'd forget something important. And now I can't even find the piece of paper." She shrugged, her voice a beat slower than it was before. "The terms, as I remember them, are that you will work with me, side by side Monday through Friday or as often as there is work to do. The shop is staffed by a college student on Saturday and we're closed on Sundays."

"I need your help because the arthritis in my hands is making my work difficult. The tailor shop has been in the family for years and we want to keep it open. There will be a great deal of responsibility on your shoulders, are you sure you can handle that?"

Gen swallowed. She didn't know if she could handle responsibility like that.

"My husband, Herman, takes care of the finances and maintenance, but I am in charge of repairs, custom orders, and placing orders for supplies. Do you have your own machine?"

"No, I don't, but I'm going home for Christmas. I'll talk with my parents about it. Is there a certain type I should have?"

"A top-of-the-line machine is far outside my price range as I imagine it is yours so any working machine will do for now." She shifted as she talked and rubbed the small of her back.

Gen nodded and wondered if Mother would let her take her machine or if they'd have time to find one at Christmas.

"Outside the business, I'll consider you and your daughter part of our family, you'll help with chores and meals. In return for your work, we'll provide food and lodging, plus a small stipend." She paused. After a minute, she asked, "I think that's it. Does that seem fair to you?"

Gen gulped and said, "Yes." Thankfulness flooded through Gen, from her head to her toes. She had a job, a place to stay, and a plan for the future. It didn't matter if she thought it was fair.

"Now, do you have any questions for me?"

"Questions for you?" She looked toward Mrs. Skloot for guidance. "Should I have any questions?" she asked the headmistress.

Mrs. Skloot laughed softly. "Well, Genevieve, you might want to ask what household goods you need to provide for yourself."

Gen nodded and looked back toward Lucy, "What about what she said?"

"Your room will have a bed, dresser, and a small nightstand. We'll find a crib for your daughter. You'll need to bring bedding and your own clothes and anything else you might need." Putting her finger to her lips, she asked, "Would you like a desk? I think we could find a desk for you if you'd like."

Gen brushed the request to the side, "No, but thank you. I'm afraid that between Kat and work there won't be time for letter writing."

Lucy spoke to Mrs. Skloot, "Well, Beverly, at least she has realistic expectations." The two shared another laugh.

"Herman and I agreed that if I liked her, she was welcome." Looking back at Gen, her face brightened with a smile, she said, "And I like you enough. Are these terms acceptable to you?"

Gen's smile was so big she thought she must look like a child on Christmas morning. "Yes, I'd say they are!" She clapped her hands together and bounced a little on her chair.

A sigh left Lucy's chest. "Good, I could really use your help. I'll leave all the information with Beverly and expect to see you after the first of the year."

She stood and held out her hand to Gen and then Mrs. Skloot. "As always Beverly, it's lovely to see you. We should have tea sometime soon. I'd love to hear what your kids are up to. Peter comes home this summer. Is James home yet? I'm sure they'd love to catch up."

Their talk faded as Mrs. Skloot led Lucy out the door. Gen sat and considered what had just happened. She had a job and a place to live! For the first time ever, things were going to work out.

A few minutes later, Mrs. Skloot returned. "You did very well, Genevieve. Congratulations." She pulled the younger woman in close and gave her a warm hug. "Things are looking up for you and little Katherine. I'm so pleased."

The day before leaving Bethany House, Mrs. Skloot, Ms. Mavis, and Mrs. Plumb gathered with Gen and baby Katherine in Mrs. Skloot's office for a send-off tea. Mrs. Skloot set a lovely table, offering her finest teacups and a steaming pot of Oolong tea. Ms. Mavis brought two plates of cookies.

The women sipped tea and passed a giggling baby around. Laughter filled the room as Kat reached for Mavis's cookies and covered her fingers and face in powdered sugar.

After their teacups emptied, Mrs. Skloot cleared her throat. The chitchat ended quickly. Turning toward Gen, she said, "Genevieve, I must say, you've been a most unusual resident here at Bethany House."

Gen felt the blush rise to her cheeks. Her hands started to tremble. "I'm sorry, Mrs. Skloot, I never meant—"

Ms. Mavis's large laughter cut her off. "That's not what she meant, child. You didn't let her finish."

Gen blushed a deeper red and stared at the dregs in the bottom of her teacup.

"Thank you, Mavis, as I was saying, Genevieve, we've never encountered someone like you. Strong, opinionated, full of passion and promise. We've very much enjoyed having you with us for the past year."

Mrs. Plumb cleared her throat and said, "Indeed. You've been a pleasure to work with."

"And I can't recall the last student I've had such fun with." Mavis's voice felt loud, especially in the closed space of the office.

Mrs. Plumb exchanged looks with the other two women who nodded. "Before you go, we have a few things for you."

Gen raised her hand in protest. "Oh no, you shouldn't have. Really."

"Nonsense. You've worked hard and you're gonna be just fine, you and that sweet little girl." Ms. Mavis handed Gen a box wrapped in newsprint. "Go on, open it."

Gen untied the ribbon and started unwrapping the paper at the seams.

"Oh no, you tear that paper open. I know you're wanting to. No need to put on a show for us."

Gen laughed a bit and tore at the paper, letting pieces fall to the floor. Inside the box was a handmade pinafore apron. Gen looked at the cook in surprise. "Mavis, did you sew this?"

"'Course I did, honey child. You think all I do is cook? I got to have somethin' to keep my hands busy at night." She looked over at Mrs. Plumb who laughed. "Well, maybe I got a bit of advice from Janice."

"A little advice?" Mrs. Plumb laughed.

"Now, I know you gonna be sewin' a bit from now on, but you're still gonna have to cook and when you do, wear this and remember all that you can do and what you've learned." She reached over and patted Gen's hand. "I'm proud of you for all your hard work. You're gonna do fine."

Gen felt tears rising in her throat. Knowing that speech would betray her emotion, she just nodded her head.

Mrs. Plumb spoke next, pulling out an embroidered carpetbag with blond wooden handles. "I wanted you to have something to carry your sewing supplies in, so I made this for you." The carpetbag had a black background and a bouquet of embroidered flowers on both sides. Gen had never owned anything like it. She hugged it to her chest. The tears were close now.

Mrs. Skloot cleared her throat. "Genevieve, deciding on one gift for you has been a difficult challenge. Through all our weeks of meetings, we've discussed many things, some easy, some hard. I've had so many ideas of things that would be useful to you in your new life." From her desk, she pulled two wrapped packages and handed them to Gen.

Gen opened the first one to find a stationery set. The second held a leather-bound journal. Mrs. Skloot said, "Write, Gen. Write out your feelings and questions. Write letters to the people you love. And if you can't think of anyone else, write to me. Let me know how you and Katherine are doing."

Gen thumbed through the pages of the journal to find they were blank, except the first one where Mrs. Skloot had written her name, address, and telephone number.

She could no longer hold back the tears. As she looked from face to face, Gen was overwhelmed by the love she'd been shown. A tear slipped down her face. "Thank you," she whispered, "for everything."

Fifteen

The next day, Gen and Kat returned to her childhood home. When she walked in the door, the relief overwhelmed her. The two rocking chairs still sat in front of the fireplace. The comforting smell of baking bread filled the air. Although she held Kat in her arms, the weight of the past year dropped off her shoulders. She was home.

The house was in the full swing of preparations for Christmas and Marie's wedding. A small pine tree sat in the corner of the living room, a few wrapped presents hidden underneath. In the kitchen, Antoinette was a flurry of floured activity.

"Hello, Mother," Gen said, holding Kat in her arms.

"Hello, dear," Antoinette said, her voice soft. After brushing the flour off her hands, she reached over and plucked the baby from Gen's arms. "You've grown so big, little Katherine. Your mama must be doing something right." The baby reached up and tried to pull at a loose strand of hair. After brushing the tendril back, Antoinette resumed baking, using one free hand while the other held her granddaughter. Lighthearted humming and baby squeals filled the kitchen with music.

Watching the two of them together, Gen smiled, "Mother, if you don't mind, I'm going to settle us in."

"Take your time. I'm just going to start her baking lessons. It's never too early to learn, you know." Antoinette turned around the kitchen, twirling the girl in her arms.

Gen watched her mother and daughter in the kitchen for a few moments. Was this her same mother? Maybe Mrs. Skloot was right and Katherine would do some good.

Gathering their bags, she headed up to her old bedroom. She and Kat would share it for the next three weeks until she moved to the Youngs'. But before that her little sister was marrying Cliff at St. Bernard's Church on Saturday the third of January.

At the top of the stairs, she glanced into Marie's room. Marie sat on the floor surrounded by papers and packages. A white satin gown hung from the closet door, the skirt draping to the floor. With scooped neckline and long sleeves, the bodice was simple and elegant. Dropping her bags in the hallway, Gen said, "Marie, it's beautiful." She ran her hands down the shiny fabric and the many buttons down the back.

"Thank you," Marie said, her cheeks were flushed with daydream. "I have something for you too." She stood and reached into the closet, pulling out a tea-length navy blue dress the same style as Marie's wedding dress. "I thought navy would be stunning on you."

Gen was speechless. She ran her hand down the shimmery fabric. The sleeves and sweetheart neckline mimicked the wedding dress. Pearl buttons ran down the back and fastened the sleeves at the wrists.

Marie took her sister's hand. "I'm afraid you'll be more beautiful than me."

Gen shook her head and laughed. "Not with you in that dress standing next to Cliff, you'll be the most beautiful bride."

"I have a dress for Katherine too." She pulled a white baby's dress out of the closet. "I know she'll probably spit up all over it, but I wanted her to have a pretty dress to wear too."

Gen threw her arms around her sister and said, "Thank you for letting us be a part of your day." She wiped happy tears away from her eyes.

Marie hugged her back. "I couldn't get married without my big sister next to me."

Even from upstairs, Gen could hear the exaggerated voice of her mother talking to Katherine from downstairs.

"But first I have to make it through Christmas and an extra week here."

"Oh, come on, it won't be that bad. Mother is the happiest I've ever seen her. She loves Christmas and now a wedding to boot. She's in heaven."

"Just you wait," Gen said to her skeptical sister. "In only a few days, things will be back to the way they were."

The beautiful white snow which fell on Christmas morning became an evil force three days later. A long-lasting snowstorm locked the family in the house for the whole day, keeping them from gaining much-needed space apart.

At first, Gen brushed off Antoinette's nagging comments. Len was able to use his playfulness to distract his wife from her frustrations. But by the end of the day the fragile facade came crashing down.

"You're still useless." Antoinette said as she left the table after dinner.

Gen's jaw dropped. "Mother, you can't be serious. I have to give Katherine her bath and put her to bed. I'll help when I'm done."

Antoinette shook her head. "Don't bother. I'll be done by then." She dropped the bowl of mashed potatoes on the counter with a thud. "You go take care of the baby while I do the rest of the work."

Len said, "You don't have to do it by yourself. I'll help you, Nettie."

She whipped her head toward her husband. "You'll do no such thing. Dishes is woman's work, it's time she learned it."

Gen sighed. "Mother, I'll come down and help as soon as I'm done. It won't take long. I promise." The defeat in her voice was loud.

But Antoinette had already turned her back on Gen.

Gen took a warm washcloth to the face of her applesauce covered daughter. Katherine blew raspberries, spraying Gen's face. She picked up her filthy daughter and headed to the bathroom.

"I'll be down in a few minutes, Mother," she said. But by the time she finished putting Kat to bed and went back downstairs, she could hear her parents sitting in their rocking chairs in front of the fire. Defeated, she turned around and headed to bed.

The next morning, Gen heard the condemnation return to every bang of the kitchen cupboard. Gen tried to remind her mother of the work it took to care for a six-month-old. There were diapers to change and wash and food to prepare. On top of all that, Gen was helping Marie with last minute preparations for the wedding. As her gift to her sister, Gen designed her sister's veil. She spent every extra minute sewing delicate pearls onto the mesh fabric. As she sewed, she stewed. *The sooner I get to the Youngs' house, the better, for all of us.*

Gen was relieved when everyone's attention turned to the final preparations for Marie's wedding. On Friday, Gen and Marie walked to the store for a few last-minute items. Katherine, bundled in thick blankets, napped in her carriage as they walked through downtown. For a January afternoon, the air was crisp and the sky was bluebird blue. The bright sun lightened their moods.

They'd completed their shopping and were heading back home. Marie's arms were full of bags and packages and Gen pushed Katherine. The sun peeked into her carriage, giving her an angelic look.

Laughter punctuated their conversation. She swerved to avoid a couple walking arm-in-arm down the sidewalk. "Excuse me," she said.

The man stopped and turned to watch Gen walk away. The woman next to him took one more step before she stopped as well. "Gen Ryder?" He stared at Gen and said, "Is that you, Viv?"

Gen stopped laughing. She knew that voice. "Hello, Bobby," she said as she turned to face him. Neither one of them moved. Soft sounds arose from the carriage as Katherine woke from her nap. Bobby looked down. "Oh my God," he whispered. Looking up at Gen, "Is that?" he couldn't complete his question.

Gen peered into the carriage and fussed with the blankets. After standing up, she said, "Yes, Bobby, this is my daughter, Katherine." Looking from him down to her, she said, "Kitty Kat, this is your . . ." She choked on the words. "This is your father, Bobby."

The little girl babbled. In the middle of the slushy, snowy sidewalk, Bobby knelt down next to the carriage. "Oh my God," he said.

Susie, standing next to him, pulled on his arm. "Come on Bobby, people are staring."

He pushed her away, eyes fixed on the little girl. "She's beautiful." His voice was strangled and quiet. He didn't look up to meet Gen's eyes. He just stared at the baby in the carriage.

Gen closed her eyes and took a deep breath. Her jaw clenched and unclenched. "Yes, she is." She stood frozen as he watched her daughter, tears glistened in his eyes.

Disgust welled up in Gen, boiling over when Bobby said in a voice thick with emotion, "Susie, look, it's my daughter." He pulled at his wife to bring her near.

Gen snapped. "She is not your daughter, you helped in her making. Nothing else. You ran off to marry Susie, without giving me a second thought."

Raising his hands against her words, Bobby stood. "Wait, Viv, I had no choice, I swear."

"Liar," Gen said, her hands gripped the carriage. She could feel the anger rising in her. Bobby was not allowed to fall in love now, not after he abandoned them. Her anger boiled over. "You had a choice. You could've fought for me, you could have visited me, you could have come to meet her after she was born." She looked at Susie with venom in her eyes. "Instead you slunk off like a dog with his tail tucked between his legs. You let your parents do your dirty work and ran off to marry Susie."

"But Viv, I'd already proposed. I didn't know."

"I was already pregnant. An engagement is easily broken off. What you knew was that I was fun to be with. Is she as good as I was?" Gen hissed. Susie blushed crimson. Bobby stepped away from the carriage to stand next to his wife and said, "Don't talk about my wife that way."

"Oh, I'm sorry," Gen said. "I forgot to offer my congratulations . . ."

Bobby lifted a hand toward Gen's arm. "Viv, can we go somewhere and talk? I'd like to visit with Katherine a bit, if you don't mind."

Gen reared back in shock. Isn't this what she wanted? As she stood on the sidewalk that cold afternoon, she felt only a burning anger. She stood watching Bobby gaze at their baby.

He looked back to Susie and asked, "Don't you think Mom and Dad would just love her? Maybe we should—"

"No," Susie said. "We are not going anywhere with her and that baby."

Turning to face his wife, Bobby asked, "Why not? That's my baby."

Susie crossed her arms and said, "No, Bobby, that's not your baby. You must be mistaken."

Confusion clouded his face.

Gen continued where Susie left off. "That's right, Bobby, you made your choice."

"Gen, please. Give me another chance."

She shook her head. "I'm sorry, Bobby," Gen said. "I can't. For her sake, I won't." Deep sadness took the place of her anger. She looked him in the eyes. "You made your choice, I am making mine," she said. Gen looked at Marie who used a gentle hand to guide her away. Susie tried to pull Bobby from the place where he stood rooted to the sidewalk.

"Goodbye, Bobby. Have a good life," Gen said as she walked away from the man she once wanted to have a future with.

He raised a hand to call them back. "Wait, Viv . . ." his voice faded as the distance between them grew.

When Gen and Marie turned the corner onto Madison Avenue, Gen's strength failed. She slumped against the carriage as her bravado gave way to tears. Marie wrapped a supportive arm around her shoulders and held her as she cried.

That night when the house was still, Gen sat alone, the sound of Kat's breathing filling the room with soft noise. In the quiet, Gen brooded over the meeting with Bobby. Her questions swirled around her head. No one was interested in her anguish.

Recalling Mrs. Skloot's words of encouragement, she remembered the gifts she'd been given. She opened the journal, pressing hard against the spine to keep it open. Placing the book on the corner of her bedside table, she held a pen and was poised to write.

Taking a deep breath, she put her pen to paper. "January 2, 1948, Dear Bobby," she wrote. "We met on the street today and you fell in love with the little girl who captured my heart the day she was born."

Her pen scratched across the paper, capturing her broken dreams and her resolution to move on and live life to fullest. When her heart was emptied, she concluded, "Bobby, I wish with all my heart we had turned out differently. But we didn't. Goodbye."

Closing the journal, Gen was at peace. She fell asleep with ease knowing Fate owed her a happy future which she intended to claim as soon as she could.

The day of the wedding dawned bright and cold. The January sun lent warmth to a day filled with excitement. Marie and Gen giggled through their preparations, finishing hair and perfecting makeup. Gen's fingers were red from the many pearl buttons on the back of Marie's dress.

Antoinette was full of smiles and unexpected beauty. The girls had convinced her to buy a stylish dress and hat and to wear a lower, looser bun. In the living room before they left for the church, Len twirled Antoinette around.

"Marie, I don't think you can be any more beautiful than my Nettie," he said as they danced.

"Oh stop, Len," Antoinette tapped her husband with her handbag. He stopped to dip her and kiss her on the lips. Antoinette blushed.

The girls enjoyed their parents' affection. With laughter hanging in the air, Gen gathered up Katherine and left for the church.

Gen floated through the next few hours as if in a beautiful dream, helping her sister ready herself for marriage. She watched Marie and Cliff stand before the altar and repeat their vows. She wiped away a tear as they promised to love and cherish each other until death parted them.

Yet envy panged her heart. Her joy for her sister was tempered when she saw Katherine in her mother's arms. She should be in her daddy's arms. I deserve a wedding like this, a man to love me and Katherine.

When Marie and Cliff walked down the aisle as man and wife, Gen swept Kat up in her arms and followed. She smiled as Marie and Cliff stole a kiss in the church entryway.

Her smile vanished when she turned the corner. Dressed in a dark wool overcoat and a black hat, Caroline McFadden was standing next to the wall.

Gen stopped, Katherine babbling in her arms, and said, "What are you doing here?"

Caroline's face contorted with malice. "How dare you. You show up here with that baby in your arms." She pointed her gloved hand in Katherine's face, "and set out to ruin Bobby's marriage."

Gen's mouth dropped open with shock as she pulled Kat into her chest, shielding her from the spewing anger. "I did no such thing," she said. By now, Len and Antoinette had exited the sanctuary, faces aglow.

"Caroline," Antoinette said from behind her daughter, "you were not invited."

Caroline's eyes refused to leave Katherine. Her shrill voice filled the foyer. "How dare you come back to this town with that baby, when we paid to fix everything."

Antoinette stepped in front, blocking Gen and Kat from Caroline's view. "You considered the matter handled and wanted nothing else to do with it. Left alone to her own devices, Genevieve chose to raise Katherine . . . without your son's help."

Caroline pointed an accusatory finger past Antoinette toward Gen. "He was just settling in with Susie when you waltz back in and stir the pot."

Gen stood helpless under the woman's verbal barrage. She listened as Caroline called her a home wrecker, accusing her of ruining Bobby's young marriage. Caroline described how Bobby came to their home talking about "his baby." Her venom grew fiercer and louder.

Antoinette responded in kind, recalling his culpability and guilty retreat.

Wedding guests entered the foyer, intent on offering their well-wishes to the bridal party, but they stopped to stare. The two women stood nose to nose, spittle from one landing on the other's face. Neither stopped to wipe it off.

Len wedged between the two women to keep them from coming to blows. "Both of you, stop this!" he commanded. "I'll not have you ruin this happy day." Looking at Caroline, he said, "I think it's time for you to leave."

Antoinette stood up straighter behind him. Gen rocked her daughter in her arms. Caroline snorted, vented her anger, and left.

Gen couldn't resist a parting shot. As Caroline walked out the door, she said to Katherine, "Thank goodness that woman will never be your grandma."

The heavy church door slammed shut behind her. Gen looked around in horror, realizing Marie and Cliff and all their guests had witnessed the confrontation.

Her face filled with shame. "Oh no," she said, turning toward her sister. "Marie, Cliff, I'm so sorry. I didn't mean . . ."

Cliff stepped forward, "Don't worry about it, Gen. Let's go celebrate our marriage." He guided Gen toward Marie where they hugged: Gen in congratulations and Marie in consolation. When they parted, they posed for a picture and headed to the VA hall for a dinner celebration.

Part
TWO

Sixteen

At last, Gen was moving out of her house, away from Medford. With the turn of the new year came her chance to start a new life, away from the constraints of Bethany House, away from the judging eyes of her mother.

It was a crisp winter day when Len drove Gen and little Katherine and all their worldly possessions to the building housing the home and business of Herman and Lucy Young in Eau Claire. The snow on the ground glittered under their feet. Gen and Len were burdened with everything she owned and thought she could need. Her mother had agreed to give her the old sewing machine, which was encased in a hard suitcase like box. Gen also carried with her the new carpet bag and the green sewing basket. Each held a different, important aspect of her future plans. The sewing basket had all of Gen's plans: sketches of dresses, half-created patterns, samples of fabrics she liked. The carpet bag, on the other hand, held her creations-in-process: a new dress for Kat, the start of a skirt for her.

Between this new opportunity and the plans Gen had for her future, Gen shivered with excitement. Kat, bundled so only her tiny face showed, watched her mama with wide green eyes.

As Gen raised her hand to knock, the door flew open to reveal two brown-haired girls. Lucy Young's voice called down the stairs. "Well, don't just stand there, welcome them in. And shut the door; it's freezing outside."

As she stepped over the threshold, a new sense of excitement flooded through Gen. She had done it, gotten out of Medford without being forced to become a farmer's wife. Here, in Eau Claire, a whole new world was open to her. New men. New possibilities. A new life.

As part of her agreement with Lucy, Gen arranged that twice a week, after Kat was in bed for the night, she could go out. Gen was eager to see who and what Eau Claire had to offer, certain the offerings were superior to the slim pickings in Medford. The world was full of men better than Bobby McFadden.

Before the grand tour of the building or the unpacking of suitcases, Len swooped Kat out of Gen's arms and smothered her with kisses, "Don't grow up too fast, little one, or I'm gonna have to come get you." Katherine squealed as her grandfather blew soft kisses into her ears. Gen caught his glistening eyes. "These are good people, Gen. You'll do well here." Pulling her into a three-way hug, he squeezed the girls tight. "I love you both, very much."

"Love you too, Dad." Gen walked her dad to the door and watched him from an upper window as he drove away. She moved Kat's arms to wave bye-bye, but her voice cracked at the words.

When his car had turned from sight, Gen felt a tug on her skirt. "Come on, Mamma wants you." Laughing, Gen followed the two little girls into the kitchen where Lucy stood at the stove stirring a large pot of spaghetti sauce. Hair pulled back in a kerchief, her cheeks were flushed with effort and sauce splattered across the apron. She beamed when Gen entered the room.

"Welcome, welcome," she said from her place at the stove. She pulled her wooden spoon from the pot and used it to introduce the two girls, Elizabeth and Sarah. Running around the table with a wooden airplane was three-year-old David. "While the sauce simmers, let me show you around the place." Lucy and her husband, Herman, owned the three-story brownstone building. The ground level housed the shop, 'The Young Tailor' which had been opened by Herman and his father after the First World War. The family lived on the second and third floors.

After the tour was completed, the family sat down to dinner. The space around the table was full of joyful chaos. At the head was Herman. Next to him, on his right, was Lucy. Sandwiched between her and Mary, who had just returned home from her after-school job, David sat on top of a telephone book. John, fourteen, was next to Mary. Elizabeth and Sarah were on the left-hand side of their dad with Anna, eleven, next to them. Gen was given the spot at the foot of the table with Kat in a highchair next to her.

As they ate, Sarah leaned forward to look straight at Gen, "That's Peter's spot. He got hurt in the war."

A frown crossed Lucy's face. "Sarah," she said quietly, "that's enough now. We'll figure out what to do when Peter and Abigail come to visit." She gave Gen an apologetic smile.

After dinner the family worked together to clean up. Before long, the little ones were tucked into bed and the older kids were doing homework in their rooms. Gen found herself sitting in an armchair in the quiet living room with Lucy and Herman, each holding a steaming cup of tea.

Lucy groaned, her feet resting on an ottoman. She'd taken the kerchief off her head and was leaning back fully, her eyes closed. Her hands were wrapped around her steaming teacup.

Sitting next to her, Herman read the day's paper. His brownish-gray hair was combed over to cover his bare scalp.

Every few minutes, he turned the newspaper page, filling the room with rustling noise. Without opening her eyes, Lucy said, "I'm so glad you're here, Genevieve. Tomorrow we'll start right away in the morning." Opening one eye at Gen, she said, "It must be a lot to take in. Do you have any questions?"

Gen didn't even know where to begin. She wondered how Lucy did it all, how her family worked, if she was happy. She wondered if a full and happy life awaited her, including her own full, noisy table.

"Well, Mrs. Young—"

"Please, call me Lucy."

Gen gulped a sip of hot tea and winced as it burned down her throat. "Okay, Lucy. What will happen tomorrow?"

Pulling her legs off the ottoman and placing them on the floor, Lucy sat up and looked Gen in the eyes. "I'm so glad you asked," she said and launched into a detailed description of Gen's many responsibilities.

When the morning arrived, feet started moving around the house before the sun was up. It was a flurry of activity: breakfasts, backpacks, and brown-bag lunches. After the kids left for school, Herman and Lucy spent the morning introducing Gen to the shop. Herman showed her the back office. Lucy toured her around the front half of the shop, including a reception area, their workspace and a baby room. "This room has everything you'll need to care for Katherine during the workday. Ever since we opened, there's always been a baby in there. It will be sweet to have little Katherine be the last babe for a while."

Katherine squirmed to be put down. Gen set her down in the gated-off space. Kat scooted around, exploring the toys and playthings scattered around the room. David was already running around the room with his wooden plane.

Part of settling in including setting up a station for Gen, with a space for her sewing machine and to store her bags. It wasn't the neatest arrangement, but Gen had a table and was able to put her carpet bag and basket underneath. She couldn't wait for a chance to work on her projects.

However, for the rest of the morning, Lucy and Gen worked through the backlog of projects. Piled throughout the workshop were stacks of dresses, pants, and coats. She worked by Lucy's side until the shop closed at 4:00 p.m., only taking breaks to care for Katherine. Back upstairs, she helped make dinner and put children to bed. Thinking she'd have some time after supper to work on her dress for Kat, Gen brought her two bags back upstairs and put them in the corner of her room.

At the end of the evening, Gen meant to appear in the living room as she did the night before, but fell asleep on her bed after putting Katherine down for the night. The days and weeks that followed were similar to the first. Gen and Kat adjusted to the routine of work and a busy family life.

Her life fit into the pattern built by the Youngs. Wake, work, family, sleep. Katherine settled into the routine, knowing exactly when to expect her meals and naps. But it wasn't even two weeks before Gen felt the restless tugs of boredom. It'd been so long since she'd been out on the town that she was just itching to go. So on a Friday night in late January, Gen put on a nice dress, gloves, and hat and took herself to the movies. Sitting in the dark theater surrounded by strangers, Gen felt a thrill of anonymity. No one knew her or her past or that she was a mother. No one was her father's friend or customer or thought that Marie was such a lovely girl. Here, she was who she wanted to be—a lovely, free woman looking for a partner in life.

Gen hummed to herself the entire way home from the movie. Eau Claire held so much possibility. The Teacher's College filled the streets with handsome, eligible men, most of whom were decorated veterans of the war. Surely Gen would find a husband among the many.

Returning home to her cozy room, Gen found sanctuary and escape from the chaos of the family. Although it was a generous space, being filled with a bed, crib, and dresser made it a tight fit. As a surprise, Herman had found a small table and chair for the wall near the window that overlooked the street. A few wooden blocks and a fabric ball cluttered the braided rug in the center of the room while Gen's bed and Kat's crib ringed the walls.

As she settled into her new life, Gen found herself wanting to talk to Bobby again. For all of his obvious flaws, she missed his listening ear. She knew it was foolish and sentimental but the urge to talk with him was strong nonetheless, so she poured out her heart to him in a letter she would never send. For three days in a row, she sat at her little table and emptied her head onto paper, describing how quickly Kat had grown and all the promise that her life now held.

At the end of each letter, she tucked the papers into an envelope and buried it in a hatbox she used for storing mementos. She laughed after reading another letter she'd written just after Katherine's birth. Maybe she'd show them to Katherine someday. Placing the new letter with the old, she tucked the hatbox safely away under her bed.

During their hours in the shop, Lucy and Gen developed an uneasy camaraderie. Sometimes they worked on individual projects, other times they worked together. In the warmth of the shop, winter thawed into spring. As Lucy's arthritis in her hands worsened, she spent less time working and more time supervising Gen's work.

Gen knew that her work was sufficient. At the beginning she welcomed Lucy's guidance and correction, wanting to please her new boss and landlady. But after weeks of critiques on the invisibility of a hem, Gen began to resent Lucy's help.

However, as the spring progressed, Lucy's arthritis became too painful to manage at the shop. Many days she helped start the day, but by noon, she was overwhelmed and needed to retire to bed. Lucy acknowledged that Gen's work was "good enough" and allowed her to keep the shop open in her stead.

Fridays were quiet and uneventful. As usual, Gen finished all the waiting projects and tidied the workroom. The early April afternoon beckoned Gen, who hated the idea of spending it locked away in the dark confines of the sewing shop. It wasn't proper for her to sit by the front window to soak in the sun. No one would blame her for closing early. Her deliberations were interrupted by the bell above the door. A tall, slender man walked in.

Standing at the front desk, his eyes swept past Gen into the back room. "Is Lucy working today?" he asked, looking confused.

Gen shook her head, "No, I'm sorry, she's off this afternoon. Is there something I can help you with?"

He patted his pockets and looked inside his blazer. A lot of people visited the shop, but he was different. Dark hair parted on the side, he wore a tweed suit coat, dark trousers and a wide, embarrassed smile with a dimple on one side. His dark brown eyes sparkled behind his glasses. Gen watched as he elegantly slipped the coat down his shoulders. He moved so smoothly Gen was taken aback to see that his right arm ended at the wrist.

"Oh, yes, I remember," he said, draping his coat over his shortened limb. "The sleeves on my coat are too short. Could you please lengthen them one inch?"

Gen studied the coat given to her, "Sir, the sleeves are the right length."

He held his arms together behind his back. "No, please, one inch. I'll come back to pick it up after the weekend." His voice was firm. Without another word, he turned and walked out the door.

As the door shut, Gen realized she hadn't gotten his name or phone number. She ran out of the shop, calling "Sir, wait, I didn't get your name." She looked in all directions, but she couldn't see him anywhere.

She spent the rest of the afternoon pondering the mysterious stranger. She held his coat in her lap, turning it over, hoping to find some clue. There was no label and the pockets were all empty.

The incident convinced Gen to keep the shop open. Closing it might make her miss another new customer. After Kat woke up from her nap, Gen shook toys in front of her daughter but the handsome stranger preoccupied her thoughts. She tried to get out the Easter dress she was finishing for Kat. Holding the pink cotton in her hands, she worked to concentrate on the final details, but instead found herself staring off into the distance.

Finally at four o'clock, she gave up and closed the shop, Gen gathered Katherine into her arms and headed upstairs, wondering if Herman would know who the gentleman was. Entering the family's dwelling, the sound of laughter filled the air. She turned into the living room to see the handsome stranger holding a cup of coffee across from Herman on the couch.

"Oh Gen, I'm glad you're home. How'd it go at the shop today?" Herman's voice was bright.

Gen stared at the man. His eyes met hers and didn't turn away. Her voice was measured as she said, "Fine, except for a gentleman who left his coat without leaving a name or phone number."

The man and Herman laughed. Herman stood and said, "Genevieve Ryder, may I introduce my oldest son, Peter Young."

"I guess you won't want that extra inch in the cuffs after all?"

Peter stood and laughed, looking straight into her eyes, "No, I guess not. It's a pleasure to meet you." Gen wanted to hide. Her heart started pounding in her chest. She could feel the blood rising to her cheeks.

Katherine squealed in Gen's arms. "This is my daughter, Katherine."

He grabbed her flailing hand, "It's very nice to meet you, Katherine, I've heard so much about you." In reply, Katherine leaned over and snatched Peter's glasses right off his face. Sometimes babies were a great distraction.

The two eldest Young children, Peter and Abigail, had come home from college for an extended weekend to celebrate the Easter holiday. The table was crowded, but the house was filled with laughter.

After dinner, easy conversation filled the living room as Peter and Abigail regaled the family with their tales of college life. Identical to each other, they were tall with dark hair and wide smiles. Peter was in his last semester, studying accounting. Abigail also had one semester left, but she was studying English.

"Are you twins?" Gen asked.

"Not identical," Peter said as he flashed his stump arm. The table erupted in nervous giggles.

Abigail rolled her eyes at her brother and said, "No, we're not twins. I'm twenty-one and he's twenty-three."

"Almost twenty-four and I'm missing a hand."

"Peter," Lucy gasped, "you mustn't joke like that."

"Why not, Mother? It's as plain as the nose on my face, so why not make light of it?" He flashed a smile across the table, but leaned close to Gen and whispered, loud enough for the table to hear, "Mother would have me live a life of a monk, but she doesn't know how I charm all the girls." He winked.

The table erupted in giggles.

Over the laughter, Abigail said, "You know, I think we should go to a movie. How about it? I've been dying to see *The Bishop's Wife.*"

"You know, I've been told that I look just like Cary Grant. What do you say to that?" Peter winked at Gen.

Abigail laughed. "I'd say someone needs to get their eyes checked, that's for sure." Looking over at Gen, she asked again, "So what about a movie?"

Gen's nerves came alive and her body started tingling with anticipation. A night out with a handsome man at her side, Gen liked the idea very much. Having Abigail tag along gave the outing a sense of legitimacy.

"I would love that. Going to the movies alone is a bit disheartening. All those couples there together . . ." Gen stopped, fearing that she had said too much. She didn't want to scare him off before she'd even gotten the chance to know this new handsome stranger.

Peter stood and said, "That settles it. We're off to the movies." He pulled Gen and Abigail to their feet. After a flurry of coats and hats, the three went off to the movie theater.

After the Easter holiday, Peter and Abigail returned to school and the house lost its sparkle. Gen carried the work of the shop on her shoulders. Between that and the demands of caring for Kat, Gen felt that life had become very boring. Each morning, Gen dreaded the work of the day ahead. She was weary from being the only parent for Kat and from carrying the load at the shop. Life was the same day after day. She just wanted to quit. But as she considered her daughter, who was almost one, Gen knew quitting wasn't an option.

Gen hadn't talked about the future she wanted for herself, not with anyone, because until recently, she hadn't really thought about what she wanted. Since Kat was born, her focus had been trained on making sure she and the baby could have a life together. But hours of mending and sewing left time for her mind to wander to the idyllic life she now desired. She could picture it clearly: a cute little house, maybe one of the new ones being built in the suburbs, a handsome young man by her side, a wedding in a church, a few more kids running around. She wouldn't have to work like this to maintain her life; her husband would provide all that she needed. It was her dream. It was the American dream.

Now, she just had to figure out a way to make that dream come true.

Seventeen

As the weeks moved on, Gen built her life around caring for Kat, even though she wanted so much more. Although every week starting with Mass with the Youngs, Sunday afternoons belonged to Gen. She and Kat would spend their afternoons strolling the streets or playing at the park, always sure to dress her best because one never knew who she might meet.

Week after week, there was no one. Gen was always greeted politely at the movies or in town. At the shop, customers admired her skill and proficiency to run the shop at such a young age and amid such a difficult circumstance.

Gen complained about all the little old ladies and their comments during her weekly calls to Marie. "I've been here for five months and all I hear is how brave and strong I am to endure such a difficult situation." She let the sarcasm hang in her voice. "I haven't even been on one date yet."

Gen heard Marie's impatient breath on the other end of the line, but she didn't care. Perfect Marie had the life Gen wanted, settled in a cute house with her adoring husband. The least Marie could do was listen to Gen repeat her woes.

"I'm doing everything I can think of. I go to Mass every week, even though the priest only speaks Latin. I take my free nights and go to the movies, but there is never anyone there—at least no one worth my time."

"Gen, you mustn't say that. I'm sure the perfect guy is out there. He's just going to show up when you least expect it."

Gen sighed loudly, "If you say so."

Despite Marie's assurances, nothing changed in Gen's day-to-day life. She worked. She played with Katherine. She took her free nights in town. She managed her monotonous life with as much grace as she could. Until Peter and Abigail returned home flaunting their newly stamped and signed degrees. Although it was a terrible burden on everyone, both Peter and Abigail squeezed into the house until they could secure their next steps.

"It's just for a month or so," Abigail said in the living room one night. She and Peter had joined Lucy, Herman, and Gen for their nightly cup of tea. After taking a sip of her tea, she added, "I can start work after the Fourth of July. My girlfriends and I are going to look for a place to live in Madison next week."

"That's great, dear," Herman crowed. "Your mother and I are so proud. Government work, did you say?"

"Yes, government work. I've already told you a hundred times." Abigail sat back and pulled her teacup up to her lips. "What about you, Pete?" Have you figured out what your plans are?"

"No." He looked across the room at Gen, who was sitting in the corner, knitting an Afghan. "I've decided to stay in town a while and see if I can find anything I like."

Gen caught Peter looking her way but lowered her head to focus on her Afghan. She wasn't going to let him see her blush.

"What?" Lucy asked, "you haven't started looking for work or a place to live? Peter, that's highly irresponsible of you. Not at all what I expect from you. You don't want to stay here, it's too crowded and there's no privacy for you."

Peter laughed. "It won't be that long, Mother." I have an interview next week and am planning to use the GI bill to buy a house."

Lucy sat up, "What do you need a house for? You can just live in an apartment for now, can't you, until you have a family?"

A smile flitted across Peter's face. "I'm hoping it doesn't take that long, Mother. You know, all the ladies out there looking for their own injured vet to nurse back to full health," he said, waving around his stumped arm.

Abigail threw a pillow at her brother's head. Peter erupted in laughter. Herman followed suit. Even Gen giggled a bit at his outrageousness.

But the evening was too much for Gen. The day had been long and she didn't belong in this fun family conversation. After gathering her needles and yarn into the basket stashed next to her chair, Gen stood. "Well, if you would excuse me, I think it's time to call it a night. It's been a long day."

She walked across the room. When she passed Peter, sitting near the doorway, he raised his arm to stop her. "Stay a bit longer, wouldn't you, please?"

Gen stopped to consider but brushed him aside. "No really, I have to get some sleep. Maybe another night."

Peter grabbed her hand, "Promise?"

She yanked it back, unsure of the origin or intention of this attention. "Maybe," she said, then turned to address the rest of the room. "Good night, all."

Choruses of "Good night" followed her down the hall to her room.

Once alone in the quiet of her room, Gen flopped on her bed, her mind racing. Peter had been flirting with her. All these months she'd been waiting for the attention of an eligible bachelor, and now one was here under the same roof. She wasn't sure how to feel.

Lying in bed, replaying the evening over in her head, Gen felt a nagging question, the one she'd held at bay for so long: Was she willing to just let a relationship with Peter become what it was meant to be without her forcing it into something it was never meant to be?

She'd forced Bobby. That hadn't turned out well for her.

Then and there, Gen decided. In the dark quiet of her room she said, "If there is going to be anything at all, it'll be because Peter pursues it."

She smiled widely at the mention of his name, her body flooded with the tingling anticipation of what was to come.

From that night on, Gen's experience at the Young household changed. Wherever she went in the house, she could feel Peter's eyes on her. Passing each other in the hall or sitting at dinner, Peter was always a polite gentleman, holding out her chair, asking for her opinion.

Gen could sense his interest. She started fixing her hair and adding a dab of fresh perfume before dinner each night. After dinner, he would play with Katherine, while Gen finished cleaning up.

A week later, as Gen was making her nightly cup of tea, Peter stood in the doorway of the kitchen watching her. Kat had gone to bed and Gen was looking forward to a few quiet moments away from the crabby baby. As she moved to walk past him, he stopped her.

"So?" He cocked his head to one side and lifted an eyebrow.

"So what?" It was cute the way he thought she could understand what he was thinking with only a one-word question. Cleary, he was a guy who was used to being in charge. Gen didn't mind that at all.

"So, how about we go out for a nice dinner on Friday? I'd like to talk to you away from all the listening ears in this house."

A wide smile broke across Gen's face. At last. It took her a moment to catch her breath. While she'd been waiting for him to make this move, the reality of it took her breath away. "I would love to," she said, but then stopped. "It's not one of my usual nights out. Who will watch Katherine?"

"Are you serious? You've got a whole houseful of willing babysitters." A wide smile split his face. Gen felt weak in the knees as he looked at her. His eyes were intent. Without breaking eye contact, Peter yelled up the stairs to the third floor, "Hey Mary or Abigail, could one of you watch Katherine on Friday night so I could take Gen to dinner?"

Laughter erupted from a bedroom upstairs. "Sure, Pete. You can even take her to a movie too!"

"See, I've got it all worked out." He leaned toward Gen, but she pulled back, even though she felt drawn to him.

"Well then, I guess it's a date," she said while walking away. Finally, a man who was willing to be in control.

As she primped in the bathroom before their date, Gen studied her reflection in the mirror. Staring into her own eyes, she knew this time would be different. Peter wasn't Bobby and she wasn't the old Gen. Still, though she wanted to be married, she wasn't willing to risk anything to get it. This time there wouldn't be any hanky-panky before a wedding.

Meeting her in the living room, Peter's gaze traveled up and down Gen's body. She'd chosen an emerald green dress and white sweater. "I love your dress," he said.

Gen blushed and brushed her skirt with her hands. Bobby had never been so complementary. Peter wore a neat suit with the right cuff hanging empty, but Gen only noticed how his eyes were trained on her. They walked to Grayling's, where the tables were set with linen and fine China.

Despite her nerves, conversation between the two was easy. Gen was thankful that they weren't strangers to each other. Even before the salad course was served, they were exchanging life stories, talking more deeply than they ever had in the Young's house.

With an absent-minded swipe at his arm, Peter started. "I was part of the 84th Infantry during the Battle of the Bulge. We were engaging the enemy when there was an explosion. Everything went dark and I woke up in the field hospital with my arm in bandages." He looked down at his arm resting on the table. "I got lucky," he said quietly. "Some of my friends lost more than their hand."

Gen laid her hand across the injured limb. "I'm sorry, Peter."

Peter covered Gen's hand with his own. "It's not so bad, most of the time. It aches now and again, like it's still there, but," he looked straight into Gen's eyes, "when I'm with you, I feel like a whole man."

Their eyes held until the waiter brought their dinners. As they ate, Gen shared her story.

"This past Christmas, when I saw him again, I realized I didn't want him to love me just for Katherine. I want to be loved for me." Looking up at Peter, she said, "What I don't regret is keeping Katherine."

Peter set down his fork. "Gen, Katherine is a beautiful little girl. Too bad for Bobby. I would consider it an honor to be her dad." He blushed but watched Gen's reaction. She hid her face in her coffee cup and smiled.

"Thank you," she said.

Gen liked how Peter pursued her. Not pushy or over the top, yet, he was often near her, talking, smiling, laughing, helping with Katherine. His presence brought comfort and excitement.

Quickly, and without meaning too, Gen's thoughts race ahead to a dimly lit church and a white dress with her handsome veteran by her side. Talk about marriage was far off as the two began the process of getting to know one another, even if Gen's thoughts already had her walking down the aisle.

Peter was persistent. The week after their first date, he knocked on her bedroom door shortly after she had returned upstairs from the shop. Standing in the doorway, he presented Gen with a single white daisy in a simple vase.

"Put this on your bedside table, would you?"

Gen blushed as she received the flower from him.

"And grab your coat, we're going out tonight."

"But Peter, I haven't even fed Katherine yet." She looked down at Katherine who was stacking some blocks on the floor.

"I have it all worked out already. My sisters have it covered." He held out his hand to her. "Please?"

Gen couldn't fight the warm tingly feeling racing through her body. She could feel the blush rise to her cheeks. "Of course, I'd love to."

From then on, every Friday night Peter arrived in her doorway with a new flower and an invitation to dinner. The evenings were filled with laughter and easy conversation as they spent hours getting to know each other. Each night would end with a chaste kiss on the cheek in her doorway.

Their conversations meandered in long Sunday strolls, pushing Kat in her pram around town. Often they brought a blanket and picnic to spend the afternoon in the park. Peter would recline across the blanket while Kat toddled about within Gen's watchful view. Together they looked like a perfect family of three.

Late in the summer, as the trees were just starting to hint at the change in season, when the sky was bright blue, but the trees were dotted with random yellow and orange leaves, Gen took Peter to Medford to meet her parents at the farm.

The plan for the day was to have Sunday lunch with them and then leave Kat in their care. Gen wanted to show Peter the town where she grew up. Gen was surprised by how nervous she was as they drove. Everything needed to go right this afternoon. Her parents needed to approve of him, in a way that they never approved of Bobby. And she wanted Peter to know and approve of her family, as much as she didn't always like them. She filled the car with her nervous chatter.

What she was really hoping was that Peter was going to seek out a private conversation with her dad and then later in the day propose to her.

But then, they hadn't really talked about marriage much, at least not directly. While Gen had been frank in her desire to have a stable family for Katherine, she'd let Peter drive any conversation about a future together. He hadn't offered Gen much.

Looking at him driving the car, his left hand on the wheel, his right arm resting on his leg, Gen thought he was the most beautiful man. Dark hair combed neatly, his silhouette was sharp and strong. They would make beautiful babies together someday.

Katherine jostled in the back.

After a quick glance back, Gen reminded herself that all notions of babies would wait until after she was married. But then, looking at Peter again, she blushed crimson, imagining what that day would be like.

Before she even knew it, they arrived at the farm. Len and Antoinette came out to greet them. Katherine toddled to her grandparents and let herself be caught in Len's strong arms and gushed over by Antoinette.

Kat giggled in her grandpa's arms as Gen introduced Peter to Antoinette. "Mother, this is Peter."

He extended his hand, "It's very nice to meet you, Mrs. Ryder." He looked around the entryway where they were gathered. "You have a lovely home."

Antoinette brushed away the compliment as she pushed everyone into the kitchen where Sunday lunch was waiting.

Gen had prepared herself for an uncomfortable meal peppered with her mother's biting judgments and piercing questions. Never had she endured a meal without her mother's harsh words souring the entire event.

The four adults sat with Katherine in a highchair between Gen and her mother. After grace was said, Len started by serving himself then passing bowls around the table.

"Roast and potatoes, you spoil me, Mrs. Ryder." Peter said as he put heaping servings on his plate. His eyes glistened greedily at the prospect.

"Well, Peter," Antoinette said in her prim voice, "Anytime you need a good meal, you're welcome here. I'm not sure you'll ever get one from Gen."

Gen took in a deep breath and locked eyes with Peter.

"Oh don't, worry about that, Mrs. Ryder, Gen's a good enough cook."

Antoinette snorted and Gen's look turned into a glare. Peter looked from woman to woman and then to Len for help.

Len stifled his laughter with a cough. Once his throat was clear, he turned to Peter, "So, tell me about how your work is going these days." With a grateful look, Peter launched into a description of his current work project that stifled any further between the women that let the meal finish in relative peace.

As they had prearranged, after lunch, Gen left Kat in the capable and greedy arms of her parents and took Peter out on a walk to show him the farm and surrounding areas.

After a few minutes of Gen's enthusiastic guiding, Peter took her hand and pulled her in a different direction. They followed a track Gen knew well, but was surprised Peter knew was even there.

"Where are we going?" Gen asked as he pulled her down the path.

Peter looked at her with a twinkle in his eye. "You really don't know?" He motioned his head toward a large rock down the path. "You know where we are headed. I think the better question is why?" he winked.

Gen blushed. "Okay. Peter, why are we headed this way?"

He turned back to the path, pulling her along. "It's a surprise."

Suddenly, Gen's heart threatened to pound itself out of her chest. They rounded a corner to find a blanket laid out with a picnic basket on top.

"Surprise," Peter said, his voice quiet. "I thought we could use a little privacy while your parents watch Katherine. You can show me Medford later."

Gen perched on the corner of the blanket, her legs tucked primly to the side. Her breath came shallow and quick as her nerves prickled with anticipation.

Opening the picnic basket, Peter pulled out two pieces of chocolate cake and two cold bottles of beer.

"Peter, how did you manage all this?"

He smiled broadly. "I have helpers." He scooted close to Gen and pulled her hands into his. He took a deep breath.

"Genevieve, I love you."

"Oh Peter, I love you too."

He leaned over to kiss her, which she eagerly returned. In a few moments, his hands were traveling up and down her back. He pulled Gen in closer and for a moment, Gen sank into his embrace, but then, Peter's kiss changed. Intensity coursed through his body to hers. Alarm bells sounded in Gen's head. Quickly, she pulled away from him and took a moment to catch her breath.

"Peter," she said, her voice raspy. "I can't."

Peter pulled Gen back toward him. "We're all alone out here, there's no one around for miles. Kat is safe at your parents' house." He leaned in to kiss her neck.

Gen pulled away again. "It's not that." Gen looked at Peter and took a deep breath. She looked around Peter, wishing suddenly to avoid his gaze. "It's just that I told myself I wouldn't do this until after I got married." Tears sprung into Gen's eyes. "I just can't risk getting pregnant again." She looked at Peter. "Please understand."

"But Gen, I love you."

"I love you too, but until I'm married, the answer is no."

Peter's eyes flashed rage as he threw Gen's hand away. "What do you mean no? You can't tell me no."

Gen backed away. She'd never seen Peter like this. "But Peter, why don't we just get married, then none of this is an issue?"

"I'm not ready yet, Gen, I have a plan. You're just going to have to wait." He ran his hand through his hair, "I just thought that you loved me too."

"I do. How could you even think that I don't? I just said that we should get married."

"And we will. . . I just thought that . . . well . . . since you're already experienced, you wouldn't mind."

Recoiling as though she'd been slapped, Gen's blush grew crimson red. "How dare you! You would risk me getting pregnant again?"

"I never got anyone else pregnant," Peter spat at her. "I'm pretty sure I know how to keep that from happening." He stood up and started pacing along the edge of the blanket. "Don't you trust me?" He took a long look at Gen and drew a steadying breath. "Look, I need to go. Do you think your parents can bring you back home?" Without waiting for her answer, he turned and walked back down the path they'd come up only minutes earlier.

Eighteen

After returning from her parents' house, Gen tried to seek out Peter. He wasn't home when she got back, late Sunday night. Nor did she see him again in the next few days. But with their work schedules and his bowling league, she wasn't too worried. But when Friday night came and Peter arrived late and disheveled to her door without a flower in his hand, Gen knew something was different.

"I'm moving out," Peter announced without preamble at dinner that night.

"What? Peter, why?"

He took a long sip of his coke. "Well, it's high time I had a place of my own. I'm a grown man and it's embarrassing that I still live with my parents."

"Where will you go?" Gen swirled a fry in a pool of ketchup, focusing on the path it made. "You aren't leaving Eau Claire, are you?" She fought to keep the tremble of fear from her voice.

Peter's eyes widened. He reached across the table to her, laying his hand on Gen's arm. "No, I can't leave Eau Claire, not without you."

Gen looked down at his hand, "So you're not mad at me? About last weekend?"

Peter's hand retracted to his hamburger. He quickly grabbed his burger and stuffed it into his mouth. He shook his head. "No," he mumbled through his chewing. After swallowing he continued. "It's fine. I was just surprised, that's all." He looked at Gen. "If that's what you want, I'll wait for you."

A smile bloomed across Gen's face as the tension released from her shoulders. She hadn't realized she was carrying so much over this. She'd been so afraid that somehow, he would be angry enough to break up with her, to find some other girl to sleep with. She bounced out of her seat to Peter's lap where she threw her arms around him. "Really, you'll do that for me?"

Peter blushed and pulled back from Gen a bit. "I will, but you sure aren't going to make it easy on me though, are you?"

"What? Oh sorry," Gen jumped up off his lap and returned to her seat, embarrassment flooding her face. But also, relief and embarrassment. Peter was the one, she just knew it!

As the fall progressed and the nights grew colder and darker, Peter's absence from the Young home was like a gaping hole in the window. Of course, she knew he had his own things to do: bowling league and beer with the guys, and work that kept him busy. But she missed his nearness. She sat in front of the fireplace in the evening and wished she could cuddle up next to him, also knowing that she hoped for so much more.

Gen couldn't shake the feeling that something was strained between her and Peter. On one hand, she couldn't find any noticeable differences in their time together. He still held her hand and kissed her breathless, but he didn't like to be alone with her. They always had to be out on the town or near other people.

Other than a brief visit, Gen hadn't even spent any remarkable time in the house he was sharing with friends. It was a gray and cloudy Saturday afternoon when she stopped over to say hello and bring Peter a small housewarming gift. She'd brought a basket of muffins and a jar of freshly canned applesauce. No one else was home and Katherine was back at the house napping.

"Oh, how nice," Gen said with a mischievous grin. "We have the whole place to ourselves."

Peter grinned back, but rubbed the back of his neck while looking around. "Gen, honey, I don't think this is a really good idea. I mean . . . we're all alone here."

"I know," Gen pulled herself in close to Peter and purred. "I'm happy to have you to myself for once."

Peter brushed her away. "What do you mean? You always have me to yourself. I'm not with anyone else."

Gen filled with confusion. She hadn't expected him to be upset at her visit. "What? Shouldn't I have come?" She looked around for some sort of an explanation, but there wasn't one apparent. Hurt bloomed from her gut as though she'd been sucker punched. She found a small table off to the side and set her gifts there. As tears crept into her eyes, she said, "Well, then, I guess I'll go. Sorry I came to see my boyfriend unannounced." She turned to leave. "Next time, I'll . . ."

"Gen, stop." Peter grabbed her arm with a strong grip. "That's not what I meant." He pulled her back to him and wrapped her up into his arms. He spoke into her hair, "It's just that, well, I can't handle being alone with you. All I want is to take you to bed and ravish you. I'm trying to do as you asked, but you're making it damn hard to do so."

Gen pulled away to look at Peter. His eyes glistened and Gen loved them for it. She could stare at them for hours.

"Peter, I . . . I didn't know."

"You have no idea the effect you have on me." He met her eyes. "You've been through so much already, I didn't want to give you reason to hate me too."

"I could never hate you, Peter Young. I love you." Gen stood up and kissed Peter, trying to convey all her love and passion and trust into that kiss.

As the holidays neared, Gen dreamed of finding a black box with a gleaming diamond under the Christmas tree, wondering if that was in his thoughts as well. But when Christmas came and went without any hint of a proposal, Gen fought to keep a level head. If he wasn't ready for a lifetime with her, she wasn't about to force him. But she was beginning to feel impatient.

The Saturday after New Year's Day 1949 she got her first glimpse into his true feelings for her. It was a normal afternoon and Gen was ready for a cup of tea. Just before entering at the kitchen door, Gen stopped. People were talking inside.

"Peter, we know you have strong feelings for her, but is she the type of woman you want for a wife?" Lucy's voice was soft.

"Mother, I've never brought home another girl. She lives here, for goodness' sake."

"Yes, but we brought her here as a mission of mercy."

"Son, she's already a mother. Don't you understand what kind of person that is?" Even in kindness, Herman's voice demanded the respect of his family. Gen pulled herself tight against the wall and held her breath.

Peter banged his fist on the table. "Of course I do, but do you understand what kind of man I am? I may not be whole anymore, but I can love her."

A chair pushed away from the table and footsteps fell across the room.

"But Peter . . ."

Someone filled the teakettle with water and lit the stove. More footsteps followed by the scrape of the chair.

"Is that what this is about? Because she's a mother, I can't marry her? What about all those poor war widows? They can marry and she can't? That's foolishness."

"Peter, son, wait. This isn't the way we wanted this conversation to go."

"Oh really?" Peter's voice was angry. Gen smiled a bit, knowing that he was angry in her honor.

Lucy's voice was soft again. "Yes, we just want what's best for you. And we wanted you to make sure you thought long and hard about this decision."

Footsteps came near the kitchen door. Gen shrank back before she turned and ran down the hallway to her room. After shutting the door, she slid down and lowered her head to her knees. Tears rolled down her face, the outward sign of her heart crumbling.

Her heart was in turmoil. She thought Peter had defended her and declared his intentions to his parents, but she wasn't quite sure. She knew how much he respected Herman and Lucy Young.

As her body shook, Kat toddled over and climbed up onto her momma's legs. "Mama sad," the little girl said.

"Yes, little one, I'm sad."

Chubby arms wrapped around Gen's lowered head. Toddler kisses turned Gen's cries into a light smile. She swept her daughter into her arms and squeezed her into a tight hug. Kat squirmed away.

Gen released the hug and pulled Kat into her chest cuddling her close. Kat rested her head on her mother's shoulder. As Gen rocked from side to side, she said, "Looks like it's just going to be me and you from now on, little one."

Gen kept her distance from Peter for the next few days. She declined a dinner invitation, feigning illness. The next Friday night, she poked at her dinner salad as Peter regaled her with tales of his client's financial woes.

Taking a break from his hamburger, Peter laid his hand across Gen's. "Honey, is everything okay? You've been quiet."

Gen poked at a piece of iceberg lettuce on her plate. She looked up into his brown eyes. Sadness overtook her and she dropped her eyes again. She didn't think she could handle the pain of his rejection.

Stabbing a limp cucumber slice she said, "Everything's fine."

He squeezed her hand. "Tell me what's wrong. Let's see if we can fix it."

"Fix it?" Her laugh was sad. "You can't fix how your parents feel about me, can you? You can't fix who I am to make me marriageable. You can't marry me because of what I am. Why haven't you broken this off already?" She waved her free hand between them.

Shock traveled across Peter's face. He grabbed the waving hand out of the air and gripped it. "Genevieve, what are you talking about?"

Gen kept her head down and voice quiet. "I overheard you and your parents in the kitchen a few days ago."

Peter pounded his fist on the table. Gen jumped. "My parents. Always concerned about doing the right thing." He ran his fingers through his hair and said, "I'm sorry you overheard that, they were just looking out for me."

"But Peter, what they said, it's all true. I am that kind of woman, I have a child."

"I love you, Gen, but it's me that's the problem. I'm less than whole. You deserve a whole man, who has two hands, to love you and to care for Katherine." He held up both arms. "I'm not the man you deserve."

She looked up at him, allowing hope to rebloom. "Peter, it wouldn't matter if you were missing both hands and a leg." Gen's face exploded in a grin. He grabbed her hands again and leaned across the table. In the middle of the cafeteria, he kissed her.

Nineteen

On a cold Monday afternoon in late February, Peter ran into the shop to find Gen mending a pair of tweed pants.

"Quick, grab your coat and put on some boots."

Gen set down her mending. "But Peter, I'm working."

"Come with me, please?" His eyes grew round and his lower lip pouted.

Gen laughed. "Put those puppy dog eyes away, Peter Young. All right, I'll come with you." As she stood up, she asked, "What about Katherine?"

"All taken care of." He winked at her. "Come on, let's go." He ushered her to his waiting car.

"Where're we going, Pete?"

He put the car in drive and headed down the road, but smiled and said nothing.

Five minutes into their drive, Peter motioned to the glove compartment. "Open it," he said. Opening the glove compartment, Gen found a small black box wrapped with a red ribbon.

Gen's heart started thumping. This wasn't the romantic proposal she'd envisioned, but she didn't care. Her hands shook as she picked it up.

The ribbon fell off in one easy pull. She opened the box to find a key. Her shoulders sagged as she turned it over in her hand. "A key? Not what one usually finds in a little black box." Her voice dripped with disappointment she refused to mask.

Peter stopped in front of a building site in a new subdivision. Turning toward her and grabbing one hand, he said, "You don't like it?" He smiled his crooked grin. "But Gen, it's the key to my new house."

"What? You don't have a house."

He gestured toward a poured cement foundation, the outlines of a new home. "Now I do. I signed the papers this morning. It's mine. And I'll move in when it's finished." The footprint of the house was visible under a fresh coat of snow.

Gen could hear the thrill in his voice, but her stomach felt heavy with dread. A house was a major life purchase. Weren't these decisions they should make together?

"Come on, I want to show you." While holding Gen's hand, Peter led her around the structure, pointing out the different rooms. Their boots left a maze of footprints around and through the property. "This here's the garage. This is the living room. Here's the kitchen." A few steps into a new room. "And this is the main bedroom." He swooped Gen into his arms and kissed her. She sank into his embrace, wrapped in his strong arms.

After a moment he released her but then grabbed her hand. "Come on, I have another surprise for you." He tromped through the snow, following a single line of tracks.

"Another one?" Gen wasn't sure she wanted another of Peter's surprises. Not if he was just going to make decisions for her. She wanted to be part of his life. She wanted to make these decisions with him, together as couples normally did. As they walked, Gen could see other houses in various stages of construction. There wasn't anyone else around. "Peter, where are we going?"

The back of the subdivision bordered Half Moon Lake, a popular swimming area in the summertime. But now, in the dead of winter, no one was around. They were totally alone. The air had a crystalline feel to it, their breath billowing up in soft clouds of smoke. The frozen snow crunched loudly under the silence of the gathering dusk.

Up ahead, Gen could see the Half Moon Lake Resort Private Clubhouse. A comforting swirl of smoke rose up out of the chimney. Peter walked straight toward it. When they reached the landing, Peter stomped off his feet and opened the front door.

Gen held back, stopping on the welcome mat. "Peter, we can't go in here. You're not a member."

He pulled her all the way into the door and closed it behind her. The slam of the door echoed in the empty room. The place was deserted. In front of a roaring fire was a table set for two decorated only with a red rose in a vase.

"Peter what's going on? Where is everyone else?"

"The Club is closed on Monday nights and I'm a member since I bought the house." He winked at Gen. "I told the man in charge that I wanted to impress my girl, so he let me use the club tonight. There's no one else here."

Peter led her to the table and sat her down.

Gen scanned the room as she sat. The large bay of windows opened onto the lake, the rose and purples of dusk filling the view. He walked away and disappeared behind swinging doors. He returned carrying a tray holding two chocolate mousse desserts and another little black box.

After setting down the tray, he kneeled in front of Gen. She pushed her hair behind her ear, tears already glistening in her eyes. This was it. Gen's heart thumped in her chest. She felt him take her hand. "When I was laying in the hospital, I thought my chance for a happy life was ruined. I would always just be a broken man, seen only for my injury. But you changed all that. You make me feel like a whole man."

As if in a dream, she heard the words she'd been waiting for. "Genevieve Antoinette Ryder, I love you, will you marry me?"

She nodded.

Peter slipped a slim gold ring with a square diamond on her hand. The diamond glinted in the firelight.

"Oh Peter." Gen didn't even try to hide her tears. "Yes, yes I will." She knelt down beside him and wrapped her arms around his neck.

They kissed.

With a ring on her finger, a new freedom arose in Gen. No longer would she have to hold back her feelings. An engagement ring was more than a promise. She was as good as married. Peter was hers, now and forever.

Their kiss opened the floodgates of their stored-up desire. Suddenly, she couldn't get enough of him: his scent, his touch, his nearness. She wanted him to be as close to her as her own skin. In the quiet of the empty clubhouse, in front of the warming fire, Gen gave herself to Peter, knowing it wouldn't be long before they would be husband and wife.

Twenty

After his proposal, life exploded with excitement and responsibilities. Besides both of them keeping their own jobs, there was a new house to get ready for and a wedding to plan. It seemed to Gen that she had barely blinked and six weeks had passed in a swirl of activity.

As a new day dawned, the sun filtering through Gen's curtains brought with it the early promise of spring. As she turned her head toward the warm light, Kat's cheerful morning singing rose up from her crib. The sound of that sweet voice brought joy to Gen's heart. Katherine was the best thing to happen to Gen, giving her purpose and identity.

A smile curved on Gen's lips as she thought about the other great part of her life: Peter. They were planning their wedding for the summer, dreaming about the glories of being man and wife. Thinking over the past two years, she realized that the beauty of her life wasn't luck, it was her due. The Fates owed her this happiness.

And nothing could spoil it.

Later in the week Gen sat in the shop mending a shirt. Her stomach gurgled in discomfort. Sometimes tuna fish sandwiches did that to her. She held her hand to her stomach to still the queasiness.

Ten minutes later the queasiness was back, coupled with a strange hunger. She shrugged it off. Not everything settles well, especially not tuna fish. Taking a break, she headed to the kitchen for a glass of ginger ale. That always did the trick.

But the pit in her stomach kept coming back at strange times for the next week. She sat around the table for meals with the family, but simply pushed the food around her plate.

That night, Gen could feel Peter watching her as they sat on the living room sofa.

Peter looked around the room before turning toward Gen. "Gen, I've been thinking." He sighed. "There's one thing we've never talked about." Peter took a deep breath.

Gen looked up from her magazine. "What's that?" She tried to act calm, but a warning tingled down Gen's spine. Whatever was coming filled her anxiety.

"Our family."

"Oh." Gen didn't know what to think. She hadn't given much thought past the man and the wedding. "What do you mean?"

Peter tapped his stump on his thigh. Gen smiled, knowing that was his nervous tendency. He was nervous too. "I don't want to be my parents with eight kids. They have a toddler when their oldest is getting married. I want to have a life with you. We're still young. Let's live a little."

"But what about Katherine? You're already getting a ready-made family, complete with a two-year-old daughter."

He reached across to grab Gen's hand. "And I'm excited for what our life is going to be, you, me, and Kitty Kat. I just don't want more than that for a while. Can you understand?"

Gen was speechless. She'd never imagined this. Since they never spoke about it, Gen always thought he'd want a large family like the one he grew up in. Being around the energy of the Young household made her want a large family someday.

"You girls, you have ways to keep that from happening, don't you? For only a year or so. Okay?"

Gen could hear his words, but the sound of his voice left no question. This wasn't a kind request. It was a command. She swallowed and shifted in her seat, laying her hands across her abdomen. His tone made her nervous.

"Pete, I'll do what I can, but there're no guarantees. It's just that some women . . ." Gen stood, looking to flee the conversation.

"Well, then, let's just hope you're not one of those." Peter stood and winked as he walked away.

Gen sat immobilized for a moment. She had no idea Peter was against more children. Maybe she didn't know Peter as well as she thought.

As the next days passed, Gen kept a bit of distance from Peter. She was still figuring out what, if anything, their conversation changed. They'd been dating for more than six months and engaged for two. Gen wasn't sure how to feel. If they hadn't talked about this very important topic already, what other things had they ignored?

In the midst of these thoughts, her upset stomach persisted. Gen had never realized that mental unease could cause such physical discomfort. But she knew things would settle and so would her stomach. To help her calm her mind, Gen threw herself into planning for the wedding. A thousand different decisions demanded her attention. Her time outside of work and Katherine was consumed with wedding planning.

A few days later, her stomach offered her a reprieve, but now she was ravenous. For potatoes and chocolate milk. At dinner that night, Gen scooped a generous second portion onto her plate. In between bites, she said, "Lucy, these potatoes are delicious. You must give me the recipe."

Lucy laughed and said, "Gen, you've eaten them at least a hundred times, they're just roasted potatoes."

Gen waved her fork at Lucy, "If you say so, but I think they're heavenly."

The people around the table laughed. "Well, Genevieve," Lucy said, "I don't think I've ever seen you eat like this. Wedding planning suits you."

Gen smiled so widely she had to cover her mouth to keep potato pieces from falling out.

Lucy looked across the table and nodded, "Well, good. I've often thought you needed a little more meat on your bones."

Blushing, Gen lowered her head to her plate and devoured the rest of her meal.

Another week passed but the empty pitted stomach feeling persisted. The idea that pregnancy was the root of her discomfort settled in her mind. As she sat alone in the tailor's shop, panic rose up in her throat. She tried to focus on the suit coat she was hemming, but couldn't pay attention. Eight weeks had passed since Peter proposed. 'Aunt Ruby' hadn't visited in that time. Pregnancy was out of the question. Peter made it clear he didn't want a child just now.

Gen closed her eyes and took some deep breathes to steady herself. After a few more weeks, she would be sure. Nothing needed to happen yet.

But in the days that followed, Gen grew confident about what was happening inside her body. She was pregnant again. She spent her every moment worrying about her future. Peter. She couldn't tell him. He'd made his feelings clear. A child right now would ruin everything.

Around her, life continued as normal. She spent as much time as she could in the shop, mending and sewing. Free moments were consumed with the daily necessity of caring for Katherine. Any extra time she tried to fill with wedding plans, but her thoughts were distracted by her growing situation.

Her tightly waisted dresses grew uncomfortable. Even after loosening the belts as far as she could, she knew sweaters would not be able to hide her growing belly for much longer.

A decision needed to be made.

Gen didn't know what to do. She prided herself on being a woman who knew her own mind and did what she set out to do.

Now, however, everything was ruined. Gen was pregnant again, and she still wasn't married.

What a disaster.

Gen couldn't think of what to do. In the long hours at the shop, she sat in the silence and thought about her new situation. She was engaged and planning a wedding. Peter loved her and she loved him back and they were going to make a family together. But he had made it abundantly clear that a family was for someday—not now. A baby now would ruin everything.

Her mind spiraled. She knew an engagement wasn't enough to save her from her situation. She'd lived for a year with Carol, who had been engaged, deeply in love and still had to face the indignity of a year at Bethany House. Gen wouldn't stand for that.

But Peter . . . he was a man who knew what he wanted and got what he wanted. Gen loved that about him. But in this moment, it terrified her. Would he still love her?

Gen was going to burst for the need to talk with someone about all this, to make sense of her thoughts and feelings. Her mind traveled back to the only place where she'd been able to share all of that without judgment. Mrs. Skloot's office.

On the following Saturday, Gen found herself in front of those large oak doors she'd left behind. Even though she'd left more than a year ago, it was as if she was here for the first time, again. Standing paralyzed in front of them, Gen fought to maintain control of her breath. Feelings of abandonment washed over her. Her breath came raggedly. Gen stood and stared unable to force her body to move. She'd called ahead, thinking if that if Mrs. Skloot knew to expect her she'd have an easier time showing up. But she hadn't expected this flood of emotions. She didn't have to do this, she didn't need to be here.

As she turned to go, the door opened in front of her. A young, and moderately pregnant, woman, greeted her. "May I help you?"

"Yes." Gen's eyes darted as she took a tentative step through the doorway. The lobby was empty, but old feelings lodged in her throat. Echoes of the girls eating breakfast filled her ears. She remembered it all, in her bones. "This is a mistake," she said, mostly to herself and turned to walk back out the door.

"Genevieve," Mrs. Skloot's voice rang through the foyer. "I'm so glad you've come." She nodded toward the girl who opened the door. "Thank you, Betty, that'll be all for now. I'm going to be spending some time with Ms. Ryder in my office."

At the name Betty, a giggle escaped Gen's lips. "Another Betty?" she asked.

Mrs. Skloot smiled, "Yes, dear, there is always another Betty. Both the same and different as all the other Bettys this place has seen." Putting her hand on the small of Gen's back, she guided Gen up to her office, where tea was already waiting.

After the office door had been firmly closed, Gen let out the deep breath she'd been holding in.

"I never thought I would have reason to come back to this place."

"A visit to an old friend is a perfectly reasonable reason."

"It just"—Gen paused, looking around the room searching for the right words to say—"it just brings back a lot of memories."

Mrs. Skloot nodded, "I understand. And I'm sure there are both pleasant and unpleasant memories mixed together." Mrs. Skloot offered Gen a chair and a cup of freshly poured tea. A plate of Ms. Mavis's best cookies sat next to the tea service. "When I told Mavis you were coming, she made sure to send up your favorite cookies to enjoy."

"I'm touched." Gen held her teacup in her lap, unmoving.

"So, I am quite sure this isn't a regular visit. While I am most grateful for your presence, most girls don't ever step foot back at Bethany House. There must be quite an extraordinary reason for your visit here."

Gen stared at the drab liquid in her teacup. Her hands, holding tightly to the saucer, trembled a little. Mrs. Skloot glanced at Gen's hands, but said nothing. Silence as large as the desolation of all of Gen's life filled the room.

Finally, when she thought she would burst with the truth of it, she blurted out, "I'm pregnant again."

Mrs. Skloot answered in her calm, measured tone, "Congratulations, dear. What a happy occasion to celebrate with you."

Gen moved her teacup and saucer back to the small table between their chairs. "It is anything but happy news, Mrs. Skloot, you don't understand. I'm not married yet." A deep flush colored her cheeks red with shame. She held up her left hand, showing her precious diamond ring. In the next harried breath she added, "I am engaged though. It happened on the night Peter proposed."

"What exactly is the problem? Surely you've told Peter and you've both just decided to move the wedding up a touch. It's not an unusual situation for people your age."

"I haven't told Peter yet."

Mrs. Skloot gasped. It was a very slight gasp, but Gen still noticed.

Gen rushed to add her justification. "It happened in February when he proposed. We were alone, it was very romantic. I'd made him mad saying no other times, so once I had a ring, I thought it wouldn't be a big deal."

"Apparently, pregnancy comes easily to you."

"Ha." Gen's laugh was tinged with pain. "Apparently. The problem now is that Peter has made known very clearly his desire to not start a family right away."

"That doesn't make sense. In marrying you, he's getting a family right away with you and Katherine. How is she, by the way?"

Gen smiled weakly, but reached for her purse. She'd brought a recent picture of she, Kat, and Peter at the park and handed it to Mrs. Skloot. "Kat? She's a lovely child, but still a toddler, into everything, always on the go, but very snuggly. Sometimes the days with her are so long, I can't even imagine what it would be like to have another one already."

The elder woman took her time admiring the picture. "You've done an admirable job raising her, she's a beautiful child. I've heard from Lucy that you are a valuable employee for them and the Kat isn't a burden at all."

Gen sat up straighter at the complement. "Thank you. She is everything I've lived for these past few years."

"Your young man is rather handsome too, I should say."

Gen's shoulders sagged back down and her face fell into her hands. "What am I going to do?" Looking up at the older woman, Gen bit her lip to fight back tears. "What options do I have?" Her voice was hardly a whisper. "I'm not coming back here. I won't do it."

"Why ever would you need to come back here? Tell Peter about your situation and simply move the wedding up."

Gulping, Gen said, "He won't like that."

"Well, of course he won't be happy, but it is a situation that both of you created. You should not be the only one to manage it."

"I don't think he'll see it that way."

"Oh I do. He may be upset, but he'll take responsibility for his actions. Marriage should be like that, a give and take, where sometimes one person doesn't like it, but does it for their spouse anyway. That's part of loving another person."

Gen shook her head, knowing that Peter's anger was not something she wanted to face. The woman just didn't understand. She wanted to forget all about this, like it never even happened. Not this pregnancy, not this conversation. She didn't want to live in fear of Peter's wrath for something she didn't really know how to control.

With great purpose, she turned the conversation to more pleasant topics and grew animated at talk of the wedding and all the planning involved. Gen prattled on about the details about the dress and veil she was designing and flower arrangements. She was also sure to tell Mrs. Skloot all about the new house and Peter's job and the life she was going to build once they were married. All of it as if there wasn't an unexpected pregnancy getting in the way.

When the hour was over, Mrs. Skloot set her empty teacup down. "Well, Genevieve, you are a remarkable young woman, raising a daughter on your own, getting ready for a wedding and a life with Peter. I'm sure you will be an excellent wife."

"Thank you, Mrs. Skloot. Your words mean a lot to me."

Gen leaned down to gather her purse.

"But one thing before you go." Mrs. Skloot's voice had shifted somehow, from friend to mentor.

She sat back up. Gen knew this was something she needed to pay attention to.

"In the middle of all your planning for your new life, I want you to remember two things. First, as much as married life in a new house will be wonderful for you and Katherine, understand that a new house and a wedding will not make your life perfect. It takes a lot more to make life actually wonderful. And second, if you truly do not think you can tell Peter about this pregnancy, I just wonder if he is a man worth marrying in the first place."

Gen absorbed these words, shocked that Mrs. Skloot would say such a thing about Peter. Of course he was worth marrying. He was worth everything. And Gen wouldn't lose him or Kat. She would make the necessary choices to get what she wanted.

Gen prided herself on being a confident woman, of knowing what she wanted and getting it. Against the odds, she had kept her daughter. She knew she wanted Peter, to have and to hold and she was willing to do the unspeakable to ensure nothing stood in the way.

However as she stood at the back door of the doctor's office she was petrified by what she was about to do. She'd gotten the day off work, telling Lucy that she was going to the doctor about the trouble with her stomach. Lucy narrowed her eyes at Gen, but nodded and sent her on her way.

To Gen, the baby growing in her stomach wasn't real yet. She hadn't felt it kick or move or wake her up in the middle of the night with its hiccups. It didn't have bright green eyes or thick dark hair like Katherine. Its giggles didn't ring in her ears.

Gen had heard stories of others who had visited offices like these. Her friends at Bethany House told her about girls who found "other" ways to get out of pregnancy. It was a shameful way to handle the situation, even more than giving a baby up for adoption. But she had a daughter to raise. There was no room for this. She could keep it secret, no one would ever know.

She gripped the doorknob and walked into the back room of the doctor's office. Gen sat on the cold steel chair in the back room as she waited. Her foot tapped the tile floor, filling the room with nervous sound. She sat with a grim face as the doctor agreed to treat her while berating her for ending up in the situation. She handed him his demanded pay with clenched fist.

She lay still as he used sharp tools to scrape inside her without anesthetic. She gritted her teeth in pain and gripped the sides of the table to keep from screaming.

With the pain came the panic. Inside she screamed, *WAIT! STOP! Don't take my baby. Please, please, don't take my baby!* But it was too late. A few minutes later, which felt like an hour, the doctor stood up, placed his bloodied tools on the tray and covered Gen with a blanket.

He mumbled something about resting for a few days and under what circumstances she should visit the hospital and that she should dress and go home.

With that, he vanished, leaving Gen laying on the examination table. She moved from her prone position and curled up into herself, trying to remove the memory of what had just happened. Her eyes flooded with tears of pain, tears of knowledge, tears of loss. Gen wanted to run away as fast as she could and never look back.

As she dressed, pain emanated through every pore of her body. The doctor must have used nails to scrape her insides. Putting pressure on her legs to stand was excruciating. After collecting her purse and sweater, she hobbled out the back door by keeping one hand clenched on the chair rail of the hall.

When she pushed open the door that led to the back alley, bright spring sunlight overwhelmed her. She shielded her eyes to protect her from its penetrating glare. It decimated any sense she still had of having done the right thing, but instead exposed the reality that her baby had been ripped from her body. She wanted to cocoon up inside herself and only come out again when the world was safe.

Twenty-One

Gen dragged herself back home and collapsed in the doorway. Her brow was slick with sweat and her face pale. After one look, Lucy sent for Herman who carried her to bed. He tucked the blanket up to Gen's chin and closed the door as he left. "Let her sleep for a while. She'll tell us what the doctor said after she wakes," he said. Lucy watched the closed door before going back to the kitchen.

Lucy peeked in on Gen at least once an hour. By late afternoon, the room smelled stale and metallic. The sheets were twisted around Gen. Laying a gentle hand on her brow, Lucy felt a soaring fever. She dabbed at Gen's sweaty brow with a cool washcloth, but the girl thrashed. Lucy took special care to close the door quietly.

As the family sat at dinner, Gen's painful moans could be heard through closed doors. Wide eyes searched for the source of the noise while older children fixed their stares at their soup bowls.

"Herman, I'm worried about Genevieve. I think she's really sick," said Lucy.

Herman nodded.

A moan echoed through the room. Every head whipped in the direction of the sound. "Shouldn't we call for the doctor?"

"Let's give her a little more time. After all she did see one this morning and we don't even know yet what he told her."

Lucy nodded and lowered her head to her soup.

Peter's eyes were fixed in the direction of the sounds. "I don't know, Dad. Gen's a pretty tough gal. This isn't like her."

"Sometimes nature needs to take its course, there may be nothing we can do." Peter's face was tight with concern. He'd hardly touched his dinner. Lucy sat to his right, tapping her foot on the floor. "All right," Herman said, "if she hasn't broken through by the morning, you can call the doctor." Relief washed over their faces.

"Thank you, Herman," Lucy said.

The night was difficult for everyone. Katherine slept fitfully in a crib that wasn't hers. Peter spent his night dozing in the chair in the corner of Gen's room. When he wasn't sleeping, he applied cold compresses and tried to make her comfortable. Gen thrashed in discomfort. When she relaxed in sleep, he held her hand. It was all he could do.

In the hour just before sunrise, Gen awoke, heavy-headed, groggy, and sore. "Water." The word eeked out of her parched throat.

Peter jumped up and ran to get her a glass of tepid water. He lifted the glass to her lips so the liquid could run down her throat. After just two sips, she lay her head back down, exhausted with the effort.

"Gen, darling. Are you all right? Can I get you anything?"

"No, not okay." She turned her head away and drew up into a ball. Everything hurt. No position lessened the pain.

"Father said we can take you to the doctor this morning."

"No," she said in a raspy voice. "No doctor." She tried to put strength into her words. She couldn't go to the doctor now. She'd rather die on this bed than face the truth of what she'd done. She hadn't checked under the sheets, but she was sure they were soaked with blood.

"But Gen, you're sick. You need help."

Gen closed her eyes as a flood of memory washed over her. "No, no doctor," she said again. Her voice was weaker than before.

"Damn it, Gen. I'm not going to lose you for your stubbornness." Gen closed her eyes and sank back into fevered sleep.

When the house started stirring, Peter insisted Gen needed immediate care. While Herman got dressed, Peter went to get Gen. When he pulled back the covers, he discovered a dark red pool soaking the bed. Panic rose in his throat.

Without any further hesitation, he wrapped Gen in a clean blanket and hefted her into his arms. He flew through the house and down to the car, placing her in the back seat of the car.

Peter drove to St. Anne's Hospital as fast as he could. The emergency attendant rolled Gen away. As she disappeared behind swinging doors, Peter was left standing in the entryway, feeling helpless.

Peter paced the waiting room for a few hours before anyone came out to talk with him. A doctor in a white coat approached and asked, "Are you next of kin for Genevieve Ryder?"

Peter ran his hand through his hair, "No, fiancé, Peter Young."

"In that case, all I can say is this: She's going to be okay. She suffered from some blood loss and an infection. We've treated her with antibiotics. You should be able to see her in an hour or two."

Relief flooded through him.

"Where is she?" he asked. "Can I go see her now? I want to be there when she wakes up."

The doctor cleared his throat. "Mr. Young, she's had a traumatic couple of days, she needs time to heal. You may see her in a few hours." He turned on his heel and walked away, his shoes clacking across the tile floor.

Two agonizing hours later, Peter ran to find Gen's room on the fifth floor. He pushed open the door to Gen's room without bothering to knock. Covered by a thin hospital blanket, Gen rested on the hospital bed. Peter drew in his breath at the sight of her. A tube leading to a drip bag was inserted in her left arm. Her face was pale, her hair unkempt and greasy.

The air in the room smelled of antiseptic. Peter's nose wrinkled at the smell. Seeing Gen lay in that bed scared Peter. He had to do something, make it better somehow. He spied the window on the far side of the room. He went to open it, to usher in some fresh spring air. But the birds were chirping, and the noise which offered such hope of spring offended Peter. He slammed the window shut. Gen didn't move at the disturbance.

Peter moved the lone chair in the room next to Gen's exposed arm. In the quiet, he slid his hand under hers.

Her skin didn't burn anymore. The normal heat of her skin overwhelmed Peter with relief. In the silence of the room, the realization that she almost died overwhelmed him. At this flood of relief, he bent over and sobbed against the bed.

A quiet tap on the door interrupted his lament. The nurse had come to check on Gen. After a brief glance in his direction, she said, "She's a tough one, isn't she?"

He nodded.

"The fact she's still with us proves she has a lot of strength."

He looked up at her and asked, "Is she going to be okay?"

She flipped over the metal chart hanging off the edge of the bed and studied it with pursed lips. Her finger traced down the page and onto the next. "The antibiotic is working well. She should make a full recovery."

Peter sighed. "Thank you," Looking over at Gen, his heart surged with relief and love. "Thank you," he whispered again.

When the nurse was ready to leave the room, she put her hand on Peter's shoulder. "I hope she's worth it."

"Oh yes, she's worth the world to me."

The nurse shook her head. "Ms. Ryder needs rest to heal fully, please remain quiet to let her sleep."

Peter asked, "Excuse me, ma'am, but can her daughter come and see her?"

The nurse pulled back. "Her what?" She looked at Peter with accusing eyes.

"Her daughter, Katherine. She's just a baby and misses her mama."

"Miss Ryder needs all the rest that she can get, especially if she has a daughter to get home to."

The sparkle in Peter's eyes dimmed, "Oh, it's just that—"

"I understand, little girls need to see their mamas, but not like this. Wait a couple days until Ms. Ryder is awake and talking. Until then, you may sit with her now, but since you aren't family yet, you'll have to leave after visiting hours."

"Yes, ma'am." Peter said. He turned back toward Gen. Leaning over, he kissed her on the forehead and said, "I won't leave until they make me."

Peter stayed next to Gen's side. As she dozed, she felt his presence near. When she woke, his was the first face she saw. After two days in the hospital, Peter recounted to her the story of the past few days.

Her face blanched as he described his early morning discovery and the agonizing wait. "I was so afraid. I thought I was going to lose you." She gripped his hand and studied his face for any hint that he understood why she was lying in a hospital bed. So far, he didn't suspect. Together, the days passed in a rhythm of pain medication, sleep, and quiet conversation. She was glad for his presence and care.

But the nights, alone in the hospital, were dark. The hours crept by as tears flowed. She grieved the loss of her child and her close brush with death. The darkness spiraling inside her threatened to consume her. *Should I even be surprised? It's just my lot in life, nothing but misery and suffering.*

In a rare daytime moment when Peter was gone, Doctor Henderson laid out the truth of what happened to Gen. She had suffered an infection as a result of her abortion. Maybe the tools had been dirty, maybe the room wasn't disinfected. Regardless, the infection, which started in her uterus, spread throughout her system.

He sat down in the chair next to her bedside. "Ms. Ryder, there is good news and there is bad news. The good news: through the aggressive use of antibiotics, we've killed the infection."

Gen nodded. That was good news indeed. She swallowed, afraid of the bad news to come.

"The bad news: the doctor who performed your procedure caused a lot of physical damage. Most likely, you'll never become pregnant again."

Gen bit her lip as grief washed over her. The realization that she'd never be able to give Peter a child sat on her chest like a lead weight. What had she done?

The doctor's voice broke into her thoughts. "Do you have any questions?"

Surprising even herself, Gen was candid with the doctor, telling him about Peter and their relationship.

"Most men don't understand the workings of a woman's body. It may be best not to tell him at all." He made a couple notes in her chart. "You have a daughter?"

Gen forced herself to swallow. "Yes, sir, I do."

His face softened with a wide smile. "What's her name?"

"Katherine," she said. "She's almost two."

"I'm sure you miss her a great deal." Looking at Gen over his glasses, he said, "You know, the kisses and hugs of a child heal many wounds."

Gen nodded, holding back tears. The doctor's manner was so kind, she was overwhelmed. She'd never experienced anything like it.

"Mr. Young may bring Katherine to see you tomorrow. You'll be discharged in a couple days."

Gen gained strength at the thought of seeing Kat. She could even pretend the doctor's sad words didn't matter because Katherine was such a beacon of joy. She would be enough.

The doctor set down the chart and headed toward the door. "Excuse me, Dr. Henderson?"

He turned. "Yes?"

"Thank you," Gen said, "for everything."

Doctor Henderson left. Gen was alone with only two bouquets of flowers as companions, one from Peter and one from her parents. Peter had brought many things to make her stay more comfortable, including her robe and slippers and some of Lucy's homemade vegetable and chicken soup.

As she looked around the room, Dr. Henderson's words echoed in the silence. "Never become pregnant again." They rang in her head like a death knell, a reality she'd have to keep secret.

He had accepted her story of Katherine without question, and he'd made clear his feelings on children. Would Peter still love her if she could never give him his own child?

With the doctor's permission, Peter brought Katherine and Lucy to visit the next afternoon. After they entered the room, the little girl hid behind Lucy's skirts.

Gen burst into a smile at the sight of her daughter. Wearing a hand-me-down red pea coat against the spring breeze, she looked like a little doll. She wanted to scoop her up and squeeze her and never let her go. "Hey there, Sweetie, want to come sit on my bed?" Her voice cracked with emotion. Gen almost missed out on the rest of Katherine's life. She'd never again make a decision that threatened to tear them apart.

At the sound of Gen's voice, Kat ran up and hopped at the side of the bed, but she wasn't tall enough to reach the top. Peter's strong arms lifted her and placed her next to Gen. Gen wrapped her arms around her and pulled the little head in close. She breathed in the scent of her skin and patted her soft, dark pigtails.

"Oh, I missed you, my Kitty Kat." Gen said. She gave her daughter another tight squeeze. The girl squirmed underneath it.

"Mama, stop."

Gen, along with Lucy and Peter, laughed, filling the room with happiness.

The girl fought to get free from Gen's arms, and Gen held her tight to keep the warmth of her close.

From the chair next to Gen, Lucy said, "Kat, tell Mama about the park."

Kat's eyes lit up as she delved into a story about her trip to the park the day before. The pigtails bounced as she babbled to Gen. Kat started using her hands and jumping a bit as she remembered the swing and slide. The girl's jostling sent shocks of pain shooting through Gen's body. She gripped the side railing to keep from jumping and startling her daughter. But the joy she brought to Gen was immense. She was so full she felt her heart would burst for love of the little girl.

After a few minutes, Peter pulled Kat away from Gen. The little girl zoomed around the room, sniffing flowers and opening cupboard doors. Her laughter sounded up and down the hallway. After an hour Peter corralled Kat and passed her to Lucy who would take her home.

"No go home, Mama Lucy. Wanna stay, Mama." Katherine cried as she was carried down the hall. As the door closed and Kat's sad protests faded, Gen sunk into her pillow. The visit took a toll on Gen's healing body. After the joy and energy exuded by her little one, Gen only wanted to sleep.

With gentleness and care, Peter pulled her blanket up and adjusted her pillow. After tending to Gen, he dragged the chair over and sat down next to her. A thin smile spread across her lips as Peter took her hand in his.

Peace filled the room. "You know, Gen, Katherine is a wonderful child. I do love her," Peter said.

Her smile strengthened.

"Watching you with her, knowing how good she is and how much you love her"—Peter paused and looked at the floor—"I'm sorry."

"Whatever are you talking about, Peter?"

His words were halting. "About me not wanting more kids. I was wrong."

Gen swallowed the lump rising in her throat. "You are?" Gen looked at Peter. His eyes had bags underneath them and shimmered with tears. His hair wasn't perfect. These past few days had taken a toll on him too.

Peter looked into her eyes. "Gen, let's have lots of babies. Let's be madly in love for the rest of our lives with a house full of children."

"But, Peter . . ."

"No buts. I mean it, Gen. I love you and I almost lost you. But I want little girls and little boys with your smile, your eyes, your laugh."

"You've given this a lot of thought."

"Gen, I've watched you here for the past four days thinking about what it'd be like to lose you. The pain was greater than anything I've ever experienced. I can't lose you or Katherine." He reached over and took her hand and played with the engagement ring on her finger. "We're going to have a big, happy family.

Gen couldn't ruin this moment by dashing his dreams. After all, the doctor did say "maybe." There'd be time to tell him later. He kissed his beloved on the forehead and turned the lights out as he left. Gen laid her head back and fell asleep, exhausted but thrilled. Her life was going to work out after all.

Twenty-Two

For Gen, returning to her room at the Young's home was exhausting. Just the effort it took to walk up the flight of stairs to the house sapped her small reserve. To be surrounded by the noise and activity of a busy household taxed her to the limit. For the next week, Gen rested, as much as she could, letting her body heal. But her grief was raw and the invisible wound was gaping. Her eyes burned from tears she fought not to cry.

She returned to the shop in small doses, using the time when Katherine liked to play as work time. Kat stood at the gate to the nursery room, a rag doll hanging from her hand. Sitting in her chair in the workroom, pangs of guilt ripped through Gen. Tears stained her little face. Gen knew what the little one wanted—to be held and loved and played with by Mama, but Gen couldn't bring herself to do it. That sweet child deserved a good mother. And Gen knew she wasn't anything like a good mother.

She sat paralyzed in her chair and watched her daughter cry. The door connecting the house to the shop opened and closed. Gen didn't register the sound and jumped when she felt a hand on her shoulder.

"Let me get her, Gen. You just stay there." Lucy's voice was soft.

"Oh, Lucy, I didn't hear you come in."

Lucy bounced the girl in her arms. "I know. You're deep in thought." The words were a statement with a question attached.

Gen forced a smile to her face. "I was just thinking about the wedding."

Lucy returned with a weak smile of her own. "I'm sure." She spent a few minutes calming Katherine before setting her down and picking up her alteration project. The two worked in silence, the happy noise of Kat playing their background noise.

Gen set down the black shirt she was hemming and sucked in her breath. "Lucy, I'm sorry." The words were unexpected, but Gen breathed a sigh of relief having said them.

Startled, Lucy looked up from the shirt she was mending, "For what, dear?" she asked.

"I'm not the pure and innocent bride you dreamed of for your son."

Lucy looked at Genevieve with a stern eye. "You have nothing to apologize for, Gen."

"But . . . ," Gen's voice was insistent.

Lucy drew in a breath and said, "I'm so relieved you've recovered from your illness. Women don't always bounce back from such a loss."

Gen looked up at Lucy with quiet fear in her eyes.

Lucy put her hand on Gen's knee. "I've lost two babies. Herman didn't even know about one of them. After the first one and how he grieved, I couldn't put him through that again." Her eyes glistened when she looked up. "I've never told anyone about the second one."

Gen stuttered, "Lucy, I . . ."

"Don't worry, your secret is safe with me." She wiped her face with her hands. After a moment, she said, "I hope you two have a long and happy life together. After all you've been through, you deserve as much."

She gave Lucy a tender look. "Thanks, Lucy." Gen blushed and looked down at the black shirt resting in her lap.

Lucy coughed to clear her throat, "Have you and Peter settled on a date yet?"

"Yes, just last night. Katherine turns two on the first day of summer, so we thought to make it a week of celebrations and get married on that Friday—June 24.

Lucy looked at the tattered calendar hanging on the wall. "About three months, enough time to get everything in order, don't you think?"

The conversation shifted from dates to details. With heads down to their mending, Gen described to Lucy the dress she was designing. "A simple A-line, nothing fancy." She tied off the thread on her needle. "I might be able to find time to add some brocade detail on the sleeves and bodice."

Hanging up her finished item, Gen kept talking, "I'm going shopping for fabrics this weekend."

Lucy excused herself and disappeared into the storage room. She returned with an entire bolt of ivory satin in her arms. The creamy colored fabric shimmered as she unwrapped the paper off the bolt.

Gen gasped. "Lucy, it's beautiful, but I can never pay you back." She fingered the fabric lightly, not wanting to snag it. It must have cost a fortune.

Joy shone on Lucy's face. "No dear, it's my wedding present for you." She paused. "I thought you'd look lovely in cream."

Gen wrapped the fabric back up and set it aside. She wiped her eyes. She stood to hug Lucy. After a quick embrace, Lucy pushed Gen off, rubbing her aching hands, "I have to go . . . my hands." As she left, Gen saw Lucy brush tears out of her eyes.

Between the demands of her work and the demands of her family, two months slipped away for Gen. In May, the small bungalow Peter bought was finished and he moved in. He and Gen added paint and collected furniture, transforming it into their home. They didn't have much, but they already loved it.

On a Wednesday in late May Peter pulled Gen away from work in the middle of the afternoon. Outside the shop's front door, Kat waited in her carriage. The day was warm enough for a stroll through town, although Gen couldn't imagine where the three of them would go.

"What's all this?" Gen asked.

"You'll see," Peter said, pushing the pram down the street. Gen followed, curious and eager. The afternoon sidewalks were empty of people, children had not yet gotten out of school. Birds twittered, filling the air with cheerful noise. After a few minutes, Gen realized they were walking to their new house. When they turned onto Sunset Hills drive, Gen gasped. A familiar car was parked in the driveway.

"What? Why?" Gen peppered Peter with questions, but bubbled over with excitement. "Are they here?" She looked at Peter. He just smiled.

Gen broke into a run toward their new home. When she passed by the familiar car, she saw her mom and dad sitting on the porch swing, waiting for her to come home.

She was so happy to see her parents that Gen ran up the porch and fell into their arms. Involuntary tears rolled down her cheeks as she clung to them. Her father held her, rubbing her back as she relaxed in his arms. Antoinette sat nearby, a reluctant hand on Gen's shoulder.

"Mother!" Gen cried. "You came too?"

"Of course I came, you silly girl." Antoinette snapped, but a smile spread across her face. "I just had to be here today."

Finally reaching the house, Peter and Katherine joined the happy reunion. Gen pulled herself back, looking at both her parents. "Why are you here?" All three adults grinned at Gen. He fished the house keys out of his pocket and made a show of opening the door for Gen. "What is it? What's inside?" Her excitement bubbled over and sparkled in her eyes.

Stepping through the front door, Gen saw a Shaker-style dining set. She walked up to the table and brushed her hand along the smooth finished top. The oak was stained with a dark red finish with ladder back chairs to match.

Len spoke into her ear, "I wanted you to have a table to build family memories around."

"Dad, you made this?" Gen's hand brushed the table top again. "It's beautiful."

Len patted Gen on the hand. His eyes fixed on the diamond engagement ring on her hand. "I made enough chairs for all my grandchildren." He coughed to clear his throat and looked around. "So where is my little Kitty Kat?" Len stomped off in the direction of giggles playing on the porch.

Left alone with her mother, Gen stood staring at the table. "Mother, it's beautiful. How long did it take him to do this?"

"It's been his special project since you left last year." Her voice was heavy with judgment. "I never imagined it'd be a wedding present," Antoinette said. She ran her gloved hand across the table and examined her fingers for evidence of dirt.

Gen couldn't believe what she was hearing. She dropped her voice and said, "Mother, Peter is wonderful." Gen paused and considered her response, wanting to stoop and speak her own barbs. Instead, she stood up straighter and jutted out her chin. "I won't let you ruin my happiness. I've found what you've always wanted for me. Isn't that good enough?"

Antoinette's face soured and a grunt escaped her lips.

Gen didn't have to put up with harsh words any longer. She turned and walked out the door, letting it hang open behind her. She sat on the porch swing next to Len who had Kat in his arms. Peter leaned against the porch's supporting column. Closing her eyes, the happy laughter of the three calmed Gen's anger. Peace filled her.

Firm footsteps stomped out the front door and stopped on the porch. Pulling the door shut did not interrupt the fun the others were having. Antoinette opened and reslammed the door, stomping her foot on the ground. Peter, Gen, and Len looked up. Antoinette stood with her one hand planted on her hip, the other waving in her daughter's direction. "Pardon me for interrupting your jolly time out here, but you and I have unfinished business." Antoinette shot a pointed look at Gen.

"Mother, how dare you." She started to rise, but Peter's firm hand kept her in her seat.

Antoinette's chest heaved with furious breaths. Len reached his hand out to calm his wife. She shook him off and looked at Peter, "Do you understand who she is?"

Peter stepped between his fiancée and her mother and said, "With all due respect, she is my fiancée who's worked hard to provide for herself and her daughter. Please, speak to her with the respect she deserves."

"Oh I am," Antoinette said, her lips curled into a fierce snarl. "She became pregnant by another man, that's his child," she said, pointing to Katherine on the porch swing. "If you're willing to accept that, fine. But are you sure it won't happen again?"

Len plopped Katherine in her mother's lap and rose to stand next to Peter. "Antoinette!"

Gen had no idea her mother had such a low opinion of her. "Mother! Is that what this is about? Because Bobby didn't choose me, no one should?"

Peter crossed his arms across his chest to hide his clenched fists. After a deep breath, he said, "Mrs. Ryder. I have chosen. And I have chosen well." Turning toward Len and extending his hand, he said, "Listen, Len, this isn't going the way I'd hoped."

Len shook Peter's hand, "You're right, I'm sorry this visit is ending like this." Looking toward his daughter, he said, "Gennie, I'm sorry. I hope you love the table." He paused and then added, "Peter is a worthy man. He'll take good care of you and Katherine." He picked up his granddaughter and smothered her face with kisses. Finishing with a loud smack on her cheek, the little girl squealed with delight.

Antoinette already stood next to the passenger side door of their car with her hands folded primly on her lap, waiting for Len to open it. As she and Len pulled out of the driveway, Len waved while Antoinette sat rigid in her seat.

When the car had turned out of sight, Gen collapsed into Peter's arms. He held her without any words. She didn't want to face him, didn't really want to talk about it. So instead of letting him make awkward conversation, she took control. "Peter, listen—"

"Listen to nothing. There's nothing to say except, I'm sorry." She buried her face into his chest. They stayed on the porch in each other's arms until the demands of a certain almost-two-year-old could no longer be ignored.

Twenty-Three

The final weeks of preparation for the wedding were a conflicted time for Gen. The excitement of preparing for a wedding and life with Peter filled her with hope. Yet, a nagging remained. Even as she watched people scurry to fill her requests for last minute preparations, she knew something wasn't quite right. Her parents were in Eau Claire often helping with final preparations. One night, Antoinette stood at the stove making dinner. Gen watched from the doorway she saw one hand stirring the pot with practiced ease and the other hand that rested in disappointment on her aged hip. Without any words, Gen heard the telegraphed message from her. *This was wrong. She was wrong. Marrying Peter was wrong.* She never really believed her mother would bless any man or marriage, so that didn't fully explain the unease settled in Gen's stomach. One couldn't be disappointed not to receive something they never thought they'd get.

If she were honest with herself, Gen knew what was wrong, it walked around with her, she wore the guilt in her conscience like a shawl. A cry she would never hear. A weight she would never carry. A smile she would never see. How long could she keep from Peter the secret of her deepest shame? Forever, if she needed to, because Kat needed a Daddy, just like Gen needed a husband. Gen had decided that Peter was the man for the job. She wouldn't allow anything to interrupt her happily ever after.

But in the quiet moments of the day, when there was no one around her needing direction, the sad kindness of the doctor's words rang in her ears—"Mostly likely . . . never become pregnant again." They were a death knell. Gen was determined to build a happy life for the three of them. Peter would never need to know about the family that wouldn't ever exist.

These thoughts tumbled around Gen's head as she watched two-year-old Katherine eat a slice of chocolate birthday cake. Looking from her chubby-cheeked daughter to the circle of loving faces surrounding her, Gen was overwhelmed at the love and support she had. But fear crept in. Could she handle their whispers and glances and well-meaning words when the happy family of three did not become four?

When these thoughts threatened to overwhelm, Gen threw herself into the work of moving her and Kat's belongings to the new house. The effort of packing, unpacking, and arranging was enough to distract from her intrusive thoughts. Kat raced from room to room exploring as Gen folded her clothes into the new bureau in Kat's freshly painted pink room.

Gen knew that if she could create a life with Peter and Kat in this house, all the pain would vanish. She could learn to make the perfect meals, make sure they were dressed well and host flawless gatherings. She would fill her life with tasteful decor, a well-manicured lawn, and every expectation of a modern, middle-class wife and mother. That would be enough. The guilt and emptiness would be filled if she had such things.

In the midst of her plans, replacing guilt with comfort, Peter would catch Gen for a private moment, where a soft touch or quiet conversation would bring her back to the good that was right in front of her.

The days passed in a flash.

Gen had barely blinked before she found herself standing in front of a mirror in the corner of a plain room in the basement of a church.

For one blessed moment, she was alone with her thoughts. The room was empty of the bridesmaids primping and preening, her mother fussing over little details, Katherine whining at the dress and the shoes she was forced to endure for the evening. Gen could hear the organ playing music above her head. Soon, it would be time to meet Peter at the altar.

But not yet.

This was her moment.

She hummed as she ran her hands down the neatly fitted satin of her dress. She and Lucy has spent their extra time getting it just right, sewing pearls onto the veil netting, adjusting the lace at the bodice and hem. This dress was her dream come true. A one-of-a-kind beauty created by her own hands.

Studying her face in the mirror, Gen saw everything this day meant to her and what it had cost. This night was hers to celebrate, to savor, and to relish. No longer would she live under the domineering hand of her mother's impossible expectations, but also, she now had the freedom to make her own choices to get what she wanted.

She'd done that twice now, first to keep Kat, second to keep Peter. A knowing smile crossed her face. She wouldn't ever need to do that again. Peter would always fight for her needs. He was exactly the man she'd hoped for: kind, considerate, and loving. He loved her. He loved Katherine. He wanted to provide a good life for them both and he wasn't going to let his injury keep him from that.

A quiet knock interrupted her thoughts. "Gen, honey. It's time." Len stood in the doorway holding out his arm to escort his eldest daughter down the aisle.

"Hey, Dad." She grabbed her bouquet from a vase of water on the table and linked arms with his. "I guess so."

Stopping in front of the open doorway to the sanctuary. She looked down the long aisle. Covered in white fabric and a small smattering of rose petals, the path led to Peter. Seeing him there, down the aisle, Gen couldn't believe it was real. He was handsome in his suit, one arm neatly hemmed to hide the missing limb. But Gen didn't see any of his imperfections, instead his smile filled her line of sight.

But the first clear note of the wedding processional filled the high-ceilinged room and every head turned to watch her entrance. The sound of the processional was drowned out by the crackle of a hundred people rising to their feet from the wooden pews. She looked up to see Peter's face locked on hers, a smile as wide as the sky plastered across it. A tear threatened in the corner of her eye. Without warning, Gen felt the tiniest hint of unease in the depth of her being. Focusing away from that, to Peter, Gen knew it was just nerves. Excited as she may be, getting married is a forever thing. She knew that. Her parents and Lucy and Herman had shown her that although marriage wasn't always perfect, love could outlast the storms of life. A commitment before God and friends in the church was forever. With a deep breath to steady her nerves, Gen took her first step down the aisle and into the rest of her life.

What followed, in Gen's mind, was the wedding of which stories are written. The chapel was illuminated by the summer evening's light and the flicker of candles. Len walked Gen down the aisle, but to her it felt like floating. Meeting Peter at the altar, he took her hand and never let go. Gen repeated words and accepted a thin gold ring on her finger. She listened as Peter promised to love and cherish her and she slid a gleaming gold band on his finger on his right hand. In a daze of joy, they were pronounced man and wife. Peter took her in his arms and kissed her to a rowdy cheer from their friends.

The rest of the evening was a blur of feasting, smiles, kisses, hugs, and laughter. Gen had never felt such joy in her entire life. Guests swirled around her, toasting the couple's complete happiness. The midsummer sun set late, casting long shadows across the VA hall where they gathered. Whoops and laughter filled the hall as Peter swooped Gen into his arms for a long, passionate kiss.

By the time the evening was wrapping up, Katherine had fallen asleep in Grandma Lucy's arms and was whisked off to spend the week at the Young's house. With a final wave to her parents and sister, Gen was pulled into Peter's car, decorated with cans and streamers, and they drove off for a week of wedded bliss as man and wife.

Twenty-Four

Gen lay in bed listening to the birds singing. The sun had already risen. Peter was taking a shower, whistling as he readied himself for work. She wanted to pinch herself, her life felt like an incredible dream.

The weeks after the wedding had been a time of transition, but the most blissful kind. She and Lucy had agreed to a brief hiatus as she adjusted to the combined rigors of married life and motherhood.

Gen enjoyed the work she'd put into making their house a home. Before they married, Gen and Peter had talked about the life they wanted to build: Peter providing for his girls, Gen making a happy home for him. Since then, she'd made a tablecloth and new curtains for the living room. She and Katherine indulged in long walks and playtimes at the park. During Kat's afternoon naps, Gen spent time paging through her old notebook from Ms. Mavis, planning perfect menus for each night's dinner.

As she lay in bed thinking through the day ahead, Gen realized she was bored. She didn't have any projects that couldn't wait a day or two. The other mothers at the park weren't that interesting, they only talked of pot roasts and their virtuous husbands and perfect children.

She got out of bed and went to the kitchen to fix coffee and breakfast for Peter. He loved his eggs, over easy, with toast and butter. She hadn't yet gotten the eggs right, but he was being patient.

His smile was weak as she presented him with another less-than-perfect egg. Using his fork, he poked his egg and said, "Not again. It's overdone. I thought you had learned to cook at the home you went to?" The words, while calm, were delivered in a lightly ominous tone.

"Oh Peter, I'm sorry. I'll try again. I'll get it right." Gen stood by the table and reached for his plate. "It's been a while since I have actually been in a kitchen."

He poked at her hand with his fork. "No, I'll eat it. We're not going to waste the food that you don't get right." With that he dove into the overdone egg and focused on the front page of the morning paper.

"Peter, I was wondering"—Gen stopped, her heart thumped in her chest. Was he past the financials yet? Peter hated to be interrupted when he read the financial section.

She pulled out the chair next to him and tumbled into her words. "I was wondering if it'd be okay if I spend a few hours at the shop, helping your mother this week." She snapped her mouth shut and waited. Her hands sat in her lap beneath the tablecloth, but she picked at her fingernails.

Long moments passed as Peter took slow sips of his coffee and continued to turn the pages of the paper.

"Peter?"

"Yes, I heard you."

"Well, may I?"

Peter rustled his paper one last time before he folded it and set it next to his empty breakfast dishes. "Aren't you pleased with the life I provide for you?"

Gen was taken aback. She'd expected a quick answer, but not this. "Yes, Peter, I love the life we've got."

"Then this should be enough."

"I need to do something other than stay in this house all day."

"You can take care of our home and our daughter." Gen sat frozen in her chair.

Peter sat thinking. "It'd be shameful for my wife to work; I provide for all my family's needs."

"Of course you do." Gen lowered her eyes. She didn't want to demean him, but she needed something more. Staying at home all day with a two-year-old had been her life's dream, but now it felt lacking. The house was settled and there was little else for her to do. "Your mother called and asked, she said she could use the help."

The room was silent again.

Peter pushed himself away from the table and threw his napkin onto his dishes. "Fine, but don't let it get in the way of your responsibilities here. I expect dinner on the table when I get home from work. It's the least a man can expect from his wife."

Gen hopped up and clapped. "Of course, Peter, I will make you proud." She leaned over to kiss him on the cheek.

"I hope so." He flicked his wrist to check his watch and grunted. "I'm going to have to speed to make it on time. Where's my briefcase?"

She brushed off his shoulders and straightened his tie. "In the hallway, dear, where you put it last night when you got home."

He kissed Gen in a way that left her breathless. Before he turned away, he said, "Oh Gen, one more thing, Steve from the office invited us over for dinner this weekend. Call his wife and arrange the details." Then, he walked out the door and drove away. For a moment, Gen reveled in the silence that followed. The thought of dinner at another couple's house excited Gen. This cemented their status as a newly-married couple, accepted despite their unconventional arrangement.

At the end of that week, on Saturday night, Peter and Gen went to the home of Steve and Judy Swanson in one of the other new developments in town. Gen put on pearls and high heels and Peter wore an evening jacket. Together they kissed Kat good night, leaving her in the care of his sister Mary.

As they drove to Steve and Judy's house, Gen was full of nervous anticipation. She'd never been invited to dinner. This was the sophistication she'd dreamed about when growing up on the farm.

Steve welcomed them at the front door, greeting them with mojitos. Peter was invited to the back deck with Steve, while Gen was ushered into the kitchen with Judy. She leaned against a corner counter and watched. Stirring, chopping, checking the contents of the oven, Judy was a whiz in the kitchen. Gen sighed, knowing she'd never have that level of proficiency. However tonight was about impressing Peter's friends, not her insecurities, so she pasted a smile onto her face and asked, "Can I do anything to help?"

A few minutes later Gen carried a steaming bowl of white rice out to the back patio. Lit by tiki torches and the low hanging summer sun, the patio was cast in a warm sunset light. The men were standing next to the grill, watching the steaks. After she set the rice on the table Gen noticed her surroundings. The backyard was a lawn of lush green grass. She longed to slip off her shoes and run through it. The smell of charcoal on the grill and heady rose bushes mingled in Gen's nose.

When Judy asked if she'd like another drink, she nodded her head and accepted the glass. She'd never tasted alcohol before tonight, but she wasn't going to admit that to these sophisticated people. She endured a bitter sip and set it down. Although Gen didn't care what people thought about her, she wanted to make a good impression.

Peter continued accepting the drinks Steve offered, one after another. As the evening wore on, Peter's behavior changed. He leaned full back in his chair in fits of laughter and pounded the table for emphasis of his own humor.

When Steve and Judy stepped away from the table to prepare dessert and another round of drinks, Gen leaned over to her husband and whispered into his ear, "Peter"—her voice low and quiet—"haven't you had enough to drink tonight?"

Peter yanked his head away and hissed, "Am I embarrassing you? I'm sorry." Gen winced at the force and volume of the words.

"Peter, knock it off. You're making a fool of yourself."

He pushed himself into Gen's space, grabbing her by the shoulder. "I'm a grown man, Gen. I'll stop when I damn well please." His face was within an inch of Gen's. His breath reeked of alcohol. "Mind yourself, woman."

When she couldn't pull away, Gen turned her face away from him. Hot tears pricked her eyes.

"Everything okay out there?" Judy called from the kitchen window.

Gen said, voice quavering, "Yes, just fine."

Gen looked into the kitchen window, but Judy's face had already disappeared. Had her host seen the exchange? No time to dwell on that now, she and Steve were walking through the patio door.

Seeing the beautiful, handmade cherry pie in Judy's hands, Gen said, "Oh Judy, I don't know how I could eat another bite."

"Oh Gen, there's always room for pie," Judy winked at her guest and served everyone a healthy slice. The night ended with forced conversation. Peter dominated every point, leaving Gen to offer Steve and Judy an apologetic look.

Finally, Peter stood to leave. He wobbled, catching himself on the edge of the table with his left arm, exposing his stump. "Whoa. Leg's feeling a bit unsteady tonight. Been a while since I've had this much to drink."

Steve looked Peter over. "Listen, Pete buddy, I don't think you should drive tonight. How about letting Gen take the wheel?"

Peter pulled his car keys out of his pocket and shook them in his hand. "Nah, man, I'm steady as a sailor. I did this all the time in the service."

Steve put his arm around Peter and reached for the car keys, "No really, let someone else drive. You're in no condition—"

"Who are you to tell me I can't drive? The police?"

"No, I'm just a friend—"

"Like hell you are!" Peter jammed the keys back into his pocket. He motioned for Gen. "Come on, honey, I think it's time for us to go."

Gen had never seen her husband like this, she shivered but went to stand by him. She looked him full in the face and put her hand on his arm. "Peter, Steve's right. I can drive us home tonight."

"Like hell you can. I'm not trusting my life to a tramp like you." His voice filled the silence of the summer night. Gen held her breath. Even the birds stopped chirping. "It's clear our welcome's worn out, let's go!"

Gen looked over to Steve and Judy, both their faces were red. Gen smiled weakly, but Judy wouldn't meet her eyes.

Peter attempted a step toward the door, but his legs buckled. "Gen . . ." She wrapped her arm around his waist as he stumbled toward the door.

"Thank you. We had a wonderful time." Gen said to Steve and Judy. She swallowed to hold back her tears. "You have a lovely home." She turned and escorted her husband to the car.

Somehow, Gen maneuvered Peter into the driver's seat. When the engine roared to life, Peter sat up, threw the car into reverse, and sped away.

The drive home was quiet and tense. Peter focused on driving. Gen hardly drew in a breath. She didn't want to break his concentration.

Peter pulled the car into the driveway and slammed it into park. Gen braced herself from crashing into the dashboard. As she reached to get out of the car, Peter's arm stretched across the seat, pinning her against the back.

With teeth gritted, a growl rumbled in his throat. "Don't ever do that to me again."

Gen glared at her husband, his accusation set her temper on fire. How dare he accuse her of anything! "Do what? Get rip-roaring drunk at someone else's house? I didn't do that, you did."

He leaned over into her space and said, his voice mocking. "Oh, what a lovely home you have. What delicious food this is." Returning to his snide, drunken voice, he said, "Come on, Gen. It was steak on the grill and a cherry pie."

"And you!" Gen's voice rose. "You stumbled out of your coworker's house. You should be ashamed of"—the sharp sting of Peter's hand across her face silenced her.

Peter spoke through gritted teeth. "Don't ever speak to me that way again. I'm your husband. I'll not be shamed by you! You should be thankful I even married a woman like you."

The sting on her cheek spread across her entire face and over her entire body like a wave of electricity. Holding onto her remaining dignity she pulled away from Peter and escaped the car.

Slamming the car door behind her, she stood in the night air. Letting the freshness wash over her, she closed her eyes to what happened. With her back to the car she said, "You can stay out here for all I care. Good night." She walked into the house with head tall and back straight.

After paying Mary and seeing her out, she locked the door, leaving Peter to sleep it off in the car. Without taking time to do anything at all, Gen went into her bedroom, shut the door, lay down on the bed in all her clothes. Every time she closed her eyes, the incident replayed itself across the back of her eyelids. The sting flushed through her again and again. If it weren't for her body's memory, she wouldn't have believed it ever happened.

Surely it was just a one-time thing. Peter had survived the war, he even had a major injury. Of course, his reactions would change if he had too much to drink. Gen's last thought before sleep overtook her was, "Well, I'll just keep him away from alcohol. That'll fix it."

The next morning, Gen woke to a quiet, insistent knocking. Opening her eyes to the first rays of morning light sunshine, she saw Peter, ruffled and in last night's clothes, standing outside the bedroom window. He smiled weakly and waved to her. "Good morning, Beautiful. Could you let me in?" He disappeared from view, presumably to walk around to the front door.

Gen stretched her arms and rubbed her face. After getting her robe she walked to the door where Peter was. She opened the solid front door, leaving the screen door closed in between them. Patchy stubble on his cheeks and mussed up hair accentuated his bloodshot eyes. Lines covered his cheek from sleeping on the car's vinyl seating. He looked so rumpled and pathetic, she felt sorry for him, until she yawned and the bruise on her cheek stretched. Then the hurtful words and the sneering looks of the night before flooded her memory.

From behind the glass, Peter rubbed his head and said, "It feels like a train ran over my head."

Frowning, she hesitated to open the door. Slowly, she reached her hand toward the handle when he asked, "What happened to your face?"

If she hadn't been so angry, Gen would have burst out laughing. Trying to contain her many emotions, she said in a flat tone, "You hit me last night when we got home."

First his jaw dropped, then realization washed over his face. Finally, penitence settled in his eyes. His shoulders dropped and he refused to lift his head. "I'm so sorry, Gen. I can't believe that happened. That's not like me, you know that."

Gen crossed her arms as she leaned on the window. "That may be true, but you still hit me. You hit me!" she said. "What do you have to say for yourself?"

"I'm sorry. I don't know what happened. It'll never happen again, I promise. I love you."

She stood still, watching him for a long moment.

"Please, please forgive me."

From the other side of the door Gen studied Peter's countenance—his downcast eyes, his slumped shoulders. He didn't look like a man proud of his actions. She cleared her throat. "Do you promise it will never happen again?"

Peter's words shot out of his mouth. "God as my witness, I will never hit you again." He raised his stumped arm over his heart.

Gen knew she couldn't leave him outside much longer, the neighbors would notice him, rumpled and standing in the flower bed as the sun started to rise. Gen chose to believe that the threat of public whisperings and humiliation would move him to good behavior. "I'm of half a mind to let you stay out there for the neighbors to see."

Peter froze. "You wouldn't do that to me, embarrass me like that, would you?" The earnestness in his eyes made Gen's heart melt. "It won't happen again. I promise."

When she finally cracked open the screen door, he pushed his way in and wrapped his arms tightly around her waist. Burying his head in her hair, soon his body shook with silent sadness. Gen's tears soon joined his. "I'm sorry," he whispered. "I'll never hit you again. I love you Genevieve Young. Always."

Twenty-Five

ummer faded into fall and threatened to become another dark Wisconsin winter. The newlyweds fell into a predictable household routine. Gen spent Tuesdays at the shop with Lucy and the rest of her time at home with Katherine. Peter worked five days a week at the office. Every day had its plan. Every week had its rhythm and, Gen felt, no variety.

Sitting at the table loaded with a dinner of meatloaf, mashed potatoes, and applesauce, Gen watched her husband eat with gusto. This meal was one that usually sated him. She had trouble being successful in the meal department. Forkful after forkful of food shoveled into his mouth. His words were few. Katherine fed herself from her highchair, shrieking with delight as the peas rolled around her tray. Gen poked at the food on her plate with her fork.

She looked outside. The sun had already set, night was coming. The house felt cold and dull. How boring. This whole life was boring. She threw down her fork in frustration. The clatter broke the silence of the room.

Peter looked up from his plate. "What's wrong, dear?"

She looked into his eyes. "Peter, I'm bored."

He tilted his head to look at her. "Would you like to play a game of checkers after dinner?"

Gen blew out a breath. "No, not that kind of bored." Looking around the room, her eye was drawn to the drab, gray decorations. "Don't you ever crave some excitement around here?"

Peter went back to eating his food. "No, I don't."

"I mean, don't you think our life is a bit boring?"

"You don't like the life I provide for you? Is it not good enough for you?"

Gen could feel Peter's temper rising, and fought to keep it down. "No, that's not what I meant. It's just that"—Gen bit her lip as she thought—"let's do something, I don't know, different."

"Like what?"

Gen thought for a moment. What could break the doldrums of their routine? What could add some energy? Her eyes opened wide with excitement. "I know, let's have a party."

Peter set his fork down and stared at her. After a few moments he said, "You know, Gen, I think that's a great idea."

The broad grin on Gen's face said it all.

Gen started planning right away. The first weekend of December was still a month away, but it'd be part of the Christmas party season. She reviewed her worn notebooks from Ms. Mavis, looking for clues on hosting a party. She cracked open her Better Homes & Gardens Cook Book for recipes and guidance.

For a week she made her lists, trusting that a thorough plan would compensate for any lack of experience. She decided to present a table full of cheese balls, crackers, stuffed olives, crab dip with a sweet finale of red velvet cakes covered with powdered sugar. Patiently, Peter listened as she prattled on at the dinner table each night about her party decisions.

The day before the party, she scooped up Kat from under the table after breakfast. Pulling her close, Gen said, "We're going to have a party, darling!"

"Ohhh, party, party!" Kat clapped her hands.

"We need to go to the grocers for some last-minute supplies," Gen said. Glancing at the clock on the wall, "If we're out to run some errands, why don't we stop by Daddy's office to say hello?"

Katherine wiggled out of Gen's arms and ran to the coat closet. After a few minutes of rummaging, she emerged wearing Peter's clunky work boots and a knitted winter cap. "Daddy hi!"

Gen laughed at Kat's antics and then helped her find the right boots, coat, mittens, scarf, and hat. When they were bundled up, they loaded into the car for the drive to Peter's office on the other side of town.

Holiday spirit, which smelled of evergreen boughs tied to lampposts, filled the air. Women carrying wrapped packages crowded the sidewalks. The mood of the day was jolly and light. Gen hummed as she drove.

Parking in front of Peter's building the two girls skipped into his office. After a brief chat with the secretary, Gen knocked on Peter's door.

"Come in," sounded the voice from inside.

Katherine pushed open the door and squealed. "Daddy!" She ran into the office, stopped in front of a large desk in the middle of the room. Her little head just peeped over the edge.

Although swamped with papers and folders, Peter's face lit with a joyous smile. Looking down, he said, "Come here, little Kitty Kat." She ran around the desk and into his arms where he smothered her with kisses. "Hey there, good lookin'," he said to his wife. "Fancy meetin' you here." With Kat in his arms, he walked over and kissed her.

Gen blushed. "Peter, what will people think?"

"That you're my beautiful wife and I'm madly in love with you."

She pushed him away and looked out the door to make sure no one had seen. "You're embarrassing me."

"I'm not the one who stopped in unannounced." He walked back around his desk and sat down with Kat in his lap. "So, to what do I owe this pleasure of seeing my girls?"

"We're headed to the store to pick up a few things for tomorrow night and we wanted to come say hi." She smiled at him.

"I'm glad you did. What have you decided on, anyway?"

"As if I haven't been talking about it all week," she scolded, but a wide smile broke across her face.

Reaching into her purse, Gen pulled out her list. She rattled off her plans again. A giggle from Kat interrupted her words. Undeterred, Gen kept talking. After finishing her recitation, Gen looked up and frowned. Peter wasn't paying attention at all. "Peter Young, you haven't heard a single word I've said, have you?"

Peter laughed as Kat blew a raspberry onto his cheek. "Yes I did." Without hesitation, he repeated Gen's menu plan back to her.

"Ha," Gen said, hands on hips but a grin on her lips. "You weren't listening. You missed the cheese ball and stuffed olives."

Glancing up at the clock, it was already ten o'clock. The morning was passing too fast. She had too much to get ready. "Playtime with Daddy is over, Katherine, we have to go to the store now."

"No," she said. "Play Daddy." She set her lip out in a two-year-old pout.

Peter looked at the little girl, "Kitty Kat, we'll play later tonight," he said with a kiss on her nose.

"Otay, Daddy." Kat said. "We play tonight."

Looking over to his wife, Peter asked, "How much is all this going to cost me?"

"Depends, how much can I spend?"

"I want this to be a great party, so buy what you have to, but I still want to buy you a Christmas present or two," he said with a wink.

"Okay Darling," she leaned over to give him a goodbye kiss. "I'll do my best, I want to make you proud." She gathered Kat up in her arms. Just before they walked out the door, Gen turned back to her husband. "I'm thinking of buying a new dress for the party, is that okay with you?"

"Sure," Peter said, but he had already turned back to the pile of papers on his desk.

The next day, party day, arrived with a furious blizzard. Being unable to go anywhere, Peter rearranged the furniture, while Gen scurried about the kitchen, finishing the food. As the day turned to evening, the storm subsided. After dinner, Peter took Katherine to his parents for a sleepover. By the time of the party, the clear, cold sky was full of twinkling stars, but the house was warm and cheery.

Gen took a final glance in the mirror, her long dark hair brushed to a bright sheen. She fastened in her pearl earrings and checked her makeup. Smoothing her dress with her hands, she stepped into the hallway.

Gen cleared her throat, but Peter did not hear her. He was busy testing the rum punch.

Finally, she called out, "Peter, come help me?"

He turned toward her with the glass raised to his lips and he nearly spit it out. "Gen, you are ravishing."

Gen wore a fitted cranberry red cocktail dress that cut straight across her chest. The skirt flared at the end. She held out her pearl necklace, "Could you help me?" she asked.

Setting down his punch, he grinned and walked over. Taking her necklace, he wrapped it around and kissed the back of her neck. Gen shivered.

"If we didn't have guests coming—"

"If we didn't have guests coming, Katherine wouldn't be at your parents and I wouldn't be wearing this dress."

"You're right," he grinned, "you wouldn't be wearing this dress, at least not for very long." Gen blushed but got the reaction she wanted. Everything about this night was going to be perfect.

The guests started arriving just after seven o'clock. Peter received them at the door. Gen stood behind and welcomed them in. Shining like a beacon against the dark night, Gen knew she looked beautiful, if not a bit flamboyant. With a wide smile and swinging hips, she guided each guest into her home.

Soon, the house filled with Peter's coworkers and their wives. The air was warm and noisy. The stuffed olives and cheese ball disappeared from their platters. Although she didn't have a chance for real conversation, Gen overheard snatches of others' talk. Everyone was having a wonderful time. Gen enjoyed the swirl of energy around her. Heads followed as she walked from room to room, checking on her guests.

Peter was also a capable host, neither allowing his guest's glasses to empty, nor his. As the night progressed, Peter's laughter increased and his stories filled the entire house. His guests listened to him as he held court in the living room. His glass of rum punch filled and emptied many times throughout the night.

Punctuating the end of a story, he slapped the man standing next to him on the back. Only the quick hands of others around kept the bystander from crashing into a table lamp. The group erupted into roars of laughter. One of the wives leaned over to Gen and said, "Looks like your husband's had a bit much to drink tonight, Gen."

Another laid a hand on Gen's arm, "Better hope he passes out before he gets his hands on you. Too much always turns my husband into a maniac." The other wives nodded in agreement. Gen cast a wary look at her husband who was now leaning against the wall. The wives near Gen gathered their husbands to leave.

The next twenty minutes were a flurry of coats and hugs, handshakes and air kisses. By the time she shut the door against the cold of the evening, Gen was exhausted. She leaned back against the door and let out a deep breath. Brushing a loose hair out of her face, Gen said to her husband, "I think that went pretty well, don't you?"

When she opened her eyes again, Peter was sitting on the couch with a scowl on his face. "What?" she asked as she moved toward him. "What's wrong?"

His voice came out sharp, "I can't believe you."

"What? What did I do?"

"I watched you tonight, with all the wives. Why can't you be as dignified as them?"

"What do you mean?" Gen studied her husband. The other wives were right. "Peter, you've had too much to drink tonight, perhaps you should just go to bed."

Peter leaped off the couch at his wife, "How dare you accuse me!" Peter grabbed the table lamp and threw it toward his wife.

"Peter!" She ducked as it smashed against the wall. "What are you doing?"

Peter's voice roared over the echo of shattering pottery. "I can't believe I've got a wife like you! All I wanted was to host a respectable party for my coworkers. I wanted my wife to be a respectable woman, not a tramp for other men to stare at." His fists clenched at his sides.

Gen inched away, trying to shrink into herself.

"You didn't hear what the other men said about you. Do you think they would've been so friendly if they knew the truth about you?"

Fear stole the words from her mouth. She backed further away, but was stopped by the wall. She put her hands against it, feeling for something to grab.

He advanced toward her, closing the space between them. He stood inches from her face, spittle flying from his mouth. "Sometimes I can't believe I actually married you."

Gen put up her hands against his chest, tears threatening. "Peter, stop, you don't know what you're saying. It's the alcohol talking. Please, just go to bed." She let the tears run down her face, but fought to keep her voice from shaking. "Please."

He spoke through gritted teeth, "You disgust me, sniveling like that. You're not a respectable woman. Get out of my sight."

Gen ducked away and ran into her bedroom, locking the door behind her. Throwing herself down on the bed, she sobbed into her pillow.

She could hear him in the living room, pacing and stomping like a caged animal. After a few minutes, he tried the knob of the bedroom door. He pounded and yelled for Gen to open up. But she shoved her head under the pillow, refusing to hear his angry words. The longer he stood at the door the softer his words became, begging for her to open the door. An hour passed before he gave up. Silence filled the house. Gen wondered where he went, but didn't dare open the door to find out, memories of his last drunken outburst burned across her cheek.

The next morning, Gen woke rumpled and sad. The morning light showed stains on her beautiful dress. She rubbed the sleep from her eyes and changed into a house dress. Checking over her face in the mirror, she grimaced. Her tears left ugly streaks of mascara down her face. Her hair was a rat's nest of snarls from a night of restless, alcohol-tinged sleep.

She wanted to hide in the bathroom forever, perhaps curl up in the bathtub for a while. Turning on the sink's faucet, she let the hot water run until steam covered the mirror. She wiped the steam away and stared at her reflection. Peter'd spoken truth last night. In his drunken state, he spewed filth, but Gen knew he was right. She was not a respectable woman. A virtuous one would never have done what she did, not the first time, or the second. She washed her face in the scalding water, hoping it would also wash the stain from her soul.

When she came out of the bathroom, she steeled herself for a confrontation with Peter. Instead, she found him sitting at the kitchen table nursing a hot cup of coffee.

He looked at her through bleary eyes. "Hi."

"Hi," she said quietly.

He stared down into his coffee cup. Without looking up he said, "About last night . . ."

Gen stood silent in the kitchen doorway. He looked so sad to her, his droopy face falling into his coffee, but the sting of his words was fresh. And the truth . . . she could not escape their truth.

He looked up from his cup and said, "Gen, I only remember bits and pieces about what happened. I had a bit to drink."

She walked into the kitchen and poured herself a hot mug of coffee. With her back turned to Peter, she said, "There wasn't a moment where you didn't have a glass in your hand." Turning back to him, searching for words. "I think you were the life of the party."

He ran his hand through his hair, his wedding ring glinting in the light. "What about after the party?" He looked over to the coffee table where the lamp used to stand. "Not so great, huh?"

"No," she answered. "Not so great."

"I already cleaned up the lamp. Did I break anything else?"

"No, just the lamp." Gen kept her voice flat, fighting the emotion swelling up in her.

"Did I really say horrible things to you?" Peter locked his eyes on hers.

Gen gulped and nodded. "Yes, you did."

"Gen, listen to me." He rose out of his seat, stretching his hand toward her. "If I said what I think I said, I didn't mean any of it. I'm sorry."

She lifted her hand toward his, but drew back. "Peter, you wouldn't have said it if it wasn't true. Deny it all you want, but I know you think I'm a hussy." Spite and sadness mixed in her voice.

He protested, "No, Gen, you're not that. I don't even remember all that I said. But I promise . . ."

Gen's voice mimicked her husband's drunken rage. "Oh stop your sniveling. It makes you look weak." He shrunk under his repeated words. Having begun to give voice to her anger, she kept talking. "If you wondered why you married such a worthless woman, I wonder why I married such a weak man. You can't even hold your own liquor."

Peter drew himself up straight, chest puffed with instant outrage. "Gen, you can't mean that."

She recoiled from him, raising her hands in defense and said, "Stay back from me. Don't lay a hand on me."

"Gen, I would never lay a hand on you."

"Really? That lamp missed me by just inches last night. And the last time you drank, your hand marked my face for a week."

"I never meant to hurt you, I swear it. I'll never raise another hand to you again."

"No, I won't let you." Gen knew Peter's wrath endangered more than just her. "And if you ever threaten my daughter, we'll leave so fast you won't know what happened."

"I could never hurt our daughter, never." Disgust filled his face. He sank onto his chair and rubbed his day-old stubble with both hands. Quiet moments passed before he asked, "Gen, how did we get here?"

"We only get here when you drink." She spat the words and let them hang in the air.

"Then I swear to you, I'll never drink again, not so much as a sip. Nothing."

These words made Gen start to soften. He was willing to change, for her. Gen took a step forward.

He rose out of his seat and took a step toward her, arms out.

Gen took his open arms as repentance sought and forgiveness given. She fell into them, ready to put this episode behind them. As she settled into him, her head on his shoulder, the doorbell rang. It was Lucy, bringing Katherine home to be with her mom and dad.

Twenty-Six

Winter melted into spring and blossomed into summer. Sunshine and flowers greeted Gen each warm summer day. Life had fallen into a comfortable pattern. Gen learned to love the routine of her days, both at home and at the shop. Time spent in Lucy's companionable presence were her favorite.

Marriage added a new dimension to their friendship, but because Lucy was her mother-in-law, Gen only shared select struggles and joys of a young marriage. Many days laughter rang through the shop. In quieter moments, Lucy offered soft words of guidance.

The week before her anniversary, Gen sat next to Lucy, as normal, but sensed something different about this afternoon. The air felt more constricted. Lucy kept looking up and staring at Gen, but whenever their eyes met, Lucy dropped hers back to her work.

In the lull of the midafternoon, Lucy broke the strained quiet by saying, "You know, Gen, I'm a bit surprised you haven't turned up pregnant yet." She didn't even look up from her sewing. "Is everything okay between you and Peter?"

Gen's face flooded with embarrassment. Keeping her eyes locked on the blue dress in her lap, she cleared her throat and said, "Things are fine."

Lucy looked up and said, "I thought there'd be another baby on the way by now."

Gen shook her head, "No, not this month, at least."

Lucy covered her mouth. "Oh Gen, I'm so sorry, I thought having more babies would be easy for you, given everything . . ."

Gen's defenses started to rise, "Well, I guess it's not that easy." She fought to control the sudden shaking of her hands. Wanting to say more, she opened her mouth, but no words came out.

Lucy, unaware of Gen's emotions, continued, "I know Peter is eager to have a child of his own."

Gen closed her eyes and inhaled. After releasing her breath, she said, in the calmest voice she had, "Katherine is his child."

"No, I'm not saying that Peter isn't like Katherine's father, he's all but adopted her. It's just that . . . well, I know Peter would like to have his own child with you, one of his own flesh and blood."

Gen couldn't speak. She had no defense to offer without giving herself away, but it was none of Lucy's business. Instead, she focused on the blue silk in her hands, rubbing it between two fingers. The soothing motion calmed her and refocused her on the work at hand, not Lucy's meddling. After a few moments, her jaw unclenched and she could stitch again.

A blush rose on Lucy's face. She sat silent for a moment before reaching over to pat Gen on the knee. She looked Gen in the eyes, her smile wide and encouraging. "Don't worry, honey, these things take time, I guess."

Gen accepted Lucy's truce. "Yes, Lucy, I guess they do."

Later that week, Gen and Peter celebrated their first anniversary with an elegant dinner at the Half Moon Lake Clubhouse, this time walking through doors held open by uniformed doormen. Gen gazed around the lodge room, flooded with memories of the first time she walked into it. This time, the stone fireplace was cold and empty and other diners filled the room with noise. Gen reached over and grabbed Peter's hand. She caught his eyes. He winked.

She held onto the joy from that night, warding away the nightmare that followed. If only she could erase select parts of the past.

Their table overlooked Half Moon Lake. A highly trained staff saw to their every need. Gen was delighted to have chicken cordon bleu while Peter enjoyed a porterhouse steak. A flaming Bananas Foster was placed in front of them. They clapped with delight.

As they ate their dessert, Peter reached across the table and grasped Gen's hand. "Gen," he said, "I love you."

Gen smiled. She never tired of hearing him say that. "I love you too, Peter."

"I love Katherine, too, with all my heart." He took a long drink of coffee.

She nodded and said, "Yes, I know. You're a wonderful father."

"We have a great family of three," he said and took another draw on his coffee. He cleared his throat and said, "I wondered if it was time to make it a family of four. We could have a little boy, it would be perfect."

Without a moment's hesitation, Gen said, "You're right, Peter, that would be perfect."

"So, what do you say? Can we have a baby of our own now?"

Her heart sank despite the smile on her face. She took a large bite of her dessert.

"I mean, even if it takes a little while, at least we'd have fun trying?" He winked and squeezed her hand.

Even in the dim light of the restaurant, Gen blushed. "Yes, of course, we can try."

Peter smiled at his wife, joy radiating from his face. Gen pasted a flat smile onto her face but knew his dreams weren't to be. His hopes, already, were too high. It was too late to tell him now. It was all going to come crashing down to the ruin of them all.

The first six months of trying were fun. Peter and Gen snuck away during Kat's nap time whenever they could. The Youngs even kept Katherine for a few overnight excursions. In the beginning, Gen's monthly cycles were not discouraging.

But when Christmas neared and Gen was still not pregnant, Peter suggested she visit the doctor. Maybe he could figure out what was wrong. An appointment after New Year 1951 brought no answers. The doctor declared her a fit young woman who should have no problem conceiving. He did, however, offer her some pills that could help her feel better, if she took them regularly.

As they neared their second anniversary, Peter begged Gen to have another child, as if his words could influence her body. But his frustration rose with each month. Every time Gen's cycle started, he sunk lower, growing heavy with disappointment.

Their inability to conceive a child affected their marriage. Small conflicts became quarrels. Leaving the toothpaste uncovered became fodder for an argument. Peter took every opportunity to express his displeasure at minor annoyances as if he knew all their problems were Gen's fault. Gen held on to every insult, never fully forgiving him for his harsh words of anger.

The years passed. The family of three lived within the routine of Peter's work, Gen's work, and their home life. After trying to get pregnant for so long, the strain of the conversation was too painful. Although it remained the elephant in the room, Peter stopped speaking of it. Gen felt immense relief when it stopped coming up, though her heart raged with guilt. This was all her fault, not his. She could tell him, but then their marriage would be over. She'd be left with nothing.

But even without mentioning her fault, she knew their marriage was treading on a precipice, one small footstep in the wrong direction would doom it. He may not be the perfect man, but he was who Gen had, to love her and to protect Katherine. She wouldn't go down without a fight.

Twenty-Seven

I n the midst of the turmoil in her marriage, life around Gen continued to go on. She spent her days with Kat, but knew those were numbered. School was starting in the fall and her baby was five already! How did she get so big already?

During the hot summer months, the monotony of her life oppressed her. Every day it was the same thing. She made three square meals a day. She cleaned the house that wasn't even that dirty. She made sure Katherine had all that she needed, but really, that little girl was really good at playing by herself, as if she was born to be an only child. Sometimes, she rearranged the furniture, just for fun. But that was so much work for such little satisfaction. They never had any guests over. All her great hopes about being a couple that hosted cookouts or parties had never come to fruition.

Restless as ever, Gen sat on the couch paging through the latest Vogue magazine during Kat's resting time. She'd been through the pages before and hardly registered what she was seeing anymore. She stopped again on the spread of summer dresses. Their pink and blue colors made her so happy. In her mind's eye she could envision the construction of those pieces. A dart here. A series of pleats there. The one-inch hem at the bottom. How neat she would look in those dresses. Peter would never allow such an extravagant purchase, but it didn't matter. The stores in sleepy Eau Claire didn't have such beautiful dresses.

She'd have to travel to Madison or even Chicago to find a Neiman Marcus or Lord & Taylor.

Her fingers twitched at the thought of running a smooth cotton through the feeder of her sewing machine. She thought back to the spot in the back room that held the machine, boxed up yet still collecting dust. In the business of watching Katherine, she'd neglected that machine. Her work with Lucy was usually just hand hemming or detail work on various projects that Lucy couldn't do with her arthritic hands.

Standing, she walked to the back room. The machine sat on a small wooden table in the back corner. The light green case beckoned her. After removing the lid and her machine, she held her Singer in her hands and looked for a place to put it. Obviously, she was going to need a workspace. Cradling her machine to make sure it didn't fall, she brushed the box to the floor. She needed the space to work, the box didn't matter anymore. She took the next five minutes fidgeting with the bobbin and the pedal. She rolled the wheel to make sure the needle and feed dogs still rose and fell.

If the machine still worked, she could create for herself the stylish clothes she wanted to wear. And Peter would be proud of her resourcefulness. Anything to bring a bright spot to their marriage was a welcome relief from the near constant tension that vibrated between them. Rummaging through her old carpet bag, she found a scrap from a time before she got married. With a second's work, she ran a straight line through it. Folding it over, she made a seam between two pieces and examined her work. She tugged and pulled and inspected. The stitching held. There were no knots or gaps in the thread. It was perfect.

She went back to the carpet bag and dumped it out on the floor. Sitting down on the floor, she sorted through the pile. Papers with sketches of dresses for pregnant bodies. She spread them out in front of her. She stared at them, remembering what it was like to want to be fashionable when she felt she was the size of a house, wondering if she would ever get to feel that way again. Shaking her head to rid herself of such thoughts, she found old pattern papers pinned to fabrics, a tin of straight pins, a few spools of thread, sturdy sewing scissors. It was all here.

Feverishly, Gen went to the kitchen and grabbed a pad of paper and pencil from the counter then walked back to the living room where her issue of Vogue lay open on the sofa. She started making a list of what she knew she needed to make those dresses from the magazine. Her foot bounced as she wrote and only stopped when she started to imagine, again, what possibilities lay in front of her. Her heart pounded as she looked to the clock. Two hours until Peter was home. Plenty of time to visit the fabric store and return in time to make dinner. Kat would love a trip to the store with all the pretty colors.

Gen jumped up with anticipation for the projects at home.

Gen took extra care with dinner that night. Peter was always receptive to her unusual thinking when dinner was pleasing. Kat was freshly cleaned and dressed when Peter walked in the door. Gen came from the kitchen wearing nice clothes, a stained apron and a dab of perfume.

"Mmm, something smells good," Peter said with his usual kiss on Gen's cheek.

"Oh, it's just the chicken in the oven, nothing special." She winked as she walked back to the kitchen to finish the little details.

In five minutes, the three were seated at a perfectly set table before a simple Tuesday night feast of lemon chicken and rice. To

Gen the minutes it took to serve everyone took hours, as she was so anxious to talk with Peter. However, he was an orderly man for whom things needed to happen in a certain way.

After his perfunctory response to his first few bites, "It's delicious, honey," Gen burst out, "Peter, I have something I want to ask you."

She'd prepared for this moment, rehearsing in her head the exact words to say to get Peter to allow her to start making clothes. In her head she'd outlined the cost value, how it would help her stay busy, and it would look good among the neighbors to have such a stylishly adorned wife and child. But when she opened her mouth to speak, all that came out was, "So, I had an idea."

Peter put his fork down and waited. "Yes?"

"Today I was looking at this month's issue of Vogue and I saw these beautiful dresses." She jumped up and grabbed the issue from the counter in the kitchen where she'd been staring at it all through dinner.

"Gen," Peter's voice was exasperated. "You know we don't have money for those kinds of things. You know that."

"Oh, of course I do." She lay her arm across his. "And I know you work very hard for us. I appreciate the work you do, you know that right?" He nodded his ascent. "So I was wondering if I could have a few dollars to start making some clothes for myself."

Shoving the magazine under his nose, Gen continued. "These dresses are $18 at Neiman Marcus. I think I can make it for myself for less than $5." She stopped talking. There was a balance between pushing just enough and pushing too far with Peter.

The noisy silence of chewing filled the room while Peter cleared his mouth. "I think that's a great idea. If you make dresses like that at such a discount, won't you look smart. And that will make all of us look good."

A wide smile broke across Gen's face.

"In fact," Peter continued, why don't you get enough to make a few outfits for yourself. The way I see it, a wardrobe full of handmade quality dresses beats store bought goods anyway. And with the prices the way they are these days, we'll come out ahead."

"Yes, dear." Inwardly, Gen crowed with delight. Finally something that she could do, for herself. She couldn't wait to get started.

Twenty-Eight

Gen got right to work making her new clothes. She decided she could make at least one dress and then a pedal pusher outfit and a sweet little outfit for Kat, all for about ten dollars. She and Kat spent hours at the fabric store perusing the fabric, touching each one, choosing exactly the right fabric for value and looks.

It was a new bright spot in her otherwise monotonous days. As she sat at the park with the other moms watching the little ones play, Gen kept thinking about her next steps and how far she was from completing her project.

"Gen, you seem a little distracted today?" said Carla, a mom with two rambunctious little boys.

Gen brought her attention back to the park, "Oh do I? I'm sorry. I'm just preoccupied with a project I'm working on at home."

"What kind of project? I love projects."

She lifted her chin as she spoke to the gathered group of women. "I saw some dresses in this month's Vogue and I'm working to recreate one for myself." The eyes of the group were on her. "It's simple, really, just a dress with a natural gather at the waist, a high neck, and cap sleeves. I made my own bias tape to finish it. I just can't believe it was $18 at the department store. I'll been able to make it for about $4."

"Sewing has never been my strong suit," said Carla. "And besides, I already have a nice dress."

Gen felt unleashed. "Oh, but a pretty dress for such a bargain is worth it. Sewing is the one thing I'm actually good at as a housewifely duty. Peter loved the idea of being able to get a fashionable piece of clothing for just a portion of the retail price.

"I'd love to see it when you're done," Carla said. The rest of the moms agreed. Gen finally had something to share.

It was only a couple days later when Gen wore her freshly completed dress to the park with Kat. They walked with an extra skip in their step. She'd compared the dress she'd made with the magazine picture and the comparison was flawless. Kat even had her own version in a play dress. Gen had thought long and hard about fabric choices and chose a new cotton blend in light blue that was supposed to wash well. Hopefully she could be a good enough laundress to get out any stain that Kat put on it.

When they arrived at the park, Carla was the first to notice. "Gen, that dress is amazing! Where's it from?"

"Oh this?" Gen put on an air of mock humility, looking down as if examining the skirt for the first time. "This is the dress I was telling you about, the one I made."

Quickly, Gen was surrounded by the moms all oohing and aahing. "You would never know this was handmade." "I could never make anything this neat." "How'd you do it Gen? What pattern did you use?"

She listened to the questions and only responded to one. "Oh, I didn't buy a pattern. I made my own." She kept her head lifted high as they examined, even pushed out her chest a bit. The attention was exactly what she wanted from them.

Leaving the park, Gen was full. It had worked, her ability had made the other women admire her. She never really needed to be liked, but admired was useful.

To her great dismay, Peter didn't seem to notice anything about her, other than her ability to make dinner and care for their home. She just needed him to see her, trying so hard to make herself beautiful for him.

In the minutes before he was due to arrive home, Gen double-checked her appearance in the mirror. Her lipstick was fresh and shiny, not a hair was out of place. For dinner, she added some jewelry, a bracelet and necklace, something she didn't usually fuss with at home during the day.

Hearing the garage door open, Gen walked over to the door and waited to greet her husband. He stomped in and slammed the door behind him. Seeing Gen standing there, he handed her his briefcase and coat and went off muttering.

Gen stayed put. There was no need to get in his way when he was in a mood. Her presence usually made things worse. From her spot, she heard him walk to the bedroom and slam that door too. She put his briefcase by the hall closet.

Five minutes later, he was back, dressed for home life. "Difficult day, dear?"

"It was fine." Peter's curt reply wasn't unusual, but the clipped tone set Gen on edge.

"Would you like to talk about it?" Gen stood in the doorway to the dining room where he had just sat down at the dinner table. "Dinner could wait for a few minutes."

"No, let's eat now. Where's Kat?"

"Outside playing yet. I'll call her in."

It only took a few minutes before the three were seated at the table and dinner had begun. Amid the clattering of dishes and the noise of eating, Kat prattled on about her day, telling her dad all about her adventures at the park and in the backyard. She had quite the imagination for one so little.

The nervous knots in Gen's stomach grew tighter as the evening went on. Peter hadn't really noticed her yet that evening.

For some reason, Gen wasn't sure she wanted to call attention to herself at that moment. His creased brow wasn't relaxing.

At a break in Katherine's conversation, she tried again. "Peter, how was work today?"

"It was fine." He set down his fork and looked over at Gen. "How was your day?" A smile broke across his face as he looked at her. "You look lovely tonight."

Gen blushed her approval. He'd noticed. "Fine," she replied. He noticed. That was enough.

Twenty-Nine

A s that summer wore on, Gen worked hard to build a thin veneer of happiness in her home. She pretended she was fulfilled as a mom and housewife. After Kat started kindergarten, even though it was for only half the day, Gen found more freedom to do the things she pleased. While she maintained the image of the perfect family with a well-kept home, Gen was able to devote more time to her own personal pursuits which she kept from Peter. He worked respectable and predictable hours at the office, giving Gen the freedom and luxury to do as she pleased.

Kat's first year of school passed in a flash and before Gen blinked again, she had started first grade. After that first school bell rang in September, Gen truly found her freedom. She had the whole day to herself. Peter was at work, Kat was at school until three. With those hours without any accountability, Gen found her rhythm. After saying goodbye to Kat, who walked to school with neighborhood friends, Gen did the morning chores: the laundry, the floors, any morning dishes. Once the house was tidy, she did as she pleased, some days were errand days, but some days she spent hours in her sewing room designing and sewing. Other days, she got dressed up and went out.

On a late morning on a Tuesday in the fall of 1953, Gen had finished her morning chores. Kat wasn't due home until after three. Inhaling the scent of her tea, Gen smiled. No one expected anything of her that afternoon. Complete freedom was hers.

After sitting for a few minutes, she made up her mind. She'd take herself out to lunch at the counter at the department store. It'd be a splurge, but a deserved one.

After clearing her teacup, she went to the bathroom for a final check on her reflection. Married though she be, the thought of turning a handsome man's head made her smile. She applied her dark red lipstick with a practiced hand, her teeth glowing white against the color. As she puckered her lips, she imagined the gossiping biddies' jealous whispers. She hadn't had a positive interaction with the school moms in ages. Ever since Katherine entered kindergarten, it was clear Gen wasn't good enough for them. Those women did the math, they knew Kat wasn't Pete's child and once they learned she wasn't a war widow, their only goal seemed to be learning more about Gen's sordid past.

She'd just finished applying a coat of hair spray to her hair when a car pulled up into the driveway. Curious, Gen thought back across her day. She wasn't expecting any visitors.

Peeking through the front curtain, she saw the back bumper of Peter's car. She dropped her purse and coat next to the front door and straightened her dress, readying herself to greet her husband. Soon she heard the opening of the garage door and a voice from the entryway. "Surprise!"

She turned toward him with a forced bright smile, "Honey! What an unexpected surprise!"

Peter grinned, a wolfish look on his face, "I just finished a morning meeting at the other office, so I thought I'd swing over to have lunch with my favorite lady." He set down his briefcase and walked toward Gen with arms extended. He swung her up in a big hug and kissed her without reserve. She returned his affection without passion.

Peter kept kissing his wife, sweeping her off her feet and taking her into their bedroom. Gen wasn't thrilled at the idea of a midafternoon rendezvous, but acquiesced. Better to play along than to fight Peter's desire. When it was over, he looked over to Gen and asked, "So, what's for lunch?"

Incredulity passed over her face. "Excuse me?" she asked, as she got dressed.

He looked at her with wide eyes. "What do you mean?"

Gen tried to control her rising temper. "How do you know I didn't have any plans for my afternoon?"

"Oh no, did you have somewhere you needed to be?" His voice was contrite. "I don't want to ruin your plans."

She shook her head, "No, not really, but . . ."

Peter's face relaxed. "So then, what's for lunch?"

Gen clenched her fists, trying to remain calm. "I don't know. I didn't have plans for you for lunch," she said through gritted teeth. "Let me see what's in the kitchen, it won't be fancy," she promised. She kept her voice light and sweet, in spite of her growing frustration.

"Don't worry, I don't need much," he smiled. He straightened his tie in front of the mirror. On her way to the kitchen, she spoke under her breath, "The nerve of that man, come home and break up my day and then ask me to fix his lunch." She slammed the cupboard door. "Least he could do is take me out to lunch." When Peter came into the kitchen, Gen stood at the cutting board wielding a butcher's knife chopping up carrot sticks with extra fury. Plates and utensils were scattered across the counter. She wore her rage as an apron.

He walked up behind her and set his chin on her shoulder. She felt him flinch at the violence of her chopping. "Gen, are you okay?" he asked.

She blew steam out of her nostrils and her eyebrows flared. "No, I am not okay."

"What's wrong? Is there anything I can help with?"

"No, just go wait at the table."

After removing his arms from her waist, Peter backed away. "Okay, I'll wait over here."

After a couple tense minutes, she slapped a plate with a sandwich and carrot strips in front of him. "Here," she said. "Enjoy." She hovered next to him holding a fresh cup of tea.

"Aren't you going to eat?" he asked. "I came home to enjoy lunch with you, not to have you watch me," he said. His voice was soft. She could hear a quiet pleading in it.

The puppy dog look in his eyes made her cringe. He didn't get to ruin her day and fix it with a few kind words. "No, I've lost my appetite." She said and continued to stand right behind his shoulder.

He took a bite of his sandwich and chewed it without thought. His face contorted. He spit out his food and wiped his mouth with his napkin. "What did you put in this sandwich?"

"Sardines and mayonnaise," she said with mock sweetness. "Like it?"

"That's it." Peter slammed his hand on the table. "What is it? What have I done this time?"

Gen steeled herself for their confrontation. Could he even understand how his choice affected her? "You really want to know?"

"Yes, yes I do. It can't be worse than this simmering anger."

She leaned into his face and crossed her arms in front of her chest. Her voice held an evil undertone. She didn't even care if he understood her words, he'd get her meaning. "I wanted to take myself out for lunch, but now I can't, because of you."

Peter's eyes nearly popped out of his head. "Are you kidding me? You're angry because I surprised you by coming home?" He continued muttering under his breath.

"What? I'm sorry I didn't hear you. Would you like to say that again?"

Peter stiffened. He set his jaw and glared at his wife. "Fine, I wondered if you were about to have your 'time' again, if that's why you're acting this way."

Gen hit the roof. She focused her eyes on her husband and snarled. Leaning into his space, she spoke with a low voice. "Of course, you would blame me for this." Her anger was growing larger than the fight. She had a weapon to use and she was determined to be triumphant. "Haven't you figured it out yet? I will only ever cycle, never be pregnant. Time you got used to the idea."

Peter's features softened and he reached a hand out to touch her arm. His voice was quieter when he said, "Gen, I'm sorry. I didn't mean that."

Gen flinched at his touch. But she'd finally said it, the relief of the truth flowed over her like a waterfall, but she hadn't hurt him with it yet. Her anger had taken control of her senses. She wasn't stopping now. She shook his hand off and waved her hands at him, "Aren't you listening, Peter? I will never be pregnant again."

"I don't understand, Gen. What are you talking about?"

"Why haven't you figured it out yet?" She saw the blank look on Peter's face. Her words crashed out. "The problem isn't you, it's me. You got me pregnant once already, before we were married. But after I got rid of the baby, I got an infection. I'm never going to get pregnant again."

Peter shook his head, disbelieving the words he was hearing. "What? You were pregnant by me?"

"Yes, I was. And I wasn't going to let a pregnancy ruin the relationship that we had, so I got rid of it. I ended up in the hospital, surely you remember?"

"Of course, I remember." Peter studied his hands for a moment before he looked up again. His face was changed, full of sadness. His voice matched; his words were whisper quiet. "I almost lost you, I couldn't have borne the pain if you had died."

His sadness enraged her, venom spilling from her mouth. "Well, aren't you a helpless romantic? Too bad it's not like that anymore." She turned away, taking his plate to the kitchen.

"You loved our story, Gen. What's happened to you? To us?"

His words stopped her in her tracks. Tears sprung into her eyes, the sadness of years of the greatest secret fell off her. When she turned to speak, her anger had faded, replaced by grief. "Peter, it's time to face facts, we're not going to have any more kids."

Peter sat dumbfounded as he stared at his wife. His brow creased as he sought to hold back tears. His mouth hung open, slack-jawed. When he spoke, his voice was hardly more than a whisper. "Why didn't you tell me this before? That was years ago. Why has it taken you so long to tell me the truth?"

Gen was silent. She turned her head back and finished walking to the kitchen. After dropping the entire plate into the trash, she leaned over the kitchen sink, staring at the shiny porcelain. Her eyes darted across the tiny gray cracks visible in the finish. She traced one with her hand. Even with cracks her sink still worked, maybe marriage worked that way too. But she had no good answer for Peter. She couldn't admit her deepest fear, not even to her husband. She didn't want to be alone with her shame.

"Is there anything else you haven't told me?" he asked. Bitterness seeped into his voice. Gen could hear it growing.

She slammed down her hand on the edge of the counter. "What do you mean? Don't you trust me?"

Peter vented his rage. "Trust you? I did trust you, until about two minutes ago when I discovered that you've been keeping secrets from me. Tell me, Gen, if you'd just learned what I did, would you?" He pushed himself away from the table. "I'm going back to work." Picking up his coat and briefcase, he rushed out the door.

Peter's car squealed out of the driveway. The sound of the slamming door lingered in the empty house. She stood staring at the door. She sat down on the couch in a daze, replaying the conversation. It was all Peter's fault, wasn't it?

She gave him an hour to be angry, then she called him at work. His secretary said he was still at lunch. An hour later, he was in a meeting and couldn't be disturbed. A few minutes before Kat was due home from school, the secretary told Gen that Peter wasn't taking any phone calls. With each denied phone call, panic grew in Gen's belly. Within a few minutes, however, Kat was home from school full of the tales of her day, and Gen attended to her daughter's needs. But Gen listened to Kat's stories with half an ear. Every five minutes, she checked the kitchen clock to see how long it would be until Peter came home.

Katherine went off to play with the neighbors, leaving Gen staring at the clock and brooding. She fixed a lackluster dinner of beans and franks, but still set three plates at the table, expecting Peter to arrive at any minute.

She spent a few extra minutes in front of her wardrobe, choosing the perfect dress to wear for Peter's homecoming. Surely, a beautiful dress would smooth over any hard feelings, especially if she was extra loving.

The hands of the clock passed five and Peter did not return. Gen convinced herself that he was just running a few minutes late. Smoothing her hand down her hair, she repeated to herself, "He'll be home soon. He always comes home for dinner."

Usually he called to let her know if he was going to be late. Maybe he went out with the guys after work and he forgot to call.

Gen fought back her fear as she went about the nightly routine. After the evening turned dark and Katherine had been tucked into bed, her fear grew into terror at what had happened to Peter and her marriage that day.

Peter would come home . . . he always came home.

But Peter did not come home that night.

Thirty

When Peter finally returned home the next night, Gen ran to meet him at the door, her heart overflowing with relief. Holding the door open for him, he didn't even make eye contact and just handed her his briefcase. When he did look at Gen, his glare was icy,

She stood in front of the swinging door, alone, as he ran and scooped Katherine into his arms. "Hey, Kitty Kat."

"Daddy," she said as he swung her around in circles. "I missed you. Where were you last night?"

His eyes crinkled with a smile when he looked down at the little girl. "I'm sorry I didn't come home last night. I stayed at Grandpa and Grandma's last night."

"No fair!" She gave him another hug. "Next time, you have to take me."

They laughed together. She took his hand and guided him to the table where dinner was sitting, hot and ready. During dinner, Katherine told stories from her past two days with great joy. Peter focused all his attention on his daughter, speaking to Gen only when necessary.

As they ate dinner at the table, Gen kept glancing over at her husband, looking for a sign. She wanted to run into his arms and hear him reassure her. She wanted to know that her fears of rejection had always been baseless.

Her relief at having Peter home made her simple pot roast dinner seem as grand as a king's feast. Despite her joy, her food sat like a lead weight in the pit of her stomach. Watching him as he ate, the tension in his brow shouted at her. Although his laughter was boisterous, his movements were stiff and methodical. All his attention was purposefully turned to Katherine.

Together, Gen and Peter tucked their daughter into bed just like they'd done since she was young. The routine was soothing to Gen. Gen helped her get ready for bed. Peter read to her for a few minutes. When it was time to say good night, they both stood at her bedside for final kisses. Gen wanted to stay in this perfect moment. Dreading the moments yet to come. Eventually, Peter walked out of the room. Gen followed and shut the door behind her.

Gen went to the kitchen and started fixing two cups of coffee. The water was percolating on the stove when Peter walked in. "Gen, we need to talk."

She gulped and nodded. "I know," was all she could say. She couldn't control the shaking in her hands as she poured the coffee. Gen would do anything to earn Peter's forgiveness and was determined to fight for her marriage. Her nerves were shot.

Five minutes later, they settled on opposing chairs in the living room, each cradling a steaming mug. Peter lost himself in the black depths of the hot liquid before setting the cup down on the table next to him. Gen sat waiting, too nervous to taste her coffee. She watched him, looking for any sign. He was unreadable.

He blew out a breath. "I hardly slept last night," he started. "My parents were surprised when I showed up, but they didn't say anything and just let me go to bed."

She leaned toward him, hands wrapped around the coffee.

"I'm so angry at you and I think I'm justified in it. How could you keep a secret like that? From me? I don't understand."

She nodded, knowing she would have to bear full responsibility. None of it was going to be his fault.

"When I stood before you and the priest and our families I made some promises. I'm going to stand by them, however much it hurts."

Gen flew off her chair and into Peter's lap in profound relief. As she wrapped her arms around his neck, he pushed her off, saying, "Wait, I'm not done yet."

She stood up, but had heard enough. The words bounced around, making her feel light as a balloon. Hope was here. A wide smile, the first in two days, fixed itself onto her face.

The look on Peter's face remained stern and serious. "This is unlike anything I've ever imagined and I am wounded, more than the war, more than any fight we've ever had." Rubbing his stumped arm, he closed his eyes. "Not all wounds can heal fully."

Gen fell to her knees, "Peter, I'm sorry. I'll do anything . . ."

"Gen, you've done enough."

She held her breath. He reached down and pulled her up from her knees. Looking straight into her eyes, he said, "Gen, I promised to love you and Katherine and I'm going to do that, because I do. But I don't know if I can forgive you for what you've done."

"What can I do to make it up to you? I'll do anything, I swear it, Peter. Anything."

He shook his head. "There's nothing you can do." He sighed. The sound of his breath weighed on her like a ton of bricks. She could barely draw a breath. "Gen, I just need time, I need to adjust my vision of our future. I always pictured"—his strong voice cracked. Pushing tears away from his eyes, he said, "I always imagined I'd have a house full of kids. And now"—his voice broke again, letting the tears flow. Peter's grief and sadness mingled.

Gen sat on the couch next to his chair. She put her hand on his knee, afraid to offer more or be outrightly rejected. As his tears diminished, he grasped her hand and turned to look her. "You broke my heart, Gen." With that he dropped her hand, stood, and walked into his office, closing the door.

In the remaining silence, Gen watched the door for two hours, waiting for Peter to emerge. Her joy at his return was dampened with this fracture in their marriage. She was unprepared for another night alone in their bed or for playacting for their daughter. She didn't want to have a marriage like her parents. Gen refused to accept that things could never return to the way they were. Peter was her husband, and she was determined to return to their previous bliss.

But rebuilding took time. For days, Gen tiptoed around Peter, finding ways to compliment or touch him, not pushing him. She fixed his favorite foods and wore his favorite clothes. The conversation was always neutral, simply reports of Kat's day. She held her tongue and her growing list of grievances. She worked hard to earn his forgiveness. She couldn't give him the family he wanted, but maybe she could make his family perfect.

After weeks of patient waiting, Peter pulled her aside. Holding her by the waist, he kissed her on the forehead. "Thank you," he said. "Thank you for your effort and love and patience." He released her and went on his way.

The next night at dinner, he reached across the table to hold Gen's hand as Katherine's chattered. Peter winked. Gen's heart soared.

Within another week, their marriage fully mended. When Peter welcomed Gen back into his arms in bed, she breathed an audible sigh of relief.

The new normal came with one new condition. Every Friday night after dinner, Peter went to the bar with some friends.

"Don't worry Gen, it's just me and a few guys sitting around talking."

"Yeah, but at a bar?" she said. "Are you sure that's a wise idea?" Inside the panic started to build. Alcohol made him crazy. Her hand automatically cradled her cheek. Even her body couldn't forget.

"Come on, Gen. It's been years since anything happened. Trust me?"

Gen took a deep wifely breath to cover her nerves with indecision. Putting her hands on her hips and keeping her voice light, she said, "What if you drink too much and then try to drive home? What if you get in an accident and die?"

Peter kissed her on the cheek. "My little worrier. Nothing will happen. Besides, how are we going to know if I can handle it if I never get a chance to try?"

Gen wasn't sure, but somehow, she knew his logic was faulty. However, she couldn't forbid him. He was a grown man, able to make his own decisions. And even if she said no, he'd still go anyway. For all she had taken from him, she could give him this one thing.

"Okay," she said. "But promise you won't do anything foolish."

He kissed her again, this time with more passion. "I promise, besides, I have you to come home to." He winked, then grabbed his coat and headed out the door.

When the door clicked shut behind him, she said to the empty room, "I know, that's what I'm worried about."

A few hours later, Peter came home from the bar, smelling of cigarette smoke and beer. She was just getting ready for bed. His greeting was kind and warm, not threatening as she feared. Because her worries did not materialize, she gave him permission to continue meeting with the guys.

So he did, every Friday night. At first he came home early in the evening and Gen would wait up for him to come home. She enjoyed the homecoming. But soon his nights stretched into the wee hours. When that happened, she couldn't stay up that late. She still had to wake up in the morning with Katherine.

Gen monitored his behavior like a paranoid parent. Every time he came home, he was her Peter, never violent, never cross. Perhaps he was a bit more amorous than usual, but Gen rather enjoyed those homecomings.

Eventually Gen began to relax about Peter and alcohol. He was proving himself one Friday at a time. One Tuesday evening after dinner, she surprised him, not with his usual cup of coffee, but with an old-fashioned on the rocks. Peter looked first at the drink in his hand, then took a long sip.

"Not bad," he said after his first mouthful, "for your first try." He lifted his glass to her. "Why don't you keep trying and I'll let you know when you've got it right." He winked.

She smiled and went back to cleaning the kitchen for the night. As she turned out the light to the kitchen, Peter grabbed her from behind and pulled her into an aggressive hug. She fought him off, hitting his arms to loosen his grip. Looking into his face, she expected to find a look of evil intent. Instead she saw a goofy, lopsided grin.

So began a new nightly ritual at the Young household. After dinner, Gen would present her husband with a drink, sometimes familiar, sometimes out of the ordinary. He would taste each one and give her feedback. Together they spent the nights laughing and sampling first the drink, then each other, enjoying the fun that alcohol brought to their marriage.

Thirty-One

Evenings were dark early in the winter in Wisconsin. Gen and Peter kept their home cozy with a fire in the fireplace and a warm fire in the bellies. As had become their habit, Gen served drinks at dinner, a Tom Collins to go with the pot roast and potatoes. After dinner, they enjoyed a second drink while dancing around the living room with Kat. After finishing her second drink, Gen was done. Two was her limit, especially when Katherine was around.

Gen excused herself to get Kat ready for bed. When Gen returned, her husband sat on the couch listening to boxing on the radio. His eyes were closed and his head leaned back. In his hand he gripped a glass, empty except for two melting pieces of ice. On the side table next to him sat a nearly empty bottle of brandy.

She studied the scene for a moment. The bottle had been full just last night. Gen didn't believe that Peter could have drunk that much already. She reached across him to take the empty glass from his hand when his eyes snapped open and he pulled his hand back. Gen jumped back. "Peter, you startled me."

"Don't take my glass," he snarled.

Gen moved her hand back as if she were walking away from a threatening animal. She'd taken a step backward when Peter shot off of the couch and into her face.

"Ahhh!" she screamed. "Peter, are you all right?"

He snarled again, his voice surly. "I'm fine. Get out of my way. My glass is empty."

Gen reached for his cup. "No," she stood against him. "You've had too much to drink tonight. That bottle was full," she said, pointing to the brandy.

"Step aside, woman." He strong-armed her out of the way. The strength from his push threw Gen across the room and into the wall. Her shoulder collided with the wall, followed by her head. With a loud thud, she fell to the floor.

When she opened her eyes, she couldn't see Peter, but heard the cupboards in the kitchen open, the sound of liquid pouring, and the sound of a bottle slamming down on the table. Then silence broken by a contented sigh.

Gen stood up and straightened herself. When Peter walked back into the room, she was prepared for the coming confrontation. She stood tall with her head held high and her fists clenched at her sides, ready for a fight. Peter looked at her and laughed. "You're pathetic," he said. "You think you could fight me, even for one minute?"

Gen pulled her head up higher, puffed her chest out. She wasn't afraid.

Peter sneered at her and said, "I'm not going to beat you, woman. You're not even worth my time. Besides," he added nodding toward the radio, "the fight is back on, that's the only one worth caring about." He brushed by her on his way back to the couch but she stood her ground, not allowing him to budge her one inch. He flopped onto the couch and took a long sip of his drink. Closing his eyes, he laid his head back.

Gen kept her head high, but she went straight into the bathroom, locked the door, and sat down on the toilet to cry. When she was finished, she washed her face with cold water and went to bed.

She kept the door closed but unlocked. She lay in her bed, curled into herself, but not really sleeping. Her eyes were shut tight when Peter opened the door. He moved clumsily around the room, knocking his shin into the bed frame and bumping his shoulder into the dresser. She tensed her body, ready for an attack. But instead, he loosened his belt, dropped his pants and shirt on the floor, and collapsed onto the bed. Gen hadn't even counted to fifty before she heard the soft snores of his sleep.

In the months that followed, Peter's uncontrolled drinking at home grew more frequent. Although Gen tried, she couldn't protect Kat from her father's poor example.

On the first warm evening of spring, the family ate dinner on the back deck. Peter swirled his tumbler with gold liquid, his third drink of the night.

The conversation focused on Katherine and her day, as it usually did at the dinner table. "And then, Marge's dad said in front of the whole class that he loved her. She was so embarrassed."

Gen leaned over and patted Kat's hand. "Well, I'm sure he didn't mean to embarrass her."

Peter lowered his glass and looked at the girl, "And what's wrong with a father declaring his love for his child." He took a long sip and then said, "Even though I wasn't there when you were born, I've still loved you."

Kat turned to him and asked, "What do you mean, Daddy?"

"I didn't even know your mother back then." Peter laughed and said, "But I've always loved you as if you were my real daughter."

Horror raced through Gen. They never spoke of Gen's past or Katherine's parentage. Such conversations were not healthy for young ears. "Peter," she cried.

Kat was almost seven and the words didn't slip past her ears. Gen yanked Kat away from the table, leading her toward the door.

"What?" he asked, "Don't you think she should know the truth about us?" he called as they walked away. Gen and Kat headed around the house to the porch swing. They'd spent plenty of afternoons on this swing, chatting about the day. But tonight there was no chatter. Gen waved a tense hello to neighbors taking after-dinner strolls. She sat straight and alert, aware of Kat's movements without looking at her. Kat fidgeted with her hair. While she examined a particular strand, she asked Gen, "Mom, what did Dad mean when he said he wasn't there when I was born?"

Gen's shoulders sank. She didn't want to have this conversation, but it'd been forced upon her. Damn him for putting her in this position. "Oh, Kat, honey, he is your father because he's married to me and he loves you very much, but when you were born, I didn't know him."

"Why not?"

"He hadn't come into my life yet."

"So who's my dad?"

Gen gulped and said, "A man named Bobby. I loved him with my whole heart and thought we'd be together forever. But when I became pregnant, with you, everything changed."

"How?"

"Oh, my Kitty Kat, so full of questions." Gen studied her for a moment. In the past months, Katherine's face had grown up. Her childhood was flying by, too fast. Gen didn't want to steal the rest of it with the truth. "Bobby wasn't ready to be a daddy."

Kat looked at her mother, "And you? Were you ready to be a mom?"

"No." Gen laughed bitterly. "No one else thought I should be a mom either, but I fought hard to make sure no one would take you away from me. You've always been my little girl." She wrapped her arm around her daughter. "Kat, I've always wanted to be your mama. I could never imagine my life without you."

Kat nodded. "Me either, Mom."

Gen rubbed her daughter's cheek. "Thanks, sweetie. Peter loves you very much too, but when he drinks, he . . ."

Kat rubbed her mom's hand. "I know, Mama. I've heard him yelling at you some nights."

Gen's eyes opened wide. "You have?" Kat nodded, wide-eyed. Gen pulled her daughter close. How could she have been such a fool? She hadn't protected her from anything.

The two of them sat on the swing, watching some neighbor boys pass by on their bikes.

"Mama?"

"Yes?"

"Does Daddy ever hurt you? He sounds pretty angry sometimes."

Rubbing her hand over her jaw, Gen winced at the memory of that first night. "No, honey. Sometimes he throws things, but he doesn't hit me." Gen turned to look at her daughter and said, "Don't worry. I don't think Daddy would hurt you."

Kat leaned in toward her mom and rested her head on Gen's shoulder. "Okay, Mama." The two sat in silence, swinging gently, until it was time for Kat to go to bed.

As she tucked her daughter into bed, Gen added one last thing. "Kat, you can ask me anything at any time, okay?"

"Yes, Mom," the girl said. "I love you and Daddy, a whole ton."

Tears brimmed in Gen's eyes as she bent over to kiss her little girl good night. "Me too, sweetie, a whole ton."

Gen was haunted by their porch conversation. It was only a few years ago when protecting and providing for Kat was Gen's most important task. She had fallen into a daze lulled by the ease of playing housewife, and Kat had been paying the price.

She needed to get out.

It wasn't time to leave yet. Gen didn't have any money or a plan. She wouldn't be able to provide Kat with the life she deserved.

This time, there was no one to talk to. No Mrs. Skloot to run to for advice. She didn't have any friends to whom she could entrust her story. She could tell her parents, she would have to, but only when the time to leave came.

How could she earn some money in a way that Peter wouldn't question? She paced the house with her dust rag in hand, absent-mindedly swiping it over lamps, tables and picture tops. From the living room to the dining room, back to her sewing room, Gen just moved. She wasn't paying attention to what she was doing. Her brain was spinning, swirling to find some answers.

After dusting her beloved sewing machine, she stopped in the middle of the room. It had been a few years, but she could start sewing again. Now that Kat was older, she had more time available. She could make dresses again. This time, for others.

Prices had changed, but not that much. Style had changed in the past few years. Whereas a few years ago, skirts were full, now skirts were straighter and more form fitting. Grabbing a scratch of paper and her recent vogue, she started sketching. She could make a dress that was an exact fit for the body that wore it. That was an option a dress from a department store didn't have.

Hope started to bud within her. There was a lot to do to make this all work, but she knew she could do it. A few dollars would be enough to start. Going to the other room, she grabbed her purse where the grocery money was in her wallet. Over the next few weeks she could siphon a few dollars each week from the grocery money and Peter would never know. After about a month, she could start working to find her first customer. It would take some time, but she would find a way to escape.

She would find a way to get her and Kat to safety.

Thirty-Two

Gen ran around the house breathless. Throwing the coverlet up off the edge of her bed, she pulled out two hard-sided suitcases. From under Kat's bed she grabbed a small red one. The next minutes were a flurry of frantic activity as she pulled essentials out of dresser drawers. She jammed shirts, skirts, underwear, socks, stockings, shoes, hats, and whatever else she could think of into the cases. She emptied Katherine's dresser and much of her closet. She threw treasured stuffed animals and books into grocery bags. Running through the bathroom, she dropped into the toiletry case anything that was theirs: shampoo, soap, brushes, curlers, hairspray, makeup, the hair dryer. She rummaged underneath the beds, pulling out her old hatbox. Opening it up, she found her old letters and the journal from Mrs. Skloot. She closed the box back up and added it to the stack.

After running through her and Kat's rooms, the stack of suitcases piled next to the door was growing. She glanced at the clock.

Only two thirty. Peter left just over an hour ago.

She rubbed the tender spots on her cheek. Without pausing to look in a mirror, she knew the area was puffy and discolored, shades of bright red dulling into purples and pinks.

Katherine gets off the bus at three twenty. I have an hour left.

She resumed her packing at a breakneck pace. She ran from room to room, gathering things important to her or Katherine.

Her hatbox with photos in it. The Afghan that was a gift from Lucy and Herman during happier times. Kat's piggy bank.

She found herself in the kitchen. "Cookies," she said aloud. "I should make Kat some cookies."

With the speed of a practiced housewife, Gen whipped up a batch of chocolate chip cookies. When she slipped the dough into the oven, she glanced again at the clock.

Three o'clock. Enough time to get it all in the car. She'd been planning this for so long. She'd sewn and sold dozens of dresses. She'd squirreled away every extra grocery penny, occasionally even managed to sneak an extra dollar or two. It had taken almost two years, but she was ready.

She wiped her hands on her worn apron. Untying it, she threw it on the counter, a disgusting symbol of the life she was leaving.

She hurried to load all the luggage and gathered things into the trunk and back seat of her powder blue car. Peter bought that car for her last year as an apology for a different beating, back when he was still sorry. He beamed when he brought it home, thinking it would be enough to heal her wounds. It was an uncommon decadence to have two cars. Gen hated how it made them stand out, but loved that it now afforded her this route to freedom.

She slammed down the overstuffed trunk, laying across it with her body to shut it. She stood back, surveyed the scene, and nodded. Nothing looked out of the ordinary. Later, when they drove down the street and waved to the neighbors no one would suspect.

She heard the faint ding of the kitchen timer and ran inside to pull the cookies from the oven. She washed the dishes automatically, not consciously thinking about any part of the process. As she did, her mind wandered. She played back the lunch hour in her mind. She saw, as if watching from the corner, the two of them sitting at the table sipping soup in silence.

Gen kept her head low so as not to attract his attention. Peter sat at his chair, crisply ironed napkin tucked into the collar of his buttoned shirt. He slurped his soup, allowing tiny dribbles to drip down his chin onto the napkin. Keeping her head low, yet raising her eyes, Gen sneered. Disgusting.

"What did you say?" Peter looked up, his forehead marked with fierce lines. His eyes narrowed into menacing slits behind his glasses.

"Nothing," Gen said.

Peter glowered at her, but returned to his soup. Pushing back his empty bowl, he grabbed a roll and tore into it. Crumbs littered the table and the floor.

"Could you please keep the crumbs on the table?"

Peter stared at her. With deliberate precision, he brushed the crumbs into a neat little pile in front of him. "That work for you?" he asked.

Gen smiled. "Yes, thank you," she answered.

He sneered again.

"Something bothering you?" Gen asked, her head tilted to the side.

"You know what's bothering me." His voice was tight and tense. He looked like a tightly wound spring, ready to explode.

"Really?" Gen didn't try to hide her exasperation. But she'd stopped caring about what Peter thought. His opinions weren't worth two cents to her anymore. "Are you still hot under the collar about our fight last night? I thought that we'd come to a resolution."

"That's what you thought. I don't think it's okay for you to dress like that. You're my wife."

Gen's eyes flared. "You're just jealous that I look damn good and other men can't stop staring."

Peter raised his hand and shook his finger in her face. Gen flinched. "You're right! Other men shouldn't look at you! You're mine, do you understand?"

"Really? If I'm so yours," she said with a sneer, "then why don't you want anything to do with me? Or Katherine, for that matter? Don't think she hasn't noticed how you've been treating her."

"How?" Peter's eyes opened wide. "I haven't done anything to her."

She narrowed her eyes at him, "You barely speak to her, other than saying the things that you must." Katherine was still an area of their life that Peter cared about. Gen wasn't afraid to use that as a barb to dig into his heart. "She still thinks of you as her father, maybe you should act like one."

Gen was not prepared for the strike of Peter's hand across her cheek. She shrank back, knowing she'd pushed as far as she dared. Even without a drink, Peter wasn't afraid to hit her anymore.

Gen grabbed her empty soup bowl and retreated to the kitchen, allowing Peter a few minutes to cool down. From the safety of the kitchen, she called out, working hard to mask the tears from her voice, "Peter, it's almost one o'clock, you don't want to be late back to work." Although he could drive back to the office in only a few minutes, he never liked being late after lunch.

She stood from the table, lunch dishes in her hand, and walked into the kitchen.

The thought occurred to her: she should leave.

She'd had that thought a thousand times before, but this time, things were different. Things between her and Peter were only getting worse, and she refused to let a man who didn't love her hold command over her life. She was a grown woman who shouldn't have to put up with this. She could take Katherine and run away and not look back. Gen knew she could take care of both of them, she'd done it before.

From her spot at the kitchen sink, she asked in her most neutral voice, "When do you think you'll be home tonight?"

Peter stood from the table and gathered his coat, hat, and briefcase. "I have an after-work meeting tonight with a client, so probably late, after Katherine's bedtime." He put his hat on his head and made for the door. With one hand opening the door, he turned back to Gen, "Make sure to give her a kiss goodnight for me." Then, he walked out, slamming the door. Gen stood in place until she heard his car back out of the driveway.

She let out the breath she had been holding.

Today. She was leaving today.

The sound of the bus brakes snapped Gen back to the present. The happy sounds of kids fluttered in through the open window. Kat's voice mingled with the other boys and girls. Joy bubbled in her words. For a moment, Gen doubted the wisdom of her plan. There was no way to keep Katherine from harm forever. She shook her head. It was simply a matter of time before Peter would strike out at Katherine, Gen was sure of it. A man who couldn't control his liquor soon couldn't control the venting of his rage. She was not willing to risk Katherine coming to any physical harm. Besides, Katherine was young and resilient, she'd make a new life for herself wherever they ended up.

Gen blew out a deep breath. She knew that once she loaded Kat in the car and they started driving, there was no turning back.

The front door opened and closed with Kat's arrival. "Hey, Mom! I'm home," she said. Gen poked her head out of the kitchen to greet her daughter holding the plate of cookies as a beacon.

"Oh yum, chocolate chip cookies, my favorite," Kat said. Dropping her satchel on the floor, she grabbed a cookie and started telling the stories of the day. "Oh Mom, you'll never guess what happened to Betty during gym class today. I would have died, it was so embarrassing . . ." Gen's eyes stayed focused on her daughter, but her mind wandered to the preparations she had made. Food, clothes, toiletries, favorite things.

The sounds of Katherine's sweet laughter broke into her thoughts. "She fell off the top of the monkey bars?" Gen said and pursed her lips. "I hope she didn't hurt herself."

"Of course she didn't hurt herself, Mom," Kat said as she reached for another cookie. "Did you just get back from somewhere?" she asked nodding toward the living room. "You didn't put your stuff away."

Gen's coat and purse were laying on the arm of the couch. "Oh that," she said. She forced laughter into her words to cover the tremor in her voice. "We're going out after you finish your snack."

"Really? Where are we going?"

Gen looked into her daughter's face and smiled, "I thought that we could take a trip to go visit Grandma and Grandpa Ryder."

Kat started jumping up and down. "Really? I love going to the farm."

"I know, and it's been a while since we visited them."

"Is Dad coming too?"

Gen brushed Kat's straight black hair behind her shoulder. "Not this time, Sweetie, he has to stay late at work. We'll be at Grandpa's for a few days."

Concern crossed Kat's face. "But what about school?"

Gen waved her hand in dismissal, "Don't worry about that. I've already talked with your teacher. Everything's all set. You'll get any work you miss after we're back."

"Okay," Kat said, but looked thoughtful for a moment. "Is everything okay? I mean, are they okay? They aren't sick or anything?"

"Oh no," Gen said to reassure her. "They're fine, your grandparents are healthier than some of my friends." Gen laughed, "Now Kat, I've already packed most of the things we'll need for our trip, but feel free to grab whatever else you think you might need. Anything special."

Kat nodded. "Sure, Mom." She walked to her room to see what else she might need. Gen watched her go. Do I need anything else? She ran from room to room, peering her head in to make sure she hadn't forgotten anything. In a few minutes, there would be no turning back.

Kat came out of her room, a puzzled look on her face, "Mom, all of my clothes are gone. And all my favorite books."

Gen blew a sigh of relief, "Good, so I didn't miss anything?"

Kat looked at her mother. She spoke with cautious words. "No, I guess not. How long are we going for anyway?"

"I told you, we're going to Grandpa Ryder's farm just for a few nights."

"All right," Kat said, "but then we're coming home, right?"

Gen nodded and finished her final sweep of the house.

Kat followed her mom around. "Mom, why is all my stuff packed up?"

Gen remained tight-lipped as she poked her head into Peter's office where he often spent the night. The whole room had a dark, closed-off feeling. She closed the door behind her. No reason to go back to that dark place ever again.

She ran back to her sewing room, to grab her sewing basket and carpet bag. Checking inside she did a quick count of the cash that was stored inside. A few hundred dollars was going to have to be enough.

Kat watched her mother with wide eyes. When Gen removed a stack of bills from the safe, she cried out, "Mom! What is all that money for?"

Gen turned, a guilty look in her eye and cash in her hand, "This is in case we have an emergency while we're on the road. We need to be prepared."

Kat nodded, but kept silent.

Picking up her sewing supplies, she looked around the room. "Well then, I think that's about it. I'm just going to jot your father a quick note . . ."

"Daddy doesn't know we're going on this trip? I knew something was fishy."

"Kat, honey, could you bring these bags to the car? I'll be right there."

Gen set the supplies in her daughter's arms and started walking her to the front of the house. A hysterical daughter wouldn't help her escape, so she kept her voice calm and soothing. "Oh yes he does, I talked with him when he was home for lunch. Don't you worry." She looked down into the girl's eyes. "Now, grab yourself a couple cookies for the road and head out to the car."

Kat was not convinced, but she trudged toward the door. "Is it okay if I do my homework on the way?"

"Of course," Gen said.

She herself went to the dining room and sat in front of a pad of paper. Sitting with pen in hand, Gen was suddenly without words. How do you say goodbye forever to the man you loved? She stared at the paper for a few minutes before she had any words. Tears started to fall as she said goodbye. When she finished, she blotted her tears from the paper, folded the paper in half and walked away.

She did her normal routine before she left, as if she was going to return to this little home. Nostalgia washed over her like a tidal wave. She and Peter spent their happiest days and their most wretched moments in these rooms. These four walls had seen a marriage built and destroyed. But now it was time to leave, before the marriage destroyed her.

Sliding behind the wheel of the car, Gen checked her wristwatch. Three forty. They would be on the road for more than an hour before Peter got home. Maybe he'd stop by the bar first. They should be at her parents' house before he made it home and realized they were gone. She shuddered to think about how angry he'd be.

Backing out of the driveway and turning onto the road, Gen fought her nerves. She smiled and waved at the neighbors as she drove past them.

Katherine sat in the front seat with her nose buried in her history book. She didn't look up from her book until the car was heading down the highway. The air in the car was thick with silence and tension until Kat said, "I bet America was really cool when they first discovered it."

Gen was startled from her brooding thoughts. "What's that, honey?"

"Columbus and DeSoto. They're the first guys who came here. I wonder what it was like back then."

"Wouldn't that be fun to find out?" Gen said, hoping that history homework would provide enough distraction.

"I wonder if the Indians ever hit their wives," Kat said, looking at her mother.

Gen sighed and her shoulders fell. "Don't be too hard on him. Alcohol makes him do crazy things."

"He hit you again today, didn't he? Was he drinking? That's why we're leaving, isn't it?"

Gen caught in her breath. Kat had sharp eyes for a ten-year-old. She realized that lying to her daughter wouldn't work, she hadn't missed much. Sighing, she asked, "How did you know?"

"I can still see the red on your cheek. You didn't cover it with makeup like you normally do."

Gen's hand rose to her cheek which was still sore and puffy. Shame flooded her face.

"Mama, don't worry. I won't tell anyone. I haven't yet."

Fear rose and she asked, "Kat, tell me the truth, did Daddy ever hurt you?"

"No, Mom. He's never even raised his voice." She shook her head. In a lower voice, she added, "Actually, he hasn't even talked to me lately."

"Oh honey, I'm sorry." She reached one hand off the steering wheel and laid it on Kat's knee. The two were silent for a time.

"Where are we really going?"

Gen gulped and said, "We're going to Grandpa Ryder's house."

"How long are we going to stay there?" She looked at her mom. "Do they even know we're coming?"

"Damn, I forgot to call them." She breathed deeply and said, "Don't worry, they won't turn us away." She turned her head away from her daughter and spoke to herself. "Not in our time of need. Grandma may be a bit mean, but she'd never wish real harm on me."

"Huh?" Kat looked at her mom.

"Oh nothing. It'll be okay."

"How long will we stay? When will we go home?"

Gen blew out a breath, trying to calm her dread. She saw an exit for a rest stop and pulled off the highway. When she had stopped the car, she turned to face her daughter. She put her hand to Kat's face. This was going to break her daughter's heart. But Gen couldn't go back, she couldn't live that way. And she was determined to protect her little girl. Her eyes were shining with tears.

Fear crept into Kat's eyes. Her voice trembled as she said, "Mom, what's wrong?"

Gen grabbed her hands. "Katherine, listen to me." She sucked in one last breath before her words changed everything forever. "We're not going back."

"What? Why?" Kat shook her head. "What did you say?"

"We're never going back. Your father has lost his mind, and it's not safe for us anymore."

"No, Mom," Kat yelled. "That's my home. I have to go back, I have school tomorrow and Linda said that we could have a sleepover this weekend and . . ." Hysteria grew in her voice. Her eyes darted around the car.

"Katherine, honey," Gen soothed her daughter by rubbing her arm and stroking her hair.

"What about Daddy? How will he be okay without us? Will I ever see him again?"

Tears streamed down Kat's cheeks. With each tear came a new question or concern. "What about my stuff? My special bear? What is Daddy going to say? Is he ever going to forgive me?"

"You don't need to worry about him anymore." She wiped some tears off Kat's face and kissed her forehead. "Besides, he wasn't your real dad anyway."

Kat burst into a fresh round of tears, but by then Gen had already resumed driving. When they were back on the highway, Kat let her history book fall to the floor and curled up into a ball in her seat. And she cried until they arrived at Grandpa's farm.

Thirty-Three

The sound of tires on the gravel driveway echoed through the darkening night. Gen tried to park as quietly as possible, but out in the middle of the country, every sound seemed to boom through the night.

Gathering her courage, Gen got out of the car and walked to the door. Standing on the front porch in front of the door, her courage faltered. She was doing the right thing for her and her daughter, but would her parents see that. Her hand shook slightly as she raised it to knock on the farmhouse door. At first her knock was quiet. She hoped that somehow her parents already knew she was there, knew that she needed them, and were already at the door.

But no one answered. She knocked louder.

"Mom, why don't you just walk in?" Kat looked impatiently at her mother. This evening had already been enough for her and she just wanted to go to sleep.

A minute later the door opened. Len filled the doorway, with Antoinette standing right behind him. His eyes were wide. "Gen! Kitty Kat! What a surprise!" Gen's face was stained with tears and a red mark covered her cheek. Kat's eyes were red and swollen from crying. He wrapped them both up in his arms. Katherine burst into a fresh round of crying as Gen sagged into his arms.

"What is it? What has happened?"

Len led the crying girls into the living room and sat them down, Gen in a rocking chair, Kat on his lap. He held the girl until her cries simply were hiccups matched with tears.

He asked, "Gen, what's happened?"

Rocking in the chair, Gen lost her gaze in the fireplace. She let the crackle and pop fill her senses as she tried to put words to the tragedy of her life. One pop of the wood sent a spark which landed in front of Gen's feet. She held still and watched as the ember flickered and lost its glow, dying at her feet.

When the ember lay dark and motionless, Gen unrolled the story of her marriage's demise and why she'd run away from her home.

Antoinette sat at the table and clucked her tongue. "I should have figured something like this would happen eventually."

"Mother!" Her rage at her mother mingled with deep sorrow. Even now, in her moment of grief, her mother passed judgment.

But Antoinette's voice was soft and sad. She looked into Gen's eyes and said, "I'm sorry, Gen, but I saw how things were changing and the marks on your face and arms." She sighed and looked down into her teacup. "What did you do to provoke such a response? Surely, you had something to do with it."

Gen's eyes flared, but her mouth remained shut. There was nothing to say to her. If she couldn't see Peter's fault in it, no amount of arguing would convince her of the truth. She dropped her eyes back to the fire.

Len barked at his wife. "Antoinette, now is *not* the time." He looked at Katherine who lay against his chest and said, "You look hungry, Little Miss. Go ask Grandma to fix you a plate of something yummy." He pinched her nose and winked. "And I'll bet, that if you look, you'll see the cookie jar is full."

Antoinette reached a hand toward the child who jumped off her grandpa's lap. Katherine settled in the kitchen with a bowl full of soup, a slab of bread slathered with butter, and a cold glass of milk. When Antoinette returned to the living room, she pushed a hot bowl of soup into Gen's hands.

"Today at lunch, I realized that I couldn't live with it anymore and that I shouldn't live with it, not for my sake or for Kat's. So I packed up everything we need and came here."

"Does Peter know?"

Gen glanced at the wall clock. Five thirty. "He will in a couple hours." she said. "I left him a note on the table, but I didn't tell him where we were going."

Antoinette crossed her arms, "Of course you came here and you'll stay here. In times of trouble, there's always family."

Genuine gratitude flooded through Gen. After the events and emotions of the day, her mother's no-nonsense strength was a balm to her weary soul.

But then Antoinette said, "However, we would expect you'll go home to Peter in a couple of days."

Gen looked aghast at her mother. "What are you talking about?"

"You will go home in a few days, after tempers have cooled and you will work things out."

"Mother, I left him because he's hit me, more than once. There's nothing left to work out." She looked over at Katherine eating at the table. She dropped her voice to a low murmur. "Besides, I'm pretty sure he doesn't love me anymore."

Antoinette looked horrified. "Whose fault is that?" she spit out. "Men don't fall out of love with their wives for no reason at all. There's always a reason." She glowered at her daughter.

"How dare you accuse me?" Gen's voice rose. Her anger threatened to boil over at her mother's harsh words. Her eyes locked on Kat who watched the scene in front of her. She dropped her voice. "Nothing should matter to you except that we're running away from a man who hurts me. Nothing warrants that kind of treatment."

Len lifted his hands, placing them between the two women. Looking from Antoinette to Genevieve, he asked, "So Gennie, what *are* you planning to do now?"

She shrugged her shoulders and said, "I don't know. I hoped to stay here for a couple days until I can figure something out."

Len nodded, "Of course, take as much time as you need." Raising his voice, "It looks like I'm going to have some help in the b—"

The shrill ring of the telephone in the hallway interrupted him. Every head whipped in the direction of the phone, but no one moved toward it. The ring was sharp and insistent. Fear descended on Gen like a blanket. Each ring of the phone was a warning. He was coming to find her.

After ten rings, Antoinette looked at her husband and said, "You'd better answer it, it might be Marie. She knows we're not always near the phone." Gen shrugged her shoulders. If Peter wanted to find her, he would. Not answering the phone wouldn't keep him from coming.

Len answered the phone with force. "Ryder residence," he said into the receiver. "Hello, Peter. Yes, they're here, they're safe." He listened. He looked to Gen but she shook her head.

"No, I'm sorry, she doesn't want to come to the phone right now."

He listened some more. He pulled the receiver away from his ear. Peter's shouting could be heard into the living room.

"Peter, I don't think that's a good idea right now. Wait until tomorrow, then you two can talk."

More yelling, this time laced with obscenities. "Peter, you need to calm down. I can give Gen a message for you."

He listened, then turned toward Gen and asked, "Do you have a message for Peter?" She shook her head again. The thought of speaking to Peter petrified her. The fear in her voice would give him power over her. She refused to let him use her weakness.

"Okay, I'll tell her." He covered over the receiver on the phone. "Peter wants me to tell you that he would like it if you came home tonight."

Gen lifted a skeptical eyebrow. "Really? That's all he said?"

Len gave her a wry smile. "No, but I thought I'd spare you the finer points of his argument."

Gen folded her arms across her puffed-out chest, defiant from her place on the couch. "You can tell him I'm not coming home. Ever."

Shouts and curses emanated from the phone. Even Kat could hear what was going on, her eyes widen at the knowledge that her father cursed at her mother. Uninvited tears sprang to her eyes once again. Antoinette held her against the storm of her tears. Kat buried herself in her grandmother's chest.

From her spot on the couch Gen surveyed the carnage as if watching it on the movie screen. Her daughter convulsing in grief and fear. Her mother tucking the girl into her arms, offering comfort, rocking her back and forth, stroking her hair, and cooing soft sounds. Her father fighting to maintain a civil discourse with a man who'd caused her harm.

Thoughts swarmed through her head. Could she reverse the pain she'd caused her daughter if she just went back? Was her marriage worth saving? Was the man on the phone who she wanted to spend the rest of her life with? For each question, she knew the answer was no, but she refused to let him cower her, in what might be their last moments. She had had enough.

Amid the chaos, she strode to the phone and held out her hand for the receiver.

"Are you sure?" her father asked. Gen nodded.

Putting the receiver to her ear, Gen said, "Hello, Peter."

She closed her eyes to his first angry words. Soon they calmed to flow like warmed honey. "I love you, darling, why did you leave like this? Please come home."

Gen took a look around the room as she considered her answer. Her daughter still weeping in her mother's arms. The crackling fire spreading warmth. Her father standing close to her side. After a moment's silence, she said, "No, Peter, I can't come home. I don't trust you anymore." She choked on the words.

He erupted. Curses and threats. "You'll regret this, Gen. I'll be there in two hours and I'll drag you home myself. I won't let you do this to me. How could you? All the love I've shown you?"

"Love? Ha!" her words were tainted with bitterness. "I know you loved me once, but I also know you don't anymore. You only love one thing—that bottle." She spit the words at him, hoping he received them with all the spite she intended. "You expect me to come home so you can hit me again? How stupid do you think I am?"

More curses and threats. Gen's face paled. "Don't you do that. If you come here, Peter, I'll be gone. And you'll never see your daughter again!"

She listened again.

"Goodbye, Peter!" she said, slamming down the receiver. She stood with her back to her family, collecting herself and calming the rage that Peter had invoked. After a minute's silence, she turned back toward her family, face white with fear.

"Mom, Dad, we have to leave. Peter's on his way here. He'll be here in two hours."

Len walked to the back of the house and opened the cabinet where he kept his rifle. Picking it up, he checked to be sure it was loaded and ready. "Don't worry, Gen. He won't put a hand on you or Katherine."

Antoinette threw her hands up in the air. "Well, I guess after that conversation, any hope for reconciliation is out, at least for the time being." She pulled Katherine up and started to lead her toward the stairs. "The least I can do is think of the child in a time like this. It's more than her mother is doing."

Gen watched her daughter disappear around the corner and up the stairs. The sound of her mother's chattering faded with each step they climbed. Soon she could hear the water running in the bathroom upstairs.

She found her way to her father's rocking chair and plunked herself into it. For the next few minutes Gen sat still while her thoughts raced a mile a minute. *Where will I go?*

She tried to clear her head enough to come up with a decisive answer, her brain was a jumble of doubt. She put her face into her hands and groaned. The reality of what she was doing washed over her. There wasn't any going back. She could feel her father's presence near her, but wasn't sure where he was. "Dad?"

"Yes, Gennie," she heard from behind her. His hands were tinkering with something metallic.

"Dad, we have to leave."

He sighed. "I was afraid you'd say that. Are you absolutely sure?"

After a long moment Gen raised her head and turned toward him and said, "Yes, I'm sure."

He set down the rifle he'd been cleaning and asked, "Where do you think you'll go?"

After wanting to control her own destiny for so long, she now felt immobile to act. "I don't know," she said, a mixture of sadness and desperation in her voice.

Her father walked to the place where she sat. He rested his hand on her shoulder. "Do you have any money? That'll help determine how far you can go."

Gen's face brightened. "I do," she said as she went to retrieve her purse from the front door. She'd dropped it there when they came in. "I've been saving here and there for a long time. I've known it would come to this."

As she counted the bills for the second time that day, her shoulders dropped. She blew out a breathe of relief. "I've managed to save over $500."

"You sure were planning for some rainy day."

Gen's faced dropped. "I guess I was." The sound of her voice tinged with regret. "I never thought I would actually have to do this though."

"I know you didn't, honey, but with that amount of money you can afford to go almost anywhere."

"Really?" Gen was pleased, but now had too many options. Where could she and Kat go to build a new life? "But Dad, where can we go to be safe?"

Len shrugged his shoulders. "Wherever you want to go."

She hated carrying this weight alone, knowing the decision would affect both her and Katherine. She sat upright as a thought occurred to her. Kat should be part of the choosing. Of course! Kat was a responsible and helpful ten-year-old. She'd have some insight as to where to go. Gen smiled as she put her hands to her mouth and called up the stairs, "Kat, could you come down here? I need to talk to you about something."

Thirty-Four

From upstairs Gen heard her mother's voice. "She'll be down in just a minute."

A few moments later, Kat bounded down the stairs, a small smile on her face. "Grandma just showed me where we'll sleep tonight. I helped put fresh sheets on the bed. I chose the red plaid ones, they're really soft." Her words tumbled into each other, the excitement a welcome relief from her earlier tears. "I'm sleeping on the side with the lamp so I can read tonight." Her eyes shined with hope.

Gen held her hand out to her daughter, sad she had to ruin even this. "I'm sorry, Sweetie, we can't stay tonight. We have to leave in about an hour."

All color drained from Kat's face. "But Mom, we can't leave already, we just got here. Where are we going to go?" Katherine's chin quivered as she spoke.

Bending down, Gen grasped her daughter by the shoulders. She looked right into her daughter's eyes. "I know, Sweetie. I wish we could stay, but we can't. Your Dad's on his way."

A smile lit Kat's face. "Dad's on his way, great. So, we can go home?"

Gen took a deep breath. Her words would send a dagger through her daughter's young heart. She led her over to the couch and sat her down. Looking her in the eyes again, she said, "Katherine"—she stopped. There was no way to make this easy. She tried again. "Katherine, we're not going home."

Kat's chin quivered. "Why not? Can't you go home and give Dad a hug and make it all better? Please." Tears brimmed at the edges of her eyes.

Gen turned away from her daughter's pain. What a horrible mother she was proving to be. She had no words of comfort, for either of them. Tears rolled down her cheeks too.

They sat together on the couch crying. Gen reached over to wipe Kat's tears, but Kat pushed her hand and turned away. Gen froze. She hadn't expected anger. She was working to save her daughter, not hurt her on purpose.

"Kat, honey," Gen spoke through her tears and fears. "I need you now, I can't do this without you."

Kat looked back to her Mom. "What? You've already made the biggest decisions. I'm just supposed to go along with it?"

"No, no." Gen wanted to soothe and reassure Kat. She wasn't a monster. "I need you to make the most important choice of all."

Kat watched her. Gen forced herself to not look away.

"I want you to choose where we go."

Kat sat stunned. "Me? You want me to choose where we go? How am I supposed to choose?" She sat for a few minutes before asking, "Really? Wherever I say, we'll go?"

"Yes," Gen said, "As long as we can drive to it."

Kat's eyes widened. "I want to go to Florida, to see where DeSoto landed, like I'm learning about in history."

Gen gulped then said "Okay, how far away is that?" Looking over at her father, "Dad, do you have a map of the United States?" In the silence that followed his leaving, Gen reached over to hold her daughter's hand, but Kat pulled away from her. A fresh round of heartbreak grabbed hold of Gen. Fighting back tears, she focused on the burning log in the fireplace. The flames engulfed the bit of the log that was left. Gen wanted to rescue that small piece of wood to keep it from being destroyed by its circumstances. It never asked to be firewood, but here it was, charred beyond recognition.

As her thoughts swirled, Gen knew she was that log. The fire was burning her up and she was powerless to keep it from happening. She knew that to her core. Peter's love had used her up, there wasn't anything worth loving left in her heart. She was a ruined woman.

Shaking her head to clear away the dismal thoughts, she turned back to Katherine. She, too, stared into the fire, quiet tears rolling down her cheeks, her hands folded in her lap. But there was still hope for her. She was young and resilient, she'd make new friends and grow up safe and have a great life. Gen could do that for her.

After a few minutes, Len returned with a hardbound atlas. Using great care, Len set the atlas, open to the US map, on the coffee table. Gen watched as Kat pointed to a small bay on the western side of the Florida Peninsula. "There. I want to go there." The sound in her voice begged for a fight.

"Really Kat? This is where you want to go?" Gen gulped when she looked at the map. "It's awfully far from Wisconsin."

"I know, Mom, they've got beaches." Kat looked down at the map. "But you said I could choose anywhere, so I choose Florida." Her voice was steely as if she was trying to pick a fight.

Gen opened her mouth, preparing to argue, but then shut her mouth. She gave the decision to Kat, she'd no right to disagree now. She looked to Len and asked, "Dad, what's the best way to get down there?" She traced a general route south with her finger.

Grief ripped through Len's eyes. "Are you sure?" he asked, pleading in his voice for the girls to stay.

"I can't stay. I won't put you in the position of defending me against Peter. We'll be fine. We'll drive and he won't find us until we are ready to be found." Circling Florida with her fingers, she said, "Peter will move on, find someone else to love him, and give him the family I couldn't."

Marching into the room, Antoinette snapped at the two adults, "That's enough. Len, you know full well that Genevieve will do whatever she wants, even if it is the worst decision in the world." She slammed her hand onto the atlas. "What are you thinking?" Antoinette turned toward Gen. "Putting your future into the hands of a child? I've never heard such foolishness, even from you."

Gen pulled herself upright, "You may have spoken to me like that when I was a child mother, but no more. I am a grown woman."

Antoinette's face turned red, set with fury. "Your best decision is to run away? And then you put your decision into the hands of a child." She waved over to Katherine sitting on the couch. "You're a coward. You could call the police, you could shame him in public, you could stay here and face him, but you're going to run away and leave me to clean up your mess, again." She stomped away into the kitchen, banging cupboards and knocking pots and pans.

Len looked from his daughter to his wife and said, "Antoinette, that's enough. Our daughter will not also be beaten with your words."

The banging in the kitchen continued.

"What are you doing?" he asked.

"I'm preparing some food for the road, I'm not going to let my granddaughter starve just because her mother's lost her mind."

Gen gritted her teeth. Even her help was a criticism. "Thank you, Mother," Gen said with strained gratitude. "I'm sure we'll appreciate such consideration." Len wrote down basic directions for Gen and retrieved a driving atlas from the car. Using paper clips, Len clipped the states of their route together to make navigation easier.

Within a few minutes, all the preparations were made. After Antoinette brought Katherine into the kitchen, Len beckoned Gen into the study. Rifling through his desk, Len pulled out his own safe. "Here," he said, thrusting a wad of bills at his daughter, "you're going to need this."

"Dad, no, I can't. You're going to need that."

He demurred, shaking his head. "We'll be fine, you're going to need this long before we will."

He pushed the money toward her. Again, she shook her head. "Dad, I don't want to take this from you."

"Well then this is for the Christmas presents we can't buy you this year." Len wiped his eyes with the back of his hand. His voice strained to keep from cracking. "Call me when you arrive. Even if I can't be near you, I want to know you're safe."

"Thanks, Dad," Gen said, accepting the cash. She turned to leave before her own emotions overcame her.

"One more thing," Len said, "if you need more, or anything, just call. I can always wire you more."

His overwhelming generosity was more than she could handle. Instead of turning away, she wrapped her arms around her father in a tight hug. The tick of the clock counted down their moments left together and filled the room with sadness.

Breaking away from her father, Gen said, "I think it's time to go."

Len nodded, eyes shining with tears.

The sight of her father's pain ripped through her anew. She was hurting every person she held dear. Only horrible people hurt the ones they loved. Unable to bear witness to the grief she caused, she turned and walked out of the room. From the hallway she called, "Katherine, sweetheart, it's time to go."

The next minutes were filled with tearful goodbyes. Katherine wept into her grandmother's bosom. Len wrapped himself around her too, enveloping the girl. All three cried together. Gen busied herself to avoid the little girl's pain. When the tears calmed, Gen took her by the hand and pulled her away.

Before walking out the car, Gen said goodbye to her parents. Len held her for a long moment, before looking her in the eyes and saying, "I love you."

Gen couldn't speak, but gave him a kiss on the cheek.

Her mother was next. She leaned in to say goodbye with a hug.

Whispered words filled her ears. "Don't you go and ruin her life, Genevieve. God will never forgive you for it."

When her mother released her, Gen looked at her mother's eyes. They betrayed no animosity. Gen played along, pretending there was no threat. Guiding Katherine with a hand on the back, the two of them headed to the car.

Len and Antoinette followed, getting them settled. Len walked around the car, kicking the tires and peering under the hood.

"Dad," Gen asked, "what are you doing?"

"I'm just trying to look after you, making sure you're safe." He shrugged. "It's what dads do."

Gen laughed weakly. "Thanks, Dad. I love you too."

The car doors slammed shut. After a long pause, Gen started the engine and put her hands on the wheel. With a final deep breath, she backed out of the driveway. Her last glance was of her parents standing together on the porch waving goodbye.

Part

THREE

Thirty-Five

The next hours were a blur of driving south on miles of local interstates. Gen drove into the night, across the state line into Illinois. Stars twinkled in the clear night sky by the time they pulled off and stopped at a small motel for the night.

The next day was more long miles. Hour by hour, the scenery changed. As they traveled further south, the air warmed and she removed layers of clothing. First her overcoat, then her sweater until she was wearing only a short-sleeved shirt. With each passing mile, Gen's worries fell off her shoulders like the layers of clothes. As she relaxed, hope infused her spirit. Never mind that Kat sulked in the seat next to her. Peter didn't know where she was and couldn't find her now. Now he was simply another part of her past that she would work to forget.

On their fifth day of driving, they crossed into Florida. She looked at her daughter and smiled. For the first time in days, Kat gave a small smile back.

After a few more hours of driving they arrived in Tampa. The sun blazed high overhead, the air was warm and thick. Gen looked at her daughter. "Well, we made it. where should we go now?"

Kat grinned and said, "The beach, Mom. Let's go to the beach!" She looked at Gen with excited, pleading eyes.

Having nowhere else to go, she shrugged. "Might as well."

They drove across the causeway and followed the signs to the beach. As they drove through town toward the beach, Gen saw rows of small squat houses with stucco walls and tile roofs.

Palm and palmetto trees poked their branches in every direction. To Kat she said, "Those branches look sharp enough to poke your eye out." The girl giggled for the first time in days. Gen was glad of that, no child should have to wear an adult's burden.

They found their way to a public access beach. As they walked to the beach, Gen's hopes sank. The sight and the sound was awesome, but nothing like she had imagined. In the miles since the city, the weather had changed, boding ill.

Dark clouds were whipped by fierce winds. In front of her, the waves pounded the shore, one right after another. Constant and roiling, the shore, which was not covered with smooth white sand, but small, cutting broken pieces of shell, was edged with a sickly yellow foam. The waves crashed down one right after another. The Gulf of Mexico looked angry, as if sensing an intruder was near.

Disappointment rose in Gen. The beach was supposed to be beautiful and calming, blue skies and palm trees. She had expected calm like Half Moon Lake, where the water lapped against the smooth sandy shore and the edges tickled the toes. Instead, she was surrounded by a frenetic energy, a constancy that made her feel anxious.

Much to her mother's dismay, Katherine removed her shoes and socks and rolled up her pants. She took tentative steps toward the water. The instant her toes hit the edge of it she squealed and hopped back out. "That's cold," she said. "I never would have thought the water would be cold."

"I didn't expect this either," Gen told her daughter. Nothing was as she thought it should be. This was supposed to be sunshine and happiness. Gen's heart sank. Of course, life hadn't turned out the way she expected, why should Florida be any different?

Gen and Kat settled into a little seaside motel and paid for a week's stay. The two girls took long drives into town searching for a neighborhood that would welcome a single mother and her daughter and allow them to live in safety. Driving through historic districts, they stared open-mouthed at the spacious seaside mansions. They traveled through seaside neighborhoods, some little more than run-down fish shanty towns. They found the grocer and the fishmonger. They located the department store and purchased clothes more suitable to the Floridian climate.

In the dark of the night, Gen sat awake, unable to sleep. The constant pounding of the surf echoed the unease in her head. Her thoughts turned back to her decision to leave, to run away from Peter.

When sleep was illusive, Gen sat on the balcony of their room and penned a letter to Peter, pouring out her heart on motel stationery. She wrote her sadness over their broken dreams, her rage because he caused this, her sorrow for her responsibility.

She left the papers on the desk.

In the morning light, she reread her words. They were all true, but her courage failed her. She would never send it to him. She sat at the desk, holding the papers in her hand. Oh Peter, how did it all go so wrong? She folded the papers and sealed them inside an envelope. As she had so many times before, she opened her hatbox and placed it inside.

Gen and Kat filled their days pouring over the classifieds, circling any job that looked interesting. Gen spent hours sitting behind the motel clerk's desk calling potential employers, embellishing her phone and typing skills. It didn't take long to find a job as a secretary at a law firm in downtown St. Petersburg, in a building that overlooked Mirror Lake.

At work, Gen shared her story with anyone who would listen. Being an abused housewife who'd escaped her drunken husband brought Gen attention she craved. Compassion overflowed. As her story spread to the wives of the lawyers in her office, they plead with their husbands to pull strings to get the girls out of the hotel and into a real home in a decent neighborhood.

Two months later, Gen signed the paperwork on a small bungalow in a neighborhood which the wives deemed "respectable." Pushing open the door, Gen laughed out loud. "I own a home," she said into the dark, empty rooms. Her boss, Charles Anderson, had given her the day off for the house closing. After receiving the keys from the realtor, she drove to her new home on Dartmouth Avenue. The street was quiet and treelined. Every home had a neatly manicured lawn in front of it. A large palmetto tree filled the front yard of Gen's house.

Her new home was a two-bedroom bungalow made of cream stucco. But the empty house didn't seem as nice without all the previous owner's things in it. Her meager belongings wouldn't be as sweet as the house demanded. She walked through the rooms. The living room, kitchen and dining room sat at the front of the house. Down a short hallway were the two bedrooms, one for each her and Katherine, with a bathroom in between. The room she'd chosen for herself had a thick gray carpet and windows opening to the backyard. Kat's room also had gray carpet, but only one widow to offer any light to the outside.

As she walked through the main rooms, the air echoed with her footsteps. She dragged her hand against the wall, imagining the life she and Katherine could build here.

Here she could make a fresh start, begin again, give Kat the advantages she deserved. Maybe she could even find true love for herself.

Standing in the kitchen surrounded by cupboards that were now hers, Gen jumped when she heard a knock on the door.

Upon opening the door, she was greeted by a woman holding a plate covered with tinfoil.

"Welcome to the neighborhood," she said as she put the plate into Gen's hands. "Hi! I'm Gina Davis. I live just down the street and I saw your car in the driveway and I had just pulled these cookies out of the oven so I thought I'd just bring some to you."

Gen gulped. This woman talked a mile a minute and her voice had that thick southern accent that Gen was still trying to get used to. "Hello," she said. "I'm Gen Ryder."

Gina stood before her with a neat brown bob wearing a thick dark blue headband. A clean apron covered her blue dress. She tilted her head and smiled. "When are ya'll movin' in?" she asked.

Gen smiled at her. "My daughter and I will start moving in tonight. We don't have much. We should be all settled in a day or two."

"What about your husband, won't he be doing the heavy lifting for you?" she laughed, a high-pitched assuming laugh.

"No, there isn't a husband to do that, so I'll do all the heavy lifting myself." Gen lifted the plate in Gina's direction. "Thanks for the cookies. Katherine will love them." She closed the door with Gina standing dumbfounded on the porch. The door gave a satisfying click and Gen went back to the kitchen. Tossing the plate of cookies onto the counter, she berated herself. *She was just asking a simple question. Of course people are going to wonder if I have a husband.* Gen was going to have to come up with better answers than that.

Gina's visit was the first of many visits over the next few days.

Gen found a way to be gracious, even though she decided that the women in her neighborhood were grating in their perfection. Never did she encounter a hair out of place or a stain on a dress, like the women were preening peacocks showing off their finery. Whenever she was home, someone was standing on the porch with a plate to welcome them to the neighborhood. As news of her single-motherhood spread, the plates became baked goods and casseroles. Gen accepted every offering, despite her desire to hide away from these perfect women. In their presence, every single one of her flaws was on display.

As life settled, Gen relaxed into her relief. She had a job that would provide enough. She owned her own home. Peter had no idea where she was. Kat was settled in a good school and had made some nice friends. Everything was going to be okay.

After a few months, Gen loved that life was now controlled by her and no one else. Besides her work and Kat's school, their time was their own, to be used as they pleased.

During trips to the department store, Gen reveled in the chance to buy new clothes worthy of her status as an attractive, confident, and single thirty-five-year-old woman. She chose flirty skirts and revealing shorts, midriff shirts, and large sunglasses. Gone were the house dresses and bulky nightgowns of her late marriage.

Gen spent extra time studying the models in magazines. Fashion in Florida was so much more relaxed than in Wisconsin. Or was it her position as a free and easy single woman instead of a dour married drudge? Either way, Gen loved it.

She and Kat would often shop together, buying similar pieces in their respective sizes. A pair of teal capris and large sunglasses. An open-backed red-polka-dot dress. Two-piece gingham swimsuits.

When they walked down the streets together, Gen held her head high. Kat would skip along next to her, chatting about the day's business. Gen listened, but paid more attention to the looks she received from well-tailored businessmen. When a handsome, dark-haired man whistled, she'd follow him with her eyes, sending the message of desire.

Other than shopping, Gen and Kat took regular trips out to the public beaches north of St. Petersburg. They would drive over on a warm Saturday morning and spend the day. Gen favored the touristy St. John's Pass and its accompanying beaches. While she relaxed in the sun she pretended not to notice the hungry looks of desperate men burdened with their wives and children. She perched herself as seductively as possible, relishing in their lust.

One sweltering Saturday afternoon, the two girls decided to visit the beach again. A perfect fall day wasn't to be wasted at home.

"Come on, Mom, let's go to Indian Rocks. I love it there."

Gen sighed. The beach was covered in rocks and few people visited. "Katherine, we just got new suits, we should go to the Pass. Maybe some of your friends will be there." Gen gathered their towels into her beach bag.

Kat turned her lip down. "But Mom, I don't want to be seen." Her tone was belligerent. "I want to be just with you."

Gen let out a huffy breath. She hated it when Kat pouted this way. If Gen insisted on the Pass, Kat would sulk all day and ruin her fun. "Fine. We'll go to Indian Rocks."

Kat jumped up and down and gave a little clap. "Yeah! I'll go get my stuff."

Two hours later they laid their towels on the gravel and sand beach. The beach, lined with vacationer's condominiums, was empty. Tourists didn't visit in mid-September even though the weather was still beachworthy.

Today there was no one to impress or tempt, just her and Kat, all by themselves. She pasted a smile on her face and tried to play with Kat who still delighted in play. Gen indulged in the simply joy of digging her feet into the sand and chasing the seagulls away from their picnic lunch. Most of their time was spent lying across beach towels accepting the generous rays of the warm sunshine. During their silent companionship Kat's face radiated peace but Gen was tormented by the silence.

Laying on her towel, Gen fought to remain still. Her thoughts wandered across the past few months, the life she'd built. Although it was a safe existence, Gen's spirit cried out in anguish. It's too quiet and lonely with just Katherine. I need to be loved and desired. I'm going to wither away into an old woman—miserable and alone.

Driving home from their day in the sun, Kat hummed along to the car radio, tapping her fingers on the dashboard. She caught the eyes of her mother who smiled. In the relaxing warmth of the car, Katherine started to talk.

"You know, Mother, when I grow up, I want to be a fashion designer. I really like clothes, especially the way you wear them. You know, I'm getting pretty good at making them too"—she paused—"or maybe I'll go to college and learn to be a writer. I would love to be a poet someday."

On and on Kat rattled, constantly indecisive about which life dream to pursue. One minute she was a family woman and the next, a woman of the world.

When she stopped talking, Kat turned to her mother and asked, "Mother, what's your dream?"

From the dazed lull of driving, Gen said, "My dream was for a man to love me and to stay with me forever." Her words drifted in from far away. Attached to them was her longing for a man to love her right now.

Kat's voice grew excited. "Me, too, Mom. I have that dream too. Do you think it can happen like in the movies?"

Waking from her own personal daydream, Gen shook her head. No sense filling her daughter with false hope. Her sadness at life's disappointments bubbled into bitterness. "Dreams? I don't have any dreams anymore. Life is only pain." She shut her mouth and refused to say anything else.

Kat sat in shock at her mother's bitter words, biting her lip to hold back the tears. A life of pain like her mother's was not what she wanted for herself, but those words kicked the life out of her youthful dreams. The car ride home, stripped of childlike joy, finished in silence.

Thirty-Six

Four years later life had changed for both Kat and Gen. Kat had grown up and was thriving in high school. She'd earned a place on the cheerleading squad and joined the literary club. Happy, bright-eyed and smart, Kat made friends with a group of kids who had grown up in the neighborhood, chief among them Anne Miller. Katherine became Anne's shadow, joining her at weekly teen's club meetings.

Gen couldn't have cared less about what Katherine did for after-school activities. Gen worked late every night, so Katherine had to fend for herself. She was pleased that Kat had found such a good friend in Anne, spending many afternoons at her house. Even though Gen herself couldn't stand the Millers with all their righteous goodness, she didn't begrudge Kat the chance to have good people in her life.

But Katherine was changing. Something was different about her daughter. Maybe it was her hair. No, her clothes. Maybe her smile, it seemed bigger these days. Maybe her laughter, it was richer and more generous somehow. Her joy was infectious. Gen liked the change she saw and if it was the Miller's influence, all the better.

But as Kat developed an active social life, Gen decided it was high time she made a few of her own friends as well. She hadn't really tried to make any lasting connections yet. The other secretaries at the office weren't exactly her type and they all had families to tend to. Gen was looking for a different type of connection anyway.

A short drive from the house was a rotating restaurant with a night club and lounge, Sunset Grill. Gen started spending her evenings watching the sun set over the Gulf of Mexico with a cocktail in her hand. After a few weeks of just the view, she was pleased to meet men who bought her dinner and drinks. On these nights, she did not always make it home to sleep in her own bed.

Gen wasn't a neglectful mother. She just needed to be loved in a way her daughter could not understand. If Kat spent the night at a friend's house, she could do the same.

She never mentioned her overnights to Katherine; she'd be mortified if she knew. That's it, Gen thought, Kat had gained a new sense of morality. All those church services and youth meetings had burned religion onto her brain. As the realization grew stronger, Gen's fear did too.

To stave off any wagging tongues, Gen accepted any invitation for dinner or coffee with the neighborhood ladies. She could pretend to be in the same society as these ladies, if it kept her in Kat's good graces. But while sitting in finely decorated living rooms nibbling cookies, Gen only revealed parts of her sad story while matching their exaggerated hand motions and overdone laughter. Gen smirked as each one laid her hand over her heart and gasped, "Gen, I've never heard anything so horrible in all my life" Gen lowered her head to accept the words, false modesty winning over.

"Since then, it's just been me and Kat, making it on our own, without the help of a man in the house."

"You poor thing. Well, don't worry, a woman as stylish as you is sure to meet someone soon." Patting her on the leg, her host would say, "And won't he be a lucky man to marry someone like you." Gen nodded, knowing she wouldn't have any trouble finding men to spend her time with. The trouble came in that the most attractive men were often married, seeking escape from their mundane lives. Further, while she was eager for a relationship, she wasn't even considering marriage. She'd tried that already and it wasn't as lovely as everyone made it seem.

So Gen didn't hide her varied relationships, especially with single men. If a man she was dating wanted to take her on a walk on the Pier she'd hold his arm and smile at passersby. From spring until fall, there was a different man every month. It wasn't long before the concerned gasps dissolved into the busybody clucks of neighborhood tongues. At the market, she'd hear the exaggerated whispers of women behind her back. Their compassionate discussions with each other mutated into vicious gossip. Gen sneered in disgust at their coffee invitations, her supposed friends wanting only the latest news to turn into gossip. Though they turned their backs on her in public, she laughed at their hypocrisy in private. And yet, while she heard their non-verbal judgment wherever she went, she yearned for complete acceptance from them.

During her lunch break at work, she often stepped out of the office for some fresh air, usually with another secretary from her office. But one day as she walked toward the break room to find a companion, she overheard her name being mentioned. She stopped in her tracks a few feet from the break-room door. "Maybe if we don't talk about it, Gen won't come to the Christmas party." Sniggers filled the room.

One secretary, a new blonde named Martha, asked, "Why? That's not very nice."

An older woman named Ruth, answered, "She's such a floozy. She'll spend the entire night drinking, pawing our husbands." Her red lacquered nails waved through the air like flames. "It's embarrassing to watch."

"Maybe she just needs a friend?" Martha said, her voice nervous and sad.

Coming out from behind the door, Gen answered the women, "Not friends who talk about me behind my back." She whipped her head away. "See you at the party, girls," she sang as she walked away, waving her own painted nails at them in farewell.

Gen blew her disgust out of her nose. Typical. Pronouncing her guilt without knowing her life. Those women went home to ugly husbands every night. Gen's bed would remain cold and empty, unless she did something about it. She wasn't about to let their haughtiness put a damper on her life.

Gen looked forward to the holiday party for weeks. She loved the opportunity to have fun, especially when someone else paid for it. When the night of the party finally arrived, her excitement bubbled out of her. After applying a final coat of bright red lipstick to her lips, she called into the kitchen, "Kat, honey, remember I have my work party tonight. I'll be home late. You all set?"

"Yeah, Mom, I'm going to a rally and then spending the night at Anne's house. We'll go to church in the morning and I'll be back by lunch."

Gen snorted, blowing hot air onto the mirror. With a single swipe, she wiped it off and said, "You're sure getting enough churchin'. They still let you in with a sinner like me as your mother?"

Kat rolled her eyes, "Jesus doesn't care who my mother is. He loves me anyway." She drew in a deep breath and said, "He loves you too, Mom."

After puckering her lips in the mirror, Gen laughed, a bitter sound. "Kat, honey, if he loved me, things would be a bit different. As it is, I've got things figured out right now." She picked up her purse and overcoat and walked into the kitchen.

Kat was standing in front of the stove, holding a book, probably an English assignment. The look on her face startled Gen. Although she thought their conversation was typical mother daughter banter, Kat's face was filled with loathing. Flipping from bitter to flippant, she tried to make her next words light and eye-opening, wanting to change Kat's opinion. Looking Kat in the eyes, she said, "I've heard their cruel words about me, not one bit loving. Isn't that what Jesus was all about anyway?"

"What do you mean, Mother? Just because they don't approve of your flirting all over town, drinking and putting your hands all over whatever man gives you the time of day?"

Gen's anger flared. Her daughter, no matter how precious, had no right to speak to her that way. "How dare you! You have no right to talk to me like that, I'm your mother!"

Kat slammed down her cup. Her voice shook. "Then act like my mother. Make cookies for the bake sale. Come to the football games to watch me cheer. Talk to me about what's going on in my life, not yours."

Instantly wounded, Gen's face flushed bright red. "But Kat . . ."

"I'll not walk away from the people who accept me just because you feel guilty. Your actions are your own choosing." Kat turned back toward the stove where a pot of water boiled, dumping in the waiting macaroni noodles.

"No, Katherine, you have that wrong. I didn't choose this life, Fate handed it to me. I'm going to make the best of it and I'll not let you or anyone else condemn me for it."

"Fine then, I'll stop defending you. If you don't care . . ." Kat's voice had risen.

Gen snapped, "That's right, my life is none of their damn business. They can stick their noses somewhere else."

"Well, I will care even if you don't, they're my friends and their opinions matter to me." Kat turned back to the stove and stirred her pot. Her stiff shoulders and clenched jaw declared the conversation over.

Gen didn't want to leave with anger between them. She closed her eyes. When she opened them, her voice regained its even tenor. "Someday, Katherine, when you're a mother like me, you'll understand." She wanted to hug her girl, wrap her arms around her, send her love in spite of their disagreements. But Kat stood frozen, her posture rigid.

She raised her hand to touch her girl, but let it hang in the air. Any affection now would be denied. She sighed and said, "Have a good night, Kat."

As she walked away and closed the front door behind her, Katherine said, "You're wrong, Mom. I will never be a mother like you."

Thirty-Seven

The living room was dark. Gen reclined against the back of the couch, her fingers picking at some loose threads on the arm. In her other hand she held a burning cigarette. The ashes dropped onto the floor while a thin trail of smoke rose into the air. On the side table next to her a tumbler waited, its golden liquid offering a dulling to her senses.

She set the still-burning cigarette onto her ash tray and leaned back. Closing her eyes, she ran her hand through her hair. Without looking, she knew she was a mess.

Stuart had just left.

The slam of the door still echoed in her ears. Their fight had been vicious and she knew he was never coming back.

Good riddance.

Her face tightened in pain as she thought back over the past few men. Kent. Neil. Brian. Victor. Each one began with such promise, yet ended so badly.

Gen pretended it wasn't true, but she'd fallen into a horrible pattern.

What was going wrong?

She would meet men at Lucky's Lounge and after some conversation, the new guy would ask her out to dinner. They'd have a lovely time, laughing and talking, finding they had so much in common. The night would end with a chaste kiss on the cheek, she did have a daughter to get home to, after all.

Within a couple weeks, Gen would invite him over for dinner. She couldn't be in a relationship with a man whom her daughter hadn't met. At sixteen, Katherine was more than just a daughter, she was a friend as well, even if they didn't always agree.

Gen winced at the memories of those dinners. Kat would paste on a scowl as Gen served up her best meals. Mr.-of-the-Hour would crack lame jokes and Gen would laugh extra loud to make up for the discomfort and drink an extra gin and tonic or two. Even though he wanted to stay, she'd make him leave, out of respect for Kat and her studies.

But after the next week's dinner, he wouldn't leave so early. They'd sit on the couch and talk and laugh and kiss and drink until the wee hours of the night. But suddenly remembering her daughter in the house, she'd shoo him out around two or three in the morning. But she wanted him to stay, all night, every night.

Gen smiled as she remembered Stuart's first night staying at her house. How they laughed and loved. They tried to keep the noise down, but the walls were thin and she can't be sure Kat didn't know. Gen was a grown woman with a right to do as she pleased, even if Kat didn't approve.

Gen lit a new cigarette. She took a long drag on it before thinking about Kat's reaction to the news that Stuart would be staying in their house for a while. Yes, he had his own place, but he wanted to be close to Gen right now. No tears, no fighting, no words. Kat just turned her back to her mother. Even now, the memory stabbed her heart.

Gen lifted her glass and tipped it back into her mouth. She swirled the liquid in her mouth before swallowing it, savoring the burn on the back of her throat.

The memories rose up to the surface.

She and Stuart lay in bed, her head on his chest, as she cried over her broken relationship with Katherine. Stuart offered to help, maybe some of his words could build a bridge. Gen relaxed into sleep at the hope of his help.

But Kat and Stuart's interactions were never comfortable. His deep voice would boom across the breakfast table, "You know, Katherine, your mother is hurt by the way you treat her." Gen leaned over the kitchen counter a cup of hot coffee in her hand. Hope beat strong in her chest.

For a moment, Kat would regard the man sitting across the table from her. Then she would look over to her mother. Gen gave a welcoming smile. "Well, Stuart." Kat used such venom to pronounce the words that Gen flinched. "Maybe my mother should consider my feelings before she brings another man like you into our house." She rose and dumped her cereal bowl into the sink. Before leaving, she'd stop in the kitchen doorway and speak into the living room, although Gen was behind her in the kitchen. "I'm spending the night at Anne's tonight, Mother."

When the door closed behind her, Gen dissolved into a puddle of tears. Stuart comforted her for a few minutes before rushing out the door to work.

Gen closed her eyes. From her current position on the couch, she could see that this was the moment when it all started falling apart. Her heart broke anew as she remembered Stuart's excuses to arrive later and leave earlier. Their lovemaking was less laughter and more business. Their words morphed from all those things they had in common to the differences that colored their lives.

His last words before he walked out the door that night were "I'm sorry, Gen. This isn't working for me. I'll call you." What she recalled the most wasn't the words he spoke so much as the quiet vitriol behind them.

But Gen knew he'd never call. He was gone.

And now, she was sitting on her living room couch, picking at the loose threads on its arm. Alone. And miserable.

Her brooding was interrupted by the slam of the front door. "Mother, I'm home."

Gen didn't move. She listened as Kat's footsteps traveled to her room, then to the kitchen. "Mom?" she called.

"In here," Gen said from the darkness.

Kat flipped on the light. Raising her hand up to her eyes, Gen squinted against the harsh light.

"Sorry, I didn't see you there," Kat said. She surveyed the room. "Where's Stuart?"

Gen snorted. "Gone."

Kat stood in the doorway, silent.

Gen closed her eyes and leaned her head back again.

"I'm sorry, Mom, I know he was special to you." She walked forward and grabbed Gen's empty tumbler. "Can I refill your drink for you?"

"Thanks, Kat, you've always been such a good girl."

Kat put the refilled tumbler back in front of Gen. "Don't worry, Mom, I'll always be here for you."

Thirty-Eight

O nly a few months later, Gen reclined on a mustard-yellow love seat at Manhattan Casino, nursing her gin and tonic. Her eyes studied the way the melted ice and alcohol swirled within each other. She'd been waiting for Ken for more than an hour. Gen didn't know how much longer this fling would last. Going from man to man was getting tedious, she needed a permanent solution, a relationship that would last. As much fun as she had with Ken, she knew he wasn't the one.

She thought that meeting him here, in the center of the black part of town, would make him feel safe. No one would know him here. Joe at the bar knew her by name, but no one would ever suspect that Ken was straying from his wife. He'd just have been another man meeting a beautiful woman at the Casino.

Her thoughts wandered back through her past, through the misery and loss that littered her life. She lingered on the loss still more painful than any other, the baby she never knew. She wondered how life would have been different if she had kept that child and been honest with Peter.

At her doctor's appointment that afternoon, Dr. Barclay suggested she take the new birth control pill to avoid another unplanned pregnancy. He knew her history and her chances, but given her current habits, he didn't want her taking unnecessary risks. She was getting too old to handle another pregnancy.

Gen scoffed at the thought. She was only thirty-eight. Lucy Young had had babies well into her forties. Old, my foot.

The doctor warned that as she neared her "change in life" that some women experienced surprise pregnancies. Unexpected things happened. Gen nodded, but declined. "Don't worry," she said. "Nothing's going to happen, hasn't so far."

She refocused on the now-empty glass in her hand. Lifting her tumbler up to eye level, she studied the reflection. The distorted image of a woman reflected back at her. Something about her posture intrigued Gen. She was angled toward her, almost staring at the back of Gen's head.

She turned around to find that an attractive black woman was leaning over toward the barkeeper, in conversation. Before she could turn back, the woman stood, collected her glass and walked in Gen's direction.

"Excuse me," the woman said. "Is this seat taken?"

Gen looked at the woman for a moment. Usually, no one other than Joe spoke to her. Being the only white face in the entire club garnered her a lack of personal attention. Lots of awkward stares, but never conversation. "Do I know you?"

Without another word, the woman sat down across from Gen, sat back, and crossed her ankles, one over the other. She took a long sip from her glass of water. "Don't you remember?"

"Remember what? You?" Gen stared at the woman who wore a fitted white dress that contrasted with her chocolate skin. Even in the dim lights of the casino, there was a familiar spark in those brown eyes.

She leaned forward and stared at Gen full in the face. "Don't tell me that life's been so hard that you've forgotten a full year of your life?"

Realization dawned across Gen's face. "Carol?! What! How? What are you doing here? How did you recognize me? You live here in Florida? I never would have thought."

Carol put down her drink and stood, arms open for a hug. "First, come in here and give me a hug. It's been a long time."

Gen rose to fall into the safety of old friendship.

They spent the next hour catching up. Mostly, Carol just listened to Gen talk about the tragedy of the past fifteen years. Once Gen started talking to someone who actually cared about her, she just couldn't stop. Details about life with Peter and raising Kat on her own and all her various failed relationships came pouring out of Gen.

"And now, here I am, alone again, sitting at a bar, sipping a drink."

Carol sat silent for a moment, a blank look across her face. "Now that is a story," she said, "one that I would have never wished for you. Remember back at Bethany House when we would talk about what our futures would be?"

"Of course I remember," Gen kept her eyes trained on the melting ice left in her tumbler. "I was so jealous of you, with your fabulous Jimmy who was ready to whisk you off to marry you." Looking up, she finished, "And then you left. And I never heard from you again. How in the world did you find yourself here?"

A slight smile winked across Carol's face. "Well, after we got married, Jimmy and I moved down here to start a new life together, to get away from the gossipy church ladies back home, so we could just be two newlyweds, deeply in love."

"You just moved down here and forgot all about your baby?"

Carol winced as if she'd been slapped across the face. "Of course not. You have to believe me, I think of him almost every day. We have other kids now, two boys and a girl, and I wonder if he looks like Jimmy Jr. and Billy. I'll see a shining flash of a white smile and wonder if he's got a smile like that. If he's happy. " She looked directly at Gen. "But I know I could have never kept him just for myself, that would have been choosing my best over his and I couldn't have done that, especially not now that I know."

"Know what?"

"Know what it means to be a mom, to be married, to do things together, as a whole family."

"I wish I could have offered Kat that kind of life."

Carol leaned across the chair and patted Gen on the knee. "Well, what's done is done. And now it's best to just move forward."

"I'm trying, but it's hard." Gen shifted away from Carol and looked at her more closely. "But now I'm wondering, is it an accident that you were here tonight? I would have never thought I'd see you again."

"Well"—Carol hesitated and Gen thought she could see a blush creep up her face—"truth be told, Jimmy and I don't live too far from here, you are in my part of town. A few weeks ago, I was at a football game and the opposing team had some really great cheerleaders and there was one young lady who looked mighty familiar to me. So I asked around and found out her name was Katherine, but a lot of people called her Kat."

"I've heard Kat is a very talented cheerleader."

"Haven't you ever seen her cheer?"

Gen blushed, "Oh, Kat doesn't really want me around her friends too much. And I don't really want to be at high school football games."

Carol stopped for a beat. "Anyway, I thought it was unusual and she looked so much like you when I knew you at Bethany that I just had to know. So I asked around. Eventually, I learned that you come here a lot. I thought I'd take a chance and see if you'd stop by here."

"Wow. You must not have much going on to just spend time here waiting to see if I show up."

"Oh, I had a good feeling."

"Are you sure you haven't had too much to drink tonight?"

Carol shook her empty glass. "Club soda. I'm perfectly fine."

"So what do you want with me now?"

"Nothing much."

Gen's face fell. She didn't see the playful smile that crossed Carol's face.

"I'm just teasing. If I'm going to be honest, Gen, my friendship with you was what got me through that terrible time at Bethany House. You were honest to a fault, unconcerned with what others thought, and fully willing to do what you wanted regardless of what others wanted for you. My life here is great, but I've missed you and I'm wondering if we could be friends again."

Gen had to set her tumbler down on the side table. She couldn't believe her luck. Tonight, of all nights, feeling lonely and alone, she suddenly had a friend. It was too good to be true, but she was not such a fool as to pass it up. "Of course," she nearly shouted, her excitement making her voice shake.

"Well, good," Carol said succinctly as she stood up. "I've been gone way too long. Jimmy knew what I was coming here to do tonight, but I'm sure he's wondering where I've gotten off to." Gathering her coat, she offered Gen another hug. "It was so good to see you tonight. I'll be in touch with you soon."

She started to walk away.

"Wait," Gen called. "Do you want my phone number? So you can call?"

Carol's laughing voice traveled back to her. "Oh honey, I already looked you up in the phone book. I know exactly how to get ahold of you." With those final words, she stepped into the elevator and was gone.

Gen sat back in her chair. The bartender poured her one more gin and tonic as she considered what had just happened. What luck she'd finally had, to have Carol back in her life.

Thirty-Nine

Before the next weekend, Gen and Carol had made plans to meet again at the Manhattan. As they sat across each other at a small table, Carol cupped a steaming mug of coffee. Gen fiddled with the straw in her gin and tonic.

"What are you doing here in Florida, anyway?" Gen spent so much of their unexpected meeting talking about herself that she hadn't even discovered what Carol was doing in St. Pete in the first place.

"Well, what I told you was true. After I left Bethany House and Jimmy graduated, we got married and decided to move down here. We did it to escape the gossip, but also because it's cold in Wisconsin. I wanted sunshine and sunny beaches and a fresh start."

"Is your Jimmy a pastor?"

Carol huffed a small chuckle. "No, not here. There were plenty of churches and pastors by the time we got here. They didn't need another one, no matter how good the preacher. No, Jimmy's been working as an undertaker for the funeral home."

Gen took a hard swallow of her drink, working not to choke on her laughter. "He does what?"

Carol swatted a hand at Gen. "Don't laugh. It's good work. People respect my Jimmy. He's a leader in our community."

"Okay, okay, I'm sorry. I guess, I'm surprised. I'd never have guessed you would be the wife of an undertaker." After drawing in a quick breath, Gen asked, "What about you? I can't imagine that you are content just sitting at home waiting for the kids to come home from school?"

"Well, that is very reasonable to do, if you are in the position to do it. I, however, work at the Day School for Workers, watching other people's babies while they are at work."

Gen watched her former roommate. "Oh I see, you're doing penance. Or punishing yourself."

"What are you talking about?"

"You know, you're watching other people's babies. Maybe you're hoping to catch a glimpse of him in one of those sweet faces?"

"Genevieve, how dare you." Carol's nostrils flared in anger. "I did what I was told to do. Yes, I regret it, but I also have a life I'm proud of. And I'm sure that little Charlie is happy."

"That's what you tell yourself."

"Yes, it is what I tell myself. Because I have other people to think about, people other than myself. Unlike you."

Gen was so stunned she dropped her glass onto the table. "What!?"

"Come on, Gen, when's the last time you thought about someone other than yourself?"

"What do you mean, everything I've done has been in service of someone else. I kept Katherine because I couldn't give her away. I married Peter because Kat needed a Daddy. I left him to keep her safe. Everything I've done since I've gotten her has been in service of that little girl."

"Oh Gen." Carol reached her hand across the table in a peace-making gesture. "Listen to yourself. You're using Katherine as an excuse for all the choices you've made. It was for her . . . and even now, you and all your men, those are for her to?" Carol arched an eyebrow as she finished the question.

Gen flinched, pulling her hands into her lap. Staring into her drink for a long minute, she couldn't think of a thing to say. Shame welled up in her, billowing through her chest, rendering her mute.

"Can't you see what you're doing? You're lying to yourself. And if no one else is going to tell you, I am."

Gen wasn't going to take this. She didn't need Carol back in her life just to tell her all the things she'd done wrong. "You have some nerve. You walk back into my life offering to be my friend and this is the way you treat me?" Gen stood and looked to find her purse.

"What? No one else ever speak to you like this? Don't like it much? Of course you don't, 'cause the truth hurts sometimes, honey. And up until now either no one has said it to you or you've been too full of yourself to listen."

"Well, I don't have to listen now." Gen pushed away from the table, and walked away.

"From what I hear, if you don't start listening, you're going to lose your reason for any of this in the first place." Carol's voice was still as calm as it ever was.

Gen stopped, a few steps away from the table. She turned back to Carol and asked, "What do you mean?"

"C'mon Gen, you can't tell me that Katherine loves the way you're living now, can you? Loves that you are constantly out, dating a different man every couple of months, even bringing some home so they can play 'daddy' to her? How long do you think any sixteen-year-old is going to be okay with that?"

"Katherine loves me. We have an understanding."

"Oh, you do?" Carol's voice reflected skepticism. "An understanding that you can do whatever you want?"

"I don't have to stay here and listen to this."

"No, of course you don't."

"Well, then, I'm going."

"Fine, then, go. I'm not keeping you here."

"You're right."

"But it'd be nice to see you again soon."

Gen blew out her nose as she turned away again and walked out the door. The door closing firmly behind her.

All the way home, Gen couldn't stop thinking about what Carol had said.

Nor the next day, nor the week after that.

After two weeks of stewing over Carol's words, Gen picked up the phone to call her.

"Hey, Carol, it's Gen. Can we meet again soon?"

Gen stood silent as she listened to Carol's silence.

A sigh came over the phone line. "Okay. How about we meet at Old Johnson Park, we can walk and talk for a while."

Relief washed over Gen. "Yeah, sure. I'll meet you there on Saturday at 10 a.m., does that work for you?"

"Well then," Gen could hear the smile in Carol's voice, "I guess, it's a date."

Saturday dawned bright with the promise of the warm mugginess that was central Florida's calling card. Gen was so anxious to meet Carol again that she spent the morning fussing around the house. As she was scrubbing the counter, Kat came into the kitchen to get breakfast.

In the few minutes that Kat took to gather her bowl of corn flakes and milk, Gen moved from the counter to the cabinets, scrubbing every inch of exposed surface.

"Mom," Kat said, "what's gotten into you?"

Gen brushed her cloth to the side to wipe an old coffee stain. "What?"

Kat looked around the kitchen, which was almost as clean as when they moved in. A smile lit her face. "Seriously, what's going on?"

Gen followed Kat's eyes around the room. She laughed. "I'm a bit nervous this morning. I'm meeting someone after lunch and . . ."

Immediately, Kat's face fell. "Oh."

"Oh no, Kitty Kat, it's not like that this time. It's, well, I'm meeting a friend for a walk." She leaned against the counter.

"A friend? You mean, a new man?"

"I'll have you know, I'm meeting a friend named Carol at Old Johnson Park."

Kat's eyes grew wide. "I didn't know you had friends. You've always said that the ladies around here . . . "

"Well, for your information, young lady, Carol is an old friend. Someone I knew before you were born, back in Wisconsin."

"I see"—Kat paused—"and does she know about . . . you now?"

"And what, young lady, is that supposed to mean?" Gen stood and put her hands on her hips. Even as she stood there, she knew she looked exactly like all the women she said she despised, condescending and above all others.

Kat rolled her eyes as she turned away from her mom. "You know, about Stuart, and all the other guys before him?" Kat took her bowl of cereal back into her room and slammed the door.

Gen couldn't believe what she had just heard. Exactly what did Katherine think of her? She knew Kat didn't like her mom hanging out with her friends, all teenage girls are embarrassed by their moms. Gen stood in the kitchen worrying the rag in her hands thinking over what Kat believed about her.

In her mind, she fought through all the arguments.

Everything I've done has been for her. To give her a better life.

You mean, to give yourself a better life. First, you stubbornly kept a baby you had no right to raise to escape from your domineering mother. Then you ran away from a marriage that could have been saved, if you had even tried.

Tried? Tried what?

How about being honest for a change. Giving Peter what he deserved: the truth.

In growing frustration, Gen threw her rag into the sink and tore off her apron. She needed to escape the thoughts in her own head. She knew she'd chosen the right path, even if Katherine didn't think so.

Two hours later, Gen found herself sitting on a bench watching the world go by at Old Johnson Park. Actually, she sat as stylishly as she could, her ankles crossed neatly beneath the bench. From behind the shield of her sunglasses, Gen surveyed the goings on of a Saturday afternoon. While there were plenty of young families or teenagers hanging out, Gen couldn't find any eligible bachelors.

She wasn't waiting long before Carol arrived with two young boys in tow. As she stood to greet her friend, she heard Carol say, "All right then, you two go on, Ms. Gen and I are just going to sit here and talk while you boys play."

Gen walked to Carol and stood, watching her two young sons as they started to climb a sprawling jacaranda tree. "Wow, you're a mom to three kids—and two boys, no less. How do you do it?"

Carol laughed, "Oh, well, let's just say I'm pretty good at the laundry. Grass stains ain't got nothing on me."

Gen tried to match Carol's easygoing laugh, but couldn't. All that escaped her lips was a sardonic *ha*.

Carol turned to her friend, "What is it?"

"Of course you're good at laundry. You can probably cook good too."

"Well, I'm no gourmet chef, but I manage to put dinner on the table."

Turning away, Gen looked over to the edge of the pond and spoke softly. "I'm not good at any of those things." Gen looked up to see Carol a step behind with a look of concern on her face. "No really, I mean it. Even with those lessons I got back at Bethany House, I'm not good for much in the kitchen or the laundry. For a while, I was a tailor's apprentice, but I left that behind when I left Wisconsin and Peter."

Carol stayed in step with Gen. Her silence urging Gen on.

"There's so much I wish was different. I wish I could keep house. I wish I could make Katherine proud. I wish . . ."

"Let me stop you right there." Carol put her hand on Gen's arm, halting them both. "You could make Katherine proud. You could, Gen, I know it."

Gen's face started to wilt at the thought "No, I can't. She's got church in her and I'm not good enough for that crowd. And besides, why would I change for any of them anyhow."

"But what if"—Carol paused—"what if you changed for you? For Katherine? It doesn't have to be for anyone else."

Gen put her hands behind her back and stared at the ground as she took slow steps around the edge of the pond. She walked like that for a few moments before looking up. "And how exactly, would you propose I do that?"

The answer flew from Carol's lips. "Well, you could stop sleeping with men you aren't married to, for one."

Gen studied her friend. The steely look in her eye indicated to Gen that Carol wasn't one to be trifled with and maybe her words were worth heeding.

She continued, "You're tempting fate, Gen. And lowering yourself in your daughter's eyes. Why don't you stop? Or at least wait a bit, meet a man who is worth your time and affection, not just any man."

Shaking her head, Gen said, "You don't mince words, do you Carol?"

A bright smile split Carol's face as she laughed. "That's not even the half of what I've said to Jimmy in our years together. I was being gentle with you."

"That was gentle?"

"Would you prefer not gentle?"

"No, ma'am." Gen laughed a bit. "But I will think about it. I won't make any promises, but I will at least think about it."

Carol reached out to pat Gen's arm. "Oh honey, I know you will."

Forty

For the next few weeks, Gen couldn't get Carol's words out of her head. Never in her life had anyone spoken to her with such forthrightness. On one hand, who was Carol to look into her life and demand change? She'd survived the impossible—escaping her abusive husband and building a life for herself. Gen had the right to build the life she wanted, even one that included lots of men.

But Carol was right. The rotating cast of gentleman wasn't raising her worth in her daughter's eyes, and that was what really mattered. If she'd really given everything up for that girl, the least she could do is act like it.

Staring at herself in the mirror, Gen said to the aging reflection, "All right. I'll change. No more men. For Katherine." Then with grim determination, she colored her lips with her a matronly mauve, put her hair up into a tight bun and walked out the door to work.

Immediately, Gen tried to change. She threw away her cigarettes and avoided the alcohol in the cupboard. Katherine had her own full life, so Gen filled hers with Carol and her family. Gen became a fixture of their family, having dinner at their home and accompanying Carol and Jimmy to the Manhattan. Before long, Gen had also met some of their friends, mostly couples, but a couple of handsome, single men.

One man, Hank, kept pushing her for dinner. He just happened to be at the club every time she was and always made conversation. Gen liked the attention, it'd been a long time since she'd been flirted with. And besides, he was easy on the eyes. With his dark eyes, rugged tan skin and his hair slicked back, she couldn't help but watch the way he moved.

It was so wholesome, the way he talked with her. He'd called five times in the past weeks. Gen laughed whenever they spoke, but always turned down his advances.

As time marched on, she felt her reserve weakening. She'd made a promise to herself that she was going to change. One date couldn't hurt. Besides, she reasoned, she was turning from her old ways. Hank was different from the other guys. For one, he wasn't married already. And he was interested in a long-term relationship, not a bedroom fling. Finally, after months of badgering, Gen consented.

Before he was to come and pick her up for their first date, Gen was in the bathroom pulling curlers out of her hair. "Mom, are you sure this is a good idea?" Kat sat on the bathroom counter next to Gen. She and Kat had forged a real relationship, sharing with each other some of the ups and downs of their daily lives. Gen looked at her daughter through the mirror's reflection. She recognized the smoothness of the skin and the sleek dark hair from her own youth, but the smile and curious eyes were completely Kat's.

Gen puckered her lips to apply lipstick. "Why wouldn't it be?" Her smile was wide in anticipation. "How will I find anyone if I can't even go out on a date?" Her first date in this new life. "He's taking me to the Club at Sunset Beach. I've never been there before."

"I don't know, Mom," Kat said, her eyes watching Gen primp.

Gen turned to her daughter and said, "Listen, Kat, I'll be fine. I'm not like I was before. I promise." She rested her hand against her daughter's cheek. "Besides, you're starting your senior year of high school next week. You're leaving next year, do you want me to be alone forever?"

Kat sighed, her words reluctant. "I guess not." She checked her own reflection next to her mother's. "Just remember that the Back-to-School Rally is tomorrow morning and I really want you to see me. I'm head cheerleader, remember?"

Gen smiled at her daughter. Building a bond with Kat had been the highlight of the past few months. She worked hard to remember Kat's important events and attend as many as possible. Through shared moments they'd built a real life together, one that included trust and friendship. She wouldn't let a single date with a good-looking man ruin that. "Of course I remember, I'll see you there, bright-eyed and bushy-tailed." She kissed her on the nose and said goodbye. "I shouldn't be out too late. Night."

Gen's date with Hank went better than she'd hoped. The two of them laughed and danced and talked until the wee hours of the morning. She left the club with a smile on her face and the lingering feel of a kiss on her cheek. She couldn't remember the last time she'd had such good fun.

The next week when Hank called her for another date she said yes, without a moment's hesitation. Soon she filled as much of her free time as she could in his presence, pushing both Carol and Kat to the background.

It didn't take long for them to tumble into bed together. And within a month, she'd fallen back into her old pattern. Hank made his first appearance at the house for Sunday dinner.

After he left, Kat cleared the table, dropping dirty dishes on the counter. Fury was evident in her voice as she said, "Mom, what are you doing? I thought you weren't going to do this anymore."

Gen fought to remain calm, but her joy fizzled as she scraped and washed the dinner dishes. "Katherine, honey, I don't expect you to understand." She took a deep breath. "Hank is a good man." She looked up from the sink and peered into her daughter's eyes. With one look at the anger brewing on her face, Gen dropped her eyes back to the suds-filled sink. "He may start spending more time here."

The trivet she carried dropped onto the kitchen floor, clattering loudly. "What?" Kat's voice rose above the din. "Are you sleeping with him?"

"That, young lady, is none of your business. You should be pleased that I've found a worthy man to spend my time with. He's not like the others, I promise. This time it's different."

"But Mom, what are people going to say?"

"It's none of their business and I'm not talking. People will only find out if you tell them." She shot an accusing look to Kat who recoiled from it.

"Are you accusing me of something?"

"Should I be?"

Kat clenched her fists before speaking again. "You haven't heard what I've heard, but your behavior, well, no one approves of it. Sleeping with a man who isn't your husband and drinking and smoking—these are all sins and not allowed."

"Sins? Sounds like you've had a little too much church with your friends. I've read the Bible too and learned that gossiping, lying, cheating, and lusting are sins too. Is anyone condemning those? Or are they just waiting to pick on me?"

"Who's picking on you?"

"You are, using their words against me. I'm your mother Kat, how could you judge me? Don't you remember what we've been through?"

"You mean, how we left Dad? How we packed our bags and ran away? How I haven't spoken to him in seven years because you two made a mess of things? Did you ever stop to think about me? About what it meant for me to leave my Dad?" Gen opened her mouth to speak, but Kat cut her off. "Even if he isn't my real Dad, he's the only one I've known and way better than all these other men who try to chum up with me. I don't need another father. I had a great one."

"Katherine, you must be delusional, he hardly even spoke to you in the months before we left. He was an angry drunk."

"He was my father and you took me away from him." Kat looked down at her wristwatch. "It's getting late, I have homework to finish."

"You aren't running away from this now, Kat."

"Running away? You're running away. You're so scared of people that you can't manage to form a decent relationship. Take Carol Wattson, for instance."

"Carol?! What about her?"

"You finally find a friend down here, a really good woman, and you brush her to the side the moment you meet a man. What kind of friend are you?"

Gen moved around the kitchen and sat down at the kitchen table. Remembering her daughter's innocence, her voice softened. "Kat, honey, I don't want to make you mad or embarrassed, but life is . . ." She paused and searched for words. "Katherine, life's been hard for me. I'm trying to do things right, but I'm still a woman who needs to be loved. You don't have to understand, but I'm your mother, and you need to accept it."

Kat crossed her arms in front of her. "Mother, I . . ." But she closed her mouth and shook her head. After a moment where the silence dropped like a boulder, she looked her mother in the eye, but then turned and walked away.

Although the light faded away from the room when Kat left, Gen stayed in her chair. Her heart felt leaden and shattered. Katherine was going to make her choose between her own happiness and her daughter's approval.

Her head sunk down onto the table. It had always been the two of them against the world, at least that's what Gen thought. Maybe they weren't as connected as she'd hoped. Kat spent a lot of time with her friends, but she was still her mother.

She just had to hold on to that. Kat would come around. She'd learn to like Hank. He was different from the others. It would be different this time.

Forty-One

The kitchen curtains were pulled shut against the windows. The rain pounded against them. A constant drumming. The noise angered Gen. How dare the weather interrupt her foul mood. At least the sun didn't mock her today. The counter was covered with dirty dishes. A half-empty bottle of gin sat next to her empty tumbler on the table. She couldn't tear her eyes away from the place where the red stirring straw met the melting ice cubes.

She been cursed to a life of misery. Surely, that must be it, there was no other way to explain this. This wasn't supposed to happen. How on earth did this happen?

She sat in the dark, content to allow it to mingle with the growing darkness in her soul.

She turned her straw which made the ice clink against the glass. The clock marked time with its incessant tock of the second hand.

Tick.

Tock.

Tick.

Tock.

The noise raised her ire. First the rain, now the clock mocked her with its keeping of time. A primal, guttural scream rose up inside her. "Ahh!" she yelled as she picked up her tumbler and threw it at the clock, shattering it against the wall. The rage gave way to bitter tears.

She didn't care about the tears or the mess on the floor or the drops of water rolling down the wall. She didn't care about any of it at all.

And she still had to tell Katherine.

This was going to ruin everything. Gen fought for hope. She and Kat had been through so much. She'll be angry, but only for a while, Gen was confident it wouldn't last long.

They'd get through this, together. Kat would forgive her.

She looked up at the nagging clock. Katherine would be home soon, fresh and beaming from a day of school and friends. Life held so much promise for her growing daughter. Gen swallowed her bitter envy.

Her movements while waiting were few, just a new glass for the table and kicking the shards of the last one into a pile near the wall.

She forced the ticktock of the clock to drown out all other sound until she heard Kat's key scraping the dead bolt on the front door. The door opened and closed. Feet walked down the hall. A bag thumped onto the floor. A light flicked on. Feet walked back down the hall into the kitchen. She walked straight to the refrigerator, bending low to see what was inside.

"Hello, Katherine."

Katherine jumped up to see her mother sitting at the kitchen table, turning her empty tumbler between her hands. "Mother!" Kat said, "What're you doing here? Aren't you supposed to be at work?"

Gen focused on the glass with ice in it. "I took the afternoon off," Gen said. She stared harder into the glass, hoping more gin would appear. The liquid was so soothing. She was disconnected from the present, she didn't want to be here having this conversation.

"Is something wrong, Mother? Are you okay?" Indifferent, Kat turned her back to Gen while looking through the fruit bowl.

"I took some time off to visit the doctor," Gen said. "I haven't been feeling well lately." Gen sighed when she finished her sentence. Feeling unwell wasn't even half of it.

Kat's head snapped at the sharp angle of genuine concern. "I'm sorry, Mother, I didn't know. Can I do anything to help?"

"No, Kat, you can't. I just have to let it run its course."

Kat started peeling the thick skin off her orange. "How long will that take, a couple days?"

Gen took a deep breath. She didn't want to utter these next words and open Pandora's box.

Gen was still silent when Kat looked up, "Mom?"

"No, about seven more months, after that I should be okay." Gen watched Kat to gauge her reaction.

Kat tilted her head a bit and focused on her mother. "I'm sorry, what was that you said?"

Gen stared at her beautiful daughter. This was the moment when she was going to discover how loyal Kat was. She took a deep breath and said, "Kat, I'm going to have a baby." Gen dropped her face and refused to meet her daughter's eyes. "I'm a few months along. I wanted you to know before anyone could see it in my clothes. They're starting to get a bit tight"—Gen paused. "The baby should arrive this coming summer."

Kat's eyes flashed and her lips began to quiver. "Of all the things," she said. Her icy tone chilled the air. "How could you be so irresponsible? This is what happens to girls at my school, not my mother." She clenched her jaw and bit back her words. Kat ran out of the kitchen to her room where she slammed the door behind her.

After only a few minutes, the door opened again. Gen perked up to the sound of Kat's footsteps, but they just walked to the front door. Kat's voice called, "I'm going to Anne's." The door opened and closed and she was gone.

Gen, so deep in her own despair, couldn't move. She sat at the kitchen table. Although she remained motionless, her mind swirled with thoughts. She'd devastated her daughter. Getting rid of this baby was out of the question, it wasn't worth the risk. But she couldn't care for another child. Kat was off to college next year, it'd be like starting all over again. She had no desire to do that again.

Her thoughts floated back to that quiet conversation with the doctor at the hospital all those years ago. Dr. Henderson said she'd never have any more kids. She and Peter had tried so hard and nothing ever happened. A baby would have saved her marriage in the first place. The image of a happy family of four flashed through the room. Gen watched as it floated through the room and vanished into the air.

Hank would have to be told. She had a sinking suspicion fatherhood was not something he wanted. Gen sat in her chair with the rain hammering the windows. The wind had picked up too. The house had grown cold in the rainy darkness. The emptiness made it colder.

"I hope Kat comes home soon." Out loud to an empty room, she declared with confidence she didn't feel, "We'll get through this together; we always do."

Forty-Two

n the middle of the night Gen lay awake in her empty bed. When she heard the front door open relief poured through her. She'd been so worried that Kat would never forgive her and return. The closing click raised her hope.

She tossed and turned throughout the night, wondering about the future. A baby at her age? She could hide underneath her clothes for a while. Florida winter was coming so she could get away with sweaters and bulkier clothing. But that would only buy her a few months. After a few months no amount of tricky clothing will hide a pregnant body.

Going to work tomorrow could be like every other day. She wouldn't have to let anyone know for some time. Her heart started to calm. She had time to figure out what to do, one or two months at least. She fell into an emotionally exhausted sleep.

In the morning, she and Kat moved as passing ships. Gen put on her bravest face, trying to strike up conversation, but Kat was tight-lipped.

"Do you have anything special at school today?"

"No."

"Are you cheering at a game tonight?"

Kat blew out a frustrated sigh. "No, it's Tuesday. Games are on Friday night."

"What time will you be home tonight?"

Kat just moved around the kitchen gathering what she needed for breakfast and lunch.

"Do you have any other meetings this week?" Gen was desperate for connection. Anything to know Kat was still with her. "Any church meetings?"

Kat slammed her books down on the table. "How dare you!" Her voice was full of anger. "You never cared about any of my things before. And now that you've gotten into this mess, now you care about me?"

Gen lifted her hand to Kat's, resting on her schoolbooks, and said, "What are you talking about? I've always cared about you, you're my daughter."

"Is this so that way you don't make the same mistakes and ruin another life?"

"How have I ruined your life?" Her heart crashed within her. Although things had been tough, she never set out to ruin Kat's life. Tears came to her eyes, but she didn't have the strength to put on a brave face. She sat at the table as the tears rolled down her face.

Kat just snorted. "Sorry, Mother, I have to go catch the bus or I'm going to be late." She turned her head away from her mother, grabbed her books and ran out the door.

Gen sank into a chair. After a moment staring into her cup of coffee, she rose slowly. It was time to get ready for work, whether she wanted to go or not.

If only there was a place like Bethany House where she could hide for the duration of her pregnancy. She laughed when she recalled her initial humiliation and anger at being sent away. But while there, she was hidden away from society's judgment and surrounded by people who supported her. How she could use something like that right now. Mrs. Skloot would know what to do.

Gen laughed as she tightened her belt. She still thought of that dear woman as Mrs. Skloot, not Beverly.

The next weeks in the Ryder house passed in icy silence. Gen returned to her normal routine of work and socializing, nothing else seemed to make sense to do. Maybe in doing what she always did an answer would come to her. Kat held onto her anger and spent as few words as possible in conversations with her mother.

As October turned into November, slightly cooler weather ruled the days in mid-central Florida. It wasn't quite cool enough, but she could claim that her Florida blood couldn't handle temperatures cooler than seventy degrees. Gen hid her growing belly under swing coats and light sweaters.

She gave the matter of disposing of the baby a lot of thought. She'd done it before, but it had come at too high a personal cost. A few discreet inquiries revealed that practices hadn't changed much in the intervening years. She'd asked around and learned the name of a doctor that would help her if she wanted. She even drove around town to find the office. Once she found it, she drove by it every day for a week, but never did she gather enough courage to stop and walk in. More than that, something was holding her back.

She resigned herself; she was going to carry this baby for her entire pregnancy. But then what?

As much as she tried to hide her growing belly, Gen could feel the stares as she walked down the street. She'd never hidden who she was before. But shame crept into her stride with lowered head and hunched shoulders. No longer was her smile defiant and welcoming, now she hid her face. People had figured out her secret, they whispered about her as she walked by, covering laughter with their hands.

When Hank finally broke things off, Gen cried. Not because she was so in love with Hank, but because now she was alone. She was doomed to be alone forever. The finality of her situation hit her like a ton of bricks.

And there was nothing to save her from it.

Forty-Three

The week of Thanksgiving, Carol called to invite Gen and Kat to their home for Thanksgiving dinner. Pregnant or not, Gen was always welcome in their home. But Gen knew she'd do better to have dinner by herself at the Sunset Grill watching the sun sink below the horizon at the rooftop restaurant. She wanted no part of Carol's judgment right now. Gen didn't have any answers and wasn't willing to face Carol until she did.

After Gen had dressed herself for dinner with no one, she peeked into Kat's room. "Honey, are you sure you don't want to come have dinner with me at the restaurant?"

"I told you already, I'm going to the Millers." She sounded so weary for a teenager. A deep sigh escaped her chest. "I wish you would come with me to Anne's house. They'd love to have you come." Kat snapped the lid of a hard-topped suitcase.

Gen frowned. A suitcase was a bit drastic for a weekend. Usually, Kat just packed a backpack for her time at the Miller's house. Leaning against the doorframe, she asked her daughter, "What are you doing?"

"Packing a few things." Kat stood and looked her mother in the eyes. "Mother, I'm going to stay with Anne for a while."

The comment passed by Gen without notice. Kat often stayed the night at the Millers. "That's nice, honey. Will you be home after the weekend?"

"No, Mother, I'll be home in the summer, after school ends." The icy words hung in the air. Kat straightened and held the suitcase in her hand. "But I'll come home every Sunday for dinner with you, if you'd like."

Gen remained in her place, unsure of how to acknowledge Katherine's words. In front of her stood her little girl, like she was on the first day of school. Determined to do it on her own. But now, she was determined to leave home. Gen stared at the suitcase, knowing she hadn't enough words to convince Kat to stay.

"Is that all Mother? You don't have anything to say? 'Kat, don't go.' 'Kat, I'm sorry.'" The anger rose in Kat's voice through her body. "Do you even care? What they say about you? What they assume about me?"

Gen's anger boiled over in an instant. "You care about what they say? Those hypocrites who judge us without knowing who we are, what we've been through? They preach love out of their mouths, but practice condemnation."

Kat stared at her mother. "You don't know them the way I do," she shot back. "They're people who love me and you couldn't care less, about me, about them, about anybody other than yourself."

"Listen to you, Miss High and Mighty. Sounds like you've done a good job joining their side. There isn't room for a sinner like me, is there?"

Kat closed her eyes against her mother's words. Pain flashed across her face. "There's plenty of room for you. You just don't want to be included. You can't be special if you act like everyone else."

"Kat, if you really knew the life I've had, you'd understand. But if you aren't even willing to see, how can I believe any other person in the world will either?"

"But Mom, I do understand. I've lived it with you. From the moment we left Wisconsin, it's been the two of us together."

Shame welled in Gen's heart. Tears pricked at her eyes. Her hands dropped to her abdomen. "Kat, it's too late, look at me. I'm an adulterous woman, alone. I can't step foot in a church, I have no friends to speak of. There's nothing left for me." Her spirit sank and the tears flowed. "If only you could understand."

"Mother, it's you who doesn't understand."

"Well, I don't, because I've heard enough of them—people forcing their beliefs on me, telling me how to live. I'll tell anyone who wants to listen my story and they'll come around. They'll see it my way."

Kat sighed. "No, they'll realize how miserable and sad you are. But I won't stay here and be miserable with you. I promise I'll come live here after the baby is born." She turned to walk out the door. Stopping in the doorway next to Gen, she said, "I'm sorry, Mother, for both of us." Then she walked away.

After the click of the door and the rev of a waiting car's engine, Gen's knees gave way and her body slid down the wall until she was sitting on the floor. As her head sank into her arms, she whispered to the silence, "No, Kat, don't go."

The holidays passed quietly in the Ryder house. With Katherine gone, Gen did her best to feign contentment. She tried not to care, but every kick or bit of heartburn reminded her that she had lost her daughter's presence. She was lonely. Her house was dark and cold without Kat's presence.

Kat came home once a week to share a meal at their worn kitchen table. The meal was shared out of loyalty and obligation, not love or friendship. Gen did her best, preparing what she thought were Kat's favorite foods: pot roast, lasagna, meatloaf.

Trying to make amends, she bought Kat little gifts. Standing at the makeup counter at Woolworth's, her hand grazed over the row of lipstick tubes. All the colors were bright, not what Kat liked. But that didn't matter, a small gift would begin to heal things between them. Indecision gripped her. But what if she chose wrong again? She remembered the look of disappointment that crossed Kat's face when Gen had handed her a pair of white patterned stockings. Gen loved the zigzag pattern. Kat took a look at them in her hand and rolled her eyes a bit. Her voice was anything but excited when she said, "Wow, thanks." Even remembering the sound of Kat's voice ripped Gen's heart apart.

She just grabbed a tube of Cherry Red Cover Girl. Kat would accept it, just out of politeness. At this point, Gen was desperate for any nicety from her. Little luxuries that show her love would help Kat understand how sorry she really was.

Despite her attempts at earning pardon, Gen felt her daughter pulling further away. Sitting at the table on a cold February Sunday afternoon, Gen pulled out a wrapped gift and pushed it in her daughter's direction.

Kat's voice was limp as she said, "Thanks, Mother." She opened the wrapped package, but her eyes were dull and disinterested.

Gen watched in anticipation, knowing this present would be the one. She'd spent hours perusing the bookstore shelves looking for just the right book. Since she wasn't a reader herself, this decision had been difficult. But she knew, this one would reach Kat's heart.

The briefest flicker of a smile crossed Kat's face as she opened a new copy of *To Kill a Mockingbird*. Her face lit up as she thumbed through the pages. Her joy was obvious.

Gen'd done it. A smile as bright as the sun plastered her face.

Kat looked up at her mother. Her smile disappeared and a stern look replaced it. She set the book down next to her plate. "Mother, I've made a decision," she said.

Gen's heart quickened. Looking up in anticipation, she tried not to hope Kat was coming home.

Kat gulped. "The baby is due at the end of May, in a few months, right?" She stabbed at a piece of pot roast and wiped it through the gravy on her plate.

Unable to speak, Gen nodded.

"I'm going to go live with Grandma Ryder in Wisconsin until after the baby arrives. I'll be back at the beginning of summer and then I'll stay here and go to community college so I can help you."

Gen's heart plummeted. This was unexpected. She needed Kat near her during these next few months. She didn't want to go through the end of this pregnancy and childbirth alone, again.

"Oh." The words formed on Gen's lips, but no sound came out. Gen's shoulders hunched in and she wrapped her arms around her growing belly, as if she'd been punched. Deep sadness pulsed through her. Looking up, she saw Kat had just returned to eating her food, not looking at Gen, not watching for a reaction. Instant resentment filled Gen's heart. "Not able to stay and face the truth of who I am, so you're going to run away to my parents' house?" Her eyes glazed over in anger. "You're no better than I am then, are you?

"You want me to stay here and live with your shame? Anything is better than staying here. You have no idea what I face, what people say to me because of you."

"You think I don't know? You think I haven't heard?" Gen laughed short, bitter laughs. "I hear the judgment every day. I feel it in the way people look at me. But I can't run away from it, no matter how badly I want to."

"But I'm not you." Kat lowered her head and wouldn't look Gen in the face. Her voice was whisper quiet as she said, "I never want to be you."

Gen recoiled as if she'd been slapped. The words punctured her heart. She'd tried to be the best mother she could.

"Fine, run away, see if I care." Gen flicked at her daughter with her hand and laughed, using mockery to mask her pain. "What do you hope to find in Wisconsin? The open, waiting arms of a soft grandmother? At first she'll wrap you up, but it won't take long for her to eat you up with her criticism. Just like me, you'll never be good enough, no matter how hard you try."

"She's already said I could come, even sent me a bus ticket," Kat said. "I've made arrangements with my teachers. Everything's set. I leave next Saturday."

Gen shook her head. She had no way to change her daughter's mind. She was lost to her already. Pushing herself away from the table, Gen put her head down and screamed, a deep guttural scream, emptying her rage and sadness into the empty air. Kat kept her face down. "I can't believe you, Katherine Ryder. Fine, run away, see how my mother treats you. But when she's pushed you away too, don't say I didn't warn you." With a loud clatter of dishes, Gen removed herself from the table. Before she walked away, she said as a final snub, "You know, I've never even really liked pot roast anyway."

The following Saturday Kat came home to pack some more things before heading to the bus station.

Gen's heart screamed for Kat not to go. It was horrible mistake for them to be separated by that much distance. The world wasn't safe for Gen without Kat. *Please stay! I don't want to have this baby alone.* "Do you have everything?"

Her voice was as calm as she could make it. "Here's some money in case you need anything."

"You can call anytime."

Gen held together a facade of passivity during the drive to the bus station. She kept her face grim, her eyes locked ahead, she refused to make a scene. She forced a strength she did not feel. If she was strong, Katherine could be too.

But still, she warred with herself. Maybe weakness would convince Kat that this was the worst decision of her life. If she cried and begged, maybe she wouldn't board that northbound bus.

In her heart, she knew nothing could keep her from going.

So Gen wouldn't do anything, except watch her daughter drive away.

She parked the car in a stall at the Greyhound Station. The morning was still young and seaside fog filled the air. She shivered at the grayness. The moist, heavy air seeped in through the cracks in the door.

Their goodbye was tight and restrained. Neither Gen nor Kat betrayed any emotion other than indifference.

The car door thudded shut behind her. Gen watched in stunned silence as Kat walked away from the car shrouded in mist. For a moment, right in front of the waiting bus, Kat stopped.

Gen's breath caught.

Kat turned and looked back, uncertainty on her face. Kat gripped her suitcase handle and turned back around. Thrusting her head up, she walked onto the bus. The doors closed and she found a seat next to a window. As the bus drove away, Kat gave a small wave out the window, but turned forward before the exhaust from the bus filled the air.

"Stay safe, my baby girl." Gen's head slumped onto the steering wheel as tears rolled down her face.

Kat was gone.

Gen was alone.

Forty-Four

With three months left until the baby arrived, Gen had nowhere to turn. Gen prided herself on being a woman who knew her own mind and had the courage to do whatever she wanted, even in the face of being a social pariah. But this time she was pregnant, single, alone, and middle-aged.

She considered herself a good, strong woman, but she was far from any support network. The last time she had a baby, someone else handled all the details, the doctor's appointments, delivery.

She'd made it so far on her own, depending on her own wits and determination to survive. But with Kat gone off to cry in Grandma's ample bosom, Gen had to admit, she was alone and out of ideas.

There was one person to call, her only hope. The offer to help Gen had always been extended, but she was the last person on earth Gen wanted to call. Actually, there were others Gen would less rather call, but time was running short and she was out of options.

She picked up the phone and called Carol. She was going to be angry at Gen. After becoming involved with Hank, Gen stopped calling Carol or going to the Manhattan. She'd been busy doing other things.

Her hand shook as she held the receiver to her ear. It rang three times. She held the receiver loosely trying to force herself to hang up. After the fifth ring, Gen gulped. No one home. As she lowered the receiver back to the cradle, a familiar voice answered, "Hello?"

She raised it back up to her ear, but her mouth was dry as cotton.

"Hello?"

She swallowed and her nerves returned. "Hello, Carol? This is Gen Ryder. I was wondering if you might be available to have tea some afternoon this week?"

A week later, Gen and Carol sat at Carol's worn, wooden kitchen table. Hot steam rose from the coffee that sat untouched in mugs in front of them. Gen's hands were cupped around her mug, as if the warmth could bring her any sense of sureness. Carol sat waiting for Gen to speak, the sounds of life happening beyond the kitchen.

Gen heard them too, the noises of children playing in other parts of the house. She stared into the hot brown liquid, wondering if her life would ever be normal again.

"Well?" Carol cocked her head toward Gen. "Spill it."

Gen's eyes glistened with tears. "Kat's gone. She left for her grandmas' and won't be back until the summer, so she says."

Carol's eyes spread wide. Her voice was rough, almost like a whisper when she asked. "She in the family way? Gen, I . . ."

"No, not Kat, she's pretty near perfect. She left because she is ashamed of me." Gen's voice was flat, without inflection or tone. "*I* am in the family way, again."

Carol's mouth dropped open as she stared at Gen. Her eyes dropped to Gen's abdomen where a bump could be seen under the layers of clothes and swing coat. Gen knew how to dress to conceal what she wanted hidden.

"You see, Hank and I . . ."

"Oh, I know exactly what happened. What's been happening. How could you be so irresponsible? Gen, you knew this was a possibility." As Carol talked, the anger grew in her voice.

Gen dropped her head, staring down at nothing. Shamed washed through her. "I know. I've messed everything up. Kat's gone. Hank left. I'm alone with a baby that I can't possibly care for. I'm too old to start over." She took a shallow breath. "I'm not going to a home again. I have a life, a home. I'm a grown woman."

Carol took an exaggerated sip of her coffee, picking up her coffee mug and holding it to her lips while she thought. "What then, do you propose to do?"

Gen continued through her options, which weren't many. "Well, I know what I won't do. I won't take care of it again. I will never do that again. It almost killed me the first time." Gen took a deep breath, cleansing her lungs. "I'm going to carry this baby and then give it up for adoption."

"What?!"

"Yes, I've given it a lot of thought. What else is there for me? I'm too old. Kat's going off to college next year, I'm almost done mothering. I can't raise a baby. Surely there is someone who dreams of a perfect little baby boy who could raise him for me."

"Oh, it's a boy? You know this?" Carol's voice held the defensive snarl of cat protecting her litter. "You think it's going to be that easy? Just give birth and hand a baby away?"

"What do you want me to do? Keep him? I just can't. I'm done."

"But you don't know what you're doing? Giving away a baby is like having a piece of your heart torn out from you."

"That may be, but I have no other option." This wasn't the way Gen thought it would go. Carol was supposed to be supportive of her and this decision. Of all people, Carol knew what this decision cost. Gen reached her hand across the table and lay it on Carol's arm. "Carol, please, I'm all alone. I need your help."

Carol agreed to help, but Gen still had a few more months to wait for baby's arrival. As the weeks passed and her condition became more apparent, Gen steeled herself for the whispered comments and sideways glances. She didn't go out anymore, so her time spent at home was filled with quiet boredom, until she remembered her old carpet bag and sewing basket with the patterns from her time at Bethany House. Maybe something in there could help her get through the next few months. If nothing else, she would have something to do with her hands to keep her moderately busy.

Digging through them, she found the beginnings of a smocked baby dress and some patterns for maternity wear. Having nothing better to do, she picked up the baby dress. She knew she would never see this baby in it, but it was soothing to do something useful. As her hands pushed the needle through the folds of cloth, a resolute sadness filled her and settled in her chest. All of a sudden, Gen was gasping for air as thick tears rolled down her face. She set the dress down and let the tears fall, staining her cheeks.

Her head stared straight ahead while her brain ran through the twisted path she'd walked to arrive at this place. She'd fought so hard to keep Kat, endured that year at Bethany House, which turned out to be the best year of her life. Loved and supported, the women at Bethany House made her believe she could be a mother on her own. And then Peter and love and marriage and heartache. The baby she didn't keep. Life would have been so different if she'd made a different choice. But then, she had to leave Peter, a loveless marriage was not a place she was content to stay. All of that led to here, where Gen found herself now, alone, and pregnant and awaiting an appointment at Children's Health Services to talk about giving her baby to a couple who wanted one.

Gen gave up the pretense of sewing or doing anything and just sat in the chair until Carol arrived to take her to her interview. There was nothing to live for now anyway.

Forty-five

The time had come. The pain had started in her lower back during the night. At first, Gen just thought the weight of the baby made her back ache like every other night, but by midnight Gen knew it was different. She and Carol had a plan. Gen would labor at home as long as she could before calling Carol to take her to the hospital. Carol would call Children's Health Services too, to let them know as well.

The spasms came at random intervals. Gen started pacing up and down the hallway like a tiger at the zoo pacing at the edge of its cage. With each spasm in her back, she leaned against the wall and growled a low growl. Gen thought she had a high tolerance for pain, but as the spasm moved from her back to wrap around and include her belly, she could hardly stand anymore. She'd lost all sense of time, just that it was still dark outside.

It didn't matter anymore, she groped her way down the hallway to the phone where Carol picked up after only two rings.

"It's time," Gen said through gritted teeth. She hung up the phone and let the waves of pain wash over her, she knew there was no fighting it. How long it took to get to the hospital, Gen didn't know, but it seemed like both a couple of minutes and forever before Gen found herself in a bright hospital room being told to push. Screams of effort emanated from somewhere near Gen, she couldn't be sure where, she didn't recognize them as her own. But after a few sessions of pushing, she heard the squall of a new baby and she lay down, exhausted.

In a few minutes, a wrapped bundle was placed in her arms. "Congratulations, it's a healthy baby boy."

Despite the exhaustion, Gen cradled the baby in her arms, unwrapping the blanket to discover ten perfect pink fingers and ten long pink toes. His mouth was a perfectly formed 'O' and his dark eyes searched for hers. When he started rooting, asking for food, Gen jolted. This baby was not for her. He was beautiful and perfect, but there was a lovely, longing couple in the waiting room marking the long and anxious minutes.

His rooting was becoming a bit desperate. Gen looked to the nurse. "Okay, it's time. Can you get them." The nurse nodded at Gen and walked out of the room.

In her final minute with this perfect little one, Gen wrapped him up in his blanket and kissed his little head. She held him close and whispered, "This is the best life I can offer you, little one."

The couple walked into the room, contained excitement radiated off of them. The woman, a sweet young thing with perfect blonde hair stood a few feet back from the hospital bed. Her hands reached out for the baby, but quickly pulled back in. A nervous laugh escaped her lips.

Gen followed with her own nervous laugh. But with a final kiss to his forehead, she offered him forward, giving him to the man and woman who would raise her little boy as their own. He would never know that he was the fruit of another womb, but he would be loved by three people for as long as they lived.

Forty-six

The weeks following the birth of the baby passed, that's how Gen saw them. They just were. She slept, stared at the TV, and picked at the casserole that Carol had left for her. Nothing held any flavor or temptation for her. If she fell asleep and never woke up again, no one would be saddened at the loss of Gen Ryder.

While her breasts and belly ached with healing, Gen held back every tear. She had cried all she needed to before the baby was born. She had built a wall around her heart as she handed him over to his mom and dad. That time in her life was over, it was time to move on.

She'd sent a telegram to her parents to let them know about the birth. She couldn't bear the thought of listening to their pity. Antoinette would gloat about Gene's decision-making and Kat would parrot it. She had no allies left.

It was a surprise when the delivery man handed her the mail. Her daughter's neat handwriting jumped off the envelope. Tearing it open, she read the brief note, her heart pounding in her chest. "Mother, I'm coming home. I'll be there on the last Thursday in May. I hope you get this letter in time." Those were the last words she ever expected to read. Although part of her she held hope eternal, she never really believed that Kat would ever come back home.

Gen knelt to the ground next to the letter. Afraid it was a deep longing turned into hallucination, the cream paper crinkled as she crushed it between her hands. For the first time in four long months, joy coursed through her veins. This had been the first word from Kat since she stepped on the bus four months ago. Katherine was coming home!

For Gen the next few days were full of preparation. She moved as quickly as she could, but she still ached. Her body hadn't bounced back like it did last time she'd delivered a baby. Eighteen years of hard living had taken its toll on her body. And she had three days to make the house ready.

Still she managed to get to the store to fill the cupboards and the fridge. She even cleaned Kat's room a bit, repositioning falling posters and wiping away dust. Taking an entire day, Gen even washed all of Kat's bedding.

Every couple of hours, Gen took a break, sat down and put her feet up. The doctor had said recovering from the trauma of birth took time. But she didn't have time to rest. *My girl is coming home! Everything has to be perfect. She has to know how much I've missed her.*

For each of those three nights, Gen's entire body was a bundle of nerves that kept her from sleeping. She tossed and turned as she imagined the homecoming.

When Thursday morning arrived, Gen was a wreck. As she straightened the kitchen from her breakfast dishes, she glanced up at the clock. Suddenly she realized she had no idea when Kat's bus would arrive. Panic set in as she worried about how Kat would get home. In a hurry, Gen grabbed her purse and her keys. As she raced out the door, she stopped, having no idea where Kat would arrive. Dropping her purse where she stood, she collapsed to the ground and started to sob, feeling powerless and out of control. The pressure of the past few months bore down on her. She had done all of it alone, with only Carol there for support.

She had navigated the uncertainty of delivering a baby. When her labor started, she had walked into the maternity ward with her head held high, ignoring the looks and whispers from the nurses. She did it all with forced strength.

But now, her first baby was coming home and she didn't have to be strong by herself anymore. Kat would be her strength.

Gen sat on the couch nursing her fourth cup of tea. She stared out the front window, watching the birds flit in and out of the trees. Gen had opened every curtain letting the late afternoon sun fill the house with light.

The ticktock of the clock was the only noise. Gen was fearful to even breathe, she didn't want to do anything to jinx Kat's homecoming. Setting her teacup down, she patted her hair. Oh, I forgot to do it this morning. She rose and hurried to the bathroom to freshen up, spraying a new coat of hair spray and applying fresh lipstick. She stood in front of her closet for long minutes choosing the perfect outfit, one that showed that she'd recently given birth, but still had time to care about her appearance. Although most of her clothes still didn't fit, she found a skirt that was just right.

Five minutes later she was back on the couch.

Her heartbeat loud enough that the sound of it in her ears drowned out the rhythm of the clock. She started to chew her nails. They weren't lacquered like usual, in her recovery she hadn't had the energy to do them.

Not knowing how else to occupy her time, she bowed her head and closed her eyes. Her lips moved but no sound escaped her lips. She squeezed her eyes shut focusing on her whispered words.

The roll of tires on gravel was quiet, but Gen's ears had been waiting anxiously for that sound. She picked up her head when she heard the car door open. Footsteps up the walkway. Gen stood.

For a moment, nothing.

Then the turn of the knob and the pushing in of the door. Gen flew to the doorway where she wrapped Katherine up in a tight hug. "Oh my baby, you're home." Gen burst into tears on her daughter's shoulder.

Kat wiped tears from her eyes too. She hadn't realized what this separation from her mom for all these months had really cost her or her mother.

Genevieve stepped back from her daughter and took a look. "Well, at least she fed you, didn't she? She's never happy unless everyone has food in their bellies." Gen laughed.

"Oh Mom, I'm so glad to see you, so glad to be home." She stepped away from her and took her own long glance. "You look fantastic!"

Gen blushed and said, "Thank you."

Kat looked around, "Where is the little one? Do I have a brother or a sister? What's their name? I can't wait to meet him or her."

Gen's voice sank, "Did no one tell you?" She looked from side to side and asked, "My parents didn't tell you?"

"Tell me what?" Kat's feeling of worry started to rise again. Something bad happened while she had been gone. "What is it?"

"Kat, come and sit with me on the couch. We need to talk."

Kat tried to hold an unnamed fear at bay while she walked to the couch. "What is it? Are you all right?"

Gen sat next to her and tried to figure out how best to tell her.

A wave of realization washed through Kat, "Oh no, it's the baby, isn't it? Is it okay? Is it dead?" She fought to hold back tears.

Gen found her words as she held her daughter's hand and heard the fear in her voice. Calmly, she said, "Oh no, he's not dead. He's just fine."

"Phew." The sound of her relief was audible.

Gen continued slowly.

"While you were gone, I didn't have anyone to turn to so I called Carol. She and I started meeting. She became a real support during the end of my pregnancy. Just before the baby was due, she connected me with an agency that helps women like me."

"Kat, there's no easy way to tell you this." She took a deep breath. "I gave him up for adoption shortly after he was born."

"You what!?" Kat was suddenly filled with conflicting emotions: fear, rage, relief. "What do you mean you gave him up for adoption? Do you mean I have a brother?"

"You do . . . I mean . . . did." Gen corrected herself. Turning toward her daughter she said, "Listen, Kat, when you were gone, I wasn't sure you were ever going to come back. And I already knew that this pregnancy wasn't the right thing for me"—she faltered—"well, I knew that there wasn't any other way. The agency helped me find a wonderful couple who wanted a baby."

"After he was born, they came to the hospital. You should have seen them, Kat. They loved him from the minute they heard his squeaky newborn cry. And I loved him so much that I had to give him a better life than what I could offer."

Tears rolled down Kat's cheeks. "But what about me, Mom? Didn't you think about me?"

"Yes, I did. Every single day. And I realized that you're going off to college and leaving me again. I won't burden you with my responsibility. You need to have the opportunities that I never got."

"But Mom, I said I would come home and help you. I meant that. Can't we bring him back? Please?"

"I'm sorry, Kat, what's done is done. They've had him now for a couple weeks. They're a lovely couple named Harriet and Steven. They had tried for so long to have a baby and were so happy. They let me name him Henry. It's such a good strong name."

Kat cried openly now.

"You may not understand this right now, Katherine, but I did this for our good." She stayed with her daughter on the couch as she cried for the next few minutes. Then after a time, she rose and went to the kitchen and fixed her daughter a cup of hot mint tea.

She brought it back to the couch and held it until Kat was ready to take it. When she thought Kat was ready to talk, she brightly asked, "So, how was your time at my parents' house?"

"Mother, you can't just change the subject like that. Why didn't you call me or tell me or make sure I knew?" Kat cried out. "I defended you to your mother, I yelled at her that all the things she said about you were wrong. I left to come here to be here to help you with the baby." Kat's face was red with anger.

"You're here now. We can help each other," Gen said. "It's always been you and me, Katherine. That's how it should be." She held her hands out to her daughter. "Can't you see, I did it for you, so you wouldn't have to carry this burden, so you wouldn't be humiliated every moment of the day."

"How dare you!" Kat's voice rose. "This was your choice. You made it for you: You've only ever thought about you. This was about you, your convenience, your life. You couldn't bear to live with the consequence, couldn't live with another child raining on your parade. You can barely manage to live with the one you did keep."

Katherine grabbed her bag and ran back out the door. She had nowhere to go, but she didn't care. She just ran, down the street, across the block. Tears blinded her eyes, but her footsteps ran familiar paths. In a few moments, Kat had made her way to Anne's house where she dissolved into a weeping mess.

As she poured out her broken heart to Anne, her mom overheard. "Katherine, you don't have to go back if you don't want to," she comforted.

Hope bloomed in her eyes even though doubt still remained, "But she's my mother. How can I possibly leave her?"

"Well, I didn't suggest leaving her. She's had more than her fair share of that in her lifetime." She paused to think for a moment. "How about this? Stay here tonight, and get your bearings straight. Then call home tomorrow, and see what you can work out."

Kat nodded dumbly, feeling numb to another heartache caused by her mom. She stood, walked to the picture window, and stared out it, down the street toward the house where she knew her mother was doing the same thing.

Epilogue

Katherine stood in front of her mother's house for the first time in twenty years. Her hand rested on the knob. She sighed.

Katherine hadn't wanted to come, but her husband convinced her of the good of it. "She's your mother and she could be dying. You need to make your peace." Even now, she knew he was right. She needed peace.

But she couldn't go straight to the hospital.

First, she needed to go home. She needed to step foot in the house that was never a home. Maybe, in walking through those closed off rooms and blocked memories, Kat could make sense of her childhood. The mingled scents of heavy perfume and layered dust assaulted her nose, making it wrinkle in irritation. Thick layers of dust on the shelves and dirty dishes in the sink. The heavy curtains were drawn shut, blocking out the summer sunshine making everything gloomy and sad.

She roamed from room to room opening and shutting doors. The noise echoed throughout the house, protesting the intrusion of a stranger. She walked into her old room and found the furniture exactly as she left it, but all the surfaces were now covered with boxes and packages. Examining more closely, she found they were full of costume jewelry, Christmas decorations, and kitchen gadgets. Kat rifled through the nearest box and found a brand-new plug-in wok, the invoice dated six years before. "What a waste. All her hard-earned money on junk she's never going to use."

The room she entered last was her mother's. In the intervening years, Gen had married a man named Alfred Taylor. Kat had spoken with him on the phone since her arrival in Florida. He was at the hospital standing vigil over her mother. She tiptoed through the room, afraid of disturbing it. Yet as she stood next to the dresser, curiosity overtook her sense of privacy. She started to open the drawers, fingering her mother's things. At the feel of an ivory silk slip, she had a sudden overwhelming craving to know everything and to understand.

She wanted to know who her mother was and why there'd been no meaningful contact in the past twenty years. Through her own wedding and the birth of her children, Gen had not been present. No letters, no phone calls. Only an occasional gift. A bitter laugh filled the air as she recalled the presents: boxes overflowing with baby clothes or a box of Christmas oranges. Those oranges filled the house with the fresh scent of citrus, but each bite felt like a betrayal of her own dignity. When Kat walked out the door twenty years before, she'd washed her hands of her mother. But not entirely, she never stopped wanting to know her, to make her proud, to be her friend. It took years to realize that Gen had never been capable of loving anyone but herself.

She walked into her mother's closet. As she expected it was full of fashionable clothes. Katherine looked at her own capris and T-shirt and felt underdressed for her mother's closet. After pawing through the dresses hanging on the rod, she peeked into every box on the floor. In them she found shoes for every occasion. The top shelf was lined with a mishmash of containers.

Among the nondescript white shoe boxes, Gen found three curious things: an old carpetbag, a green sewing basket, and a beaten-up old hat box. The sewing basket was exactly what Gen expected. In fact, she had a very similar vintage basket at home next to her sewing machine.

The embroidery of the carpet bag was bumpy under her fingers. Opening it, she found thin papers, discolored and frail with age, pages with sketches and notes about dresses for grown women and little girls. There were even a few half-finished projects. Most beautiful among them was a smocked baby's gown, completely finished but never worn.

Laying the carpetbag aside, she reached for the battered box wrapped in blue floral paper. Her hand shook as she pulled it down off the shelf. She sat down on the floor and set the box in front of her. Opening the box she found it filled with sealed envelopes. She ran her hands through them. The envelopes each bore a name, three names dominated them: Bobby, Peter, and Katherine. Katherine tore open the first letter she saw with her name on it.

Dear Katherine,

Today your daughter was born. What a beautiful day. You must be so happy. I wish I could come and see her. I'm sure that you're going to be a wonderful mother.

I still remember the day that you were born. How much I wanted to hold you and keep you safe from all harm.

There's so much promise in a new life. Treasure every moment with your little girl.

I can think of so many things to tell you about being a mother, but the most important is, don't be me. Love fully and without reserve.

I let bitterness guide my life and now I'm afraid it's too late. Too late for me, too late for us.

But it's not too late for you and your little one. Give her a kiss from her grandma,

Love, Mother

Katherine reread the letter in her hand four times. Tears streamed down her face. Looking over to the hatbox, many sealed envelopes sat unopened. Each one offered her a glimpse into her mother's heart and motivations, revealing more of the truth of her story.

Like a greedy child, she grabbed a handful of letters and started to read. She sat on the floor of the closet until she had read them all. And when she was done, her heart burst with sadness and love for what her mother had lived through.

It was time. After twenty years, Katherine wanted to talk to her mother. Returning all the letters to the hatbox, she stood to leave.

Clutching the hatbox, she gathered her courage and headed out of the house. "Mother, I think it's finally time for us to talk."

Author's Note

The *Unfortunate Life of Genevieve Ryder* is a work of fiction that comes, as most fiction does, from a deeply personal place.

In 2008, the grandmother I met once, but didn't remember, died. About six months later, I received a package from the estate in the mail. Inside was a stack of pictures from the 1960s and a baby's christening gown and shoes that were yellowed with age. There was no note explaining who the people in the pictures were (I knew the woman was my grandma), nor any note telling me who the gown was for. I had few biographical facts for who she was. I thought there might have been a divorce sometime in the 1950s, a time when divorce was largely unheard of. I heard whispers of a second baby besides my mom, but I found no evidence. Then again, I was a child with a vivid imagination and could have easily made up details to fill in the empty photograph in my mind.

I've always wondered who my grandmother really was. I wonder who that baptismal dress was for. I wonder who the man in those photos was, because the only thing I know is that he was not my grandfather. This novel is a spinning of my imagination, but I'm confident none of it is factual. Except one thing: there was anger and hurt, rejection, betrayal, and loneliness in my grandmother's life.

On a historical note, Bethany House is based on the historical Florence Crittenton houses. These homes for unwed mothers were started in the 1890s in New York as homes for prostitutes and other women who found themselves pregnant. The original intent of these homes was to provide for the safety and care of these women, and to equip them to raise their children. Starting in the 1920s the professionalization of social workers and shifts in attitudes toward adoption pushed these homes toward the more commonly known scenario of babies being adopted out. The shift toward adoption instead of intact mother-child pairs became the standard for all Florence Crittenton homes in 1943, although some local homes were able to retain local control.

I found myself wanting Gen to have the opportunity to keep her child in a space that believed she was capable of being a good mother, that would take the time to show her how to succeed against the prejudices of the world. While I'm not sure if a place like Bethany House existed in 1946–47, I'd like to believe it was possible. Stories of girls who were forced to give up their babies for adoption are heart-rending and well-documented. If you would like to read further about this sad history, I recommend *The Girls Who Went Away: The Hidden History of Women Who Surrendered Children for Adoption in the Decades Before Roe v. Wade* by Ann Fessler.

In the middle of his ministry, Jesus was presented with a trap by the religious leaders of the time. Those leaders were looking for a way to condemn him, so they threw in front of him a woman who had been caught in the act of adultery. They surround Jesus and challenge him. The woman has broken the law. The law says the penalty for this is death by stoning. As the story found in John 8 goes, Jesus stoops and starts writing in the dirt with his finger. He then says to the accusers, "All right, but let the one who has never sinned throw the first stone." I imagine silence. Then, one by one, starting with the oldest in the crowd, the men turn away. Soon, Jesus is left alone with the woman (and the crowd who gathered to watch). He looks around and asks, "Where are your accusers? Didn't even one of them condemn you?" She answers, "No, Lord." I imagine the compassion in his eyes, the softness of his voice as he considers this betrayed and broken woman. "Neither do I. Go and sin no more."

That's it. That's all that's written about this encounter. And I have lots of questions about that story. But the main one I come back to is this: what kind of life had she led that brought her to that moment? Was she unhappily married? Was she a widow? Had her husband divorced her? How far had she fallen from the bright-eyed young girl she once was?

What did the gift of forgiveness mean for her in that moment? Not only did she get to keep her life, but she was given the opportunity to start anew, without the guilt of the past laying heavily on her shoulders.

I believe that all of us have stories in our lives—stories of pain, of bad choices, of harming ourselves or others that we love. Personally, I am quite adept at holding onto that pain. But when I do, it threatens to make me inward-focused and bitter, much like Gen. I exclaim, "But I did it all for you," when in fact, I mostly did it to protect myself.

If I had ever met Gen in her later life, I imagine she would have had a "full" life, but her eyes would be empty and her lips full of bitterness. The world was her enemy. Without knowing what she had experienced in her life, it would be so easy to judge her and then to walk away, satisfied in my condemnation of the way she'd lived her life.

But just as Jesus asked the crowd of accusers who surrounded that unnamed woman, he says to me, "If you are without sin, throw the stone of judgment." And I realize I am as broken and guilty as she is. It's just that I've already received the gift of grace that no one offered her. And my condemnation of her is unjust.

So I've written out Gen's story for me and for you as a reminder that we cannot always know the life a person has lived, the choices they have made, the hurts and joys they carry, but we can always choose to offer grace.

To the grandma I never knew: I'm so sorry, and I love you.

Acknowledgments

This story has lived for so long in my head that the reality of having it on paper and in your hands is a bit overwhelming to me. There are circles of people who have surrounded me for years on this journey to publication. Thanks to those who have walked with me through this, whether as a Facebook friend, a newsletter reader, or a person in my physical orbit. I hope this book is equal to your constant belief in me.

In many ways, Gen's story began with a new, nervous friendship with Gail Hanson who, like me, had a story to tell. At the encouragement of her husband, we started weekly writing accountability phone calls. She and I talked about Ruby and Gen and the stories that were growing inside of us. Those times started a sister-like bond that endures even though our lives have been divided across the country. I love you, friend.

Thank you to the very earliest reader of this manuscript, Deb VanDuinen, who read it in sections and cried at the end and made me feel like Gen's story could really be something.

Thank you to C.H.A.P.T.E.R.S. Book Club for reading one of the earliest versions of this book as part of our book club in 2012, for letting me be brave and do scary things while showing me incredible kindness. Betsy, Manda, Andrea, Lisa, Janet, Anne, Heidi, Roberta, and Sarah, I still have the notes of our conversation from 2012. I will be forever grateful for your early belief in me and your willingness to read a very imperfect, sometimes awkward story. (Remember, your version included the roll in the hay, which has mercifully been cut. Really, you guys were the best.)

Like many others, 2020 gave me a chance to bring my writing and dreams back into focus after putting them on the back burner to raise my family. I pulled Gen's story out of the dusty boxes and started over. For the fourth time.

To my cupcakes: April Mack, Susan Park, Sarah Strong, Anthony Wade, and Mel Casilli. Our monthly Zoom calls make me believe that there is a way to make it in this crazy publishing world. I love that I have internet friends! While our writing is the cake we need, your friendship has become the sweetest frosting. (The best cupcake and frosting combo is still a yellow cupcake with chocolate frosting.)

To the many people who have believed and encouraged and read and re-read along the way: Jim Keener, Laura DeGroot, Kelli Burns, Meika Weiss, Gail Hanson, and my students, particularly the class of 2022 (Zach, Asher, Christian, Julia, Erika, Coco, Ceci, Mya, and Anna) and Maddie: your unwavering belief in me kept me going during some pretty hard times. Thank you for reading, for caring, for believing.

To Andrea Robinson and Laura Baker—your willingness to read this story in its end stages helped me to see how Gen's story affects each reader in different ways. Your questions, comments, and clarifications made Gen's story better and stronger. Thanks for seeing her with eyes of compassion and helping her come to life. I owe you each some really great wine.

To Patrice, who has become the dearest of friends through the miles and adventures we have walked. I love how our lives have weaved together over the years. Our walks have been life-giving as we traverse miles around our neighborhood. Thanks for not letting me live in my own head too much and for (usually) having good counsel. I am so thankful for you.

To my kids—Josh, Kai, Jaxx, and Mali—you are the best of me. You make me more proud than any mom deserves. Your constant encouragement, steady support, and grace at my failings made this book happen.

To Eric, my beloved, who gives me permission to chase my dreams when I don't feel brave enough to do it myself. Thanks for making me laugh with horrible dad jokes, intuiting when you need to step in and make dinner because I'm eyeballs deep in a revision, and for always choosing us. Now that this story is in book form, I can't wait for you to read it.

Finally, to the One who holds me with compassion and lovingkindness, who seeks and sees the goodness in and around me, thank you for the gift of storytelling and the grace to tell hard stories. May you be praised with the words from my fingers.